It captured the hearts of millions . . . shattered all the records . . . and took the world by storm.

THE HORSE WHISPERER
The blockbuster first novel by Nicholas Evans

* Over 58 weeks on the *New York Times* Bestseller List—
jumped to #1 faster than any first novel in
publishing history
* Over 10 million copies in print worldwide
* Translated into 36 languages
* Topped bestseller lists throughout the world:
#1 in Australia, Austria, Canada, England, Finland,
Germany, Italy, Spain, Switzerland,
the United States, and others

#1 *New York Times* Bestseller
#1 *Los Angeles Times* Bestseller
#1 *Washington Post* Bestseller
#1 *San Francisco Chronicle* Bestseller
#1 *Chicago Tribune* Bestseller
#1 *Boston Globe* Bestseller
#1 *Philadelphia Inquirer* Bestseller
#1 *Miami Herald* Bestseller
#1 *Seattle Times* Bestseller
#1 *Entertainment Weekly* Bestseller
#1 *Houston Chronicle* Bestseller
#1 *Publishers Weekly* Bestseller
#1 *Denver Post* Bestseller
#1 *Minneapolis Star Tribune* Bestseller
#1 *Atlanta Journal and Constitution* Bestseller
#1 New York *Daily News* Bestseller
#1 *Portland Oregonian* Bestseller
#1 *Dallas Morning News* Bestseller

A Main Selection of the Literary Guild
Please turn the page for more extraordinary acclaim. . . .

The HORSE WHISPERER

NICHOLAS EVANS

A DELL BOOK

Published by
Dell Publishing
a division of
Bantam Doubleday Dell Publishing Group, Inc.
1540 Broadway
New York, New York 10036

Verse from "On Trust in the Heart" by Seng-t'san (p.xi) translated by D. T. Suzuki, *Manual of Zen Buddhism,* Grove Press, 1960.

Cover art copyright © 1998 Touchstone Pictures

Photos by Elliott Marks

Front cover horse photography by Robert Vavra

ISBN: 0-440-22265-6

Reprinted by arrangement with Delacorte Press

Printed in the United States of America

Published simultaneously in Canada

November 1996

30   29   28   27   26   25   24   23   22   21
OPM

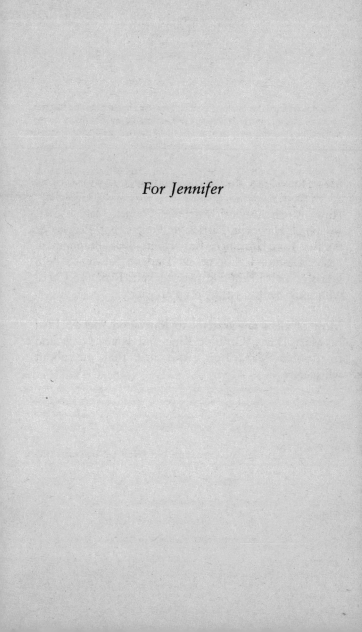

For Jennifer

Many thanks are due to the following:

Huw Alban Davies, Michelle Hamer, Tim Galer, Josephine Haworth, Patrick de Freitas, Bob Peebles & family, Tom Dorrance, Ray Hunt, Buck Brannaman, Leslie Desmond, Lonnie & Darlene Schwend, Beth Ferris & Bob Ream and two truckers, Rick and Chris, who took me for a ride in an anteater.

Most of all, I am grateful to four good friends: Fred & Mary Davis, Caradoc King and James Long; and to Robbie Richardson, who first told me about whisperers.

The HORSE WHISPERER

Pursue not the outer entanglements,
Dwell not in the inner void;
Be serene in the oneness of things,
And dualism vanishes by itself.

From "On Trust in the Heart"
by Seng-t'san (d. 606)

ONE

O N E

THERE WAS DEATH AT ITS BEGINNING AS THERE WOULD BE death again at its end. Though whether it was some fleeting shadow of this that passed across the girl's dreams and woke her on that least likely of mornings she would never know. All she knew, when she opened her eyes, was that the world was somehow altered.

The red glow of her alarm showed it was yet a half-hour till the time she had set it to wake her and she lay quite still, not lifting her head, trying to configure the change. It was dark but not as dark as it should be. Across the bedroom, she could clearly make out the dull glint of her riding trophies on cluttered shelves and above them the looming faces of rock stars she had once thought she should care about. She listened. The silence that filled the house was different too, expectant, like the pause between the intake of breath and the uttering of words. Soon there would be the muted roar of the furnace coming alive in the basement and the old farmhouse floorboards would start their ritual creaking complaint. She slipped out from the bedclothes and went to the window.

There was snow. The first fall of winter. And from the laterals of the fence up by the pond she could tell there must be almost a foot of it. With no deflecting wind, it was perfect and driftless, heaped in comical proportion on the branches of the six small cherry trees her father had planted last year. A single star shone in a wedge of deep blue above the woods. The girl looked down and saw a lace of frost had formed on the lower part of the window and she placed a finger on it, melting a small hole. She shivered, not from the cold, but from the thrill that this transformed world was for the moment entirely hers. And she turned and hurried to get dressed.

Grace Maclean had come up from New York City the night before with her father, just the two of them. She always enjoyed the trip, two and a half hours on the Taconic State Parkway, cocooned together in the long Mercedes, listening to tapes and chatting easily about school or some new case he was working on. She liked to hear him talk as he drove, liked having him to herself, seeing him slowly unwind in his studiously weekend clothes. Her mother, as usual, had some dinner or function or something and would be catching the train to Hudson this morning, which she preferred to do anyway. The Friday-night crawl of traffic invariably made her crabby and impatient and she would compensate by taking charge, telling Robert, Grace's father, to slow down or speed up or take some devious route to avoid delays. He never bothered to argue, just did as he was told, though sometimes he would sigh or give Grace, relegated to the backseat, a wry glance in the mirror. Her parents' relationship had long been a mystery to her, a complicated world where dominance and compliance were never quite what they seemed. Rather than get involved, Grace would simply retreat into the sanctuary of her Walkman.

On the train her mother would work for the entire journey, undistracted and undistractable. Accompanying her once recently, Grace had watched her and marveled that she never even looked out of the window except perhaps in a glazed, unseeing scan when some big-shot writer or one of her more eager assistant editors called on the cellular phone.

The light on the landing outside Grace's room was still on. She tiptoed in her socks past the half-open door of her parents' bedroom and paused. She could hear the ticking of the wall clock in the hall below and now the reassuring, soft snoring of her father. She came down the stairs into the hall, its azure walls and ceiling already aglow from the reflection of snow through undraped windows. In the kitchen, she drank a glass of milk in one long tilt and ate a chocolate-chip cookie as she scribbled a note for her father on the pad by the phone. *Gone riding. Back around 10. Luv, G.*

She took another cookie and ate it on the move as she went through to the passageway by the back door where they left coats and muddy boots. She put on her fleece jacket and hopped elegantly, holding the cookie in her mouth, as she pulled on her riding boots. She zipped her jacket to the neck, put on her gloves and took her riding hat down off the shelf, wondering briefly if she should phone Judith to check if she still wanted to ride now that it had snowed. But there was no need. Judith would be just as excited as she was. As Grace opened the door to step out into the freezing air, she heard the furnace come to life down in the basement.

* * *

Wayne P. Tanner looked gloomily over the rim of his coffee cup at the rows of snowcrusted trucks parked outside the diner. He hated the snow but, more than that, he hated being caught out. And in the space of just a few hours it had happened twice.

Those New York state troopers had enjoyed every minute of it, smug Yankee bastards. He had seen them slide up behind him and hang there on his tail for a couple of miles, knowing damn well he'd seen them and enjoying it. Then the lights coming on, telling him to pull over and the smartass, no more than a kid, swaggering up alongside in his Stetson like some goddamn movie cop. He'd asked for the daily logbook and Wayne found it, handed it down and watched as the kid read it.

"Atlanta huh?" he said, flipping the pages.

"Yes sir," Wayne replied. "And it's one helluva lot warmer down there, I can tell you." The tone usually worked with cops, respectful but fraternal, implying some working kinship of the road. But the kid didn't look up.

"Uh-huh. You know that radar detector you've got there is illegal, don't you?"

Wayne glanced at the little black box bolted to the dash and wondered for a moment whether to play all innocent. In New York fuzz-busters were only illegal for trucks over eighteen thousand pounds. He was packing about three or four times that. Pleading ignorance, he reckoned, might just make the little bastard meaner still. He turned back with a mock-guilty grin but it was wasted because the kid still didn't look at him. "Don't you?" he said again.

"Yeah, well. I guess."

The kid shut the logbook and handed it back up to

him, at last meeting his eyes. "Okay," he said. "Now let's see the other one."

"I'm sorry?"

"The other logbook. The real one. This one here's for the fairies." Something turned over in Wayne's stomach.

For fifteen years, like thousands of other truck drivers, he'd kept two logs, one telling the truth about driving times, mileage, rest-overs and all and the other, fabricated specially for situations like this, showing he'd stuck by all the legal limits. And in all that time, pulled over God knows how many dozens of times, coast to coast, never had any cop done this. Shit, damn near every trucker he knew kept a phony log, they called them comic books, it was a joke. If you were on your own and no partner to take shifts, how the hell were you supposed to meet deadlines? How the hell were you supposed to make a goddamn living? Jesus. The companies all knew about it, they just turned a blind eye.

He had tried spinning it out awhile, playing hurt, even showing a little outrage, but he knew it was no good. The kid's partner, a big bull-necked guy with a smirk on his face, got out of the patrol car, not wanting to miss out on the fun, and they told him to get down from the cab while they searched it. Seeing they meant to pull the place apart, he decided to come clean, fished the book out from its hiding place under the bunk and gave it to them. It showed he had driven over nine hundred miles in twenty-four hours with only one stop and even that was for only half the eight hours required by law.

So now he was looking at a thousand-, maybe thirteen-hundred-dollar fine, more if they got him for the goddamn radar detector. He might even lose his commercial driver's license. The troopers gave him a fistful of paper and escorted him to this truck stop, warning him he'd better not even think of setting out again till morning.

He waited for them to go, then walked over to the gas station and bought a stale turkey sandwich and a six-pack. He spent the night in the bunk at the back of the cab. It was spacious and comfortable enough and he felt a little better after a couple of beers, but he still spent most of the night worrying. And then he woke up to see the snow and discovered he'd been caught out again.

In the balm of a Georgia morning two days earlier, Wayne hadn't thought to check that he had his snow chains. And when he'd looked in the locker this morning, the damn things weren't there. He couldn't believe it. Some dumbfuck must have borrowed or stolen them. Wayne knew the interstate would be okay, they'd have had the snowplows and sanders out hours ago. But the two giant turbines he was carrying had to be delivered to a pulp mill in a little place called Chatham and he would have to leave the turnpike and cut across country. The roads would be winding and narrow and probably as yet uncleared. Wayne cursed himself again, finished his coffee and laid down a five-dollar bill.

Outside the door he stopped to light a cigarette and tugged his Braves baseball cap down hard against the cold. He could hear the drone of trucks already moving out on the interstate. His boots scrunched in the snow as he made his way over the lot toward his truck.

There were forty or fifty trucks there, lined up side by side, all eighteen-wheelers like his, mainly Peterbilts, Freightliners and Kenworths. Wayne's was a black and chrome Kenworth Conventional, "anteaters" they called them, because of the long, sloping nose. And though it looked better hitched to a standard high-sided, reefer trailer than it did now with the two turbines mounted on a flatbed, in the snowy half-light of dawn, he thought it was still the prettiest truck on the lot. He stood there for a moment admiring it, finishing his cigarette. Unlike the younger drivers who didn't give a shit nowadays, he always kept his cab gleaming. He had even cleared all the snow off before going in for breakfast. Unlike him though, he suddenly remembered, they probably hadn't forgotten their goddamn chains. Wayne Tanner squashed his cigarette into the snow and hauled himself up into the cab.

Two sets of footprints converged at the mouth of the long driveway that led up to the stables. With immaculate timing, the two girls had arrived there only moments apart and made their way up the hill together, their laughter carrying down into the valley. Even though the sun had yet to show, the white picket fence, confining their tracks on either side, looked dowdy against the snow, as did the jumps in the fields beyond. The girls' tracks curved to the brow of the hill and disappeared into the group of low buildings that huddled, as if for protection, around the vast red barn where the horses were kept.

As Grace and Judith turned into the stable yard, a cat skittered away from them, spoiling the snow. They stopped and stood there a moment, looking over toward the house. There was no sign of life. Mrs. Dyer, the woman who owned the place and had taught them both to ride, would normally be up and about by now.

"Do you think we should tell her we're going out?" Grace whispered.

The two girls had grown up together, seeing each other at weekends up here in the country for as long as either could remember. Both lived on the Upper West Side, both went to schools on the East Side and both had fathers who were lawyers. But it occurred to neither of them that they should see each other during the week. The friendship belonged here, with their horses. Just turned fourteen, Judith was nearly a year older than Grace and in decisions as weighty as risking the ever-ready wrath of Mrs. Dyer, Grace was happy to defer. Judith sniffed and screwed up her face.

"Nah," she said. "She'd only bawl us out for waking her up. Come on."

The air inside the barn was warm and heavy with the sweet smell of hay and dung. As the girls came in with their saddles and closed the door, a dozen horses watched from their stalls, ears pricked forward, sensing something different about the dawn outside just as Grace had. Judith's horse, a soft-eyed chestnut gelding called Gulliver, whinnied as she came up to the stall, putting his face forward for her to rub.

"Hi baby," she said. "How are you today, huh?" The horse backed off gently from the gate so Judith would have room to come in with the tack.

Grace walked on. Her horse was in the last stall at the far end of the barn. Grace spoke softly to the others as she passed them, greeting them by name. She could see Pilgrim, his head erect and still, watching her all the way. He was a four-year-old Morgan, a gelding of a bay so dark that in some lights he looked black. Her parents had bought him for her last summer for her birthday, reluctantly. They had worried he was too big and too young for her, altogether too much of a horse. For Grace, it was love at first sight.

They had flown down to Kentucky to see him and when they were taken out to the field, he came right over to the fence to check her out. He didn't let her touch him, just sniffed her hand, brushing it lightly with his whiskers. Then he tossed his head like some haughty prince and ran off, flagging his long tail, his coat glistening in the sun like polished ebony.

The woman who was selling him let Grace ride him and it was only then that her parents gave each other a look and she knew they would let her have him. Her mother hadn't ridden since she was a child but she could be counted on to recognize class when she saw it. And Pilgrim was class alright. There was no doubting he was also a handful and quite different from any other horse she had ridden. But when Grace was on him and could feel all that life pounding away inside him, she knew that in his heart he was good and not mean and that they would be okay together. They would be a team.

She had wanted to change his name to something prouder, like Cochise or Khan, but her mother, ever the tyrant liberal, said it was up to Grace of course, but in her opinion it was bad luck to change a horse's name. So Pilgrim he remained.

"Hey, gorgeous," she said as she reached the stall. "Who's my man?" She reached out for him and he let her touch the velvet of his muzzle, but only briefly, tilting his head up and away from her. "You are such a flirt. Come on, let's get you fixed here."

Grace let herself into the stall and took off the horse's blanket. When she swung the saddle over him, he shifted away a little as he always did and she told him firmly to keep still. She told him about the surprise he had waiting for him outside as she lightly fastened the girth and put on the bridle. Then she took a hoof pick from her pocket and methodically cleared the dirt from each of his feet. She could hear Judith already leading

Gulliver out of his stall, so she hurried to tighten the girth and now they too were ready.

They led the horses out into the yard and let them stand there a few moments appraising the snow while Judith went back to shut the barn door. Gulliver lowered his head and sniffed, concluding quickly it was the same stuff he had seen a hundred times before. Pilgrim however was amazed. He pawed it and was startled when it moved. He tried sniffing it, as he had seen the older horse do. But he sniffed too hard and gave a great sneeze that had the girls rocking with laughter.

"Maybe he's never seen it before," said Judith.

"He must have. Don't they have snow in Kentucky?"

"I don't know. I guess so." She looked across at Mrs. Dyer's house. "Hey, come on, let's go or we'll wake the dragon."

They led the horses out of the yard and into the top meadow and there they mounted up and rode in a slow, climbing traverse toward the gate that led into the woods. Their tracks cut a perfect diagonal across the unblemished square of the field. And as they reached the woods, at last the sun came up over the ridge and filled the valley behind them with tilted shadows.

One of the things Grace's mother hated most about weekends was the mountain of newsprint she had to read. It accumulated all week like some malign volcanic mass. Each day, recklessly, she stacked it higher with the weeklies and all those sections of *The New York Times* she didn't dare trash. By Saturday it had become too menacing to ignore and with several more tons of Sunday's *New York Times* horribly imminent, she knew that if she didn't act now, she would be swept away and buried. All those words, let loose on the world. All that

effort. Just to make you feel guilty. Annie tossed another slab to the floor and wearily picked up the *New
York Post*.

The Macleans' apartment was on the eighth floor of
an elegant old building on Central Park West. Annie sat
with her feet tucked up on the yellow sofa by the window. She was wearing black leggings and a light gray
sweatshirt. Her bobbed auburn hair, tied in a stubby
ponytail, was set aflame by the sun that streamed in
behind her and made a shadow of her on the matching
sofa across the living room.

The room was long and painted a pale yellow. It was
lined at one end with books and there were pieces of
African art and a grand piano, one gleaming end of
which was now caught by the angling sun. If Annie had
turned she would have seen seagulls strutting on the ice
of the reservoir. Even in the snow, even this early on a
Saturday morning, there were joggers out, pounding the
circuit that she herself would be pounding as soon as
she had finished the papers. She took a sip from her
mug of tea and was about to junk the *Post* when she
spotted a small item hidden away in a column she usually skipped.

"I don't believe it," she said aloud. "You little rat."

She clunked the mug down on the table and went
briskly to get the phone from the hallway. She came
back already punching the number and stood facing the
window now, tapping a foot while she waited for an
answer. Below the reservoir an old man wearing skis
and an absurdly large radio headset was tramping fero-
ciously toward the trees. A woman was scolding a
leashed gaggle of tiny dogs, all with matching knitted
coats and with legs so short they had to leap and sledge
to make progress.

"Anthony? Did you see the *Post*?" Annie had obviously woken her young assistant but it didn't occur to her to apologize. "They've got a piece about me and Fiske. The little shit's saying I fired him and that I faked the new circulation figures."

Anthony said something sympathetic but it wasn't sympathy Annie was after. "Do you have Don Farlow's weekend number?" He went to get it. Out in the park, the dog woman had given up and was now dragging them back toward the street. Anthony returned with the number and Annie jotted it down.

"Good," she said. "Go back to sleep." She hung up and immediately dialed Farlow's number.

Don Farlow was the publishing group's storm-trooper lawyer. In the six months since Annie Graves (professionally she had always used her maiden name) was brought in as editor-in-chief to salvage its sinking flagship magazine, he had become an ally and almost a friend. Together they had set about the ousting of the Old Guard. Blood had flowed—new blood in and old blood out—and the press had relished every drop. Among those to whom she and Farlow had shown the door were several well-connected writers who had promptly taken their revenge in the gossip columns. The place became known as the Graves Yard.

Annie could understand their bitterness. Some had been there so many years, they felt they owned the place. To be uprooted at all was demeaning enough. To be uprooted by an upstart forty-three-year-old woman, and English to boot, was intolerable. The purge was now almost over, however, and Annie and Farlow had recently become skillful at constructing payoff deals which bought the silence of those departing. She thought they had done just that with Fenimore Fiske, the magazine's aging and insufferable movie critic who was now badmouthing her in the *Post*. The rat. But as

Annie waited for Farlow to answer the phone, she took comfort from the fact that Fiske had made a big mistake in calling her increased circulation figures a sham. They weren't and she could prove it.

Farlow was not only up, he had seen the *Post* piece too. They agreed to meet in two hours' time in her office. They would sue the old bastard for every penny they'd bought him off with.

Annie called her husband in Chatham and got her own voice on the answering machine. She left a message telling Robert it was time he was up, that she would be catching the later train and not to go to the supermarket before she got there. Then she took the elevator down and went out into the snow to join the joggers. Except, of course, Annie Graves didn't jog. She ran. And although this distinction was not immediately obvious from either her speed or her technique, to Annie it was as clear and vital as the cold morning air into which she now plunged.

The interstate was fine, as Wayne Tanner had expected. There wasn't too much else on the road what with it being a Saturday and he reckoned he'd be better keeping on up 87 till it hit 90, cross the Hudson River there and head on down to Chatham from the north. He'd studied the map and figured that though it wasn't the most direct route, less of it would be on smaller roads that might not have been cleared. With no chains, he only hoped this access road to the mill they'd told him about wasn't just some dirt track or something.

By the time he picked up the signs for 90 and swung east, he was starting to feel better. The countryside looked like a Christmas card and with Garth Brooks on the tape machine and the sun bouncing off the Kenworth's mighty nose, things didn't seem so bad as they had last night. Hell, if it came to the worst and he lost his license, he could always go back and be a mechanic like he was trained to be. It wouldn't be so much money, for sure. It was a goddamn insult how little they paid a guy who'd done years of training and had to buy himself ten thousand dollars' worth of tools. But sometimes lately he'd been getting tired of being on the road so much. Maybe it would be nice to spend more time at home with his wife and kids. Well, maybe. Spend more time fishing, anyway.

With a jolt, Wayne spotted the exit for Chatham coming up and he got to work, pumping the brakes and taking the truck down through its nine gears, making the big four-twenty-five horsepower Cummins engine roar in complaint. As he forked away from the interstate he flipped the four-wheel-drive switch, locking in the cab's front axle. From here, he calculated, it was maybe just five or six miles to the mill.

High in the woods that morning there was a stillness, as if life itself had been suspended. Neither bird nor animal spoke and the only sound was the sporadic soft thud of snow from overladen boughs. Up into this waiting vacuum, through maple and birch, rose the distant laughter of the girls.

They were making their way slowly up the winding trail that led to the ridge, letting the horses choose the pace. Judith was in front and she was twisted around, propped with one hand on the cantle of Gulliver's saddle, looking back at Pilgrim and laughing.

"You should put him in a circus," she said. "The guy's a natural clown."

Grace was laughing too much to reply. Pilgrim was

walking with his head down, pushing his nose through the snow like a shovel. Then he would toss a load of it into the air with a sneeze and break into a little trot, pretending to be frightened of it as it scattered.

"Hey, come on now you, that's enough," said Grace, reining him in, getting control. Pilgrim settled back into a walk and Judith, still grinning, shook her head and turned to face the trail again. Gulliver walked on, thoroughly unconcerned by the antics behind him, his head moving up and down to the rhythm of his feet. Along the trail, every twenty yards or so, bright orange posters were pinned to the trees, threatening prosecution for anyone caught hunting, trapping or trespassing.

At the crest of the ridge that separated the two valleys was a small, circular clearing where normally, if they approached quietly, they might find deer or wild turkey. Today however, when the girls rode out from the trees and into the sun, all they found was the bloody, severed wing of a bird. It lay almost exactly in the middle of the clearing like the mark of some savage compass and the girls stopped there and looked down at it.

"What is it, a pheasant or something?" said Grace.

"I guess. A former pheasant anyway. Part of a former pheasant."

Grace frowned. "How did it get here?"

"I don't know. A fox maybe."

"It couldn't be, where are the tracks?"

There weren't any. Nor was there any sign of a struggle. It was as if the wing had flown there on its own. Judith shrugged.

"Maybe somebody shot it."

"What, and the rest of it flew on with one wing?"

They both pondered a moment. Then Judith nodded sagely. "A hawk. Dropped by a passing hawk."

Grace thought it over. "A hawk. Uh-huh. I'll buy that." They nudged the horses into a walk again.

"Or a passing airplane."

Grace laughed. "That's it," she said. "It looks like the chicken they served on that flight to London last year. Only better."

Usually when they rode up here to the ridge they would give the horses a canter across the clearing and then loop back down to the stables by another trail. But the snow and the sun and the clear morning sky made both girls want more than that today. They decided to do something they had done only once before, a couple of years ago, when Grace still had Gypsy, her stocky little palomino pony. They would cross over into the next valley, cut down through the woods and come back around the hill the long way, beside Kinderhook Creek. It meant crossing a road or two, but Pilgrim seemed to have settled down and anyway, this early on a snowy Saturday morning, there would be nothing much about.

As they left the clearing and passed again into the shade of the woods, Grace and Judith fell silent. There were hickories and poplars on this side of the ridge with no obvious trail among them and the girls had frequently to lower their heads to pass beneath the branches so that soon they and the horses were covered with a fine sprinkling of dislodged snow. They negotiated their way slowly down beside a stream. Crusts of ice overhung it, spreading jaggedly from the banks and allowing but a glimpse of the water that rushed darkly beneath. The slope grew ever steeper and the horses now moved with caution, taking care where they placed their feet. Once Gulliver slipped lurchingly on a hidden rock, but he righted himself without panic. The sun slanting down through the trees made crazed patterns on the snow and lit the clouds of breath billowing from the horses' nostrils. But neither girl paid heed, for they were concentrating too hard on the descent and their heads were filled only with the feel of the animals they rode.

It was with relief that at last they saw the glint of Kinderhook Creek below them through the trees. The descent had been more difficult than either girl had expected and only now did they feel able to look at each other and grin.

"Nice one, huh?" Judith said, gently bringing Gulliver to a stop. Grace laughed.

"No problem." She leaned forward and rubbed Pilgrim's neck. "Didn't these guys do well?"

"They did great."

"I don't remember it being steep like that."

"It wasn't. I think we followed a different stream. I figure we're about a mile farther south than we should be."

They brushed the snow from their clothes and hats and peered down through the trees. Below the woods a meadow of virgin white sloped gently down to the river. Along the near side of the river they could just make out the fence posts of the old road that led to the pulp mill. It was a road no longer used since a wider, more direct access had been built from the highway which lay half a mile away on the other side of the river. The girls would have to follow the old mill road north to pick up the route they had planned to get home.

Just as he'd feared, the road down to Chatham hadn't been cleared. But Wayne Tanner soon realized he needn't have worried. Others had been out before him and the Kenworth's eighteen heavy-duty tires cut into their tracks and grabbed the surface firmly. He hadn't needed the damn chains after all. He passed a snowplow coming the other way and even though that wasn't a whole lot of use to him, such was his relief that he gave the guy a wave and a friendly blast on the horn.

He lit a cigarette and looked at his watch. He was earlier than he'd said he would be. After his run-in with the cops, he'd called Atlanta and told them to fix things with the mill people for him to deliver the turbines in the morning. Nobody liked working on a Saturday and he guessed he wasn't going to be too popular when he got there. Still, that was their problem. He shoved in another Garth Brooks tape and started looking out for the entrance to the mill.

The old mill road was easy going after the woods and the girls and their horses relaxed as they made their way along it, side by side in the sunshine. Away to their left, a pair of blue jays chased each other in the trees fringing the river and through their shrill chatter and the rustle of water on rock, Grace could hear what she assumed was a snowplow out clearing the highway.

"Here we go." Judith nodded up ahead.

It was the place they had been looking for, where once a railroad had crossed first the mill road and then the river. It was many years since the railroad had closed and though the river bridge remained intact, the top of the bridge across the road had been removed. All that remained were its tall concrete sides, a roofless tunnel through which the road now passed before disappearing in a bend. Just before it was a steep path that led up the embankment to the level of the railroad and it was up here that the girls needed to go to get onto the river bridge.

Judith went first, steering Gulliver up the path. He took a few steps then stopped.

"Come on boy, it's okay."

The horse gently pawed the snow, as if testing it. Judith urged him on with her heels now.

"Come on lazybones, up we go."

Gulliver relented and moved on again up the path. Grace waited down in the road, watching. She was vaguely aware that the sound of the snowplow out on the highway seemed louder. Pilgrim's ears twitched. She reached down and patted his sweaty neck.

"How is it?" she called up to Judith.

"It's okay. Take it gently though."

It happened just as Gulliver was almost at the top of the embankment. Grace had started up behind him, following his tracks as precisely as she could, letting Pilgrim take his time. She was halfway up when she heard the rasp of Gulliver's shoe on ice and Judith's frightened cry.

Had the girls ridden here more recently, they would have known that the slope they were climbing had, since late summer, run with water from a leaking culvert. The blanket of snow now concealed a sheet of sheer ice.

Gulliver staggered, trying to find purchase with his hind feet, kicking up a spray of snow and ice shards. But as each foot failed to hold, his rear end swung down and across the slope so that he was now squarely on the ice. One of his forelegs skewed sideways and he went down on one knee, still sliding. Judith cried out as she was flung forward and lost a stirrup. But she managed to grab the horse's neck and stayed on, yelling down at Grace now.

"Get out of the way! Grace!"

Grace was transfixed. There was a roar of blood in her head that seemed to freeze and separate her from what she was watching above her. But upon Judith's second cry she reconnected and tried to turn Pilgrim down the slope. The horse yanked his head, frightened, fighting her. He took several small sideways steps, twisting his neck up the slope until his feet too skidded and he nickered in alarm. They were now directly in the path of Gulliver's slide. Grace screamed and wrenched the reins.

"Pilgrim, come on! Move!"

In the odd stillness of the moment before Gulliver hit them, Grace knew there was more to the roar in her head than the rushing of blood. That snowplow wasn't out on the highway. It was too loud for that. It was somewhere nearer. The thought was vaporized by the shuddering impact of Gulliver's hindquarters. He bulldozed into them, hitting Pilgrim's shoulder and spinning him around. Grace felt herself being lifted out of the saddle, whiplashed up the slope. And had one hand not found the rump of the other horse she would have fallen then as Judith fell. But she stayed on, wrapping a fist into Pilgrim's silky mane as he slid down the slope beneath her.

Gulliver and Judith were past her now and she watched her friend being flung like a discarded doll across the horse's rear, then jerk and twist viciously back as her foot snagged in the stirrup. Judith's body bounced and swung sideways and as she hit the ice hard with the back of her head, her foot took another twist in the stirrup, locking itself there so that now she was being dragged. In one seething, frenzied tangle, the two horses and their riders careered down toward the road.

Wayne Tanner saw them as soon as he came out of

the bend. Assuming he would be approaching from the south, the mill people hadn't thought to mention the old access road farther north. So Wayne had seen the turn and taken it and was relieved to find the Kenworth's wheels seemed to hold the untracked snow as well as they had back on the highway. When he came around the bend he saw, maybe a hundred yards ahead, the concrete walls of the bridge and beyond it, framed by it, some animal, a horse, trailing something. Wayne's stomach turned over.

"What the hell?"

He hit the brakes, but not too hard, for he knew that if he made things too sudden the wheels would lock, so he worked the trolley valve on the steering wheel, trying to get drag from the brakes at the back of the trailer. He couldn't even feel it. The gears would have to bring him down and he smacked the heel of his hand into the shift and double-declutched, making the six cylinders of the Cummins roar. Shit, he'd been going too fast. There were two horses there now, one with a rider on it. What the hell were they doing? Why didn't they get off the goddamn road? His heart was pounding and he could feel a sweat breaking out as he worked the trailer brakes and the shift, finding a rhythm in the mantra going through his head: *Hit the binders, grab a gear, hit the binders, grab a gear.* But the bridge was looming up too fast. For Christsake, couldn't they hear him coming? Couldn't they see him?

They could. Even Judith, in her agony on the ground, could see him, fleetingly, as she was thrashed around screaming through the snow. Her thighbone had snapped when she fell and in the slide to the road both horses had stepped on her, crushing ribs and splintering a forearm. In that first stumble Gulliver had cracked a knee and torn tendons and the pain and fear that filled his head showed in the whites of his eyes as he reeled and pranced and tried to free himself of this thing that hung hooked to his side.

Grace saw the truck as soon as they reached the road. One look was enough. Somehow she had managed not to fall and now she had to get them all off the road. If she could get hold of Gulliver's reins, she could lead him off to safety, dragging Judith behind. But Pilgrim was as freaked as the older horse and the two of them circled frantically, feeding each other's fear.

With all her strength, Grace tugged on Pilgrim's mouth and for a moment had his attention. She backed him toward the other horse, leaning precariously from her saddle, and reached out for Gulliver's bridle. He moved off, but she shadowed him, stretching out her arm till she thought it would pop from its socket. Her fingers were nearly on it when the truck blasted its horn.

Wayne saw both horses leap at the sound and for the first time realized what it was that hung from the side of the one that had no rider.

"Holy shit."

He said it out loud and at the same time found he had run out of gears. He was in first and the bridge and the horses were coming up so fast he knew all he could do now was go for the tractor brakes. He murmured a little prayer and stepped harder than he knew he should on the foot valve. For a second it seemed to work. He could feel the wheels at the back of the cab bite home.

"Yeah! That's my girl."

Then the wheels locked and Wayne felt forty tons of steel take charge of their own destiny.

In a stately, accelerating slither, the Kenworth snaked into the mouth of the bridge, entirely ignoring his efforts at the wheel. Now Wayne was just a spectator and he watched the cab's offside wing below him make contact with the concrete wall in what at first was but a glancing kiss of sparks. Then, as the deadweight of the trailer shouldered in behind, there was a gouging, ripping mayhem of noise that made the very air vibrate.

In front of him now he could see the black horse turn to face him and he saw that its rider was just a young girl and that her eyes were wide with fear beneath the dark peak of her hat.

"No, no, no," he said.

But the horse reared up defiantly before him and the girl was jerked back and fell to the road. Only briefly did the horse's front feet come down, for in the moment before the truck was upon it, Wayne saw it lift its head and rear again. Only this time it leapt right at him. With all the power of its hind legs, it launched itself over the front of the cab, clearing the sheer face of the radiator grille as if it were a jump. The metal shoes on its front feet came down on the hood, skidding up it in a frenzy of sparks and as a hoof hit the windshield there was a loud crack and Wayne lost all sight in a craze of glass. Where was the girl? God, she must be down there on the road in front of him.

Wayne smashed his fist and forearm against the windshield and when it shattered he saw the horse was still there on the hood. Its right foreleg was stuck in the V-shaped struts of the wing mirror and the animal was screaming at him, covered in fragments of glass, its mouth foaming and bloody. Beyond it, Wayne could see the other horse at the side of the road, trying to limp away, its rider still hanging by her leg from the stirrup.

And still the truck kept going. The trailer was coming clear of the bridge wall and with nothing now to restrain its sideways drift, it began a slow, relentless jackknife, effortlessly scything down the fence and sending up a cresting bow-wave of snow like an ocean liner.

As the trailer's momentum overtook that of the cab and slowed it, the horse on the hood made one last great effort. The struts of the wing mirror broke and the animal rolled free and disappeared from Wayne's view. There was a moment of brooding calm, as in the eye of a hurricane, in which Wayne watched the trailer finish its sweep of the fence and the edge of the field beyond and start slowly arcing back toward him. Corralled in the quietly closing angle of the jackknife stood the other horse, uncertain now where escape might lie. Wayne thought he saw its dangling rider lift her head from the ground to look at him, unaware of the wave that was breaking behind her. Then she was lost. For the trailer surged over her, scooping the horse toward the cab like a butterfly in a book and crushing it there in a final thunderous slam of metal.

"Hello? Gracie?"

Robert Maclean paused in the passageway by the back door, holding two large bags of groceries. There was no reply and he went through into the kitchen and dumped the bags on the table.

He always liked to get the weekend food in before Annie arrived. If he didn't, they would have to go to the supermarket together and would end up spending an hour there while Annie pondered the fine distinctions between various brands. It never failed to astound him how someone who every moment of her working life made snap decisions, committing thousands, even millions of dollars, could at weekends spend ten minutes wondering which kind of pesto sauce to buy. It also cost a lot more than if he shopped alone, because Annie usually failed to reach any final decision over which brand was best and they'd end up buying all three.

The downside of doing it alone was of course the inevitable criticism he would face for buying the wrong things. But in the lawyerly manner which he applied to all areas of his life, Robert had weighed both sides of this issue and shopping without his wife emerged the clear winner.

Grace's note lay by the phone, where she had left it. Robert looked at his watch. It was only a little after ten and he could understand the two girls wanting to spend longer out on a morning like this. He pushed the play-back button on the answering machine, took off his parka and started to put away the groceries. There were two messages. The first, from Annie, made him smile. She must have called right after he'd left for the super-market. Time he was up, indeed. The second was from Mrs. Dyer up at the stables. All she said was would they please call her. But something in her voice made Robert go cold.

The helicopter hung there for a while above the river, taking in the scene, then dipped its nose and lifted up over the woods, filling the valley with the deep, rever-berating thud of its blades. The pilot looked down to one side as he circled again. There were ambulances, police cars and rescue squad vehicles down there, red lights flashing, all parked in fan formation in the field beside the massive jackknifed truck. They had marked out where they wanted the helicopter to land and a cop was making big, unnecessary arm signals.

It had taken just ten minutes for them to fly down from Albany and the paramedics had worked all the way, going through routine checks of the equipment.

Now they were ready and watched silently over the pilot's shoulder as he circled and made his approach. The sun flashed briefly on the river as the helicopter followed its own shadow in over the police roadblock and over a red four-wheel-drive car also making its way toward the scene of the wreck.

Through the window of the police car, Wayne Tanner watched the helicopter hover above the landing spot and gently lower itself, whipping up a blizzard around the head of the cop who was directing it in.

Wayne was in the front passenger seat with a blanket over his shoulders, holding a cup of something hot he hadn't yet tasted. He could make no more sense of all the activity going on outside than he could of the harsh, intermittent babble of the police radio beside him. His shoulder ached and there was a small cut on his hand that the ambulance woman had insisted on bandaging extravagantly. It hadn't needed it. It was as if she didn't want him, surrounded by such carnage, to feel left out.

Wayne could see Koopman, the young deputy sheriff whose car he was sitting in, over by the truck talking to the rescue squad people. Nearby, leaning on the hood of a rusted pale blue pickup and listening in, was the little hunter guy in the fur hat who had raised the alarm. He'd been up in the woods, heard the crash and gone straight down to the mill where they called the sheriff's office. When Koopman arrived, Wayne was sitting in the snow out in the field. The deputy was just a kid and had clearly never seen a wreck this bad before, but he'd handled things well and even looked disappointed when Wayne told him he'd already put out a call on channel nine of his CB. That was the channel monitored by the state police and minutes later they started to arrive. Now the place was swarming with them and Koopman looked a little put out that it wasn't his show anymore.

On the snow beneath the truck, Wayne could see the reflected glare of the oxyacetylene blowtorches that the rescue squad guys were using to cut through the tangled wreck of the trailer and the turbines. He looked away, fighting the memory of those long minutes after the jackknife finished.

He hadn't heard it right away. Garth Brooks was singing on regardless on the tape machine and Wayne had been so stunned at his own survival that he was unsure if it was he or his ghost climbing down from the cab. There were blue jays squawking in the trees and at first he thought this other noise came from them too. But it was too desperate, too insistent, a kind of sustained, tortured shrieking and Wayne realized it was the horse dying in the closed jackknife and he'd clamped his hands to his ears and run away into the field.

They'd already told him one of the girls was still alive and he could see the paramedics at work around her stretcher, getting her ready for the helicopter. One of them was pressing a mask over her face and another had his arms up high, holding two plastic bags of fluid that were connected by tubes to her arms. The body of the other girl had already been flown out.

A red four-wheeler had just pulled up and Wayne watched a big bearded man get out and take a black bag out of the back. He slung it over a shoulder and made his way toward Koopman who turned to greet him. They talked for a few minutes then Koopman led him out of sight behind the truck, where the blowtorchers were at work. When they reappeared, the bearded guy looked grim. They went over to talk to the little hunter guy who listened, nodded and got what looked like a rifle bag out of the cab of his pickup. Now all three of them were heading over toward Wayne. Koopman opened the car door.

"You okay?"

"Yeah, I'm okay."

Koopman nodded toward the bearded guy.

"Mr. Logan here is a veterinarian. We need to find that other horse."

Now that the door was open Wayne could hear the roar of the blowtorches. It made him feel sick.

"Any idea which way it went?"

"No sir. Sure don't think he could've gotten far."

"Okay." Koopman put a hand on Wayne's shoulder. "We'll be getting you out of here soon, okay?"

Wayne nodded. Koopman shut the door. They stood there talking outside the car but Wayne couldn't hear what they said. Beyond them, the helicopter was lifting off, taking the girl away. Someone's hat blew off in the blizzard. But Wayne saw none of this. All he saw was the bloodfoam mouth of the horse and its eyes staring at him over a jagged edge of windshield as they would stare at him in his dreams for a long time to come.

"We've got him, haven't we?"

Annie was standing by her desk, looking over Don Farlow's shoulder as he sat reading the contract. He didn't answer, just lifted a sandy eyebrow, finishing the page.

"We have," Annie said. "I know we have."

Farlow put the contract down on his lap.

"Yes, I think we have."

"Ha!" Annie raised a fist and walked across the office to pour herself another cup of coffee.

They had been there half an hour. She'd caught a cab down to Forty-third and Seventh, got stuck in the traffic and walked the last two blocks. New York drivers were coping with the snow in the way they knew best, blaring their horns and yelling at each other. Farlow was already there in her office and had the coffee on. She liked the way he made himself at home.

"Of course, he'll deny he ever spoke to them," he said.

"It's a direct quote, Don. And look how much detail there is. He can't deny he said it."

Annie brought her coffee back and sat down at her desk, a vast asymmetrical affair in elm and walnut that a friend in England had made for her four years ago when, to everyone's surprise, she had given up writing to become an executive. It had followed her from that magazine to this much grander one, where it had won the instant loathing of the interior designer hired at great expense to restyle the deposed editor's office to Annie's taste. He had taken clever revenge by insisting that, as the desk clashed so badly, everything else should clash too. The result was a cacophony of shape and color that the designer, with no detectable sign of irony, called Eclectic Deconstructionism.

All that really worked were some abstract splatter paintings done by Grace at the age of three that Annie (to her daughter's initial pride and subsequent embarrassment) had proudly framed. They hung on the walls among all the awards and photographs of Annie smiling cheek by jowl with assorted glitterati. More discreetly positioned, on the desk where only she could see them, were the photographs of those she cared about: Grace, Robert and her father.

Over the tops of these Annie now surveyed Don Farlow. It was funny to see him not wearing a suit. The old denim jacket and hiking boots had surprised her.

She'd had him down as a Brooks Brothers type—slacks, loafers and yellow cashmere. He smiled.

"So. You want to sue him?"

Annie laughed. "Of course I want to sue him. He signed an agreement saying he wouldn't talk to the press and he's libeled me by saying I've faked the figures."

"A libel that'll be repeated a hundred times over if we sue. And blown up into a much bigger story."

Annie frowned.

"Don, you're not going soft on me are you? Fenimore Fiske is a bitter, twisted, talentless, spiteful old toad."

Farlow put up his hands, grinning.

"Don't hold back Annie, tell me what you really think."

"While he was here he did all he could to stir up trouble and now he's gone he's trying to do the same. I want to burn his wrinkled ass."

"Is that an English expression?"

"No, we'd say apply heat to his aging fundament."

"Well, you're the boss. Fundamentally."

"You better believe it."

One of the phones on Annie's desk clicked and she picked it up. It was Robert. He told her in a level voice that Grace had been in an accident. She'd been flown up to a hospital in Albany where she was in intensive care, still unconscious. Annie should stay on the train all the way to Albany. He would meet her there.

Two

ANNIE AND ROBERT HAD MET WHEN SHE WAS ONLY
eighteen. It was the summer of 1968 and rather than go
straight from school to Oxford University where she
had been offered a place, Annie decided to take a year
off. She signed up with an organization called Volun-
tary Service Overseas and was given a two-week crash
course on how to teach English, avoid malaria and re-
pel the advances of amorous locals (say no, loudly, and
mean it).

Thus prepared, she flew to Senegal in West Africa
and after a brief stay in the capital, Dakar, set off on the
dusty five-hundred-mile ride south in an open-sided bus
crammed with people, chickens and goats, to the small
town that was to be her home for the next twelve
months. On the second day, as night fell, they arrived at
the banks of a great river.

The night air was hot and damp and clamorous with
insects and Annie could see the lights of the town twin-
kling far across the water. But the ferry had shut down
till morning and the driver and other passengers, now
her friends, were concerned about where she would

spend the night. There was no hotel and though they themselves would have no trouble finding a place to lay their heads, they clearly felt the young Englishwoman needed somewhere more salubrious.

They told her there was a *tubab* living nearby who would surely put her up. Without the faintest idea of what a *tubab* might be, Annie found herself being led in a large posse bearing her bags along winding jungle tracks to a small mud house set among baobab and papaya trees. The *tubab* who answered the door—she later found out it meant white man—was Robert.

He was a Peace Corps volunteer and had been there a year, teaching English and building wells. He was twenty-four, a Harvard graduate and the most intelligent person Annie had ever met. That night he cooked her a wonderful meal of spiced fish and rice, washed down with bottles of cold local beer and they talked by candlelight till three in the morning. Robert was from Connecticut and was going to be a lawyer. It was congenital, he apologized, eyes wryly aglint behind his gold-rim specs. Everyone in the family had been lawyers for as long as any of them could remember. It was the Curse of the Macleans.

And, like a lawyer, he cross-examined Annie about her life, forcing her to describe and analyze it in a way that made it seem as fresh to her as it did to him. She told him how her father had been a diplomat and how, for the first ten years of her life, they had moved from country to country whenever he was given a new post. She and her younger brother had been born in Egypt, then lived in Malaya, then Jamaica. And then her father had died, quite suddenly, from a massive heart attack. Annie had only recently found a way of saying this that didn't stop the conversation and make people study their shoes. Her mother had resettled in England, rapidly remarried and packed her and her brother off to boarding schools. Although Annie skimmed over this part of the story, she could tell Robert sensed the depth of unresolved pain beneath it.

The following morning Robert took her in his jeep across on the ferry and delivered her safely to the Catholic convent where she was to live and teach for the coming year under the only occasionally disapproving eye of the mother superior, a kindly and conveniently myopic French-Canadian.

Over the course of the next three months, Annie met up with Robert every Wednesday when he came to buy supplies in town. He spoke Jola—the local language— fluently and gave her a weekly lesson. They became friends but not lovers. Instead, Annie lost her virginity to a beautiful Senegalese man called Xavier to whose amorous advances she remembered to say yes, loudly, and mean it.

Then Robert was transferred up to Dakar, and the evening before he went Annie crossed the river for a farewell supper. America was voting for a new president and the two of them listened in deepening gloom to a crackling radio as Nixon took state after state. It was as if someone close to Robert had died and Annie was moved as he explained to her in a voice choked with emotion what it meant for his country and the war many of his friends were fighting in Asia. She put her arms around him and held him and for the first time felt she was no longer a girl but a woman.

Only when he had gone and she met other Peace Corps volunteers did she realize how unusual he was. Most of the others were dope-heads or bores or both. There was one guy with glazed, pink eyes and a headband who claimed he'd been high for a year.

She saw Robert once more when she went back up to

Dakar to fly home the following July. Here people spoke another language called Wolof and he was already fluent. He was living out near the airport, so near that you had to stop talking whenever a plane went over. To make some virtue of this, he had got hold of a huge directory detailing every flight in and out of Dakar and, after two nights studying it, knew it by heart. When a plane flew over he would recite the name of the airline, its origin, route and destination. Annie laughed and he looked a little hurt. She flew home the night a man walked on the moon.

They didn't see each other again for seven years. Annie sailed triumphantly through Oxford, launching a radical and scurrilous magazine and sickening her friends by getting a brilliant First in English without ever appearing to do a stroke of work. Because it was the thing she least didn't want to do, she became a journalist, working on an evening newspaper in the far north-east of England. Her mother came to visit her just once and was so depressed by the landscape and the sooty hovel her daughter was living in that she cried all the way back to London. She had a point. Annie stuck it for a year then packed her bags, flew to New York and amazed even herself by bluffing her way into a job on *Rolling Stone*.

She specialized in hip, brutal profiles of celebrities more accustomed to adulation. Her detractors—and there were many—said she would soon run out of victims. But it didn't work out that way. They kept on coming. It became a kind of masochistic status symbol to be "done" or "buried" (that quip had started even at Oxford) by Annie Graves.

Robert phoned her one day at the office and for a moment the name meant nothing to her. "The *tubab* who gave you a bed one night in the jungle?" he prompted.

They met for a drink and he was much better looking than Annie remembered. He said he'd been following her byline and seemed to know every piece she'd written better than she did herself. He was an assistant district attorney and working, as much as his job allowed, for the Carter campaign. He was idealistic, bursting with enthusiasm and, most important of all, he made her laugh. He was also straighter and had shorter hair than any man she'd dated in seven years.

While Annie's wardrobe was full of black leather and safety pins, his was all button-down collars and corduroy. When they went out, it was L.L. Bean meets the Sex Pistols. And the unconventionality of this pairing was an unspoken thrill to them both.

In bed, the zone of their relationship so long postponed and which, if she was honest with herself, she had secretly dreaded, Robert proved surprisingly free of the inhibitions she had expected. Indeed he was far more inventive than most of the drug-slackened coolsters she had lain with since coming to New York. When, weeks later, she remarked on this, Robert ruminated a moment, as she recalled him doing before declaiming details from the Dakar flight directory, and replied in perfect seriousness that he'd always believed sex, like the law, was best practiced with all due diligence.

They were married the following spring and Grace, their only child, was born three years later.

Annie had brought work with her on the train not through habit but in the hope that it might distract her. She had it stacked in front of her, the proofs of what she hoped was a seminal State of the Nation piece, commissioned at huge expense from a great and grizzled pain-in-the-ass novelist. One of her big-shot writers, as Grace would say. Annie had read the first paragraph three times and hadn't taken in a word.

Then Robert called on her cellular phone. He was at the hospital. There was no change. Grace was still unconscious.

"In a coma, you mean," Annie said, her tone challenging him to talk straight with her.

"That's not what they're calling it, but yes, I guess that's what it is."

"What else?" There was a pause. "Come on Robert, for Godsake."

"Her leg's pretty bad too. It seems the truck went over it." Annie took a wincing little breath.

"They're looking at it now. Listen Annie, I better get back there. I'll meet you at the train."

"No, don't. Stay with her. I'll get a cab."

"Okay. I'll call you again if there's news." He paused. "She's going to be alright."

"Yes, I know." She pressed a button on the phone and put it down. Outside, sunlit fields of perfect white altered their geometry as the train sped by. Annie rummaged in her bag for her sunglasses, put them on and laid her head back against the seat.

The guilt had started immediately upon Robert's first call. She should have been up there. It was the first thing she said to Don Farlow when she hung up. He was sweet and came and put his arm around her, saying all the right things.

"It would have made no difference Annie. You couldn't have done anything."

"Yes I could. I could have stopped her going. What

was Robert thinking of, letting her go out riding on a day like this?"

"It's a beautiful day. You wouldn't have stopped her."

Farlow was right of course but the guilt remained because it wasn't, she knew, about whether or not she should have gone up with them last night. It was the mere tip of a long seam of guilt that snaked its way back through the thirteen years her daughter had been alive.

Annie had taken six weeks off work when Grace was born and had loved every minute. True, a lot of the less lovable minutes had been delegated to Elsa, their Jamaican nanny, who remained to this day the linchpin of their domestic life.

Like many ambitious women of her generation, Annie had been determined to prove the compatibility of motherhood and career. But while other media mothers used their work to promote this ethic, Annie had never flaunted it, shunning so many requests for photo spreads of her with Grace that women's magazines soon stopped asking. Not so long ago she had found Grace flipping through such a piece about a TV anchorwoman, proudly pictured with her new baby.

"Why didn't we ever do this?" Grace said, not looking up. Annie answered, rather too tartly, that she thought it was immoral, like product placement. And Grace had nodded thoughtfully, still not looking at her. "Uh-huh," she said, matter-of-fact, flipping on to something else. "I guess people think you're younger if you make out you haven't got kids."

This comment and the fact that it was uttered without a trace of malice had given Annie such a shock that for several weeks she thought of little else than her relationship with Grace or, as she now saw it, her lack of one.

It hadn't always been so. In fact until four years ago when she'd taken her first editorship, Annie had prided herself that she and Grace were closer than almost any mother and daughter she could think of. As a celebrated journalist, more famous than many of those she wrote about, her time until then had been her own. If she so chose, she could work from home or take days off whenever she wanted. When she traveled, she would often take Grace with her. Once they'd spent the best part of a week, just the two of them, at a famously fancy hotel in Paris, waiting for some prima donna fashion designer to grant Annie a promised audience. Every day they walked miles shopping and sightseeing and spent the evenings guzzling delicious room service in front of the TV, snuggled in a gilded, emperor-size bed like a pair of naughty sisters.

Executive life was very different. And in the strain and euphoria of transforming a stuffy, little-read magazine into the hottest read in town, Annie had at first refused to acknowledge the toll it was taking at home. She and Grace now had what she proudly referred to as "quality time." From her present perspective, its main quality seemed to Annie to be oppression.

They had one hour together in the mornings when she forced the child to do her piano practice and two hours in the evening when she forced her to do homework. Words intended as motherly guidance seemed increasingly doomed to be taken as criticism.

At weekends things were better and the horse riding helped keep intact what fragile bridge there remained between them. Annie herself no longer rode but, unlike Robert, had from her own childhood an understanding of the peculiar tribal world of riding and showjumping.

She enjoyed driving Grace and her horse to events. But even at its best, their time together never matched the easy trust that Grace shared with Robert.

In myriad minor ways, it was to her father that the girl first turned. And Annie was by now resigned to the notion that here history was inexorably repeating. She herself had been her father's child, her mother unwilling or unable to see beyond the pool of golden light encircling Annie's brother. Now Annie, with no such excuse, felt herself propelled by pitiless genes to replicate the pattern with Grace.

The train slowed in a long curve and came to a halt in Hudson and she sat still and looked out toward the restored verandah of the platform, with its cast-iron pillars. There was a man standing exactly where Robert normally waited and he stepped forward and held out his arms to a woman with two small children who had just climbed down from the train. Annie watched him hug each of them in turn, then shepherd them toward the parking lot. The boy insisted on trying to carry the heaviest bag and the man laughed and let him. Annie looked away and was glad when the train started to move out again. In twenty-five minutes she would be in Albany.

They picked up Pilgrim's tracks farther back along the road. There were spots of blood still red in the snow among the hoofprints. It was the hunter who saw them first and he followed them, leading Logan and Koopman down through the trees toward the river.

Harry Logan knew the horse they were looking for, though not as well as the one whose mangled carcass he had just watched them cut from the wreckage of the jackknifed trailer. Gulliver was one of a number of horses he looked after up at Mrs. Dyer's place but the Macleans used another local vet instead. Logan had noticed the flashy new Morgan a couple of times in the stable. From the blood it was trailing, he knew it must be badly hurt. He still felt shaken by what he had seen and wished he could have got here earlier to put Gulliver out of his misery. But then he might have had to watch them taking Judith's body away and that would have been tough. She was such a nice kid. It was bad enough seeing the Maclean girl whom he hardly knew.

The rushing noise of the river was getting loud and now he caught sight of it down there through the trees. The hunter had stopped and was waiting for them. Logan stumbled on a dead branch and nearly fell and the hunter looked at him with scarcely veiled contempt. Macho little shit, thought Logan. He had taken an instant dislike to the guy as he did to all hunters. He wished he'd told him to put his goddamn rifle back in the car.

The water was running fast, breaking over rocks and surging around a silver birch that had toppled from the bank. The three men stood looking down at where the tracks disappeared by the water.

"Must have tried crossing over or something," said Koopman, trying to be helpful. But the hunter shook his head. The opposite bank was steep and there were no tracks going up it.

They walked along the bank, nobody speaking. Then the hunter stopped and put his hand out for them to do the same.

"There," he said, in a low voice, nodding up ahead.

They were about twenty yards from the old railroad bridge. Logan peered, shielding his eyes against the sun. He couldn't see a thing. Then there was a movement under the bridge and at last Logan saw him. The horse was on the far side, in the shadows, looking right at them. His face was wet and there was a steady dark dripping from his chest into the water. There seemed to be something stuck to his front, just below the base of the neck, though from here Logan couldn't make out what it was. Every so often the horse jerked his head down and to the side and blew out a strand of pink froth that floated quickly away downstream and dissolved. The hunter swung the gun bag off his shoulder and started unzipping it.

"Sorry pal, they're out of season," Logan said, casual as he could, pushing past. The hunter didn't even look up, just pulled the rifle out, a sleek Winchester .308 with a telescopic sight as fat as a bottle. Koopman looked on admiringly. The hunter took some bullets from a pocket and calmly started loading the rifle.

"Thing's bleedin' to death," he said.

"Yeah?" said Logan. "You're a vet too, huh?"

The guy gave a scornful little laugh. He went on slotting bullets into the magazine with the infuriating air of someone who knew he would be proven right. Logan wanted to strangle him. He turned back toward the bridge and took a careful step forward. Immediately the horse backed away and now he was in the sunlight on the far side of the bridge and Logan could see there wasn't anything stuck to the animal's chest. It was a flap of pink skin hanging loose from a terrible L-shaped gash, about two feet long. Blood was pulsing out of the exposed flesh and streaming down his breast into the water. Logan could now see that the wetness on the horse's face was blood too. Even from here he could tell the nasal bone had been smashed in.

Logan had a sinking feeling in his stomach. This was one hell of a beautiful horse and he hated the idea of putting him down. But even if he could get near enough to control the bleeding, the damage looked so severe, it was odds on the animal would die. He took another step toward him and Pilgrim backed off again, turning to check out the escape upstream. There was a sharp sound behind him, the hunter racking the bolt of his rifle. Logan turned on him.

"Will you shut the fuck up?"

The hunter didn't respond, just gave Koopman a knowing look. There was a rapport developing here that Logan was keen to break. He put his bag down and squatted to get some things out of it, talking to Koopman now.

"I want to see if I can get to him. Could you loop over to the far side of the bridge there and block him off?"

"Yes sir."

"Maybe get yourself a branch or something and wave it at him if he looks like he's heading your way. You might have to get your feet wet."

"Yes sir." He was already going back up into the trees. Logan called after him.

"Holler when you're ready. And don't get too close!"

Logan loaded a syringe with sedative and stuffed some other things he thought he might need into the pockets of his parka. He was aware of the hunter's eyes on him but ignored him and stood up. Pilgrim's head was low but he was watching every move they made. They waited, the rush of water loud about them. Then Koopman called and as the horse turned to see, Logan stepped carefully down into the river, concealing the syringe in his hand as best he could.

Here and there among the torrent were slabs of exposed rock, washed clean of snow, and he tried to use them as stepping-stones. Pilgrim turned back and saw him. He was getting agitated now, not knowing which way to run and he pawed the water and snorted out another slick of bloody froth. Logan had run out of stepping-stones and knew the moment had come to get wet. He lowered one foot into the current and felt the icy surge over the top of his boot. It was so cold, it made him gasp.

Koopman appeared in the bend of the river beyond the bridge. He too was up to his knees in the water and he had a big birch branch in his hand. The horse was looking from one of them to the other. Logan could see the fear in the animal's eye and there was something else there too which scared him a little. But he spoke to him in a soft, soothing lilt.

"It's okay fella. It's okay now."

He was within twenty feet of the horse now and was trying to figure out how he was going to do this. If he could get hold of the bridle, he might have a chance of giving the shot in the neck. In case something went wrong, he had loaded more sedative into the syringe than he would need. If he could get it into a vein in the neck, he would have to inject less than if he shot into a muscle. In either case, he would have to take care not to give too much. A horse in as bad a state as this couldn't be allowed to fall unconscious. He would have to try and inject just enough to calm him so they could lead him out of the river and get him somewhere safer.

Now that he was this close, Logan could see the chest wound. It was as bad as anything he'd ever seen and he knew they didn't have long. From the way the blood was pumping, he figured that the horse had already lost maybe up to a gallon of it.

"It's okay young fella. No one's going to hurt you."

Pilgrim snorted and wheeled away from him, taking a few steps toward Koopman, stumbling and sending up a flash of water that rainbowed in the sun.

"Shake your branch!" Logan yelled.

Koopman did and Pilgrim stopped. Logan used the flurry to lunge nearer, stepping into a hole as he did and wetting himself up to the crotch. Sweet Jesus, it was cold. The horse's white-rimmed eyes saw him come and he started off again toward Koopman.

"And again!"

The shake of the branch stopped him and Logan dived forward and made a grab. He got the reins, taking a turn in them and felt the horse brace and twist against him. He tried to step into the shoulder, keeping as clear as he could from the hind feet that were coming around to get him and he reached up quickly and managed to get the needle into the horse's neck. At the touch of the needle, Pilgrim exploded. He reared up, screaming in alarm and Logan had a fraction of a moment to push the plunger. But as he did so, the horse knocked him sideways, driving into him so that Logan lost all balance and control. Without meaning to, he injected the entire contents of the syringe into Pilgrim's neck.

The horse knew now who was the more dangerous of these men and he leapt away toward Koopman. Logan still had the reins twisted over his left hand, and so he was whipped off his feet and pulled headfirst into the water. He felt the icy water streaming through his clothes as he was dragged along like a tangled water-skier. All he could see was surf. The reins bit into the flesh of his hand and his shoulder hit a rock and he cried out in pain. Then the reins came free and he was able to lift his head and take a lungful of air. He could see Koopman now, diving out of the way and the horse splashing past him and scrambling up the bank. The syringe was still hanging from his neck. Logan stood up and watched the horse disappearing up through the trees.

"Shit," he said.

"You alright?" Koopman asked.

Logan just nodded and started to wring the water from his parka. Something caught his eye up on the bridge and he looked up to see the hunter, leaning on the parapet. He'd been watching and was grinning from ear to ear.

"Why don't you get the fuck out of here," said Logan.

She saw Robert as soon as she came through the swing doors. At the end of the corridor there was a waiting area with pale gray sofas and a low table with flowers on it and he was standing there looking out of a tall window, the sun streaming in about him. He turned at the sound of her footsteps and had to screw his eyes up to see into the relative dark of the corridor. Annie was touched by how vulnerable he looked in this moment before he saw her, with half his face lit by the sun and his skin so pale it was all but translucent. Then he found her and came walking toward her, with a grim little smile. They put their arms around each other and stayed like that for a while, saying nothing.

"Where is she?" Annie asked at last.

He took hold of her arms and held her away from him a little so he could look at her.

"They've taken her downstairs. They're operating on her now." He saw her frown and went on quickly before she could say anything. "They said she's going to be okay. She's still unconscious but they've done all these checks and scans and it doesn't look like there's any brain damage."

He stopped and swallowed and Annie waited, watching his face. She knew from the way he was trying so hard to keep his voice steady that of course there was something else.

"Go on."

But he couldn't. He started to cry. Just hung his head and stood there with his shoulders shaking. He was still holding Annie's arms and she gently disengaged herself and held him the same way.

"Go on. Tell me."

He took a long breath and tilted his head back, looking at the ceiling before he could look at her again. He made one false start then managed to say it.

"They're taking her leg off."

Annie would later come to feel both wonder and shame at her reaction that afternoon. She had never thought herself particularly stalwart in moments of crisis, except at work where she positively relished them. Nor did she normally find it difficult to show her emotions. Perhaps it was simply that Robert made the decision for her by breaking down. He cried, so she didn't. Someone had to hold on or they would all be swept away.

But Annie had no doubt that it could easily have gone the other way. As it was, the news of what they were doing to her daughter in that building at that very moment entered her like a shaft of ice. Apart from a quickly suppressed urge to scream, all that came into her head was a string of questions, so objective and practical that they seemed callous.

"How much of it?"

He frowned, lost. "What?"

"Her leg. How much of it are they taking off?"

"From above the—" He broke off, having to summon control. The detail seemed so shocking. "Above the knee."

"Which leg?"

"The right."

"How far above the knee?"

"Jesus Christ Annie! What the hell does it matter?" He pulled away from her, freeing himself, wiping his wet face with the back of a hand.

"Well, it matters quite a lot I think." She was astonishing even herself. He was right, of course it didn't matter. It was academic, ghoulish even, to pursue it but she wasn't going to stop now. "Is it just above the knee or is she losing the top of her leg as well?"

"Just above the knee. I haven't got the exact measurements but why don't you just go on down and I'm sure they'll let you have a look."

He turned away to the window and Annie stood watching as he took out a handkerchief and did a proper job on the mucus and tears, angry at himself now for having wept. There were footsteps in the corridor behind her.

"Mrs. Maclean?"

Annie turned. A young nurse, all in white, darted a look at Robert and decided Annie was the one to talk to.

"There's a call for you."

The nurse led the way, walking in small rapid steps, her white shoes making no sound on the shining tiled floor of the corridor so that she seemed to Annie to be gliding. She showed Annie to a phone near the reception desk and put the call through from the office.

It was Joan Dyer from the stables. She apologized for calling and asked nervously after Grace. Annie said she was still in a coma. She didn't mention the leg. Mrs. Dyer didn't linger. The reason she had called was Pilgrim. They'd found him and Harry Logan had been on the phone asking what they should do.

"What do you mean?" Annie asked.

"The horse is in a very bad way. There are broken bones, deep flesh wounds and he's lost a lot of blood. Even if they do all they can to save him and he survives, he's never going to be the same."

"Where's Liz? Can't we get her down there?"

Liz Hammond was the vet who looked after Pilgrim and was also a family friend. It was she who had gone down to Kentucky for them last summer to check Pilgrim out before they bought him. She'd been equally smitten.

"She's away on some conference," Mrs. Dyer said. "She's not back till next weekend."

"Logan wants to put him down?"

"Yes. I'm sorry Annie. Pilgrim's under sedation now and Harry says he may not even come around. He'd like your authority to put him down."

"You mean shoot him?" She heard herself doing it again, hammering away at irrelevant detail as she had just now with Robert. What the hell did it matter how they were going to kill the horse?

"By injection I imagine."

"And what if I say no?"

There was a pause at the other end.

"Well, I suppose they'd have to try and get him somewhere they could operate on him. Cornell maybe." She paused again. "Apart from anything else Annie, it would end up costing you a lot more than he's insured for."

It was the mention of money that clinched it for Annie, for the thought had yet to coalesce that there might be some connection between the life of this horse and the life of her daughter.

"I don't care what the hell it costs," she snapped and she could feel the older woman flinch. "You tell Logan if he kills that horse, I'll sue him."

She hung up.

"Come on. You're okay, come on."

Koopman was walking backward down the slope, waving the truck on with both arms. It reversed slowly down after him into the trees and the chains hanging from the hoist on its rear end swung and clinked as it came. It was the truck that the mill people had standing by to unload their new turbines and Koopman had commandeered it, and them, for this new purpose. Following close behind it was a big Ford pickup hitched to an open-top trailer. Koopman looked over his shoulder to where Logan and a small crowd of helpers were kneeling around the horse.

Pilgrim was lying on his side in a giant bloodstain that was spreading out through the snow under the knees of those trying to save him. This was as far as he'd got when the flood of sedative hit. His forelegs buckled and he went down on his knees. For a few moments he'd tried to fight it but by the time Logan arrived he was out for the count.

Logan had got Koopman to call Joan Dyer on his mobile and was glad the hunter wasn't around to hear him asking her to get the owner's permission to put the animal down. Then he'd sent Koopman running for help, knelt by the horse and got to work trying to stem the bleeding. He reached deep into the steaming chest wound, his hand groping through layers of torn soft-tissue till he was up to his elbow in gore. He felt around for the source of the bleeding and found it, a punctured artery, thank God a small one. He could feel it pumping hot blood into his hand and he remembered the little clamps he had put in his pocket and scrabbled with his other hand to find one. He clipped it on and immediately felt the pumping stop. But there was still blood flowing from a hundred ruptured veins so he struggled out of his sodden parka, emptied its pockets and squeezed as much water and blood as he could from it. Then he rolled it up and stuffed it as gently as he could into the wound. He cursed out loud. What he really needed now was fluids. The bag of Plasmalyte he had brought was in his bag down by the river. He got to his feet and half ran, half fell back down there to get it.

By the time he returned, the rescue squad paramedics were there and were covering Pilgrim with blankets. One of them was holding out a phone to him.

"Mrs. Dyer for you," he said.

"I can't talk to her now for Christsakes," Logan said. He knelt down and hitched the five-liter bag of Plasmalyte to Pilgrim's neck, then gave him a shot of steroids to fight the shock. The horse's breathing was shallow and irregular and his limbs were rapidly losing temperature and Logan yelled for more blankets to wrap around the animal's legs after they had bandaged them to lessen the blood flow.

One of the rescue-squad people had some green drapes from an ambulance and Logan carefully extracted his blood-soaked parka from the chest wound and packed the drapes in instead. He leaned back on his heels, out of breath, and started loading a syringe with penicillin. His shirt was dark red and sodden and blood dripped from his elbows as he held the syringe up to flick the bubbles out.

"This is fucking crazy," he said.

He injected the penicillin into Pilgrim's neck. The horse was as good as dead. The chest wound alone was enough to justify putting him down but that wasn't the half of it. His nasal bone was hideously crunched in, there were clearly some broken ribs, an ugly gash over the left cannon bone and God knows how many other smaller cuts and bruises. He could also tell from the way the horse had run up the slope that there was lameness high up in the right foreleg. He should just put the poor beast out of its agony. But now he'd got this far, he was damned if he was going to give that trigger-happy little fucker of a hunter the satisfaction of knowing he was right. If the horse died of his own accord, so be it.

Koopman had the mill truck and the trailer down beside them now and Logan saw they had managed to find a canvas sling from somewhere. The rescue-squad guy still had Mrs. Dyer standing by on the phone and Logan took it from him.

"Okay, I'm yours," he said and as he listened, he indicated to them where to put the sling. When he heard the poor woman's tactful rendering of Annie's message, he just smiled and shook his head.

"Terrific," he said. "Nice to be appreciated."

He handed the phone back and helped drag the two canvas sling straps under Pilgrim's barrel, through what was now a sea of red slush. Everyone was standing and Logan thought they all looked funny with their matching red knees. Someone handed him a dry jacket and for the first time since he was in the river he realized how cold he was.

Koopman and the driver hitched the ends of the sling to the hoist chains and then stood back with the others as Pilgrim was slowly lifted into the air and swung like a carcass onto the trailer. Logan climbed up there with two paramedics and they manhandled the horse's limbs so that eventually he lay as before on his side. Koopman passed the vet's things up to him while others spread blankets over the horse.

Logan gave another shot of steroids and took out a new bag of Plasmalyte. He suddenly felt very tired. He figured the chances of the horse being alive by the time they got to his clinic were odds on against.

"We'll call ahead," Koopman said. "So they'll know when to expect you."

"Thanks."

"All set now?"

"I guess so."

Koopman slapped the rear end of the pickup that was hitched to the trailer and yelled for the driver to move out. It started slowly up the slope.

"Good luck," Koopman called after them but Logan didn't seem to hear. The young deputy looked vaguely disappointed. It was all over and everyone was going home. There was a zipping sound behind him and he turned to look. The hunter was putting his rifle back in its bag.

"Thanks for your help," Koopman said. The hunter nodded, swung the bag over his shoulder and walked away.

Robert woke with a jolt and for a moment thought he was in his office. The screen of his computer had gone berserk, quivering green lines racing each other across ranges of jagged peaks. Oh no, he thought, a virus. Rampaging through his files on the Dunford Securities case. Then he saw the bed with its covers neatly tented over what remained of his daughter's leg and he remembered where he was.

He looked at his watch. It was nearly five A.M. The room was dark except for where the angle-lamp behind the bed cast a cocoon of soft light over Grace's head and her naked shoulders. Her eyes were closed and her face serene as if she didn't mind at all the snaking coils of plastic tube that had invaded her body. There was a tube into her mouth from the respirator and another up her nose and down into her stomach through which she could be fed. More tubes looped down from the bottles and bags that hung above the bed and they met in a tangled fury at her neck, as if fighting to be first into the valve slotted into her jugular. The valve was masked by flesh-colored tape, as were the electrodes on her temples and chest and the hole they had cut above one of her young breasts to insert a fiber-optic tube into her heart.

Without a riding hat, the doctors said, the girl might well be dead. When her head hit the road, the hat had cracked but not the skull. A second scan however had found some diffused bleeding in the brain so they had drilled a tiny hole in her skull and inserted something that was now monitoring the pressure inside. The respirator, they said, would help stop the swelling in the brain. Its rhythmic whoosh, like the waves of a mechanical sea breaking on shingle, was what had lulled Robert into sleep. He had been holding her hand and it lay palm up where he had unwittingly discarded it. He took it again in both of his and felt the falsely reassuring warmth of her.

He leaned forward and gently pressed down a piece of tape that had come unstuck from one of the catheters in her arm. He looked up at the battery of machines each of whose precise purpose Robert had insisted on having them explain. Now, without having to move, he carried out a systematic check, scanned each screen, valve and fluid level to make sure nothing had happened while he slept. He knew it was all computerized and that alarms would sound at the central monitoring desk around the corner if anything went wrong, but he had to see for himself. Satisfied now, still holding Grace's hand, he settled back in his seat. Annie was sleeping in a little room they had provided down the corridor. She had wanted him to wake her at midnight so that she could take over the vigil but as he himself had dozed Robert thought he would let her go on sleeping.

He stared at Grace's face and thought that amid all this brutish technology she looked like a child half her age. She had always been so healthy. Apart from having a knee stitched once when she fell off a bicycle, she hadn't been in a hospital since she was born. Though there had been drama enough then to last a good few years.

It was an emergency caesarean section. After twelve hours of labor they had given Annie an epidural and because nothing seemed likely to happen for a while, Robert had wandered off to the cafeteria to get himself a cup of coffee and a sandwich. When he came back up to her room half an hour later all hell had broken loose. It was like the deck of a warship, people in green running all over the place, wheeling equipment around, yelling orders. While he was away, someone told him, the internal monitoring had shown the baby was in distress. Like some hero from a forties war movie, the obstetrician had swept in and declared to his troops that he was "going in."

Robert had always imagined caesareans were peaceful affairs. No panting, shoving and screaming, just a simple cut along a plotted line and the baby lifted effortlessly out. Nothing then had prepared him for the wrestling match that followed. It was already under way when they let him in and stood him wide-eyed in a corner. Annie was under general anesthetic and he watched these men, these total strangers, delving inside her, up to their elbows in gore, hauling it out and sloshing it in dollops into a corner. Then stretching the hole with metal clamps and grunting and heaving and twisting until one of them, the war hero, had it in his hands and the others suddenly went still and watched him lift this little thing, marbled white with womb grease, out of Annie's gaping belly.

He fancied himself as a comic too, this man, and said casually over his shoulder to Robert: "Better luck next time. It's a girl." Robert could have killed him. But after they had quickly wiped her clean and checked that she had the right number of fingers and toes, they handed her to him, wrapped in a white blanket and he forgot his anger and held her in his arms. Then he laid her on Annie's pillow so that when she woke up Grace was the first thing she saw.

Better luck next time. There had never been a next time. Both of them had wanted another child but Annie had miscarried four times, the last time dangerously, well into the pregnancy. They were told it was unwise to go on trying but they didn't need telling. For with each loss the pain multiplied exponentially and in the end neither felt able to face it again. After the last one, four years ago, Annie said she wanted to be sterilized. He could tell it was because she wanted to punish herself and he had begged her not to. In the end, reluctantly, she'd relented and had a coil fitted instead, making a grim joke that with luck it might have the same effect anyway.

It was at precisely this time that Annie was offered and, to Robert's amazement, accepted her first editorship. Then, as he watched her channel her anger and disappointment into her new role, he realized she'd taken it either to distract or, again, to punish herself.

Perhaps both. But he wasn't in the least surprised when she made such a brilliant success of it that almost every major magazine in the country started trying to poach her.

Their joint failure to produce another child was a sorrow he and Annie never now discussed. But it had seeped silently into every crevice of their relationship.

It had been there, unspoken, this afternoon when Annie arrived at the hospital and he had so stupidly broken down and wept. He knew Annie felt he blamed her for being unable to give him another child. Maybe she had reacted so harshly to his tears because somehow she could see in them a trace of that blame. Maybe she was right. For this fragile child, lying here maimed by a surgeon's knife, was all they had. How rash, how mean of Annie to have spawned but one. Did he really think that? Surely not. But how then could he speak the thought so freely to himself?

Robert had always felt that he loved his wife more than she would ever love him. That she did love him he had no doubt. Their marriage, compared with many he had observed, was good. Both mentally and physically they still seemed able to give each other pleasure. But barely a day had gone by in all these years when Robert hadn't counted himself lucky to have held on to her. Why someone so vibrant should want to be with a man like him, he never ceased to wonder.

Not that Robert underestimated himself. Objectively (and objectivity he considered, objectively, to be one of his strengths) he was one of the most gifted lawyers he knew. He was also a good father, a good friend to those few close friends he had and, despite all those lawyer gags you heard nowadays, he was a genuinely moral man. But though he would never have thought himself dull, he knew he lacked Annie's sparkle. No, not her sparkle, her spark. Which is what had always excited him about her, from that very first night in Africa when he opened his door and saw her standing there with her bags.

He was six years older than she was but it had often felt much more. And what with all the glamorous, powerful people she met, Robert thought it nothing less than a minor miracle that she should be content with him. More than that, he was sure—or as sure as a thinking man could be about such matters—that she had never been unfaithful to him.

Since the spring however, when Annie had taken on this new job, things had become strained. The office bloodletting had made her irritable and more than usually critical. Grace too, and even Elsa, had noticed the change and watched themselves when Annie was around. Elsa looked relieved nowadays when it was he rather than Annie who got home first from the office. She would quickly hand over messages, show him what she had cooked for dinner and then hurry off before Annie arrived.

Robert now felt a hand on his shoulder and looked up to see his wife standing beside him, as though summoned by his thoughts. There were dark rings under her eyes. He took her hand and pressed it to his cheek.

"Did you sleep?" he asked.

"Like a baby. You were going to wake me."

"I fell asleep too."

She smiled and looked down at Grace. "No change."

He shook his head. They had spoken softly as if for fear of waking the girl. For a while they both watched her, Annie's hand still on his shoulder, the whoosh of the respirator measuring the silence between them all. Then Annie shivered and took her hand away. She wrapped her woolen jacket tightly around her, folding her arms.

"I thought I'd go home and get some of her things," she said. "You know, so when she wakes up, they'll be there."

"I'll go. You don't want to drive now."

"No, I want to. Really. Can I have your keys?"

He found them and gave them to her.

"I'll pack a bag for us too. Is there anything special you need?"

"Just clothes, a razor maybe."

She bent and kissed him on the forehead.

"Be careful," he said.

"I will. I won't be long."

He watched her go. She stopped at the door and looked back at him and he could tell there was something she wanted to say.

"What?" he said. But she just smiled and shook her head. Then she turned and was gone.

The roads were clear and at this hour, apart from a lonely sand truck or two, quite deserted. Annie drove south on 87 and then east on 90, taking the same exit the truck had taken the morning before.

There had been no thaw and the car's headlights lit the low walls of soiled snow along the roadside. Robert had fitted the snow tires and they made a low roar on the gritted blacktop. There was a phone-in on the radio, a woman saying how worried she was about her teenage son. She'd recently bought a new car, a Nissan, and the boy seemed to have fallen in love with it. He spent hours sitting in it, stroking it and today she'd walked into the garage and caught him making love to its tailpipe.

"Kinda what you'd call a fixation, huh?" said the show's host, whose name was Melvin. All phone-ins seemed to have these ruthless wise guy hosts nowadays and Annie could never understand why people kept calling, knowing full well they would get humiliated. Perhaps that was the point. This caller sailed on oblivious.

"Yes, I guess that's what it is," she said. "But I don't know what to do about it."

"Don't do anything," cried Melvin. "The kid'll soon get exhausted. Next caller . . ."

Annie turned off the highway onto the lane that curled up the shoulder of the hill to their house. The road surface here was glistening hard-pack snow and she drove carefully through the tunnel of trees and pulled into the driveway that Robert must have cleared yesterday morning. Her headlights panned across the white clapboard front of the house above her, its gables lost among towering beech trees. There were no lights on inside and the hall walls and ceiling gave a glimpse of blue as the headlights shafted briefly in. An outside light came on automatically as Annie drove around to the back of the house and waited for the door of the basement garage to raise.

The kitchen was how Robert had left it. Cupboard doors hung open and on the table stood the two unpacked grocery bags. Some ice cream in one of them had melted and leaked and was dripping off the table into a small pink lake on the floor. The red light was flashing on the answering machine, showing there were messages. But Annie didn't feel like listening to them. She saw the note Grace had written to Robert and stared at it, somehow not wanting to touch it. Then she turned abruptly and got to work clearing the ice cream and putting away the food that hadn't been spoiled.

Upstairs, packing a bag for Robert and herself, she felt oddly robotic, as if her every action were programmed. She supposed the numbness had something to do with shock or maybe it was some kind of denial.

It was certainly true that when she first saw Grace after the operation, the sight was so alien, so extreme, that she couldn't take it in. She had been almost jealous of the pain it wrought so palpably in Robert. She had seen the way his eyes kept roving over Grace's body, siphoning agony from every intrusion the doctors had made. But Annie just stared. This new version they had made of her daughter was a fact that made no sense at all.

Annie's clothes and hair smelled of the hospital so she undressed and showered. She let the water run down over her for a while then adjusted it till it was almost too hot to bear. Then she reached up and switched the shower head to its most vicious setting so that the water pricked her like hot needles. She closed her eyes and held her face up into it and the pain made her cry out loud. But she kept it there, happy that it hurt. Yes, she could feel this. At least she could feel this.

The bathroom was full of steam when she stepped out of the shower. She wiped the towel across the mirror, only partly clearing it, then dried herself before it, watching the smeared, liquid image of a creature that didn't seem to be her. She had always liked her body, though it was fuller and bigger-breasted than the sylphs who strutted the style pages of her magazine. But the blurred mirror was giving her back a distorted, pink abstraction of herself, like a Francis Bacon painting, and Annie found it so disturbing that she turned off the light and went quickly back into the bedroom.

Grace's room was just as she must have left it the previous morning. The long T-shirt she wore as a nightdress was lying on the end of the unmade bed. There was a pair of jeans on the floor and Annie bent to pick them up. They were the ones that had fraying holes in the knees, patched inside with pieces cut from an old floral-print dress of Annie's. She remembered how she had offered to do it and how hurt she had been when Grace said nonchalantly that she'd rather Elsa do it. Annie did her usual trick and, with just a little hurt flick of an eyebrow, made Grace feel guilty.

"Mom, I'm sorry," she said, putting her arms around her. "But you know you can't sew."

"I can too," Annie said, turning into a joke what they both knew hadn't been.

"Well, maybe you can. But not as good as Elsa."

"Not as well as Elsa, you mean." Annie always picked her up on the way she spoke, adopting her loftiest English accent to do so. It always prompted Grace to come back in flawless Valley Girl.

"Hey Mom, whatever. Like, you know, really."

Annie folded the jeans and put them away. Then she tidied the bed and stood there, scanning the room, wondering what to take to the hospital. In a sort of hammock slung above the bed were dozens of cuddly toys, a whole zoo of them, from bears and buffalo to kites and killer whales. They came from every corner of the globe, borne by family and friends and now, convening here, took turns in sharing Grace's bed. Each night, with scrupulous fairness, she would select two or three, depending on their size, and prop them on her pillow. Last night, Annie could see, it had been a skunk and some lurid dragon-creature Robert had once brought back from Hong Kong. Annie put them back in the hammock and rummaged to find Grace's oldest friend, a penguin called Godfrey, sent to the hospital by Robert's friends at the office on the day Grace was born.

One eye was now a button and he was sagging and faded from too many trips to the laundry. Annie hauled him out and stuffed him in the bag.

She went over to the desk by the window and packed Grace's Walkman and the box of tapes she always took on trips. The doctor had said they should try playing music to her. There were two framed photographs on the desk. One was of the three of them on a boat. Grace was in the middle with her arms around both their shoulders and all of them were laughing. It had been taken five years ago in Cape Cod; one of the happiest vacations they'd ever had. Annie put it in the bag and picked up the other picture. It was of Pilgrim, taken in the field above the stables shortly after they got him last summer. He had no saddle or bridle on him, not even a halter, and the sun gleamed on his coat. His body was pointing away but he had turned his head and was looking right at the camera. Annie had never really studied the photograph before but now that she did she found the horse's steady gaze unsettling.

She had no idea if Pilgrim was still alive. All she knew was from a message Mrs. Dyer had left yesterday evening at the hospital, that he'd been taken to the vet's place in Chatham and was to be transferred to Cornell. Now, looking at him in this picture, Annie felt herself reproached. Not for her ignorance of his fate, but for something else, something deeper that she didn't yet understand. She put the picture in the bag, switched off the light and went downstairs.

A pale light was already coming in through the tall windows in the hall. Annie put the bag down and went into the kitchen without turning on any lights. Before checking the phone messages, she thought she would make herself a cup of coffee. As she waited for the old copper kettle to boil, she walked over to the window.

Outside, only a few yards from where she stood, was a group of whitetail deer. They were standing completely still, staring back at her. Was it food they were after? She'd never seen them this close to the house before, even in the harshest of winters. What did it mean? She counted them. There were twelve, no, thirteen. One for each year of her daughter's life. Annie told herself not to be ridiculous.

There was a low, burgeoning whistle as the kettle started to boil. The deer heard it too and they turned as one and fled, their tails bouncing madly as they headed up past the 'pond to the woods. Christ almighty, thought Annie, she's dead.

THREE

HARRY LOGAN PARKED HIS CAR UNDER A SIGN THAT SAID large animal hospital and thought it odd that a university couldn't come up with wording to indicate more precisely whether it was the animals who were large or the hospital. He got out and trudged through the furrows of gray sludge which were all that remained of the weekend snow. Three days had passed since the accident and as Logan wove his way through the rows of parked cars and trailers, he thought how astonishing it was that the horse was still alive.

It had taken him nearly four hours to mend that chest wound. It was full of fragments of glass and flakes of black paint from the truck and he'd had to pick them out and sluice it clean. Then he'd trimmed the ragged edges of flesh with scissors, stapled up the artery and sewn in some drainage tubes. After that, as his assistants supervised the anesthetic, air supply and a long-overdue blood transfusion, Logan got to work with needle and thread.

He had to do it in three layers: first the muscle, then the fibrous tissue, then the skin, some seventy stitches in each layer, the inner two of them done with soluble thread. And all this for a horse he thought would never wake up. But the damn thing had woken up. It was incredible. And what's more he had just as much fight in him as he'd had down in the river. As Pilgrim struggled to his feet in the recovery chamber, Logan prayed he wouldn't tear the stitches out. He couldn't face the idea of doing it all over again.

They had kept Pilgrim on sedatives for the next twenty-four hours by which time they thought he had stabilized enough to stand the four-hour trip over here to Cornell.

Logan knew the university and its veterinary hospital well, though it had changed a lot since he was here as a student in the late sixties. It held a lot of good memories for him, most of them to do with women. Sweet Jesus, did they have some times. Especially on summer evenings when you could lie under the trees and look down at Lake Cayuga. It was about the prettiest campus he knew. But not today. It was cold and starting to rain and you couldn't even see the damn lake. On top of that, he felt lousy. He had been sneezing all morning, the result no doubt of having his balls frozen off in Kinderhook Creek. He hurried into the warmth of the glass-walled reception area and asked the young woman at the desk for Dorothy Chen, the clinician who was looking after Pilgrim.

They were building a big new clinic across the road and, as he waited, Logan looked out at the pinched faces of the construction workers and felt better. There was even a little ping of excitement at the thought of seeing Dorothy again. Her smile was the reason he wasn't going to mind driving a couple of hundred miles every day to see Pilgrim. She was like a virgin princess from one of those Chinese art movies his wife liked. A hell of a figure too. And young enough for him to know better. He saw her reflection coming through the door and turned to face her.

"Hi Dorothy! How're you doing?"

"Cold. And not very happy with you," she wagged a finger at him and frowned, mock-stern. Logan held up his hands.

"Dorothy, I drive a million miles for one of your smiles, what have I done?"

"You send me a monster like this and I'm supposed to smile at you?" But she did. "Come on. We got the X rays."

She led the way through a maze of corridors and Logan listened to her talking and tried not to watch the delicate way her hips moved inside her white coat.

There were enough X rays to mount a small exhibition. Dorothy pinned them up on the light box and they stood side by side, studying them. As Logan had thought, there were cracked ribs, five of them, and the nasal bone was broken. The ribs would heal themselves, and the nasal bone Dorothy had already operated on. She'd had to lever it out, drill holes and wire it back in place. It had gone well, though they still had to remove the swabs packed into the clotted cavity of Pilgrim's sinus.

"I'll know who to come to when I need a nose job," said Logan. Dorothy laughed.

"You wait till you see it. He's going to have the profile of a prizefighter."

Logan had been worried there might be some fracture high on the right foreleg or shoulder, but there wasn't. The whole area was just terribly bruised from the impact and there was severe damage to the network of nerves that served the leg.

"How's the chest?" said Logan.

"It's fine. You did a great job there. How many stitches?"

"Oh, about two hundred." He felt himself blushing like a schoolboy. "Shall we go see him?"

Pilgrim was out in one of the recovery stalls and they could hear him long before they got there. He was calling out and his voice was cracked from all the noise he'd been making since the last lot of sedatives had worn off. The walls of the stall were thickly padded but even so they seemed to shake under the constant thumping of his hooves. Some students were in the next stall and the pony they were looking at was clearly bothered by Pilgrim's din.

"Come to see the Minotaur?" one of them asked.

"Yeah," said Logan. "Hope you guys already fed him."

Dorothy slid the bolt to open the top part of the door. As soon as she did so, the noise inside stopped. She opened the door just enough for them to look in. Pilgrim was backed into the far corner with his head low and his ears pinned right back, looking at them like something from a horror comic. Almost every part of him seemed to be wrapped in bloody bandage. He snorted at them then raised his muzzle and bared his teeth.

"And it's good to see you too," said Logan.

"You ever see a horse this freaked before?" Dorothy asked. He shook his head.

"Me neither."

They stood there for a while, looking at him. What on earth were they going to do with him, he wondered. The Maclean woman had called him yesterday for the first time and had been real nice. Probably a little ashamed, he thought, about the message she'd sent through Mrs. Dyer. Logan wasn't bitter, in fact he was sorry for the woman after what had happened to her daughter. But when she saw the horse she'd probably want to sue him for letting the wretched thing live.

"We should give him another shot of sedative," said Dorothy. "Trouble is there aren't too many volunteers to do it. It's kind of hit and run."

"Yes. Though he can't stay on the stuff forever. He's already had enough to sink a battleship. Let's see if I can get a look at his chest."

Dorothy gave an ominous shrug. "You've made a will I hope?"

She started opening the lower part of the door. Pilgrim saw him coming and shifted uneasily, pawing the floor, snorting. And as soon as Logan stepped into the stall, the horse moved and swung his hindquarters around. Logan stepped to the side wall and tried to position himself so that he could move into the animal's shoulder, but Pilgrim was having none of it. He surged forward and sideways and lashed out with his hind legs. Logan leapt for safety, stumbled, then beat a rapid, undignified retreat. Dorothy quickly shut the door after him. The students were grinning. Logan gave a little whistle and brushed his coat down.

"Save a guy's life and what do you get?"

It rained for eight days without taking a breath. No dank December drizzle this, but rain with attitude. The rogue progeny of some sweet-named Caribbean hurricane had come north, liked it and stayed. Rivers in the Midwest burst their banks and the TV news was awash with images of people crouched on rooftops and the bloated bodies of cattle twirling like abandoned airbeds in swimming pool fields. In Missouri a family of five drowned in their car while waiting in line at McDonald's and the President flew in and declared it a disaster, as some on the rooftops had already guessed.

Ignorant of all this, her battered cells silently regrouping, Grace Maclean lay in the privacy of her coma. After a week, they had removed the air tube down her throat and inserted one instead through a little hole cut neatly in her neck. They fed her plastic bags of brown milky liquid through the tube that went up her nose and down into her stomach. And three times a day a physical therapist came and worked her limbs like a puppeteer to stop her muscles and joints from wasting away.

After the first week, Annie and Robert took turns at the bedside, one keeping vigil while the other either went back down to the city or tried to work from home in Chatham. Annie's mother offered to fly in from London but was easily dissuaded. Elsa came up and mothered them instead, cooking meals, fielding calls and running errands to and from the hospital. She watched Grace for them on the only occasion Annie and Robert were absent at the same time, the morning of Judith's funeral. Upon the sodden turf of the village cemetery they had stood with others under a canopy of black umbrellas, then driven all the way back to the hospital in silence.

Robert's partners at the law firm had as always been kind, taking as much off his shoulders as they could. Annie's boss, Crawford Gates, the group president, had called her as soon as he heard the news.

"My dear, dear Annie," he said, in a voice more sincere than both of them knew him to be. "You mustn't even think of coming back here till that little girl's one hundred percent better, do you hear me?"

"Crawford . . ."

"No, Annie, I mean it. Grace is the only thing that

matters. There's nothing on this earth so important. If anything crops up we can't handle, we know where you are."

Far from reassuring her, this only made Annie feel so paranoid that she had to fight a sudden urge to catch the next train to town. She liked the old fox—it was he after all who had wooed her and given her the job—but she trusted him not a jot. Gates was a recidivist plotter and couldn't help himself.

Annie stood at the coffee machine in the corridor outside the intensive care unit and watched the rain gusting in great swathes across the parking lot. An old man was having a fight with a recalcitrant umbrella and two nuns were being swept like sailboats toward their car. The clouds looked low and mean enough to bump their wimpled heads.

The coffee machine gave a last gurgle and Annie extracted the cup and took a sip. It tasted just as revolting as the other hundred cups she'd had from it. But at least it was hot and wet and had caffeine in it. She walked slowly back into the unit, saying hello to one of the younger nurses coming off shift.

"She's looking good today," the nurse said as they passed.

"You think?" Annie looked at her. All the nurses knew her well enough by now not to say such things lightly.

"Yes, I do." She paused at the door and it seemed for a moment as if she wanted to say something else. But she thought better of it and pushed the door open, going.

"Just you keep working those muscles!" she said.

Annie saluted. "Yes, ma'am!"

Looking good. What did looking good mean, she wondered as she walked back to Grace's bed, when you were in your eleventh day of coma and your limbs were as slack as dead fish? Another nurse was changing the dressing on Grace's leg. Annie stood and watched. The nurse looked up and smiled and got on with the job. It was the only job Annie couldn't bring herself to do. They encouraged parents and relatives to get involved. She and Robert had become quite expert at the physical therapy and all the other things that had to be done, like cleaning Grace's mouth and eyes and changing the urine bag that hung down beside the bed. But even the thought of Grace's stump sent Annie into a sort of frozen panic. She could barely look at it, let alone touch it.

"It's healing nicely," the nurse said. Annie nodded and forced herself to keep watching. They had taken the stitches out two days ago and the long, curved scar was a vivid pink. The nurse saw the look in Annie's eyes.

"I think her tape's run out," she said, nodding toward Grace's Walkman on the pillow.

The nurse was giving her an escape from the scar and Annie gratefully took it. She ejected the spent tape, some Chopin suites, and found a Mozart opera in the locker, *The Marriage of Figaro*. She slotted it into the Walkman and adjusted the earphones on Grace's head. She knew this was hardly the choice Grace would have made. She always claimed she hated opera. But Annie was damned if she was going to play the doom-laden tapes Grace listened to in the car. Who knew what Nirvana or Alice In Chains might do to a brain so bruised? Could she even hear in there? And if so, would she wake up loving opera? More likely, just hating her mother for yet another act of tyranny, Annie concluded.

She wiped a trickle of saliva from the corner of Grace's mouth and tidied a strand of hair. She let her hand rest there and stared down at her. After a while she became aware that the nurse had finished dressing the leg and was watching her. They smiled at each other. But there was a trace of something perilously close to pity in the nurse's eyes and Annie swiftly broke the moment.

"Workout time!" she said.

She pushed up her sleeves and pulled a chair closer to the bed. The nurse gathered up her things and soon Annie was alone again. She always started with Grace's left hand and she took it now in both of hers and began working the fingers one by one then all of them together. Backward and forward, opening and closing each joint, feeling the knuckles crack as she squeezed them. Now the thumb, revolving it, squashing the muscle and kneading it with her fingers. She could hear the tinny sound of the Mozart spilling from Grace's earphones and she found a rhythm in the music and worked to it, manipulating the wrist now.

It was oddly sensual this new intimacy she had with her daughter. Not since Grace was a baby had Annie felt she knew this body so well. It was a revelation, like coming back to a land loved long ago. There were blemishes, moles and scars she had never known were there. The top of Grace's forearm was a firmament of tiny freckles and covered with a down so soft that Annie wanted to brush her cheek against it. She turned the arm over and studied the translucent skin of Grace's wrist and the delta of veins that coursed beneath it.

She moved on to the elbow, opening and closing the joint fifty times, then massaging the muscles. It was hard work and Annie's hands and arms ached at the end of every session. Soon it was time to move around to the other side. She laid Grace's arm gently down on the bed and was about to get up, when she noticed something.

It was so small and so quick that Annie thought she must have imagined it. But after she had put Grace's hand down, she thought she saw one of the fingers quiver. Annie sat there and watched to see if it happened again. It didn't. So she picked the hand up again and squeezed it.

"Grace?" she said, quietly. "Gracie?"

Nothing. Grace's face was blank. The only movement was the top of her chest which rose and fell in time with the respirator. Maybe what she had seen was merely the hand settling under its own weight. Annie looked up from her daughter's face to the stack of machines that monitored her. Annie still hadn't learned as well as Robert how to read their screens. Perhaps she trusted their inbuilt alarm systems more than he did. But she knew pretty well what the most vital ones should be saying, the ones that watched Grace's heartbeat and her brain and blood pressure. The heartbeat screen had a little electronic orange heart on it, a motif Annie found quaint, sentimental almost. The rate had stayed a constant seventy for many days. But now, Annie noticed, it was higher. Eighty-five, flicking to eighty-four as she watched. Annie frowned. She looked around. There wasn't a nurse to be seen. She wasn't going to panic, it was probably nothing. She looked back at Grace.

"Grace?"

This time she squeezed Grace's hand and, looking up, saw the heartbeat monitor go crazy. Ninety, a hundred, a hundred and ten . . .

"Gracie?"

Annie stood up, holding the hand tightly in both of hers, and peering down into Grace's face. She turned to call for someone but didn't have to because two of them were there already, a nurse and a young intern. The change had been picked up on the screens at the central desk.

"I saw her move," Annie said. "Her hand . . ."

"Keep on squeezing," said the intern. He took a penlight out of his breast pocket and opened one of Grace's eyes. He shone the light into it and watched for a reaction. The nurse was checking the monitors. The heartbeat had steadied out at a hundred and twenty. The intern took Grace's earphones off.

"Talk to her."

Annie swallowed. For a moment, stupidly, she was lost for words. The intern looked up at her.

"Just talk. It doesn't matter what you say."

"Gracie? It's me. Darling, it's time to wake up now. Please wake up now."

"Look," the intern said. He was still holding Grace's eye open and Annie looked and saw a flicker. The sight of it made her take a sudden, sharp breath.

"Her blood pressure's up to one-fifty," said the nurse.

"What does that mean?"

"It means she's responding," said the intern. "May I?"

He took Grace's hand from Annie, still holding the eye open with his other hand.

"Grace," he said. "I'm going to squeeze your hand now and I want you to try and squeeze back if you can. Try as hard as you can now, okay?"

He squeezed, looking into the eye all the time.

"There," he said. He passed the girl's hand to Annie. "Now I want you to do it for your mother."

Annie took a deep breath and squeezed . . . and felt it. It was like the first, faint, tentative touch of a fish on a line. Deep in those dark, still waters something shimmered and would surface.

* * *

Grace was in a tunnel. It was a little like the subway except that it was darker and flooded with water and she was swimming in it. The water wasn't cold though. In fact it didn't really feel like water at all. It was too warm and too thick. In the distance she could see a circle of light and somehow she knew she had the choice of going toward it or turning and going in the other direction where there was also light, but of a dimmer, less welcoming kind. She wasn't frightened. It was simply a matter of choice. Either way would be fine.

Then she heard voices. They were coming from the place where the light was dimmer. She couldn't see who it was but she knew one of the voices was her mother's. There was a man's voice too, but not her father's. It was some other man, someone she didn't know. She tried to move toward them along the tunnel but the water was too thick. It was like glue, she was swimming in glue and it wouldn't let her through. The glue won't let me through, the glue . . . She tried to call out for help but she couldn't find her voice.

They didn't seem to know she was there. Why couldn't they see her? They sounded such a long way off and she was suddenly worried they might go and leave her all alone. But now, yes, the man was calling her name. They had seen her. And although she still couldn't see them, she knew they were reaching out for her and if she could only make one final, great effort, maybe the glue would let her through and they could haul her out.

FOUR

ROBERT PAID IN THE FARM SHOP AND BY THE TIME HE came out, the two boys had tied the tree up with string and were loading it into the back of the Ford Lariat crew-cab he'd bought last summer to ferry Pilgrim up from Kentucky. It had been a surprise for both Grace and Annie when he drove it, with its matching silver trailer, up to the house early one Saturday morning. They came out onto the porch, Grace thrilled and Annie quite furious. But Robert had just shrugged and smiled and said come on, you couldn't put a new horse in an old box.

He thanked the two boys, wished them a Merry Christmas and pulled out of the muddy, potholed parking lot onto the road. He had never bought a Christmas tree so late before. Usually he and Grace would go out the weekend before and get one, though they always left it until Christmas Eve to bring it inside and decorate it. At least she would be there to do that, to decorate it. Christmas Eve was tomorrow and Grace was coming home.

The doctors weren't totally happy about it. It was

only two weeks since she'd come out of the coma but he and Annie had argued forcefully that it would be good for her and finally sentiment had triumphed: Grace could go home, but for two days only. They were to collect her at noon tomorrow.

He pulled up outside the Chatham Bakery and went in to pick up some bread and muffins. Breakfast at the bakery had become a weekend ritual for them. The young woman behind the counter sometimes babysat Grace.

"How's your beautiful girl?" she asked.

"Coming home tomorrow."

"Really? That's great!"

Robert saw others were listening too. Everyone seemed to know about the accident and people he had never talked to before asked after Grace. He noticed though how no one ever spoke about the leg.

"Well, you make sure you give her my love."

"I sure will, thanks. Merry Christmas."

Robert saw them watching from the window as he got back into the Lariat. He drove past the animal feed plant, slowed to cross the railroad, and headed for home through Chatham Village. The store windows along Main Street were full of Christmas festoonery and the narrow sidewalks, strung above with colored lights, were busy with shoppers. Robert exchanged waves with those he knew as he drove by. The crèche on the central square looked pretty—undoubtedly a violation of the First Amendment—but pretty nonetheless and hey, it was Christmas. Only the weather seemed not to know it.

Since the rain had stopped, on the day Grace mouthed her first words, it had been ludicrously warm. Fresh from pontificating about hurricane floods, media climatologists were having their most lucrative Christmas in years. The world was officially a greenhouse or at least upside down.

When he got back to the house, Annie was in the den, on the phone to her office. She was giving someone, one of the senior editors he guessed, the usual hard time. From what Robert could gather, as he tidied the kitchen, the poor soul had agreed to run a profile piece on some actor Annie despised.

"A star?" she said, in disbelief. "A star? He's the complete opposite of a star. The guy's a goddamned black hole!"

Robert might normally have smiled at this but the aggression in her voice was dispelling the seasonal glow he had come home with. He knew she found it frustrating trying to run a chic metropolitan magazine from an upstate farmhouse. But it was more than that. Since the accident, Annie had seemed possessed by an anger so intense it was almost frightening.

"What! You agreed to pay him that?" she howled. "You must be out of your mind! Is he going to do it nude or something?"

Robert put the coffee on and laid the table for breakfast. The muffins were the ones Annie liked best.

"I'm sorry John, I'm not going with it. You'll have to call and cancel. . . . I don't care. . . . Yes, you can fax it to me. Okay."

He heard her hang up. No good-bye, but then there rarely was with Annie. Her footsteps as she came through the hall sounded more resigned than angry. He looked up and smiled at her as she came into the kitchen.

"Hungry?"

"No. I had some cereal."

He tried not to look disappointed. She saw the muffins on the table.

"Sorry."

"No problem. All the more for me. Like some coffee?"

Annie nodded and sat down at the table. She looked, with no apparent interest, through the newspaper he'd bought. It was a while before either of them spoke.

"Get the tree?" she asked.

"You bet. Not as good as last year's, but it's pretty."

There was another silence. He poured coffee for them both and sat down at the table. The muffins tasted good. It was so quiet he could hear himself chewing. Annie sighed.

"Well, I suppose we ought to get it done tonight," she said. She took a sip of coffee.

"What?"

"The tree. Decorate it."

Robert frowned. "Without Grace? Why? She'd hate it if we did it without her."

Annie put her coffee down with a clatter.

"Don't be stupid. How the hell is she going to decorate the tree on one leg?"

She stood up, making her chair grate on the floor, and went to the door. Shocked, Robert stared at her for a moment.

"I think she could manage it," he said steadily.

"Of course she couldn't. What's she going to do, hop around? Christ, she can hardly manage to stand up with those crutches."

Robert winced. "Annie, come on. . . ."

"No, you come on," she said and she started to go then turned back to him. "You want it all to be the same, but it can't be the same. Just try and realize that will you?"

She stood for a moment, framed by the blue surround of the doorway. Then she said she had work to do and was gone. And with a dull turning, deep in his chest, Robert knew she was right. Things would never be the same.

It was clever the way they handled her finding out about the leg, Grace thought. Because looking back on it, she couldn't actually pinpoint the moment that she knew. She supposed they had it down to a fine art, these things, and knew exactly how much dope to pump into you so you didn't freak out. She was aware something had happened down there even before she could move or speak again. There was this strange feeling and she noticed how the nurses seemed busier there than anywhere else. And it just seemed to slip into her consciousness like many other facts as they hauled her out of that tunnel of glue.

"Going home?"

She looked up. Leaning in at the door was the woman who came each day to see what you wanted to eat. She was vast and friendly, with a booming laugh capable of passing through bricks and mortar. Grace smiled and nodded.

"Alright for some," the woman said. "Means you don't get to eat my Christmas dinner, mind."

"You can save me some. I'm coming back the day after tomorrow." Her voice sounded croaky. She still had a Band-Aid over the hole they had made in her neck for the respirator tube. The woman winked.

"Honey, I'll do just that."

She went and Grace looked at her watch. It was still twenty minutes till her parents were due and she was sitting on her bed, dressed and ready to go. They had moved her into this room a week after she'd come out of the coma, freeing her at last from the respirator so she could speak rather than just mouth. The room was small, with a terrific view of the parking lot and painted that depressing shade of pale green they must make specially for hospitals. But at least there was a TV and with every surface cluttered with flowers, cards and presents, it was cheerful enough.

She looked down at her leg where the nurse had neatly pinned up the bottom half of her gray sweatpants. She'd once heard someone say that if you had an arm or a leg cut off, you could still feel it. And it was absolutely true. At night it itched so badly it drove her crazy. It itched right now. The weird thing was that even so, even as she looked at it, the funny half-leg they'd left her with didn't seem to belong to her at all. It was someone else's.

Her crutches were propped against the wall by a bedside table and peeping around them was the photograph of Pilgrim. It was one of the first things she'd seen when she came out of the coma. Her father had seen her looking at it and told her the horse was okay and that made her feel better.

Judith was dead. And Gully. They'd told her that too. And it was just like it was with the leg, the news wouldn't quite sink in. It wasn't that she didn't believe it—why after all would they lie? She had cried when her father broke it to her but, perhaps again because of the drugs she was on, it hadn't felt like real crying. It was almost like watching herself cry. And since then, whenever she'd thought about it (and it was amazing to her how she managed not to), the fact of Judith's death seemed somehow to be suspended in her head, protectively encased so that she couldn't inspect it too closely.

A police officer had come to see her last week and had asked her questions and taken notes about what had happened. The poor guy had looked so nervous and Robert and Annie had hovered anxiously in case she got upset. They needn't have worried. She told him she could only remember things up to the point when they slid down the bank. It wasn't true. She knew that if she wanted to, she could remember much, much more. But she didn't want to.

Robert had already explained that she would have to make some other statement later, a deposition or something, for the insurance people, but only when she was better. Whatever that meant.

Grace was still staring at the picture of Pilgrim. She had already decided what she was going to do. She knew they'd try and get her to ride him again. But she wasn't going to, ever. She would tell her parents to give him back to the people in Kentucky. She couldn't bear the idea of selling him locally where she might come across him one day being ridden by someone else. She would go and see him one more time, to say good-bye. But that was all.

Pilgrim came home for Christmas too, a week earlier than Grace, and no one at Cornell was sad to see the back of him. He left tokens of his appreciation with several of the students. One now had her arm in plaster and half a dozen others had cuts and bruises. Dorothy Chen, who had devised a kind of matador technique to give him his daily shots, was rewarded by a perfect set of teeth marks on her shoulder.

"I can only see them in the bathroom mirror," she told Harry Logan. "They've gone through every shade of purple you can imagine."

Logan could imagine. Dorothy Chen, examining her naked shoulder in her bathroom mirror. Oh boy.

Joan Dyer and Liz Hammond came with him to pick

the horse up. He and Liz had always got on well, despite having rival practices. She was a big, hearty woman of about his age and Logan was glad to have her along because he always found Joan Dyer, on her own, a little heavy going.

Joan, he guessed, was in her mid-fifties and had that sort of stern, weathered face that always made you feel you were being judged. It was she who drove, apparently content to listen while Logan and Liz chatted about business. When they got to Cornell, she backed the trailer expertly right up to Pilgrim's stall. Dorothy got a shot of sedatives into him, but it still took them an hour to get him loaded in.

These past weeks Liz had been helpful and generous. When she got back from her conference she'd come over to Cornell, at the Macleans' request. It was obvious they wanted her to take over from him—a sacrifice Logan would have been all too happy to make. But Liz reported back that Logan had done a great job and should be left to it. The compromise was that she was to keep a kind of watching brief. Logan didn't feel threatened. It was a relief to share notes about a difficult case like this.

Joan Dyer, who hadn't seen Pilgrim since the accident, was shocked. The scars on his face and chest were bad enough. But this savage, demented hostility was something she'd never before seen in a horse. All the way back, for four long hours, they could hear him crashing his hooves against the sides of his box. They could feel the whole trailer shake. Joan looked worried.

"Where am I going to put him?"

"What do you mean?" said Liz.

"Well, I can't put him back in the barn like this. It wouldn't be safe."

When they got back to the stables, they kept him in

the trailer while Joan and her two sons cleared one of a row of small stalls behind the barn that hadn't been used in years. The boys, Eric and Tim, were in their late teens and helped their mother run the place. Both, Logan noted as he watched them work, had inherited her long face and economy with words. When the stall was ready, Eric, the older and more sullen of the two, backed the trailer up to it. But the horse wouldn't come out.

In the end Joan sent the boys in through the front door of the trailer with sticks and Logan watched them whacking the horse and saw him rear up against them, as terrified as they were. It didn't seem right and Logan was worried about that chest wound bursting open, but he couldn't come up with a better idea and at last the horse backed off down into the stall and they slammed the door on him.

As he was driving home that night to his wife and children, Harry Logan felt depressed. He remembered the hunter, that little guy in the fur hat, grinning down at him from the railroad bridge. The little creep was right, he thought. The horse should have been put down.

Christmas at the Macleans' started badly and got worse. They drove home from the hospital with Grace carefully bolstered across the backseat of Robert's car. They hadn't got halfway when she asked about the tree.

"Can we decorate it soon as we get back?"

Annie looked straight ahead and left it to Robert to say they'd already done it, though not how it was done, in a joyless silence late the night before with the air between them bristling.

"Baby, I thought you wouldn't feel up to it," he said.

Annie knew she should feel touched or grateful for this selfless shouldering of blame and it bothered her that she didn't. She waited, almost irritated, for Robert to leaven things with the inevitable joke.

"And hey young lady," he went on. "You're going to have enough work to do when we get home. There's firewood to cut, all the cleaning, food to prepare . . ."

Grace dutifully laughed and Annie ignored Robert's sidelong look in the silence that followed.

Once home, they managed to summon some little cheer. Grace said the tree in the hall looked lovely. She spent some time alone in her room, playing Nirvana loudly to reassure them she was alright. She was good on the crutches and could even handle the stairs, falling only once when she tried to bring down a bag of little presents she'd had the nurses go out and buy for her to give her parents.

"I'm okay," she said when Robert ran to her. She had banged her head sharply on the wall and Annie, emerging from the kitchen, could see she was in pain.

"Are you sure?" Robert tried to offer help but she accepted as little as she could.

"Yes. Dad, really I'm fine."

Annie saw Robert's eyes fill as Grace went over and put the presents under the tree and the sight made her so angry she had to turn and go quickly back into the kitchen.

They always gave each other Christmas stockings. Annie and Robert did Grace's together and then one for each other. In the morning, Grace would bring hers into their room and sit on the bed and they would take turns unwrapping presents, making jokes about how clever Santa Claus had been or how he'd forgotten to remove a price tag. Now, as with the tree, the ritual seemed to Annie almost unbearable.

Grace went to bed early and when they were sure she was asleep, Robert tiptoed to her room with the stocking. Annie undressed and listened to the hall clock ticking away the silence. She was in the bathroom when Robert came back and she heard a rustling and knew he was pushing her stocking under her side of the bed. She had just done the same with his. What a farce it was.

He came in as she was brushing her teeth. He was wearing his striped English pajamas and smiled at her in the mirror. Annie spat out and rinsed her mouth.

"You've got to stop this crying," she said without looking at him.

"What?"

"I saw you, when she fell. You've got to stop feeling sorry for her. Pity won't help her at all."

He stood looking at her and as she turned to go back into the bedroom their eyes met. He was frowning at her, shaking his head.

"You're unbelievable, Annie."

"Thanks."

"What's happening to you?"

She didn't reply, just walked past him back into the bedroom. She got into bed and switched off her light and after he'd finished in the bathroom he did the same. They lay with their backs to each other and Annie stared at the sharp quadrant of yellow light that jutted in from the landing onto the bedroom floor. It wasn't anger that had stopped her answering him, she simply had no idea what the answer was. How could she have said such a thing to him? Perhaps his tears enraged her because she was jealous of them. She hadn't wept once since the accident.

She turned and slipped her arms guiltily around him, putting her body to his back.

"I'm sorry," she murmured and kissed the side of his

neck. For a moment Robert didn't move. Then slowly he rolled onto his back and put an arm around her and she nestled in with her head on his chest. She felt him give a deep sigh and for a long time they lay still. Then she slid her hand slowly down his belly and gently took hold of him and felt him stir. Then she rose up and knelt above him, pulling her nightgown over her head and letting it fall to the floor. And he reached up, as he always did, and put his hands on her breasts as she worked herself on him. He was hard now and she guided him into her and felt him shudder. Neither of them uttered a sound. And she looked down through the darkness at this good man who had known her for so long and saw in his eyes, unobscured by desire, an awful, irretrievable sadness.

The weather turned colder on Christmas Day. Metallic clouds whipped over the woods like a film in fast-forward and the wind shifted to the north and brought arctic air spiraling down the valley. Inside, they listened to it howling in the chimney as they sat playing Scrabble by the big log fire.

That morning, opening presents around the tree, they had all tried hard. Never in her life, not even when very young, had Grace had so many presents. Almost everyone they knew had sent her something and Annie had realized, too late, that they should have kept some back. Grace, she could see, sensed charity and left many gifts unopened.

Annie and Robert hadn't known what to buy her. In recent years it had always been something to do with riding. Now everything they could think of carried an implication simply through not being to do with riding. In the end Robert had bought her a tank of tropical fish. They knew she wanted one but Annie feared even this had a message tagged to it: sit and watch, it seemed to say. This now is all you can do.

Robert had rigged it all up in the little back parlor and put Christmas wrapping paper on it. They led Grace to it and watched her face light up as she undid it.

"Oh my God!" she said. "That is just fabulous."

In the evening, when Annie finished tidying away the supper things, she found Grace and Robert in front of it, lying on the sofa in the dark. The tank was illuminated and bubbling and the two of them had been watching it and fallen asleep in each other's arms. The swaying plants and the gliding shadows of the fish made ghostly patterns on their faces.

At breakfast the next morning, Grace looked very pale. Robert put his hand on hers.

"Are you okay, baby?"

She nodded. Annie came back to the table with a jug of orange juice and Robert took his hand away. Annie could see Grace had something difficult to say.

"I've been thinking about Pilgrim," she said in a level voice. It was the first time the horse had been mentioned. Annie and Robert sat very still. Annie felt ashamed neither of them had been to see him since the accident or at least since he had come back to Mrs. Dyer's.

"Uh-huh," said Robert. "And?"

"And I think we should send him back to Kentucky." There was a pause.

"Gracie," Robert began. "We don't need to make decisions right now. It may be that—" Grace cut him off.

"I know what you're going to say, that people who've had injuries like mine do ride again, but I don't—" She broke off for a moment, composing herself. "I don't want to. Please."

Annie looked at Robert and she could tell he felt her eyes on him, daring him to show even a hint of tears.

"I don't know if they'll take him back," Grace went on. "But I don't want anyone around here to have him."

Robert nodded slowly, showing he understood even if he didn't yet agree. Grace latched on to this.

"I want to say good-bye to him, Daddy. Could we go see him this morning? Before I go back to the hospital?"

Annie had spoken just once to Harry Logan. It had been an awkward call and though neither mentioned her threat to sue him, it had hung heavily over their every word. Logan had been charming and, in her tone at least, Annie got as near to an apology as she ever got. But since then, her news of Pilgrim had come only through Liz Hammond. Not wanting to add unduly to their worries over Grace, Liz had given Annie a picture of the horse's recovery that was as reassuring as it was false.

The wounds were healing well, she said. The skin grafts over the cannon bone had taken. The nasal bone repair looked better than they had ever dared hope. None of these was a lie. And none of them prepared Annie, Robert and Grace for what they were about to see as they came up the long drive and parked in front of Joan Dyer's house.

Mrs. Dyer came out of the stable and crossed the yard toward them, wiping her hands on the sides of the old blue quilt jacket she always wore. The wind whipped strands of gray hair across her face and she smiled as she tidied them away. The smile was so odd and out of character that Annie was puzzled. It was probably just awkwardness at the sight of Grace being helped out onto her crutches by Robert.

"Hello Grace," Mrs. Dyer said. "How are you dear?"

"She's doing just great, aren't you baby?" Robert said. Why can't he let her answer for herself? thought Annie. Grace smiled bravely.

"Yes, I'm fine."

"Did you have a good Christmas? Lots of presents?"

"Zillions," said Grace. "We had a fabulous time didn't we?" She looked at Annie.

"Fabulous," Annie endorsed.

No one seemed to know what to say next and for a moment they all stood there in the cold wind, embarrassed. Clouds barreled furiously overhead and the red walls of the barn were suddenly set ablaze by a burst of sun.

"Grace wants to see Pilgrim," said Robert. "Is he in the barn?"

Mrs. Dyer's face flickered.

"No. He's out back."

Annie sensed something was wrong and could see Grace did too.

"Great," said Robert. "Can we go see him?"

Mrs. Dyer hesitated, but only for an instant.

"Of course."

She turned and walked off. They followed her out of the yard and around the old row of stalls at the back of the barn.

"Mind how you go. It's pretty muddy back here."

She looked over her shoulder at Grace on her crutches then darted a look at Annie. It felt like a warning.

"She's pretty darn good on these things, don't you think Joan?" Robert said. "I can't keep up."

"Yes, I can see." Mrs. Dyer smiled, briefly.

"Why isn't he in the barn?" Grace asked. Mrs. Dyer didn't answer. They were at the stalls now and she stopped by the only door that was closed and turned to face them. She swallowed hard and looked at Annie.

"I don't know how much Harry and Liz have told you." Annie shrugged.

"Well, we know he's lucky to be alive," Robert said. There was a pause. They were all waiting for Mrs. Dyer to go on. She seemed to be searching for the right words.

"Grace," she said. "Pilgrim isn't how he used to be. He's been very disturbed by what happened." Grace looked very worried suddenly and Mrs. Dyer looked at Annie and Robert for help. "To be honest, I'm not sure it's a good idea for her to see him."

"Why? What—?" Robert started to say, but Grace cut him off.

"I want to see him. Open the door."

Mrs. Dyer looked at Annie for a decision. It seemed to Annie that they had already gone too far to turn back. She nodded. Reluctantly Mrs. Dyer drew back the bolt on the top half of the door. There was an immediate explosion of sound inside the stall which startled them all. Then there was silence. Mrs. Dyer slowly opened the top door and Grace peered in with Annie and Robert standing behind her.

It took a while for the girl's eyes to grow accustomed to the darkness. Then she saw him. Her voice when she spoke was so small and frail that the others could barely hear it.

"Pilgrim? Pilgrim?"

Then she gave a cry and turned away and Robert had to reach out quickly to stop her from falling.

"No! Daddy, no!"

He put his arms around her and led her back to the yard. The sound of her sobbing faded and was lost on the wind.

"Annie," Mrs. Dyer said. "I'm so sorry. I shouldn't have let her."

Annie looked at her blankly then stepped closer to the door of the stall. The smell of urine hit her in a sudden, pungent wave and she could see the floor was filthy with dung. Pilgrim was backed into the shadow of the far corner, watching her. His feet were splayed and his neck stretched so low that his head was little more than a foot above the ground. His grotesquely scarred muzzle was tilted up at her, as if daring her to move and he was panting in short, nervy snorts. Annie felt a shiver at the nape of her neck and the horse seemed to sense it too, for now he pinned back his ears and leered at her in a toothy, gothic parody of threat.

Annie looked into his eyes with their blood-crazed whites and for the first time in her life knew how one might come to believe in the devil.

FIVE

THE MEETING HAD BEEN DRAGGING ON FOR ALMOST AN hour and Annie was bored. There were people perched all around her office, locked in a fierce and esoteric debate about which particular shade of pink would look best on an upcoming cover. The competing mock-ups were laid out before them. Annie thought they all looked vile.

"I just don't think our readers are Day-Glo kind of people," somebody was saying. The art director, who clearly did think so, was getting more and more defensive.

"It isn't Day-Glo," he said. "It's electric candy."

"Well I don't think they're electric candy people either. It's too eighties."

"Eighties? That's absurd!"

Annie would normally have cut it short long before it got to this. She would simply have told them what she thought and that would have been that. The problem was, she was finding it almost impossible to concentrate and, more worryingly, to care.

It had been the same all morning. First there had been

a breakfast meeting to make peace with the Hollywood agent whose "black hole" client had gone berserk at having his profile canceled. Then she'd had the production people in her office for two hours spreading doom about the soaring cost of paper. One of them had been wearing a cologne of such dizzying awfulness that Annie had needed to open all the windows afterward. She could still smell it now.

In recent weeks she had come to rely more than ever on her friend and deputy, Lucy Friedman, the magazine's resident style guru. The cover they were now discussing was tied to a piece Lucy had commissioned on lounge lizards and featured a grinning photograph of a perennial rock star whose wrinkles had already been contractually removed by computer.

Sensing, no doubt, that Annie's mind was elsewhere, Lucy was effectively chairing the meeting. She was a big, pugnacious woman with a wicked sense of humor and a voice like a rusty car muffler. She enjoyed turning things upside down and did it now by changing her mind and saying the background shouldn't be pink at all but fluorescent lime-green.

As the argument raged, Annie drifted off again. In an office across the street, a man wearing spectacles and a business suit was standing by the window, doing some kind of tai chi routine. Annie watched the precise, dramatic swooping of his arms and how still he kept his head and she wondered what it did for him.

Something caught her eye and she saw through the glass panel by the door that Anthony, her assistant, was mouthing and pointing at his watch. It was nearly noon and she was supposed to be meeting Robert and Grace at the orthopedic clinic.

"What do you think Annie?" Lucy said.

"Sorry Luce, what was that?"

"Lime-green. With pink cover lines."

"Sounds great." The art director muttered something that Annie chose to ignore. She sat forward and laid her hands flat on the desk. "Listen, can we wind this up now? I have to be somewhere."

There was a car waiting for her and she gave the driver the address and sat in the back, hunched inside her coat, as they wove across to the East Side and headed uptown. The streets and those who walked them looked gray and dreary. It was that season of gloom, when the new year had been in long enough for all to see it was just as bad as the old one. Waiting at the lights, Annie watched two derelicts huddled in a doorway, one sleeping while the other declaimed grandly to the sky. Her hands felt cold and she shoved them deeper into her coat pockets.

They passed Lester's, the coffee shop on Eighty-fourth where Robert used to take Grace for breakfast sometimes before school. They hadn't talked about school yet but soon she would have to go back and face the stares of the other girls. It wasn't going to be easy but the longer they left it, the tougher it would be. If the new leg fit alright, the one they were going to try today at the clinic, Grace would soon be walking. When she'd got the hang of it, she should go back to school.

Annie got there twenty minutes late and Robert and Grace were already in with Wendy Auerbach, the prosthetist. Annie declined the receptionist's offer to take her coat and was led down a narrow white corridor to the fitting room. She could hear their voices.

The door was open and none of them saw her come in. Grace was sitting in her panties on a bed. She was looking down at her legs but Annie couldn't see them because the prosthetist was kneeling there, adjusting something. Robert stood to one side, watching.

"How's that?" said the prosthetist. "Is that better?" Grace nodded. "Alrighty. Now see how it feels standing."

She stood clear and Annie watched Grace frown in concentration and ease herself slowly off the bed, wincing as the false leg took her weight. Then she looked up and saw Annie.

"Hi," she said and did her best to smile. Robert and the prosthetist turned.

"Hi," Annie said. "How's it going?"

Grace shrugged. How pale she looked, thought Annie. How frail.

"The kid's a natural," said Wendy Auerbach. "Sorry, we had to start without you, Mom."

Annie put up a hand to show she didn't mind. The woman's relentless jollity irritated her. "Alrighty" was bad enough. Calling her "Mom" was dicing with death. She was finding it difficult to take her eyes off the leg and was aware that Grace was studying her reaction. The leg was flesh-colored and, apart from the hinge and valve hole at the knee, a reasonable match for her left leg. Annie thought it looked hideous, outrageous. She didn't know what to say. Robert came to the rescue.

"The new socket fits a treat."

After the first fitting, they had taken another plaster mold of Grace's stump and fashioned this new and better socket. Robert's fascination with the technology had made the whole process easier. He had taken Grace into the workshop and asked so many questions he probably now knew enough to be a prosthetist himself. Annie knew the purpose was to distract not just Grace but also himself from the horror of it all. But it worked and Annie was grateful.

Someone brought in a walking-frame and Robert and Annie watched Wendy Auerbach show Grace how to use it. This would only be needed for a day or two, she said, until Grace got the feel of the leg. Then she could just use a cane and pretty soon she'd find she didn't even need that. Grace sat down again and the prosthetist bounced through a list of maintenance and hygiene tips. She talked mainly to Grace, but tried to involve the parents too. Soon, this narrowed down to Robert, for it was he who asked the questions and anyway she seemed to sense Annie's dislike.

"Alrighty," she said eventually, clapping her hands. "I think we're done."

She escorted them to the door. Grace kept the leg on but walked with crutches. Robert carried the walking-frame and a bag of things Wendy Auerbach had given them to look after the leg. He thanked her and they all waited as she opened the door and offered Grace one last piece of advice.

"Remember. There's hardly a thing you did before that you can't do now. So, young lady, you just get up on that darn horse of yours as soon as you can."

Grace lowered her eyes. Robert put his hand on her shoulder. Annie shepherded them before her out of the door.

"She doesn't want to," she said through her teeth as she went past. "And neither does the darn horse. Alrighty?"

Pilgrim was wasting away. The broken bones and the scars on his body and legs had healed, but the damage done to the nerves in his shoulder had rendered him lame. Only a combination of confinement and physical therapy could help him. But such was the violence with which he exploded at anyone's approach that the latter was impossible without risk of serious injury. Confinement alone was thus his lot. In the dark stench of his stall, behind the barn where he had known days far happier, Pilgrim grew thin.

Harry Logan had neither the courage nor the skill of Dorothy Chen in administering shots. And so Mrs. Dyer's boys devised a sly technique to help him. They cut a small, sliding hatch in the bottom section of the door through which they pushed in Pilgrim's food and water. When a shot was due they would starve him. With Logan standing ready with his syringe, they would put down pails of feed and water outside then open the hatch. The boys would often get a fit of giggles as they hid to one side and waited for Pilgrim's hunger and thirst to get the better of his fear. When he reached tentatively out to sniff the pails, the boys would ram down the hatch and trap his head long enough for Logan to get the shot into his neck. Logan hated it. He especially hated the way the boys laughed.

In early February he called Liz Hammond and they arranged to meet at the stables. They took a look at Pilgrim through the stall door and then went to sit in Liz's car. They sat in silence for a while watching Tim and Eric hosing down the yard, fooling around.

"I've had enough Liz," Logan said. "It's all yours now."

"Have you spoken with Annie?"

"I called her ten times. I told her a month ago the horse ought to be put down. She won't listen. But I tell you, I can't handle this anymore. Those two fucking kids drive me nuts. I'm a vet, Lizzie. I'm supposed to stop animals' suffering, not make them suffer. I've had it."

Neither of them spoke for a moment, just sat there, gravely assessing the boys. Eric was trying to light a cigarette but Tim kept aiming the hose at him.

"She was asking me if there were horse psychiatrists," said Liz. Logan laughed.

"That horse doesn't need a shrink, he needs a lobotomy." He thought for a while. "There's this horse chiropractor guy over in Pittsfield but he doesn't do cases like this. Can't think of anybody who does. Can you?"

Liz shook her head.

There was no one. Logan sighed. The whole thing, he concluded, had been one goddamn miserable fuckup from the start. And there was no sign he could see of it getting any better.

Two

SIX

IT WAS IN AMERICA THAT HORSES FIRST ROAMED. A MIL-lion years before the birth of man, they grazed the vast plains of wiry grass and crossed to other continents over bridges of rock soon severed by retreating ice. They first knew man as the hunted knows the hunter, for long before he saw them as a means to killing other beasts, man killed them for their meat.

Paintings on the walls of caves showed how. Lions and bears would turn and fight and that was the moment men speared them. But the horse was a creature of flight not fight and, with a simple deadly logic, the hunter used flight to destroy it. Whole herds were driven hurtling headlong to their deaths from the tops of cliffs. Deposits of their broken bones bore testimony. And though later he came pretending friendship, the alliance with man would ever be but fragile, for the fear he'd struck into their hearts was too deep to be dislodged.

Since that neolithic moment when first a horse was haltered, there were those among men who understood this.

They could see into the creature's soul and soothe the wounds they found there. Often they were seen as witches and perhaps they were. Some wrought their magic with the bleached bones of toads, plucked from moonlit streams. Others, it was said, could with but a glance root the hooves of a working team to the earth they plowed. There were gypsies and showmen, shamans and charlatans. And those who truly had the gift were wont to guard it wisely, for it was said that he who drove the devil out might also drive him in. The owner of a horse you calmed might shake your hand then dance around the flames while they burned you in the village square.

For secrets uttered softly into pricked and troubled ears, these men were known as Whisperers.

They were mainly men it seemed and this puzzled Annie as she read by hooded lamplight in the cavernous reading room of the public library. She had assumed that women would know more about such things than men. She sat for many hours at one of the long, gleaming mahogany tables, privately corralled by the books she had found, and she stayed until the place closed.

She read about an Irishman called Sullivan who lived two hundred years ago and whose taming of furious horses had been witnessed by many. He would lead the animals away into a darkened barn and no one knew for sure what happened when he closed the door. He claimed that all he used were the words of an Indian charm, bought for the price of a meal from a hungry traveler. No one ever knew if this was true, for his secret died with him. All the witnesses knew was that when Sullivan led the horses out again, all fury had vanished. Some said they looked hypnotized by fear.

There was a man from Groveport, Ohio called John Solomon Rarey, who tamed his first horse at the age of twelve. Word of his gift spread and in 1858 he was summoned to Windsor Castle in England to calm a horse of Queen Victoria's. The queen and her entourage watched astonished as Rarey put his hands on the animal and laid it down on the ground before them. Then he lay down beside it and rested his head on its hooves. The queen chuckled with delight and gave Rarey a hundred dollars. He was a modest, quiet man, but now he was famous and the press wanted more. The call went out to find the most ferocious horse in all England.

It was duly found.

He was a stallion by the name of Cruiser, once the fastest racehorse in the land. Now though, according to the account Annie read, he was a "fiend incarnate" and wore an eight-pound iron muzzle to stop him killing too many stableboys. His owners only kept him alive because they wanted to breed from him and to make him safe enough to do this, they planned to blind him. Against all advice, Rarey let himself into the stable where no one else dared venture and shut the door. He emerged three hours later leading Cruiser, without his muzzle and gentle as a lamb. The owners were so impressed they gave him the horse. Rarey brought him back to Ohio, where Cruiser died on July 6, 1875, outliving his new master by a full nine years.

Annie came out of the library and down between the massive lions that guarded the steps to the street. Traffic blared by and the wind funneled icily up the canyon of buildings. She still had three or four hours of work to do back at the office, but she didn't take a cab. She wanted to walk. The cold air might make sense of the stories swirling in her head. Whatever their names, no matter where or when they lived, the horses she had read about all had but one face. Pilgrim's. It was into

Pilgrim's ears that the Irishman intoned and they were Pilgrim's eyes behind the iron muzzle.

Something was happening to Annie which she couldn't yet define. Something visceral. Over the past month she had watched her daughter walking the floors of the apartment, first with the frame, then with the cane. She had helped Grace, they all had, with the brutal, boring, daily slog of physical therapy, hour upon hour of it, till their limbs ached as much as hers. Physically, there was a steady accumulation of tiny triumphs. But Annie could see that, in almost equal measure, something inside the girl was dying.

Grace tried to mask it from them—her parents, Elsa, her friends, even the army of counselors and therapists who were paid well to see such things—with a kind of dogged cheerfulness. But Annie saw through it, saw the way Grace's face went when she thought no one was looking and saw silence, like a patient monster, enfold her daughter in its arms.

Quite why the life of a savage horse slammed up in a squalid country stall should seem now so crucially linked with her daughter's decline, Annie had no idea. There was no logic to it. She respected Grace's decision not to ride again, indeed Annie didn't like the idea of her even trying. And when Harry Logan and Liz told her again and again that it would be kinder to destroy Pilgrim and that his prolonged existence was a misery to all concerned, she knew they were talking sense. Why then did she keep saying no? Why, when the magazine's circulation figures had started to level out, had she just taken two whole afternoons off to read about weirdos who whispered into animals' ears? Because she was a fool, she told herself.

Everyone was going home when she got back to the office. She settled at her desk and Anthony gave her a list of messages and reminded her about a breakfast meeting she had been trying to avoid. Then he said good-night and left her on her own. Annie made a couple of calls that he'd said couldn't wait, then called home.

Robert told her that Grace was doing her exercises. She was fine, he said. It was what he always said. Annie told him she would be late and to go ahead and eat without her.

"You sound tired," he said. "Heavy day?"

"No. I spent it reading about whisperers."

"About what?"

"I'll tell you later."

She started to go through the stack of papers Anthony had left for her but her thoughts kept sliding away into farfetched fantasies about what she'd read in the library. Maybe John Rarey had a great-great-grandson somewhere who'd inherited the gift and could use it on Pilgrim? Maybe she could place an ad in the *Times* to trace him? WHISPERER WANTED.

How long it was before she fell asleep she had no idea, but she woke with a start to see a security man standing at the door. He was doing a routine check of the offices and apologized for disturbing her. Annie asked him what time it was and was shocked to hear it was past eleven.

She called for a car and slouched dismally in the back as it took her all the way up Central Park West. The apartment building's green door canopy looked colorless in the sodium glow of the streetlamps.

Robert and Grace had both gone to bed. Annie stood in the doorway of Grace's room and let her eyes get used to the dark. The false leg stood in the corner like a toy sentry. Grace shifted in her sleep and murmured something. And the thought suddenly occurred to Annie that perhaps this need she felt to keep Pilgrim alive, to find someone who could calm his troubled heart, wasn't about Grace at all. Perhaps it was about herself.

Annie softly pulled the covers up over Grace's shoulder and walked back along the corridor to the kitchen. Robert had left a note on the yellow pad on the table. Liz Hammond had called, it said. She had the name of someone who might be able to help.

SEVEN

TOM BOOKER WOKE AT SIX AND LISTENED TO THE LOCAL news on the TV while he shaved. A guy from Oakland had parked in the middle of the Golden Gate Bridge, shot his wife and two kids and then jumped off. Traffic both ways was at a standstill. In the eastern suburbs a woman out jogging in the hills behind her home had been killed by a mountain lion.

The light above the mirror made his sunburnt face look green against the shaving foam. The bathroom was dingy and cramped and Tom had to stoop to stand under the shower rigged in the bathtub. It always seemed motels like this were built for some miniature race you never came across, people with tiny, nimble fingers who actually preferred soap the size of credit cards and wrapped for their convenience.

He dressed and sat on the bed to pull his boots on, looking out over the little parking lot that was crammed with the pickups and four-wheeler trucks of those coming to the clinic. As of last night there were going to be twenty in the colt class and about the same in the horsemanship class. It was too many but he never liked turning folk away. For their horses' sake more than theirs. He put on his green wool jacket, picked up his hat and let himself out into the narrow concrete corridor that led to reception.

The young Chinese manager was putting out a tray of evil-looking doughnuts by the coffee machine. He beamed at Tom.

"Morning Mr. Booker! How you doing?"

"Good thanks," Tom said. He put his key down on the desk. "How are you?"

"Fine. Complimentary doughnut?"

"No thanks."

"All set for the clinic?"

"Oh, reckon we'll muddle through. See you later."

"Bye Mr. Booker."

The dawn air felt damp and chilly as he walked toward his pickup, but the cloud was high and Tom knew it would burn off by midmorning. Back home in Montana the ranch was still under two foot of snow, but when they drove into Marin County here last night it had felt like spring. California, he thought. They sure had it all worked out down here, even the weather. He couldn't wait to get home.

He pointed the red Chevy out onto the highway and looped back over 101. The riding center nestled in a gently sloping wooded valley a couple of miles out of town. He had brought the trailer up here last night before checking into the motel and turned Rimrock out into the meadow. Tom saw someone had already been out putting arrow signs up along the route saying BOOKER HORSE CLINIC and wished whoever it was hadn't. If the place was harder to find maybe some of the dumber ones wouldn't show up.

He drove through the gate and parked on the grass near the big arena where the sand had been watered and neatly combed. There was no one about. Rimrock saw him from the far side of the meadow and by the time Tom got over to the fence he was there waiting. He was an eight-year-old brown quarter horse with a white blaze on his face and four neat white socks that gave him the dapper look of someone dressed up for a tennis party. Tom had bred and reared him himself. He rubbed the horse's neck and let him nuzzle the side of his face.

"You got your work cut out today, old son," Tom said. Normally he liked to have two horses at a clinic so they could share the load. But his mare, Bronty, was about to foal and he'd had to leave her back in Montana. That was another reason he wanted to get home.

Tom turned and leaned against the fence and the two of them silently surveyed the empty space that for the next five days would be buzzing with nervous horses and their more nervous owners. After he and Rimrock had worked with them, most would go home a little less nervous and that made it worth doing. But this was the fourth clinic in about as many weeks and seeing the same damn fool problems cropping up time and time again got kind of wearing.

For the first time in twenty years he was going to take the spring and summer off. No clinics, no traveling. Just stay put on the ranch, get some of his own colts going, help his brother some. That was it. Maybe he was getting too old. He was forty-five, hell, nearly forty-six. When he'd started out doing clinics he could do one a week all year round and love every minute. If only the people could be as smart as the horses.

Rona Williams, the woman who owned the center and hosted this clinic every year, had seen him and was coming down from the stables. She was a small, wiry woman with the eyes of a zealot and though pushing forty, wore her hair in two long plaits. The girlishness of this was contradicted by the manly way she walked. It was the walk of someone used to being obeyed. Tom liked her. She worked hard to make a success of the clinic. He touched his hat to her and she smiled then looked up at the sky.

"Gonna be a good one," she said.

"I reckon." Tom nodded toward the road. "I see you got yourself some nice new signs out there. In case any of these forty crazy horses get themselves lost."

"Thirty-nine."

"Oh? Someone drop out?"

"Nope. Thirty-nine horses, one donkey." She grinned. "Guy who owns it's an actor or something. Coming up from L.A."

He sighed and gave her a look.

"You're a ruthless woman Rona. You'll have me wrestling grizzly bears before you're through."

"It's an idea."

They walked down to the arena together and talked the schedule through. He would kick off this morning with the colts, working with them one by one. With twenty of them, that was going to take pretty much the whole day. Tomorrow would be the horsemanship class, with some cattle work later, if there was time, for those who wanted it.

Tom had bought some new speakers and wanted to do a sound test, so Rona helped him get them out of the Chevy and they set them up near the bleachers where the spectators would sit. The speakers squealed with feedback when they were switched on, then settled into a menacing, anticipatory hum as Tom walked out across the virgin sand of the arena and spoke into the radio mike of his headset.

"Hi folks." His voice boomed among the trees that

stood unstirring in the still air of the valley. "This is the Rona Williams show and I'm Tom Booker, donkey tamer to the stars."

When they'd checked everything through, they drove down into town to the place they always had breakfast. Smoky and T.J., the two young guys Tom had brought from Montana to help with this run of four clinics, were already eating. Rona ordered granola and Tom some scrambled eggs, wheat toast and a large orange juice.

"You hear about that woman killed by a mountain lion out jogging?" said Smoky.

"The lion was jogging too?" Tom asked, all big blue-eyed innocence. Everyone laughed.

"Why not?" said Rona. "Hey fellas, it's California."

"That's right," said T.J. "They say he was all in Lycra and wearing these little earphones."

"You mean one of them Sony Prowlmen?" said Tom. Smoky waited for them to finish, taking it well. Teasing him had become the morning game. Tom was fond of him. He wasn't a Nobel prizewinner, but when it came to horses he had something going for him. One day, if he worked at it, he'd be good. Tom reached out and ruffled his hair.

"You're okay Smoke," he said.

A pair of buzzards circled lazily against the liquid blue of the afternoon sky. They floated ever upward on the thermals that rose from the valley, filling that middle space between tree and hilltop with an eerie, intermittent mewing. Five hundred feet below, in a cloud of dust, the latest of the day's twenty dramas was unfolding. The sun and maybe the signs along the road had lured as big a crowd as Tom had ever seen here.

The bleachers were packed and people were still coming in, paying their ten bucks a head to one of Rona's helpers at the gate. The women running the refreshment stall were doing brisk business and the air was laced with the smell of barbecue.

In the middle of the arena stood a small corral some thirty feet across and it was here that Tom and Rimrock were working. The sweat was starting to streak the dust on Tom's face and he wiped it on the sleeve of his faded blue snap-button shirt. His legs felt hot under the old leather chaps he wore over his jeans. He'd done eleven colts already and this now was the twelfth, a beautiful black thoroughbred.

Tom always started by having a word with the owner to find out the horse's "history," as he liked to call it. Had he been ridden yet? Were there any special problems? There always were, but more often than not it was the horse who told you what they were, not the owner.

This little thoroughbred was a case in point. The woman who owned him said he had a tendency to buck and was reluctant to move out. He was lazy, cranky even, she said. But now that Tom and Rimrock had him circling around them in the corral, the horse was saying something different. Tom always gave a running commentary into the radio mike so the crowd could follow what he was doing. He tried not to make the owner sound foolish. Too foolish anyway.

"There's another story coming through here," he said. "It's always kind of interesting to hear the horse's side of the story. Now if he was cranky or lazy, like you say, we'd be seeing the tail twitching there and his ears back maybe. But this isn't a cranky horse, it's a scared horse. You see how braced he is there?"

The woman was watching from outside the corral,

leaning on the rail. She nodded. Tom had Rimrock turning on a dime, in deft little white-socked steps, so he was always facing the circling thoroughbred.

"And how he keeps pointing his hindquarters in at me? Well, I'd guess the reason he seems reluctant to move out is because when he does he gets into trouble for it."

"He's not good at transitions," the woman said. "You know? When I want him to move from a trot to a lope, say?"

Tom had to bite his tongue when he heard this kind of talk.

"Uh-huh," he said. "That's not what I'm seeing. You may think you're asking for a lope but your body's saying something else. You're putting too many conditions on it. You're saying 'Go, but hey, don't go!' Or maybe 'Go, but not too fast!' He knows this from the way you feel. Your body can't lie. You ever give him a kick to make him move out?"

"He won't go unless I do."

"And then he goes and you feel he's going too fast, so you yank him back?"

"Well, yes. Sometimes."

"Sometimes. Uh-huh. And then he bucks." She nodded.

He said nothing for a while. The woman had got the message and was starting to look defensive. She was clearly big on image, made up like Barbara Stanwyck, with all the right gear. The hat alone must have set her back three hundred bucks. God knows what the horse cost. Tom worked on getting the thoroughbred focused on him. He had sixty foot of coiled rope and he threw it so the coils slapped against the horse's flank, making it burst into a lope. He coiled the rope back in then did it again. Then again and again, making the animal go from a trot to a lope, letting it slow, then up to a lope again.

"I want him to get so as he can leave real soft," he said. "He's getting the idea now. He's not all braced up and tense like he was at the start. See the way his hind-quarters are straightening out? And how his tail's not clamped in all tight like it was? He's finding out it's okay to go." He threw the rope again and this time the transition to the lope was smooth.

"You see that? That's a change. He's getting better already. Pretty soon, if you work at it, you'll be able to make all these transitions easy on a loose rein."

And pigs will fly, he thought. She'll take the poor animal home, ride him just as she always did and all this work will have been for nothing. The thought, as always, moved him up a gear. If he fixed the horse real good, maybe he could immunize the poor thing against her stupidity and fear. The thoroughbred was moving out nicely now but Tom had only worked on one side, so he turned him around to make him run the other way and did the whole thing over again.

It took almost an hour. By the time he finished, the thoroughbred was sweating hard. But when Tom let him ease up and come to a standstill, the horse looked kind of disappointed.

"He could go on playing all day," said Tom. "Hey mister, can I have my ball back?" The crowd laughed. "He's going to be okay—so long as you don't go yank-ing on him." He looked at the woman. She nodded and tried to smile but Tom could see she was crestfallen and he suddenly felt sorry for her. He walked Rimrock over to where she stood and switched off the radio mike so only she could hear when he spoke.

"It's all about self-preservation," he said gently. "You see, these animals have got such big hearts, there's nothing they want more than to do what you want them to. But when the messages get confused, all they can do is try and save themselves."

He smiled down at her for a moment, then said:

"Now why don't you go saddle him up and see."

The woman was close to tears. She climbed over the rail and walked over to her horse. The little thoroughbred watched her all the way. He let her come right up and stroke his neck. Tom watched.

"He's not going to look back if you don't," he said. "They're the most forgiving creatures God ever made."

She led the horse out and Tom brought Rimrock slowly back to the middle of the corral, letting the silence hold for a while. He took off his hat, squinting at the sky as he wiped the sweat from his brow. The two buzzards were still hanging there. Tom thought how mournful their mewing sounded. He put his hat back on and flicked the switch of the radio mike.

"Okay folks. Who's next?"

It was the guy with the donkey.

EIGHT

IT WAS MORE THAN A HUNDRED YEARS SINCE JOSEPH AND Alice Booker, Tom's great-grandparents, made their long journey west to Montana, lured like thousands of others by the promise of land. The passage cost them the lives of two children, one from scarlet fever and the other drowned, but they made it as far as the Clark's Fork River and there staked a claim to a hundred and sixty fertile acres.

By the time Tom was born, the ranch they started had grown to twenty thousand acres. That it had so prospered, let alone endured the ruthless round of drought, flood and felony, was mainly due to Tom's grandfather John. It was at least logical therefore that it should be he who destroyed it.

John Booker, a man of great physical strength and even greater gentleness, had two sons. Above the ranch house that had long since replaced the tarred homesteaders' shack stood a rocky bluff where the boys played hiding games and looked for arrowheads. From its crest you could see the river curving around like a castle moat and in the distance the snowy peaks of the

Pryor and Beartooth Mountains. Sometimes the boys would sit there side by side without talking and look out across their father's land. What the younger boy saw was his entire world. Daniel, Tom's father, loved the ranch with all his heart and if ever his thoughts strayed beyond its boundaries, it was only to reinforce the feeling that all he wanted lay within them. To him the distant mountains were like comforting walls, protecting all he held dear from the turbulence beyond. To Ned, three years his senior, they were the walls of a prison. He couldn't wait to escape and when he was sixteen he duly did. He went to California to seek his fortune and lost a gullible succession of business partners theirs instead.

Daniel stayed and ran the ranch with his father. He married a girl called Ellen Hooper from Bridger and they had three children, Tom, Rosie and Frank. Much of the land John had added to those original riverside acres was poorer pasture, rough sage-strewn hills of red gumbo gashed with black volcanic rock. The cattle work was done on horseback and Tom could ride almost before he could walk. His mother used to like telling how, at two years old, they'd found him in the barn, curled up in the straw asleep, between the massive hooves of a percheron stallion. It was as though the horse was guarding him, she said.

They used to halter-break their colts as yearlings in the spring and the boy would sit on the top rail of the corral and watch. Both his father and his grandfather had a gentle way with the horses and he didn't discover till later that there was any other way.

"It's like asking a woman to dance," the old man used to say. "If you've got no confidence and you're scared she's gonna turn you down and you sidle up, looking at your boots, sure as eggs'll break, she'll turn you down. Of course, then you can try grabbing her and forcing her around the floor, but neither one of you's gonna end up enjoying it a whole lot."

His grandfather was a great dancer. Tom could remember him gliding with his grandmother under the strings of colored lights at the Fourth of July dance. Their feet seemed to be on air. It was the same when he rode a horse.

"Dancing and riding, it's the same damn thing," he would say. "It's about trust and consent. You've gotten hold of one another. The man's leading but he's not dragging her, he's offering a feel and she feels it and goes with him. You're in harmony and moving to each other's rhythm, just following the feel."

These things Tom knew already, though knew not how he came to know them. He understood the language of horses in the same way he understood the difference between colors or smells. At any moment he could tell what was going on in their heads and he knew it was mutual. He started his first colt (he never used the word break) when he was just seven.

Tom's grandparents died the same winter, one swiftly following the other, when Tom was twelve. John left the ranch in its entirety to Tom's father. Ned flew up from Los Angeles to hear the will read out. He had been back rarely and Tom only remembered him for his fancy two-tone shoes and the hunted look he had in his eyes. He always called him "bud" and brought some useless gift, a piece of frippery that was the current craze of city kids. This time he left without saying a word. Instead, they heard from his lawyers.

The litigation dragged on for three years. Tom would hear his mother crying in the night and the kitchen always seemed full of lawyers and real estate people and neighbors who smelled money. Tom turned away from

all this and lost himself in the horses. He would cut
school to be with them and his parents were too preoccupied either to notice or care.

The only time he remembered his father happy during this time was in the spring when for three days they
drove the cattle up to the summer pastures. His mother,
Frank and Rosie came too and the five of them would
ride all day and sleep out under the stars.

"If only you could make now last forever," Frank
said on one of those nights while they lay on their backs
watching a huge half-moon roar up out of the dark
shoulders of the mountain. Frank was eleven and not
by nature a philosopher. They had all lain still, thinking
about this for a while. Somewhere, a long way off, a
coyote called.

"I guess that's all forever is," his father replied. "Just
one long trail of nows. And I guess all you can do is try
and live one now at a time without getting too worked
up about the last now or the next now."

It seemed to Tom as good a recipe for life as he'd yet
heard.

Three years of lawsuits left his father a broken man.
The ranch ended up sold to an oil company and the
money that remained, after the lawyers and the taxman
had taken their cut, was split in half. Ned was never
seen or heard of again. Daniel and Ellen took Tom,
Rosie and Frank and moved away west. They bought
seven thousand acres and an old sprawl of a ranch
house on the Rocky Mountain Front. It was where the
high plains ran smack into a hundred-million-year-old
wall of limestone, a place of harsh, towering beauty,
which later Tom would come to love. But he wasn't
ready for it. His real home had been sold from under
him and he wanted to be off on his own. Once he had

helped his parents get the new ranch going, he upped and left.

He went down to Wyoming and worked as a hired hand. There he saw things he would never have believed. Cowboys who whipped and spurred their horses till they bled. At a ranch near Sheridan he saw for himself why they called it "breaking" a horse. He watched a man tie a yearling tight by its neck to a fence, hobble a hind leg then beat it into submission with a length of zinc piping. Tom would never forget the fear in the animal's eyes nor the stupid triumph in the man's when, many hours later, it sought to save its life and submitted to the saddle. Tom told the man he was a fool, got into a fight and was fired on the spot.

He moved to Nevada and worked some of the big ranches there. Wherever he worked, he made a point of seeking out the most troubled horses and offering to ride them. Many of the men he rode with had been doing the job since long before he was born and, to begin with, they would snigger behind their hands at the sight of him mounting some crazy beast that had thrown the best of them a dozen times. They soon stopped though when they saw the way the boy handled himself and how the horse changed. Tom lost count of the horses he met who had been seriously screwed up by the stupidity or cruelty of humans, but he never met one he couldn't help.

For five years this was his life. He came home when he could and always tried to be there for the times his father most needed help. For Ellen, these visits were like a series of snapshots plotting her son's progression into manhood. He had grown lean and tall and of her three children by far the best looking. He wore his sun-bleached hair longer than before and she chided him for it but secretly liked it. Even in winter his face was tanned and it made the clear, pale blue of his eyes all the more vivid.

The life he described seemed to his mother a lonely one. There were friends he mentioned, but none who were close. There were girls he dated, but none he was serious about. By his own account, most of the time that he wasn't working with horses, he spent reading and studying for a correspondence course he'd signed up for. Ellen noticed he'd grown quieter, how he spoke now only when he had something to say. Unlike his father however, there was nothing sad about this quietness. It was more a kind of focused stillness.

As time went by, people got to hear about the Booker boy and calls would come to wherever he happened to be working, asking if he would take a look at some horse or other they were having trouble with.

"How much you charge 'em for doing this?" his brother Frank asked him over supper one April when Tom had come home to help with the branding. Rosie was away at college and Frank, nineteen now, was working full time on the ranch. He had a keen commercial nose and in fact virtually ran the place as their father retreated ever deeper into the gloom created by the lawsuits.

"Oh, I don't charge them," Tom said. Frank put his fork down and gave him a look.

"You don't charge them at all? Ever?"

"Nope." He took another mouthful.

"Why the hell not? These people have money, don't they?"

Tom thought for a moment. His parents were looking at him too. It seemed this was a matter of some interest to all of them.

"Well. You see, I don't do it for the people. I do it for the horse."

There was a silence. Frank smiled and shook his head. It was clear Tom's father thought him a little crazy too. Ellen stood up and started stacking plates defensively.

"Well, I think it's nice," she said.

It got Tom thinking. But it took another couple of years for the idea of doing clinics to take shape. Meanwhile, he surprised them all by announcing he was going off to the University of Chicago.

It was a mixed humanities and social sciences course and he stuck it out for eighteen months. He only lasted that long because he fell in love with a beautiful girl from New Jersey who played the cello in a student string quartet. Tom went to five concerts before they even spoke. She had a mane of thick, glossy black hair which she swept back over her shoulders and she wore silver hoops in her ears like a folk singer. Tom watched the way she moved as she played, the music seeming to swim through her body. It was the sexiest thing he had ever seen.

At the sixth concert she looked at him all the way through and he waited for her afterward outside. She came up and took his arm without saying a word. Her name was Rachel Feinerman and later that night in her room, Tom thought he had died and gone to heaven. He watched her light candles and then turn to stare at him as she stepped out of her dress. He thought it strange how she kept her earrings on but was glad she had because the candlelight flashed in them as they made love. She never once closed her eyes and she arched herself into him, watching him watch his hands travel her body in wonder. Her nipples were large and the color of chocolate and the luxuriant triangle of hair on her belly glistened like the wing of a raven.

He brought her home for Thanksgiving and she said

she had never been so cold in all her life. She got on well with everyone, even the horses, and said she thought it was the most beautiful place she had ever laid eyes on. Tom could tell what his mother was thinking just from the look on her face. That this young woman, with her inappropriate footwear and religion, was sure as hell no rancher's wife.

Not long after this, when Tom told Rachel he'd had enough of mixed humanities and Chicago and that he was going back to Montana, she got mad.

"You're going to go back and be a cowboy?" she said caustically. Tom said yes, matter of fact that was pretty much what he did have in mind. They were in his room and Rachel spun around, waving an exasperated arm at the books crammed into his shelves.

"What about all this?" she said. "Don't you care about any of this?" He thought for a moment, then nodded.

"Sure I care," he said. "That's part of why I want to quit. When I was working as a hand, I just couldn't wait to get back in at night to whatever I was reading. Books had a kind of magic. But these teachers here, with all their talk, well . . . Seems to me if you talk about these things too much, the magic gets lost and pretty soon talk is all there is. Some things in life just . . . are."

She looked at him for a moment, with her head tilted back, then slapped him hard across the face.

"You stupid bastard," she said. "Aren't you even going to ask me to marry you?"

So he did. And they went to Nevada the following week and were married, both aware that it was probably a mistake. Her parents were furious. His were just dazed. Tom and Rachel lived with everyone else in the ranch house for the best part of a year, while they patched up the cottage, an old ramshackle place, over-looking the creek. There was a well up there with an old cast-iron pump and Tom got it working again and rebuilt the surround and wrote his and Rachel's initials in the wet concrete. They moved in just in time for Rachel to give birth to their son. They called him Hal.

Tom worked with his father and Frank on the ranch and watched his wife get more and more depressed. She would talk for hours on the phone to her mother, then cry all night long and tell him how lonely she felt and how stupid she was for feeling that way because she loved him and Hal so much it should be all she needed. She asked him again and again whether he loved her, even waking him sometimes in the dead of the night to ask him the same question and he would hold her in his arms and tell her he did.

Tom's mother said these things sometimes happened after a woman had a child and that maybe they should get away for a while, take a vacation somewhere. So they left Hal with her and flew to San Francisco and even though the city was hung with a cold fog for the whole week they were there, Rachel started to smile again. They went to concerts and movies and fancy res-taurants and did all the tourist things too. And when they got home it was even worse.

Winter came and it was the coldest anyone on the Front could remember. The snow drove down the val-leys and made pygmies of the giant cottonwoods along the creek. In a blitz of polar air one night they lost thirty head of cattle and chipped them from the ice a week later like the fallen statues of an ancient creed.

Rachel's cello case stood gathering dust in a corner of the house and when he asked why she didn't play any-more she told him music didn't work here. It just got lost, she said, swallowed up by all the air. Some mornings later, clearing the fireplace, Tom came across a blackened metal string and sifting on among the ashes he found the charred tip of the cello's scroll. He looked in the case and there was only the bow.

When the snow melted, Rachel told him she was taking Hal and going back to New Jersey and Tom just nodded and kissed her and took her in his arms. She was from too different a world, she said, as they had always both known though never acknowledged. She could no more live here with all this windblown, aching space around her than live on the face of the moon. There was no acrimony, just a hollowing sadness. And no question but that the child should go with her. To Tom it only seemed fair.

It was the morning of the Thursday before Easter that he stacked their things in the back of the pickup to take them to the airport. The mountain front was draped in cloud and a cold drizzle was coming in from the plains. Tom held the son he hardly knew and would forever hardly know, bundled in a blanket, and watched Frank and his parents form an awkward line outside the ranch house to say their good-byes. Rachel hugged each one of them in turn, his mother last. Both women were weeping.

"I'm sorry," Rachel said. Ellen held her and patted the back of her head.

"No, sweetheart. I'm sorry. We all are."

The first Tom Booker horse clinic was held in Elko, Nevada the following spring. It was, by common consent, a great success.

NINE

ANNIE CALLED LIZ HAMMOND FROM THE OFFICE THE morning after she got her message.

"I hear you've found me a whisperer," she said.

"A what?"

Annie laughed. "It's okay. I was just reading some stuff yesterday. That's what they used to call these people."

"Whisperers. Mm, I like that. This one sounds more like a cowboy. Lives in Montana somewhere."

She told Annie how she had heard of him. It was a long chain, a friend who knew someone who remembered someone saying something about a guy who'd had a troubled horse and had taken him to this other guy in Nevada . . . Liz had doggedly followed it through.

"Liz, this must have cost you a fortune! I'll pay for the calls."

"Oh, that's okay. Apparently there are a few people out West doing this kind of thing, but I'm told he's the best. Anyway, I got his number for you."

Annie took it down and thanked her.

"No problem. But if he turns out to be Clint East-wood, he's mine okay?"

Annie thanked her again and hung up. She stared down at the number on the yellow legal pad in front of her. She didn't know why, but suddenly she felt apprehensive. Then she told herself not to be stupid, picked up the phone and dialed.

They always had a barbecue on the first night of Rona's clinic. It brought in some extra money and the food was good so Tom didn't mind staying on, though he was longing to get out of his dusty, sweaty shirt and into a hot tub.

They ate at long tables on the terrace outside Rona's low, white adobe ranch house and Tom found himself sitting next to the woman who owned the little thoroughbred. He knew it wasn't an accident because she'd been coming on strong all evening. She didn't have the hat on anymore and had untied her hair. She was in her early thirties maybe, a good-looking woman, he thought. And she knew it. She was fixing him with big black eyes but overdoing it a little, asking him all these questions and listening to him as if he was the most incredibly interesting guy she'd ever met. She had already told him that her name was Dale, that she was in real estate, that she had a house on the ocean near Santa Barbara. Oh yes, and that she was divorced.

"I just can't get over the way he felt under me after you'd finished with him," she was saying, again. "Everything had just, I don't know, freed up or something."

Tom nodded and gave a little shrug.

"Well, that's what happened," he said. "He just

needed to know it was okay and you just needed to get out of his way a little."

There was a roar of laughter from the next table and they both turned to look. The donkey man was spinning some piece of Hollywood gossip about two movie stars Tom had never heard of, caught in a car doing something he couldn't quite picture.

"Where did you learn all this stuff Tom?" he heard Dale ask. He turned back to her.

"What stuff?"

"You know, about horses. Did you have like, a guru or a teacher or something?"

He fixed her with a serious look, as if about to vouchsafe wisdom.

"Well Dale, you know, a lot of this is nuts and bolts stuff." She frowned.

"What do you mean?"

"Well, if the rider's nuts, the horse bolts."

She laughed, too enthusiastically, putting her hand on his arm. Hell, he thought, it wasn't that good a joke.

"No," she pouted. "Tell me, seriously."

"A lot of these things you can't really teach. All you can do is create a situation where if people want to learn they can. The best teachers I ever met were the horses themselves. You find a lot of folk have opinions, but if it's facts you want you're better off going to the horse."

She gave him a look he guessed was supposed to convey in equal measure a religious wonder at his great profundity and something rather more carnal. It was time for him to go.

He got up from the table making some lame excuse about having to check Rimrock, who'd long since been turned out. When he wished Dale good-night, she looked a little peeved at having wasted so much energy on him.

As he drove back to the motel, he thought it was no accident that California had always been the favored place for any cult that blended sex and religion. The people were pushovers. Maybe if that group in Oregon —the ones who used to wear orange pants and worship the guy with the ninety Rolls-Royces—had set up here instead, they'd still be going strong.

Tom had met dozens, scores, of women like Dale at these clinics over the years. They were all searching for something. With many it seemed in some strange way to be connected with fear. They'd bought themselves these fiery, expensive horses and were terrified of them. They were looking for something to help conquer this fear or maybe just fear in general. They might equally have chosen hang gliding or mountaineering or wrestling killer sharks. They just happened to have chosen riding.

They came to his clinics longing for enlightenment and comfort. Tom didn't know how much enlightenment there had been, but there'd been comfort a fair few times and it had been mutual. Ten years ago, a look like the one Dale just gave him and they'd have been bowling back to the motel together and out of their clothes before you could even shut the door.

It wasn't that nowadays he always walked away from such opportunities. It just didn't seem worth the trouble quite so much anymore. For there was usually trouble of some kind. People seldom seemed to bring the same expectations to such encounters. It had taken him a while to learn this and to understand what his own expectations were, let alone those of any woman he might meet.

For some time after Rachel left, he'd blamed himself

for what happened. He knew it wasn't just the place that was wrong. She had seemed to need something from him that he hadn't been able to give. When he'd told her that he loved her, he'd meant it. And when she and Hal went, they left a space within him that, try as he might, he was never quite able to fill with his work.

He'd always liked the company of women and found that sex came his way without looking for it. And as the clinics took off and he traveled month after month around the country, he found some solace this way. Mostly they were brief affairs, though there were one or two women, as relaxed as he about these matters, who even to this day when he passed through, welcomed him to their beds like an old friend.

The guilt about Rachel however had stayed with him. Until at last he realized that what she had needed from him was need itself. That he should need her as she needed him. And Tom knew that this was impossible. He could never feel such a need, for Rachel or anyone else. For without ever spelling it out to himself and without any sense of self-satisfaction, he already knew he had in his life a kind of innate balance, the kind that others seemed to spend most of their lives striving for. It didn't occur to him that this was anything special. He felt himself simply part of a pattern, a cohesion of things animate and inanimate, to which he was connected both by spirit and by blood.

He turned the Chevy into the motel parking lot and found a space right outside his room.

The bathtub was too short for a long soak. You had to decide whether to let your shoulders get cold or your knees. He got out and dried himself in front of the TV. The mountain lion story was still big news. They were going to hunt it down and kill it. Men with rifles and fluorescent yellow jackets were combing a hillside. Tom found it kind of touching. A mountain lion would see those jackets from about a hundred miles. He got into bed, killed the TV and called home.

His nephew Joe, the oldest of Frank's three boys, answered the phone.

"Hi Joe, how're you doing?"

"Good. Where are you?"

"Oh, I'm in some godforsaken motel, in a bed that's about a yard too short. Reckon I may have to take my hat and boots off."

Joe laughed. He was twelve years old and quiet, much like Tom had been at that age. He was also pretty good with the horses.

"How's old Brontosaurus doing?"

"She's good. She's getting real big. Dad thinks she'll foal by midweek."

"You make sure you show your old man what to do."

"I will. Want to speak to him?"

"Sure, if he's around."

He could hear Joe calling his dad. The living room TV was on and, as usual, Frank's wife Diane was hollering at one of the twins. It still seemed odd, them living in the big ranch house. Tom continued to think of it as his parents' house even though it was nearly three years since his father had died and his mother had gone to live with Rosie in Great Falls.

When Frank had married Diane, they'd taken over the creek house, the one Tom and Rachel had briefly occupied, and done some remodeling. But with three growing boys it was soon a squeeze and when his mother left, Tom insisted they move into the ranch house. He was away so much of the time, doing clinics, and when he was there, the place felt too big and too empty. He would have been happy to do a straight swap and move back out to the creek house himself but Diane said they'd only move if he stayed, there was room enough for all of them. So Tom had kept his old room and now they all lived together. Visitors, both family and friends, sometimes used the creek house, though mainly it stood empty.

Tom could hear Frank's footsteps coming to the phone.

"Hiya bro, how's it going down there?"

"It's going okay. Rona's going for a world record on the number of horses and the motel here's built for the seven dwarfs but aside from that, everything's dandy."

They talked for a while about what was happening on the ranch. They were in the middle of calving, getting up all hours of the night and going up to the pasture to check the herd. It was a lot of hard work but they hadn't lost any calves yet and Frank sounded cheerful. He told Tom there had been a lot of calls asking if he would reconsider his decision not to do any clinics this summer.

"What did you tell 'em?"

"Oh, I just said you were getting too old and were all burned out."

"Thanks pal."

"And there was a call from some Englishwoman in New York. She wouldn't say what it was about, just that it was urgent. Gave me a real hard time when I wouldn't tell her your number down there. I said I'd ask you to call her."

Tom picked up the little pad off the bedside table and wrote down Annie's name and the four phone numbers she had left, one of them a mobile.

"That it? Just the four? No number for the villa in the South of France?"

"Nope. That's it."

They talked a little about Bronty then said good-bye. Tom looked at the pad. He didn't know too many people in New York, only Rachel and Hal. Maybe this was something to do with them, though surely this woman, whoever she was, would have said so. He looked at his watch. It was ten-thirty, which made it one-thirty in New York. He put the pad back on the table and switched off the light. He would call in the morning.

He didn't get the chance. It was still dark when the phone rang and woke him. He switched on the light before answering and saw it was only five-fifteen.

"Is that Tom Booker?" From the accent, he could tell immediately who it must be.

"I think so," he said. "It's kind of early to be sure."

"I know, I'm sorry. I thought you'd probably be up early and didn't want to miss you. My name's Annie Graves. I called your brother yesterday, I don't know if he told you."

"Sure. He told me. I was going to call you. He said he hadn't given you this number."

"He didn't. I managed to get it from someone else. Anyway, the reason I'm calling is that I understand you help people who've got horse problems."

"No ma'am, I don't."

There was a silence at the other end. Tom could tell he had thrown her.

"Oh," she said. "I'm sorry, I—"

"It's kind of the other way around. I help horses who've got people problems."

They hadn't gotten off to a great start and Tom regretted being a wise guy. He asked her what the problem was and listened for a long time in silence as she told him what had happened to her daughter and the horse. It was shocking and made all the more so by the measured, almost dispassionate way she told it. He sensed there was emotion there, but that it was buried deep and firmly under control.

"That's terrible," he said when Annie had finished. "I'm real sorry."

He could hear her take a deep breath.

"Yes, well. Will you come and see him?"

"What, to New York?"

"Yes."

"Ma'am, I'm afraid—"

"Naturally I'll pay the fare."

"What I was going to say was, I don't do that sort of thing. Even if it was somewhere nearer, that's not what I do. I give clinics. And I'm not even doing them for a while. This here's the last one I'm doing till the fall."

"So you'd have time to come, if you wanted to."

It wasn't a question. She was pretty pushy. Or maybe it was just the accent.

"When does your clinic finish?"

"On Wednesday. But—"

"Could you come on Thursday?"

It wasn't just the accent. She had picked up on a slight hesitation and was pushing hard at it. It was like what you did with a horse, pick the path of least resistance and work on it.

"I'm sorry ma'am," he said firmly. "And I'm real sorry about what happened. But I've got work to do back on the ranch and I can't help you."

"Don't say that. Please, don't say that. Would you at least think about it." Again it wasn't a question.

"Ma'am—"

"I'd better go now. I'm sorry to have woken you."

And without letting him speak or saying good-bye, she hung up.

* * *

When Tom walked into reception the following
morning, the motel manager handed him a Federal Express package. It contained a photograph of a girl on a
beautiful-looking Morgan horse and an open return air
ticket to New York.

T E N

Tom laid his arm along the back of the plastic covered bench seat and watched his son cooking hamburgers behind the counter of the diner. The boy looked as if he'd been doing it all his life, the way he moved them around the grill and flipped them nonchalantly as he chatted and laughed with one of the waiters. It was, Hal had assured him, the hottest new lunch place in Greenwich Village.

The boy worked here for nothing three or four times a week in exchange for living rentfree in a loft apartment belonging to the owner, who was a friend of Rachel's. When he wasn't working here, Hal was at film school. Earlier he'd been telling Tom about a "short" he was shooting.

"It's about a man who eats his girlfriend's motorcycle piece by piece."

"Sounds tough."

"It is. It's kind of a road movie but all set in one place." Tom was about ninety percent sure this was a joke. He really hoped so. Hal went on, "When he's finished the motorcycle, he does the same with the girl-friend."

Tom nodded, considering this. "Boy meets girl, boy eats girl."

Hal laughed. He had his mother's thick black hair and dark good looks, though his eyes were blue. Tom liked him very much. They didn't get to see each other too often, but they wrote and when they did meet, they were easy together. Hal had grown up a city kid but he came out to Montana now and again and when he did, he loved it. He even rode pretty good, considering.

It had been some years since Tom had seen the boy's mother, but they talked on the phone about Hal and how he was doing and that was never difficult either.

Rachel had married an art dealer called Leo and they'd had three other children who were now in their teens. Hal was twenty and seemed to have grown up happy. It was the chance of seeing him that had clinched the decision to fly east and look at the English-woman's horse. Tom was going up there this afternoon.

"Here you go. One cheeseburger with bacon."

Hal put it down in front of him and sat down opposite him with a grin. He was only having a coffee.

"You're not eating?" asked Tom.

"I'll have something later. Try it."

Tom took a bite and nodded his approval.

"It's good."

"Some of the guys just leave them lying on the grill. You gotta work them, seal the juices."

"Is it okay for you to take time out like this?"

"Oh sure. If it gets busy, I'll go help."

It wasn't yet noon and the place was still quiet. Tom normally didn't like to eat much at midday and he rarely ate meat nowadays but Hal had been so keen to cook him a burger he'd pretended he was up for it. At the next table, four men in suits and a lot of wrist jewelry were talking loudly about a deal they'd done. Not the normal kind of clientele, Hal had discreetly informed him. But Tom had enjoyed watching them. He was always impressed by the energy of New York. He was just glad he didn't have to live here.

"How's your mother?" he asked.

"She's great. She's playing again. Leo's fixed for her to give a concert at a gallery just around the corner here on Sunday."

"That's good."

"She was going to come along today and see you but last night there was this colossal row and the pianist walked out, so now it's all panic to find someone else. She said to give you her best."

"Well you make sure to give her mine."

They talked about Hal's course and his plans for the summer. He said he'd like to come out to Montana for a couple of weeks and it seemed to Tom that he meant it and wasn't just saying it to make him feel wanted. Tom told him how he was going to be working with the yearlings and some of the older colts he'd bred. Talking about it made him long to get started. His first summer for years with no clinics, no traveling, just being there by the mountains and seeing the country come to life again.

The diner was getting busy so Hal had to go back to work. He wouldn't let Tom pay and came out with him onto the sidewalk. Tom put his hat on and noticed the glance Hal gave it. He hoped it wasn't too embarrassing to be seen with a cowboy. It was always a little awkward when they said good-bye, with Tom thinking maybe he should give the boy a hug, but they'd kind of got into the habit of just shaking hands so today, as usual, that's all they did.

"Good luck with the horse," Hal said.

"Thank you. And you with the movie."

"Thanks. I'll send you a cassette."

"I'd like that. Bye then Hal."

"Bye."

Tom decided to walk a few blocks before looking for a cab. It was cold and gray and the steam rose in drifting clouds from manholes in the street. There was a young guy, standing on a corner, begging. His hair was a matted tangle of rats' tails and his skin the color of bruised parchment. His fingers spilled through frayed woolen mitts and with no coat, he was hopping from one foot to the other to keep warm. Tom gave him a five-dollar bill.

They were expecting him at the stables at about four, but when he got to Penn Station he found there was an earlier train and decided to take it. The more daylight there was when he saw the horse, he thought, the better. Also, this way maybe he could get a little look at the animal on his own first. It was always easier when the owners weren't breathing down your neck. When they were, the horses always picked up on the tension. He was sure the woman wouldn't mind.

Annie had wondered whether to tell Grace about Tom Booker. Pilgrim's name had barely been mentioned since the day she saw him at the stables. Once Annie and Robert had tried talking to her about him, believing it better to confront the issue of what they should do with him. But Grace had become very agitated and cut Annie off.

"I don't want to hear," she said. "I've told you what I want. I want him tó go back to Kentucky. But you always know better, so it's up to you."

Robert had put a calming hand on her shoulder and started to say something, but she shrugged him off violently and yelled "No Daddy!" They left it at that.

In the end, they did however decide to tell her about the man from Montana. All Grace said was that she didn't want to be up in Chatham when he came. It was decided therefore that Annie would go alone. She'd come up by train the previous night and spent the morning at the farmhouse, making calls and trying to concentrate on the copy wired by modem to her computer screen from the office.

It was impossible. The slow tick of the hall clock, which normally she found comforting, was today almost unbearable. And with every long hour that limped by she became more nervous. She puzzled over why this should be and came up with no answer that satisfied her. The nearest she could get was a feeling, as acute as it was irrational, that in some inexorable way it wasn't only Pilgrim's fate that was to be determined today by this stranger, it was the fate of all of them. Grace's, Robert's and her own.

There were no cabs at Hudson station when the train got in. It was starting to drizzle and Tom had to wait for five minutes under the dripping iron-pillared canopy over the platform till one arrived. When it did he climbed into the back with his bag and gave the driver the address of the stables.

Hudson looked as though it might once have been pretty, but now it seemed a sorry sort of place. Once grand old buildings were rotting away. Many of the shops along what Tom supposed was its main street were boarded up and those that weren't seemed mostly to be selling junk. People tramped the sidewalks with their shoulders hunched against the rain.

It was just after three when the cab turned into Mrs. Dyer's driveway and headed up the hill toward the stables. Tom looked out at the horses standing in the rain across the muddy fields. They pricked their ears and watched the cab go by. The entrance into the stable yard was blocked by a trailer. Tom asked the cabdriver to wait and got out.

As he edged through the gap between the wall and the trailer, he could hear voices from the yard and the clatter of hooves.

"Git in! Git in there, damn you!"

Joan Dyer's sons were trying to load two frightened colts into the open back of the trailer. Tim stood on the ramp and was trying to drag the first colt inside by its halter rope. It was a tug-of-war he would easily have lost had Eric not been at the other end of the animal, driving it forward with a whip and dodging its hooves. In his other hand he held the rope of the second colt who was by now as scared as the first. All this Tom saw in one glance as he stepped around the side of the trailer into the yard.

"Whoa now boys, what's happening here?" he said. Both the boys turned and looked at him for a moment and neither answered. Then, as if he didn't exist, they looked away again and went on with what they were doing.

"It's no fucking good," Tim said. "Try the other one first." He yanked the first colt away from the trailer so that Tom had to step quickly back against the wall as they went by. At last Eric looked at him again.

"Can I help you?" There was such contempt both in the voice and the way the boy eyed him up and down that Tom could only smile.

"Thank you. I'm looking for a horse called Pilgrim. Belongs to a Mrs. Annie Graves?"

"Who are you?"

"My name's Booker."

Eric jerked his head toward the barn. "Better go see my mom."

Tom thanked him and walked away to the barn. He heard one of them snigger and say something about Wyatt Earp but he didn't look back. Mrs. Dyer came out of the barn door just as he got there. He introduced himself and they shook hands after she'd wiped hers on her jacket. She looked over his shoulder at the boys by the trailer and shook her head.

"There are better ways to do that," Tom said.

"I know," she said, wearily. But she clearly didn't want to pursue it. "You're early. Annie's not here yet."

"I'm sorry. I got the early train. I should have called. Would it be okay if I had a look at him before she gets here?"

She hesitated. He gave her a conspirator's smile that stopped just short of a wink, meaning that she, knowing about horses, would understand what he was about to say.

"You know how sometimes it's, well, kind of easier to get a fix on these things when the owner's not around."

She took the bait and nodded.

"He's back here."

Tom followed her around the back of the barn to the row of old stalls. When she got to Pilgrim's door, she turned to face him. She looked agitated suddenly.

"I have to tell you, this has been a disaster from the beginning. I don't know how much she's told you, but the truth is, in everybody's opinion except hers, this horse should have been put out of its misery long ago.

Why the vets have gone along with her I don't know. Frankly, I think keeping it alive is cruel and stupid."

The intensity took Tom by surprise. He nodded slowly and then looked at the bolted door. He'd already seen the yellowy brown liquid oozing from under it and could smell the filth beyond.

"He's in here?"

"Yes. Be careful."

Tom slid the top bolt and heard an immediate scuffle. The stench was nauseating.

"God, doesn't anyone clean him out?"

"We're all too scared," Mrs. Dyer said quietly.

Tom gently opened the top part of the door and leaned in. He saw Pilgrim through the darkness, looking back at him with his ears flattened and his yellow teeth bared. Suddenly the horse lunged and reared, striking at him with his hooves. Tom moved swiftly back and the hooves missed him by inches and smashed against the bottom door. Tom closed the top and rammed the bolt shut.

"If an inspector saw this, he'd close the whole damn place down," he said. The quiet, controlled fury in his voice made Mrs. Dyer look at the ground.

"I know, I've tried to tell—" He cut her off.

"You ought to be ashamed."

He turned away and walked back toward the yard. He could hear an engine revving and now the frightened call of a horse as a car horn started blaring. When he came around the end of the barn he saw one of the colts was already tied up in the trailer. There was blood on one of its hind legs. Eric was trying to drag the other colt in, lashing its rear with the whip while his brother, in an old pickup, shunted it from behind, honking the horn. Tom went up to the car, flung the door open and dragged the boy out by the scruff of his neck.

"Who the fuck do you think you are?" the boy said, but the end of it came out falsetto as Tom swung him sideways and threw him to the ground.

"Wyatt Earp," Tom said and walked right on past toward Eric who backed away.

"Hey listen cowboy . . ." he said. Tom grabbed him by the throat, freed the colt and took the whip out of the boy's other hand with a twist that made him yelp. The colt ran off across the yard, saving itself. Tom had the whip in one hand and the other still clamped on Eric's throat so that the boy's frightened eyes bulged. He held him there in front of him, their faces not a foot apart.

"If I thought you were worth the effort," Tom said, "I'd whip your no-good hide from hell to breakfast."

He shoved him away and the boy's back thumped against the wall, knocking the wind clean out of him. Tom looked back and saw Mrs. Dyer coming into the yard. He turned and stepped around the side of the trailer.

As he came through the gap, a woman was getting out of a silver Ford Lariat parked beside the waiting taxi. For a moment he and Annie Graves were face to face.

"Mr. Booker?" she said. Tom was breathing hard. All he really registered was the auburn hair and the troubled green eyes. He nodded. "I'm Annie Graves. You got here early."

"No ma'am. I got here too damn late."

He got into the cab, shut the door and told the driver to go. When they reached the bottom of the driveway he realized he was still holding the whip. He wound down the window and threw it in the ditch.

ELEVEN

I**T WAS ROBERT WHO FINALLY SUGGESTED GOING TO** Lester's for breakfast. It was a decision he'd worried about for two weeks. They hadn't gone there since Grace started school again and that unspoken fact was starting to weigh heavily. The reason it hadn't been mentioned was that Lester's excellent breakfast was only part of the routine. The other part, just as important, was taking the crosstown bus to get there.

It was one of those silly things that had started when Grace was much younger. Sometimes Annie came too but usually it was just Robert and Grace. They used to pretend it was some grand adventure and would sit at the back and play a whispered game in which they took turns elaborating fantasies about the other passengers. The driver was really an android hitman and those little old ladies rock stars in disguise. More recently, they would just gossip but until the accident it had never occurred to either of them not to take the bus. Now neither was sure if Grace would be able to climb onto it.

So far she had been going to school two and then

three days a week, mornings only. Robert took her there by cab and Elsa collected her by cab at noon. He and Annie tried to seem casual when they asked her how it was going. Great, she said. Everything was great. And how were Becky and Cathy and Mrs. Shaw? They were all great too. He suspected that she knew full well what they wanted to ask but couldn't. Did people stare at her leg? Did they ask her about it? Did she see them talking about her?

"Breakfast at Lester's?" Robert said that morning, in as matter-of-fact a voice as he could muster. Annie had already left for an early meeting. Grace shrugged and said, "Sure. If you want to."

They took the elevator down and said good morning to Ramón, the doorman.

"Get you a taxi?" he said.

Robert hesitated, but only for a beat.

"No. We're getting the bus."

As they walked the two blocks to the bus stop, Robert chattered away and tried to look as if it was natural to be walking this slowly. He knew Grace wasn't listening to him. Her eyes were locked on the sidewalk ahead, surveying its surface for traps, concentrating hard on placing the rubber tip of the cane and swinging her leg through behind it. By the time they got to the stop, despite the cold, she was sweating.

When the bus came, she climbed in as though she had been doing it for years. It was crowded and for a while they stood near the front. An old man saw Grace's cane and offered her his seat. She thanked him and tried to decline but he wouldn't hear of it. Robert wanted to scream at him to let her be but didn't and, blushing, Grace relented and sat down. She looked up at Robert and gave him a little humiliated smile that smote his heart.

When they walked into the coffee shop, Robert had a sudden panic that he should have called and warned Lester so that no one would make a fuss or ask embarrassing questions. He needn't have worried. Perhaps someone from the school had already told them, but Lester and the waiters were their normal brisk and cheerful selves.

They sat at their usual table by the window and ordered what they always ordered, bagels with cream cheese and lox. While they waited, Robert tried hard to keep the conversation going. It was new to him, this need to fill the silences between them. Talking with Grace had always been so easy. He noticed how her eyes kept drifting off to the people walking past outside, on their way to work. Lester, a dapper little man with a toothbrush moustache, had the radio on behind the counter and for once Robert felt grateful for the constant, inane babble of traffic news and jingles. When the bagels arrived Grace barely touched hers.

"Like to go to Europe this summer?" he said.

"What, a vacation you mean?"

"Yes. I thought we could go to Italy. Rent a house in Tuscany or somewhere. What do you think?"

She shrugged. "Okay."

"We don't have to."

"No. It'd be nice."

"If you're good, we might even go on to England and visit your grandmother." Grace grimaced on cue. The threat of dispatching her to see Annie's mother was an old family joke. Grace glanced out of the window then back at Robert.

"Dad, I think I'll go in now."

"Not hungry?"

She shook her head. He understood. She wanted to get into school early, before the lobby was crowded with gawking girls. He knocked back his coffee and paid the check.

Grace made him say good-bye on the corner rather than walk her down to the school entrance. He kissed her and walked away, fighting the urge to turn and watch her go in. He knew that if she saw him look, she might mistake concern for pity. He walked back to Third Avenue and turned downtown toward his office.

The sky had cleared while they had been inside. It was going to be one of those icy, clear blue New York days that Robert loved. It was perfect walking weather and he walked briskly, trying to drive away thoughts of that lonely figure limping into school by thinking of what he had to do once he got into work.

First, as usual, he would call the personal injury lawyer they'd hired to look after the convoluted legal farce Grace's accident seemed destined to become.

Only a sensible person would be fool enough to think the case might boil down to whether the girls were negligent in riding on the road that morning and whether the truck driver was negligent in hitting them. Instead of course, everybody was suing everybody: the girls' health insurance companies, the truck driver, his insurance company, the haulage company in Atlanta, their insurance company, the company that the driver had leased the truck from, their insurance company, the manufacturers of the truck, the manufacturers of the truck's tires, the county, the mill, the railroad. No one had yet filed suit against God for letting it snow, but it was still early days. It was pure plaintiff-attorney paradise and it felt odd to Robert to be looking at it from the other end.

At least, thank heaven, they'd managed to keep most of it away from Grace. Apart from the statement she'd given in the hospital, all she'd had to do was give a deposition under oath to their lawyer. Grace had met the woman socially a couple of times before and hadn't seemed troubled by again having to go over the accident. Again she had said that she could remember nothing after sliding down the bank.

Early in the new year the truck driver had written them a letter, saying he was sorry. Robert and Annie had discussed for a long time whether or not to show it to Grace and in the end decided it was her right. She'd read it, handed it back and said simply that it was nice of him. For Robert, just as important a decision was whether or not to show it to their attorney who naturally would seize upon it gleefully as an admission of guilt. The lawyer in Robert said show it. Something more human in him said don't. He'd hedged his bets and kept it on file.

In the distance now, he could see the sun glinting coldly on the towering glass of his office building.

A lost limb, he'd read recently in some learned legal journal, could nowadays be worth three million dollars in damages. He pictured his daughter's pale face, looking out of the coffee shop window. What fine experts they must be, he thought, to quantify the cost.

The school lobby was busier than usual. Grace did a quick scan of the faces, hoping she wouldn't see any of her classmates. Becky's mom was there, talking to Mrs. Shaw, but neither of them looked her way and there was no sign of Becky. She was probably already in the library, on one of the computers. In the old days that's where Grace would have headed too. They would fool around, leaving funny messages on each other's E-mail and would stay there till the bell rang. Then they'd all race up the stairs to the classroom, laughing and elbowing each other out of the way.

Now that Grace couldn't manage the stairs, they would all feel obliged to come with her in the elevator, a slow and ancient thing. To spare them the embarrassment, Grace now went straight up to the classroom on her own so that she could be sitting at her desk when they arrived.

She made her way over to the elevator and pressed the call button, keeping her eyes on it so that if any of her friends came by they'd have the chance to avoid her.

Everyone had been so nice to her since her return to school. That was the problem. She just wanted them to be normal. And other things had changed. While she'd been away, her friends seemed to have subtly regrouped. Becky and Cathy, her two best friends, had gotten closer. The three of them used to be inseparable. They would gossip and tease and moan about each other and console each other on the phone every evening. It had been a perfectly balanced threesome. But now, although they did their best to include her, it wasn't the same. But how could it be?

The elevator arrived and Grace went in, thankful that she was still the only one waiting and would have it to herself. But just as the doors were closing two younger girls came hurtling in, laughing and gabbling away to each other. As soon as they saw Grace they both went quiet.

Grace smiled and said, "Hi."

"Hi." They said it together but said nothing more and the three of them stood awkwardly while the elevator made its laborious, cranking ascent. Grace noticed how the eyes of both girls examined the blank walls and ceiling, looking everywhere except at the one thing she knew they wanted to look at, her leg. It was always the same.

She'd mentioned it to the "trauma psychologist," yet another expert her parents made her visit every week. The woman meant well and was probably very good at her job, but Grace found the sessions a complete waste of time. How could this stranger—how could anyone—know what it was like?

"Tell them it's okay to look," the woman had said. "Tell them it's okay to talk about it."

But that wasn't the point. Grace didn't want them to look, she didn't want them to talk about it. Talk. These shrink people seemed to think that talk solved everything and it just wasn't true.

Yesterday the woman had tried to get her to talk about Judith and that was the last thing on earth Grace wanted to do.

"How do you feel about Judith?"

Grace had felt like screaming. Instead, she said coldly, "She's dead, how do you think I feel?" Eventually the woman got the message and the subject was dropped.

It had been the same a few weeks ago when she'd tried to get Grace to talk about Pilgrim. He was maimed and useless, just like Grace, and every time she thought of him, all she could see were those terrible eyes cowering in the corner of that stinking stall at Mrs. Dyer's. How on earth could it help to think or talk about that?

The elevator stopped at the floor below Grace's and the two younger girls got out. She heard them immediately start talking again as they went off down the corridor.

When she got to her own classroom it was as she'd hoped, nobody else had yet come up. She got her books out of her bag, carefully concealed her cane on the floor under the desk, then lowered herself slowly onto the hard wooden seat. In fact it was so hard that by the end of the morning her stump would be throbbing with pain. But she could handle it. That kind of pain was easy.

It was three days before Annie was able to speak to Tom Booker. She already had a clear enough picture of what had happened at the stables that day. After watching the taxi go away down the driveway, she'd gone into the yard and got most of the story just from the faces of the two Dyer boys. Their mother had told Annie coldly that she wanted Pilgrim out of the place by Monday.

Annie called Liz Hammond and together they went to see Harry Logan. He had just finished a hysterectomy on a Chihuahua when they arrived. He came out with his surgical gown on and when he saw the two women he said "Uh-oh" and pretended to hide. He had a couple of recovery stalls behind the clinic and, after a lot of sighing, he agreed to let Annie put Pilgrim in one of them.

"For one week only," he wagged a finger at her.

"Two," Annie said.

He looked at Liz and gave a forlorn grin.

"She a friend of yours? Okay, two then. Absolute max. While you find somewhere else."

"Harry, you're a sweetheart," said Liz. He put up his hands.

"I'm an idiot. This horse. He bites me, he kicks me, he drags me through a freezing river and what do I do? I take him in as a house-guest."

"Thanks Harry," Annie said.

The three of them went up to the stables the next morning. The boys weren't about and only once did Annie see Joan Dyer, looking out from an upstairs window of her house. After two hours of bruising struggle and three times the amount of sedative Harry felt happy giving, they got Pilgrim into the trailer and drove him back to the clinic.

The day after Tom Booker's visit, Annie had tried calling him in Montana. The woman who answered the phone—Booker's wife, Annie assumed—told her that he was expected back the following evening. The woman's tone was none too friendly and Annie thought she must have heard what had happened. She said she would tell Tom that Annie had called. Annie waited two long days and heard nothing. On the second night, when Robert was in bed reading and she was sure Grace was asleep, she called again. Again, it was the woman who answered.

"He's having his supper right now," she said.

Annie heard a man's voice asking who it was and the ruffling sound of a hand being put over the receiver. Through it she could hear her say, "It's that English-woman again." There was a long pause. Annie realized she was holding her breath and told herself to calm down.

"Mrs. Graves, this is Tom Booker."

"Mr. Booker. I wanted to apologize for what happened at the stables." There was silence at the other end so she went on. "I should have known what was going on up there but I suppose I just closed my eyes to it."

"I can understand that." She expected him to go on but he didn't.

"Anyway. We've moved him to another place, a better place, and I wondered if you could . . ." She realized how futile, how stupid this was even before she said it. "If you would consider coming back and seeing him."

"I'm sorry. I can't do that. Even if I had the time, frankly I don't know how much use it'd be."

"Couldn't you spare just a day or two? I don't care what it would cost." She heard him give a little laugh and she regretted saying it.

"Ma'am, I hope you don't mind if I speak plainly with you, but you've got to understand. There's a limit to the amount of suffering these creatures can take. I believe this horse of yours has been living in the shadow for too long now."

"So you think we should put him down? Like everyone else does?" There was a pause. "If he was your horse Mr. Booker, would you put him down?"

"Well ma'am. He's not my horse and I'm glad it's not my decision. But in your shoes, yes, that's what I'd do."

She tried again to persuade him to come, but she could tell it was no use. He was courteous and calm and totally unmovable. She thanked him and hung up, then walked down the corridor and into the living room.

The lights had all been turned off and the top of the piano shone dimly in the darkness. She went slowly over to the window and stood there for a long time, looking out across the treetops of the park toward the towering apartment blocks of the East Side. It was like a stage backdrop, ten thousand tiny windows, pinpricks of light in a fake night sky. It was impossible to believe that inside every one of them was a different life with its own special pain and destiny.

Robert had fallen asleep. She took his book from his hands, turned off his bedside light and undressed in the dark. For a long time she lay on her back beside him, listening to his breathing and watching the orange shapes made on the ceiling by the streetlamps spilling around the edges of the blinds. She already knew what she was going to do. But she wasn't going to tell Robert, or Grace, until she had it all arranged.

TWELVE

FOR HIS TALENT IN NURTURING YOUNG AND RUTHLESS recruits to run his mighty empire, Crawford Gates was known, among many names less flattering, as The Face That Launched a Thousand Shits. For this reason Annie always had somewhat mixed feelings about being seen with him.

He was sitting opposite her, eating his seared swordfish meticulously without taking his eyes off her. And as she talked, Annie was intrigued by how his fork kept finding the next piece, homing faultlessly in on it as if drawn there by a magnet. It was the same restaurant he had taken her to almost a year ago when he'd offered her the editorship, a vast soulless space with minimalist matt black decor and a floor of white marble that somehow always made Annie think of an abattoir.

She knew a month was a lot to ask but she felt she was owed it. Until the accident she had barely taken a day off and even since then she hadn't taken many.

"I'll have the phone, fax, modem, everything," she said. "You won't even know I'm not here."

She cursed to herself. She'd been talking for fifteen

minutes and was getting the tone all wrong. It sounded like she was pleading. She should be doing it from strength, just telling him straight what she was going to do. There was nothing about his manner that so far suggested disapproval. He was just hearing her out while the damn swordfish autopiloted into his mouth. When she was nervous she had this stupid habit of feeling obliged to fill the silences of any conversation. She decided to stop and wait for a reaction. Crawford Gates finished chewing, nodded and took a slow sip of Perrier.

"Are you going to take Robert and Grace too?"

"Just Grace. Robert's got too much on. But Grace really needs to get away. Since she went back to school she's started to sink a little. The break'll do her good."

What she didn't say was that even now neither Grace nor Robert had the faintest idea of what she was planning. Telling them was almost the only thing left to do. Everything else she had done, with Anthony's help, from the office.

The house she had found to rent was in Choteau, which was the nearest town of any size to Tom Booker's ranch. There hadn't been much choice, but the place was furnished and from the details the real estate agent had sent, it seemed adequate. She had found a physical therapist nearby for Grace and some stables who were prepared to take Pilgrim, though Annie had been less than frank about what the horse was like. The worst part was going to be hauling the trailer across seven states to get there. But Liz Hammond and Harry Logan had made calls and fixed a chain of places they were welcome to stay en route.

Crawford Gates dabbed his lips clean.

"Annie my dear, I said it before and I say it again. You take all the time you need. These children of ours are precious, God-given creatures and when something goes wrong, we just have to stand right by them and do what's best."

From someone who'd walked out on four marriages and twice that many children, Annie thought that was pretty rich. He sounded like Ronald Reagan at the end of a bad day and the Hollywood sincerity only served to sharpen the anger she already felt at her own miserable performance. The old bastard would probably be lunching at this same table tomorrow with her successor. She'd been half hoping he would just come right out with it and fire her.

Cruising back to the office in his absurdly long black Cadillac, Annie decided that tonight she would tell Robert and Grace. Grace would scream at her and Robert would tell her she was crazy. But they would go along with it because they always did.

The only other person she needed to inform was the one upon whom the whole plan hinged: Tom Booker. It would seem to others curious, she reflected, that this of all things worried her least. But Annie had done it many times before. As a journalist, she had specialized in people who said no. Once she'd traveled five thousand miles to a Pacific island and turned up on the doorstep of a famous writer who never gave interviews. She ended up living with him for two weeks and the piece she wrote won awards and was syndicated all over the world.

It was, she believed, a simple and unassailable fact of life that if a woman went to epic lengths to throw herself on the mercy of a man, the man would not, could not, refuse.

THIRTEEN

THE HIGHWAY STRETCHED STRAIGHT AHEAD OF THEM between converging fences for miles too many to ponder toward the thunder-black dome of the horizon. At this most distant point, where the road seemed to climb into the sky, lightning flickered repeatedly, as if reatomizing blacktop into cloud. Beyond the fences, on either side, the ocean of Iowa prairie spread away flat and featureless to nowhere, lit fitfully through the rushing cloud by vivid, rolling shafts of sun, as though some giant were searching for his prey.

In such a landscape there was dislocation both of time and space and Annie felt the inkling of what could, if she were to let it, become panic. She scanned the skyline for something to latch on to, some sign of life, a grain silo, a tree, a solitary bird, anything. Finding none, she counted fence poles or the marker stripes on the road that streamed at her from the horizon as if blazed there by the lightning. She could picture the silver Lariat and its missile-shaped trailer from above, swallowing these stripes in steady gulps.

In two days they had traveled more than twelve hundred miles and in all that time Grace had hardly spoken. Much of the time she had slept, as she slept now, curled up on the back bench seat. When she woke she would stay there, listening to her Walkman or staring blankly out. Once, and only once, Annie looked in her rearview mirror and saw her daughter watching her. When their eyes met Annie smiled and Grace looked instantly away.

She had reacted to her mother's plan much as Annie had predicted. She had screamed and shouted and said she wasn't going, they couldn't make her and that was that. She got up from the dinner table, went to her room and slammed the door. Annie and Robert sat there for a while in silence. Annie had told him on his own earlier and bludgeoned every protest he made.

"She can't go on avoiding the issue," she said. "It's her horse for Godsake. She can't just wash her hands of it."

"Annie, look at what the kid's been through."

"But walking away from it isn't helping her, it's making it worse. You know how much she loved him. You saw how she was that day at the stables. Can't you imagine how the sight of him must haunt her?"

He didn't reply, just looked down and shook his head. Annie took his hand in hers.

"We can do something about this, Robert," she said, gentle now. "I know we can. Pilgrim can be alright again. This man can make him alright. And then Grace can be too."

Robert looked at her. "Does he really think he can do it?" Annie hesitated but not enough for him to notice.

"Yes," she said. It was the first time she had actually lied about it. Robert naturally assumed Tom Booker had been consulted about Pilgrim's trip to Montana. It was an illusion she'd also maintained with Grace.

Finding no ally in her father, Grace gave in, as Annie knew she would. But the resentful silence into which her anger evolved was lasting much longer than Annie had expected. In the old days, before the accident, Annie could normally subvert such moods by teasing or blithely ignoring them. This silence however was of a new order. It was as epic and immutable as the enterprise on which the girl had been forced to embark and, as the miles went by, Annie could only marvel at her stamina.

Robert had helped them pack, driven them to Chatham and gone with them to Harry Logan's on the morning they set off. In Grace's eyes this made him an accomplice. While they loaded Pilgrim into the trailer, she sat like stone in the Lariat with her earphones on, pretending to read a magazine. The horse's cries and the sound of his hooves smashing against the sides of the trailer reverberated around the yard but never once did Grace look up.

Harry gave Pilgrim a hefty shot of sedative and handed Annie a box of the stuff along with some needles in case of emergencies. He came to the window to say hello to Grace and started to tell her about feeding Pilgrim during the trip. Grace cut him short.

"You better talk to Mom," she said.

When it was time to go, her response to Robert's farewell kiss was little more than perfunctory.

That first night they had stayed with some friends of Harry Logan's who lived on the edge of a small town just south of Cleveland. The husband, Elliott, had been to veterinary school with Harry and was now a partner in a large local practice. It was dark when they arrived and Elliott insisted Annie and Grace go in and freshen up while he saw to the horse. He said they too used to keep horses and he'd prepared a stall in the barn.

"Harry said to leave him in the trailer," Annie said.

"What, for the entire trip?"

"That's what he said."

He cocked an eyebrow and gave her a patronizing, professional kind of smile.

"You go on in. I'll take a look."

It was starting to rain and Annie wasn't going to argue. The wife's name was Connie. She was a small, subdued woman with a brittle perm that looked as if it had been done that afternoon. She took them in and showed them to their rooms. The house was large and filled with the echoing silence of children grown up and gone. Their faces smiled from the walls in photographs of high school triumphs and sunny graduations.

Grace was put in their daughter's old room and Annie in the guest room along the corridor. Connie showed Annie where the bathroom was and left, saying supper was ready whenever they were. Annie thanked her and went back down the corridor to look in on Grace.

Connie's daughter had married a dentist and moved to Michigan, but her old room looked as if she'd never left. There were books and swimming trophies and shelves herded with little crystal animals. Amid this abandoned clutter of a stranger's childhood, Grace stood by the bed and rummaged in her bag for her wash things. She didn't look up when Annie came in.

"Okay?"

Grace shrugged and still didn't look up. Annie tried to look casual, feigning interest in the pictures on the wall. She stretched and groaned.

"God, I'm so stiff."

"What are we doing here?"

The voice was cold and hostile and Annie turned and saw Grace staring at her with her hands on her hips.

"What do you mean?"

Grace took in the whole room with a contemptuous sweep of her arm.

"All this. I mean, what are we doing here!"

Annie sighed, but before she could say anything Grace said forget it, it didn't matter. She snatched up her cane and her wash bag and headed for the door. Annie could see how furious it made the girl that she couldn't storm out more effectively.

"Grace, please."

"I said forget it, okay?" And she was gone.

Annie was talking with Connie in the kitchen when Elliott came in from the yard. He looked pale and had mud all down one side of him. He also seemed to be trying not to limp.

"I left him in the trailer," he said.

At supper Grace toyed with her food and spoke only when spoken to. The three adults did their best to keep the conversation going but there were long spells when the only sound was the chink of cutlery. They talked about Harry Logan and Chatham and a new outbreak of Lyme disease that everyone was worrying about. Elliott said they knew a young girl about Grace's age who'd caught it and her life had been completely wrecked. Connie darted a look at him and he flushed a little and quickly changed the subject.

As soon as the meal was over, Grace said she was tired and would they mind if she went to bed. Annie said she would come too but Grace wouldn't let her. She said polite good-nights to Elliott and Connie. As she walked to the door, her cane clunked on the hollow floor and Annie caught the look in the couple's eyes as they watched.

The next day, yesterday, they'd made an early start and driven with just a few short stops all the way across

Indiana and Illinois and on into Iowa. And all day long, as the vast continent opened up around them, Grace kept her silence.

Last night they'd stayed with a distant cousin of Liz Hammond's who'd married a farmer and lived near Des Moines. The farm stood alone at the end of five straight miles of driveway, as if on its own brown planet, plowed in faultless furrows to every horizon.

They were quiet, religious folk—Baptists, Annie guessed—and as unlike Liz as she could imagine. The farmer said Liz had told them all about Pilgrim, but Annie could see he was still shocked by what he saw. He helped her feed and water the horse and then raked out and replaced as much of the wet, dung-soiled straw as he could from under Pilgrim's thrashing hooves.

They ate supper at a long wooden table with the couple's six children. They all had their father's blond hair and wide blue eyes and watched Annie and Grace with a kind of polite wonder. The food was plain and wholesome and there was only milk to drink, served creamy and still warm from the dairy in brimming glass jugs.

This morning, the wife had cooked them a breakfast of eggs, hash browns, and home-cured ham and just as they were leaving, with Grace already in the car, the farmer had handed something to Annie.

"We'd like you to have this," he said.

It was an old book with a faded cloth cover. The man's wife was standing beside him and they watched as Annie opened it. It was *The Pilgrim's Progress* by John Bunyan. Annie could remember it being read to her at school when she was only seven or eight years old.

"It seemed appropriate," the farmer said.

Annie swallowed and thanked him.

"We'll be praying for you all," the woman said.

The book still lay on the front passenger seat. And every time Annie caught sight of it she thought about the woman's words.

Even though Annie had lived in this country for many years, such candid religious talk still jolted some deep-seated English reserve in her and made her feel uneasy. But what disturbed her more was that this total stranger had so clearly seen them all as needing her prayers. She'd seen them as victims. Not just Pilgrim and Grace—that was understandable—but Annie too. Nobody, nobody ever, had seen Annie Graves that way.

Now, below the lightning on the horizon, something caught her eye. It started as little more than a flickering speck and grew slowly as she watched it, assembling itself into the liquid shape of a truck. Soon, beyond it, she could see the towers of grain elevators then other, lower buildings, a town, sprouting up around them. A flurry of small brown birds erupted from the side of the road and were buffeted away on the wind. The truck was nearly up to them now and Annie watched the glinting chrome of its grille get larger and larger until it passed them in a blast of wind that made the car and trailer shudder. Grace stirred behind her.

"What was that?"

"Nothing. Just a truck."

Annie saw her in the mirror, rubbing sleep from her eyes.

"There's a town coming up. We need gas. Are you hungry?"

"A little."

The exit road traveled in a long loop around a white wooden church that stood on its own in a field of dead grass. In front of it a small boy with a bicycle watched them circle by and as they did, the church was suddenly engulfed in sunshine. Annie half expected to see a finger pointing down through the clouds.

There was a diner next to the gas station and after filling up they ate egg-salad sandwiches in silence, surrounded by men who wore baseball caps emblazoned with the names of farm products and who spoke in hushed tones of winter wheat and the price of soybeans. For all Annie understood, they might as well have been speaking some foreign tongue. She went to pay the check then came back to the table to tell Grace she was going to the rest room and would meet her back at the car.

"Would you see if Pilgrim wants some water?" she said. Grace didn't answer.

"Grace? Did you hear me?"

Annie stood over her, aware suddenly that the farmers around them had stopped talking. The confrontation was deliberate but now she regretted the impulse to make it so public. Grace didn't look up. She finished her Coke and the sound her glass made when she put it down punctuated the silence.

"Do it yourself," she said.

The first time Grace had thought about killing herself was in the cab coming home that day from the prosthetist's. The socket of the false leg had dug into the underside of her thighbone, but she'd pretended it felt fine and had gone along with her father's determined cheerfulness while wondering which would be the best way to do it.

Two years ago a girl in eighth grade had thrown herself under a downtown express on the subway. No one seemed able to come up with a reason for it and like everyone else Grace had been shocked. But she had also been secretly impressed. What courage it must have taken, she thought, in that final, decisive moment. Grace remembered thinking she herself could never summon such courage and that even if she could, her muscles would somehow still refuse to make that last launching flex.

Now though, she saw it in an altogether different light and could contemplate the possibility, if not the particular method, with what amounted to dispassion. That her life was ruined was a simple fact, only reinforced by the way those around her sought so fervently to show it wasn't. She wished with all her heart that she had died that day with Judith and Gulliver in the snow. But as the weeks went by she realized—and it came to her almost as a disappointment—that maybe she wasn't the suicide type.

What held her back was the inability to see it only from her own point of view. It seemed so melodramatic, so extravagant, more the sort of extremist thing her mother might do. It didn't occur to Grace that perhaps it was the Maclean in her, those cursed lawyer genes, that made her so objectify the issue of her own demise. For blame had ever flowed but one way in this family. Everything was always Annie's fault.

Grace loved and resented her mother in almost equal measure and often for the same thing. For her certainty, for example, and for the way she was always so damn right. Above all for knowing Grace the way she did. Knowing how she would react to things, what her likes and dislikes were, what her opinion might be on any given subject. Maybe all mothers had such insight on their daughters and sometimes it was wonderful to be so understood. More often though, and especially of late, it felt like a monstrous invasion of her privacy.

For these, and a thousand less specific wrongs, Grace

now took revenge. For at last, with this great silence, she seemed to have a weapon that worked. She could see the effect it was having on her mother and found it gratifying. Annie's acts of tyranny were normally executed without a hint of guilt or self-doubt. But now Grace sensed both. There seemed some tacit and exploitable acknowledgment that it was wrong to have forced Grace to join this escapade. Viewed from the backseat of the Lariat, her mother seemed like some gambler, staking life itself on one last desperate spin of the wheel.

They drove due west to the Missouri then swung north with the river snaking broad and brown to their left. At Sioux City they crossed into South Dakota and headed west again on Route 90 which would take them all the way to Montana. They passed through the northern Badlands and saw the sun go down over the Black Hills in a strip of blood-orange sky. They traveled without speaking and the brooding sorrow between them seemed to spawn and spread until it mingled with the million other sorrows that haunted this vast, unforgiving landscape.

Neither Liz nor Harry knew anyone who lived in these parts, so Annie had booked a room at a small hotel near Mount Rushmore. She had never seen the monument and had looked forward to coming here with Grace. But when they pulled into the hotel's deserted parking lot it was dark and raining and Annie thought the only good thing about being there was that she wouldn't have to make polite conversation with hosts she'd never met and would never meet again.

The rooms were all named after different presidents. Theirs was Abraham Lincoln. His beard jutted at them from laminated prints on every wall and an extract from the Gettysburg Address hung above the TV, partly obscured by a glossy cardboard sign advertising adult movies. There were two large beds, side by side, and Grace collapsed on the one farthest from the door while Annie went back out into the rain to see to Pilgrim.

The horse seemed to be getting used to the rituals of the journey. Confined in the narrow stall of the trailer, he no longer erupted when Annie stepped into the cramped, protected space in front of him. He just edged back into the darkness and watched. She could feel his eyes on her while she hung up a new net of hay and carefully pushed his buckets of feed and water within reach. He would never touch them until she had gone. She sensed his simmering hostility and was both scared and excited by it so that when she closed the door on him her heart was pounding.

When she got back to the room, Grace had undressed and was in bed. Her back was turned and whether she was asleep or just pretending, Annie couldn't tell.

"Grace?" she said softly. "Don't you want to eat?"

There was no reaction. Annie thought about going alone to the restaurant, but couldn't face it. She took a long, hot bath, hoping the water would bring her comfort. All it brought her was doubt. It hung in the air with the steam, enfolding her. What on earth did she think she was doing, dragging these two wounded souls across a continent, in some gruesome reprise of pioneer madness? Grace's silence and the remorseless emptiness of the spaces they had crossed made Annie feel suddenly, terribly alone. To obliterate these thoughts, she slid her hands between her legs and felt herself, worked at herself, refusing to concede to the initial stubborn numbness until at last her loins twitched and swam and she was lost.

That night she dreamed she was walking with her father along a snowy ridge, roped like mountaineers, though this was something they had never done. Below, on either side, sheer walls of rock and ice plunged to nothingness. They were on a cornice, a thin overhanging crust of snow which her father said was safe. He was in front of her and he turned to her and smiled the way he smiled in her favorite photograph, a smile which said with total confidence that he was with her and everything was alright. And as he did so, over his shoulder she saw a crack zigzagging toward them and the lip of the cornice start to split away and tumble down the mountainside. She wanted to cry out but couldn't and the moment before the crack reached them, her father turned and saw it. And then he was gone and Annie saw the rope between them snaking after him and she realized the only way to save them both was to jump the other way. So she launched herself into the air on the other side of the ridge. But instead of feeling the rope jolt and hold, she just kept on falling, free-falling into the void.

When she woke it was morning. They had slept late. Outside it was raining even harder. Mount Rushmore and its stone faces were hidden in swirling cloud that the woman in reception said wasn't going to clear. Not far away, she said, there was another mountain carving they could maybe get a glimpse of, a giant figure of Crazy Horse.

"Thanks," said Annie. "We've got our own."

They had breakfast, checked out and drove back up to the interstate. They crossed the state line into Wyoming and skirted south of Devil's Tower and Thunder Basin, then over the Powder River and up toward Sheridan where at last the rain stopped.

Increasingly the pickups and trucks they saw were

driven by men in cowboy hats. Some touched their brims or lifted a hand in grave salute. As they went by, the sun made rainbows in the plumes of their tail-spray.

It was late afternoon when they crossed into Montana. But Annie felt neither relief nor any sense of achievement. She had tried so hard not to let Grace's silence beat her. All day she had hopped stations on the radio and listened to Bible-thumping preachers, livestock reports and more kinds of country music than she'd known existed. But it was no good. She felt herself compressed into an ever-shrinking space between the weight of her daughter's gloom and her own welling anger. At last it was too much to bear. Some forty miles into Montana, neither looking nor caring where it led, she took an exit off the interstate.

She wanted to park but nowhere seemed right. There was a massive casino standing on its own and as she looked, its neon sign flickered on, red and lurid in the fading light. She drove on up a hill, past a café and a low straggle of stores with a dirt parking strip in front. Two Indians with long black hair and feathers in their high-crowned cowboy hats stood beside a battered pickup, watching the Lariat and trailer approach. Something in their gaze unsettled her and she kept on up the hill, took a right turn and stopped. She switched off the ignition and for a while sat very still. She could sense Grace behind her, watching. The girl's voice, when at last she spoke, was cautious.

"What's going on?"

"What?" Annie said sharply.

"It's closed. Look."

There was a sign along the road that said NATIONAL MONUMENT, LITTLE BIGHORN BATTLEFIELD. Grace was right. According to the opening hours it gave, the place had closed an hour ago. It made Annie even angrier that

Grace should so misjudge her mood to think she had come here deliberately, like a tourist. She didn't trust herself to look at her. She just stared ahead and took a deep breath.

"How long is this going to go on, Grace?"

"What?"

"You know what I mean. How long is it going to go on?"

There was a long pause. Annie watched a ball of tumbleweed chase its own shadow down the road toward them. It brushed the side of the car as it went by. She turned to look at Grace and the girl looked away and shrugged.

"Hmm? I mean, is this it now?" Annie went on. "We've come nearly two thousand miles and you've sat there and you haven't spoken a word. So I just thought I'd ask, just so I know. Is this the way you and I are going to be now?"

Grace was looking down, fiddling with her Walkman. She shrugged again.

"I dunno."

"Do you want us to turn around and go back home?" Grace gave a bitter little laugh.

"Well, do you?"

Grace lifted her eyes and looked sideways out of the window, trying to seem nonchalant, but Annie could see she was fighting tears. There was a clumping sound as Pilgrim shifted in the trailer.

"Because if that's what you want—"

Suddenly Grace turned on her, her face savage and distorted. The tears were running now and the failure to stop them doubled her fury.

"What the hell do you care!" she screamed. "You decide! You always do! You pretend you care what other people want but you don't, it's just bullshit!"

"Grace," Annie said gently, putting a hand out. But Grace smacked it away.

"Don't! Just leave me alone!"

Annie looked at her for a moment then opened the door and got out. She started walking, blindly, tilting her face to the wind. The road led up past a grove of pine trees to a parking lot and a low building, both deserted. She kept walking. She followed a path that curved up the hillside and found herself beside a cemetery enclosed by black iron railings. At the crest of the hill there was a simple stone monument and it was here that Annie stopped.

On this hillside, on a June day in 1876, George Armstrong Custer and more than two hundred soldiers were cut to pieces by those they had sought to slaughter. Their names were etched in the stone. Annie turned to look down the hill at the scattered white tombstones. They cast long shadows in the last pale reach of the sun. She stood there and looked out across the vast, rolling plains of wind-flattened grass that stretched away from this sorrowful place to a horizon where sorrow was infinite. And she started to weep.

It would later strike her as strange that she should have come here by chance. Whether some other random place would have brought forth the tears she'd stemmed for so long, she never would know. The monument was a kind of cruel anomaly, honoring as it did the agents of genocide while the countless graves of those they had butchered elsewhere lay forever unmarked. But the sense of suffering here and the presence of so many ghosts transcended all detail. It was simply a fitting place for tears. And Annie hung her head and wept them. She wept for Grace and for Pilgrim and for the lost souls of the children who'd died in her womb.

Above all, she wept for herself and what she had become.

All her life she had lived where she didn't belong. America wasn't her home. And nor, when she went there now, was England. In each country they treated her as if she came from the other. The truth was, she came from nowhere. She had no home. Not since her father died. She was rootless, tribeless, adrift.

Once this had seemed her greatest strength. She had a way of tapping into things. She could seamlessly adapt, insinuate herself into any group, any culture or situation. She knew instinctively what was required, who you needed to know, what you had to do to win. And in her work, which had so long obsessed her, this gift had helped her win all that was worth winning. Now, since Grace's accident, it all seemed worthless.

In the past three months she had been the strong one, fooling herself that it was what Grace needed. The fact was, she knew no other way to react. Having lost all connection with herself, she had lost it too with her child and, for this, she was consumed with guilt. Action had become a substitute for feeling. Or at least for the expression of it. And this was why, she now saw, she had launched herself into this lunatic adventure with Pilgrim.

Annie sobbed until her shoulders ached, then she slid her back down the cold stone of the monument and sat with her head in her hands. And there she stayed until the sun dipped pale and liquid behind the distant snowy rim of the Bighorn Mountains and the cottonwoods down by the river melted together in a single black scar. When she looked up, it was night and the world was a lantern of sky.

"Ma'am?"

It was a park ranger. He had a flashlight, but kept its beam tactfully away from her face.

"You okay there ma'am?"

Annie wiped her face and swallowed.

"Yes. Thank you," she said. "I'm fine." She got up.

"Your daughter was getting kind of worried down there."

"Yes, I'm sorry. I'm going now."

He tipped his hat as she went. "Night ma'am. You go safely now."

She walked back down to the car, aware he was watching. Grace was asleep, or perhaps she was only pretending to be. Annie started the engine, switched on the lights and made a turn at the top of the road. She looped back onto the interstate and drove through the night, all the way to Choteau.

THREE

FOURTEEN

Two creeks ran through the Booker brothers' land and they gave the ranch its name, the Double Divide. They flowed from adjacent folds of the mountain front and in their first half mile they looked like twins. The ridge that ran between them here was low, at one point almost low enough for them to meet, but then it rose sharply in a rugged chain of interlocking bluffs, shouldering the creeks apart. Forced thus to seek their separate ways, they now became quite different.

The northern one ran, swift and shallow, down a wide, uncluttered valley. Its banks, though sometimes steep, gave easy access to the cattle. Brook trout hung with their heads upstream in its breaks and eddies, while herons stalked its shingled beaches. The route the southern creek was forced to take was lusher, full of obstacles and trees. It wove through tangled thickets of Bebbs willow and red-stem dogwood, then disappeared awhile in marsh. Lower down, meandering a meadow so flat that its loops linked back upon themselves, it formed a maze of still, dark pools and grassy islands whose geography was constantly arranged and re-arranged by beavers.

Ellen Booker used to say the creeks were like her two boys, Frank the north and Tom the south. That was until Frank, who was seventeen at the time, remarked over supper one night that it wasn't fair because he liked beaver too. His father told him to go wash his mouth out and sent him to bed. Tom wasn't so sure his mother got the joke, but she must have because she never said it again.

The house they called the creek house, where first Tom and Rachel, then later Frank and Diane had lived and which now was empty, stood on a bluff above a bend in the northern creek. From it you could look down the valley, across the tops of cottonwood trees, to the ranch house half a mile away, surrounded by white-washed barns, stables and corrals. The houses were linked by a dirt road that wound on up to the lower meadows where the cattle spent the winter. Now, in early April, most of the snow had gone from this lower part of the ranch. It lay only in shaded, rockstrewn gullies and among the pine and fir trees that dotted the north side of the ridge.

Tom looked up at the creek house from the passenger seat of the old Chevy and wondered, as he often did, about moving in. He and Joe were on their way back from feeding the cattle, the boy expertly negotiating the potholes. Joe was small for his age and had to sit like a ramrod to see over the front. During the week Frank did the feeding, but at weekends Joe liked to do it and Tom liked to help him. They'd unloaded the slabs of alfalfa and together enjoyed the sight and sound of the cows surging in with their calves to get it.

"Can we go see Bronty's foal?" Joe asked.

"Sure we can."

"There's a kid at school says we should've imprint-trained him."

"Uh-huh."

"He says if you do it soon as they're born, it makes them real easy to handle later on."

"Yep. That's what some folk say."

"There was this thing on the TV about a guy who does it with geese too. He has this airplane and the baby geese all grow up thinking it's their mom. He flies it and they just follow."

"Yeah, I heard about that."

"What do you think about all that stuff?"

"Well Joe, I don't know a whole lot about geese. Maybe it's okay for them to grow up thinking they're airplanes." Joe laughed. "But with a horse, I reckon first you have to let him learn to be a horse."

They drove back down to the ranch and parked outside the long barn where Tom kept some of his horses. Joe's twin brothers, Scott and Craig, came running out of the house to meet them. Tom saw Joe's face fall. The twins were nine years old and because of their blond good looks and the fact that they did everything in a noisy unison, they always got more attention than their brother.

"You going to see the foal?" they yelled. "Can we come?" Tom put a big hand like a crane-grab on each of their heads.

"So long as you keep quiet you can," he said.

He led them into the barn and stood with the twins outside Bronty's stall while Joe went in. Bronty was a big ten-year-old quarter horse, a reddish bay. She pushed her muzzle toward Joe, who put a hand on it while he gently rubbed her neck. Tom liked to watch the boy around horses, he had an easy, confident way with them. The foal, a little darker than his mother, had been lying in the corner and was now struggling to his feet. He tottered on comical, stilted legs to the sheltering side of the mare, peeping around her rear end at Joe. The twins laughed.

"He looks so funny," Scott said.

"I've got a picture of you two at that age," said Tom. "And you know what?"

"They looked like bullfrogs," Joe said.

The twins soon got bored and left. Tom and Joe turned the other horses out into the paddock behind the barn. After breakfast they were going to start working with some of the yearlings. As they walked back to the house, the dogs started barking and ran out past them. Tom turned and saw a silver Ford Lariat coming over the end of the ridge and heading down the driveway toward them. There was just the driver in it and as it got nearer he could see it was a woman.

"Your mom expecting company?" Tom asked. Joe shrugged. It wasn't until the car pulled up, with the dogs running around it still barking, that Tom recognized who it was. It was hard to believe. Joe saw his look.

"You know her?"

"I believe I do. But not what she's doing here."

He told the dogs to hush and walked over. Annie got out of the car and came nervously toward him. She was wearing jeans and hiking boots and a huge, cream-colored sweater that came halfway down her thighs. The sun behind made her hair flare red and Tom realized how clearly he remembered those green eyes from the day at the stables. She nodded at him without quite smiling, a little sheepish.

"Mr. Booker. Good morning."

"Well, good morning." They stood there for a moment. "Joe, this is Mrs. Graves. Joe here is my nephew." Annie offered the boy her hand.

"Hello, Joe. How are you?"

"Good."

She looked up the valley, toward the mountains, then looked back at Tom.

"What a beautiful place."

"It is."

He was wondering when she was going to get around to saying what on earth she was doing here, though he already had an idea. She took a deep breath.

"Mr. Booker, you're going to think this is insane, but you can probably guess why I've come here."

"Well. I kind of reckoned you didn't just happen to be passing through." She almost smiled.

"I'm sorry just turning up like this, but I knew what you'd say if I phoned. It's about my daughter's horse."

"Pilgrim."

"Yes. I know you can help him and I came here to ask you, to beg you, to have another look at him."

"Mrs. Graves . . ."

"Please. Just a look. It wouldn't take long."

Tom laughed. "What, to fly to New York?" He nodded at the Lariat. "Or were you counting on driving me there?"

"He's here. In Choteau."

Tom stared at her for a moment in disbelief.

"You've hauled him all the way out here?" She nodded. Joe was looking from one of them to the other, trying to get the picture. Diane had stepped out onto the porch and stood there holding open the screen door, watching.

"All on your own?" Tom asked.

"With Grace, my daughter."

"Just to have me take a look at him?"

"Yes."

"You guys coming in to eat?" called Diane. Who's the woman, was what she really meant. Tom put his hand on Joe's shoulder.

"Tell your mom I'm coming," he said and as the boy went off he turned back to Annie. They stood looking at each other for a moment. She gave a little shrug and, at last, smiled. He noticed how it made the corners of her mouth go down but left untouched the troubled look in her eyes. He was being railroaded and wondered why he didn't mind.

"Excuse me saying it, ma'am," he said. "But you sure as hell don't like taking no for an answer."

"No," Annie said simply. "I suppose I don't."

Grace lay on her back on the floor of the musty bedroom, doing her exercises and listening to the electronic bells of the Methodist church across the street. They didn't just chime the hour, they played whole tunes. She quite liked the sound, mainly because it was driving her mother crazy. Annie was down in the hall, on the phone to the real estate agent about it.

"Don't they know there are laws about this sort of thing?" she was saying. "They're polluting the air."

It was the fifth time she had called him in two days. The poor man had made the mistake of giving her his home number and Annie was ruining his weekend, bombarding him with complaints: the heating wasn't working, the bedrooms were damp, the extra phone line she'd asked for hadn't been installed, the heating still wasn't working. And now the bells.

"It wouldn't be so bad if they played something half decent," she was saying. "It's ridiculous, the Methodists have all the good tunes."

Yesterday when Annie went out to the ranch, Grace had refused to go with her. After Annie left, she went out exploring. There wasn't much to explore. Choteau was basically one long main street with a railroad on one side and a grid of residential streets on the other. There was a dog parlor, a video store, a steak house and a cinema showing a movie Grace had seen over a year ago. The town's only claim to fame was a museum where you could see dinosaur eggs. She went into a couple of stores and the people were friendly but reserved. She was aware of others watching as she walked slowly back down the street with her cane. When she got back to the house she felt so depressed, she burst into tears.

Annie had come back elated and told Grace that Tom Booker had agreed to come and see Pilgrim the following morning. All Grace said was "How long have we got to stay in this dump?"

The house was a big, rambling place, faced with peeling pale-blue clapboard and carpeted throughout in a stained, yellow-brown shagpile. The sparse furniture looked as if it had been picked up in a yard sale. Annie was appalled when they first saw the place. Grace was delighted. Its glaring inadequacy was on her side, a perfect vindication.

Secretly, she wasn't as opposed to this mission of her mother's as she made out. It was a relief in fact to get away from school and the tiring business of putting on a brave face all the time. But her feelings for Pilgrim were confused. They frightened her. It was best to block him right out of her head. Her mother however made this impossible. Her every action seemed to force Grace to confront the issue. She'd taken this whole thing on as if Pilgrim was hers and he wasn't hers, he was Grace's. Of course Grace wanted him to get better, it was just that . . . It struck her then, for the first time, that maybe she didn't want him to get better. Maybe she blamed him for what had happened? No, that was stupid. Maybe she wanted him to be as she was, forever maimed? Why should he recover and not her? It wasn't fair. Stop it, stop it, she told herself. These whirling, crazy thoughts were her mother's fault and Grace wasn't going to let them get a hold in her head.

She redoubled the effort in her exercises, until she felt the sweat trickle down her neck. She lifted her stump high in the air, again and again, making the muscles ache in her right buttock and her thigh. She could look at this leg now and accept at last that it belonged to her. The scar was neat, no longer that angry, itching pink. Her muscles were coming back nicely, so much so that the sleeve of her prosthetic leg was starting to feel a little tight. She heard Annie hang up.

"Grace? Have you finished? He'll be here soon."

Grace didn't reply, just let the words hang there.

"Grace?"

"Yeah. So what?"

She could feel Annie's reaction, picture the irked look on her face giving way to resignation. She heard her sigh and go back into the drab dining room which, as a first priority of course, Annie had transformed into her office.

FIFTEEN

ALL TOM HAD PROMISED WAS THAT HE WOULD GO
and have another look at the horse. After she had come
all that way, it was the least he could do. But he'd made
it a condition that he would go alone. He didn't want
her looking over his shoulder, putting pressure on him.
She was pretty good at that, he already knew. She had
made him promise to drop by afterward and give her
his verdict.

He knew the Petersen place, just outside Choteau,
where she had Pilgrim stabled. They were nice enough
people, but if the horse was as bad as when Tom last
saw him, they wouldn't put up with him for long.

Old man Petersen had the face of an outlaw, three
days of grizzled beard and teeth as black as the tobacco
he always chewed. He showed them in a mischievous
grin when Tom pulled up in the Chevy.

"What's it they say? If you're looking for trouble,
you've come to the right place. Damn near killed me
getting him unloaded. Been kicking and hollering like a
banshee ever since."

He led Tom down a muddy track, past the rusting

hulks of derelict cars, to an old barn, lined either side
with stalls. The other horses had been turned out. Tom
could hear Pilgrim long before they got there.

"Only fitted that door last summer," Petersen said.
"He'd have had the old one down by now. Woman says
you're gonna sort him out for her."

"Oh she did?"

"Uh-huh. All I can say is, make sure you go see Bill
Larson for a fitting first." He roared with laughter and
slapped Tom on the back. Bill Larson was the local
undertaker.

The horse was in even sorrier shape than when Tom
last saw him. His front leg was so badly wasted, Tom
wondered how he even managed to stand, let alone
keep up the kicking.

"Must have been a nice-lookin' horse once," said Petersen.

"I reckon." Tom turned away. He'd seen enough.

He drove back into Choteau and looked at the piece
of paper on which Annie had written her address.
When he pulled up outside the house and walked up to
the front door, the church bells were playing a tune he
hadn't heard since he was a kid in Sunday school. He
rang the doorbell and waited.

The face he saw when the door opened startled him.
It wasn't that he'd been expecting the mother, it was the
open hostility in the girl's pale, freckled face. He remembered the face from the photograph Annie had sent
him, a happy girl and her horse. The contrast was
shocking. He smiled.

"You must be Grace." She didn't smile back, just
nodded and stepped aside for him to come in. He took
off his hat and waited while she shut the door. He could
hear Annie talking in a room off the hallway.

"She's on the phone. You can wait in here."

She led the way into a bare, L-shaped living room. Tom looked down at her leg and the cane as he followed, making a mental note not to look again. The room was gloomy and smelled of damp. There were a couple of old armchairs, a sagging sofa and a TV playing an old black-and-white movie. Grace sat down and went on watching it.

Tom perched himself on an arm of one of the chairs. The door across the hallway was half open and he could see a fax machine, a computer screen and a tangle of wires. All he could see of Annie was a crossed leg and a boot that bobbed impatiently. She sounded pretty worked up about something.

"What! He said what? I don't believe it. Lucy . . . Lucy, I don't care. It's got nothing to do with Crawford, I'm the bloody editor and that's the cover we go with."

Tom saw Grace raise her eyes to the ceiling and wondered if it was for his benefit. In the movie, an actress whose name he could never remember was on her knees, hanging on to James Cagney, begging him not to leave. They always did this and Tom could never understand why they bothered.

"Grace, will you get Mr. Booker a coffee?" Annie shouted from the other room. "I'd like one too." She went back to her phone call. Grace flicked the TV off and got up, clearly irritated.

"It's okay, really," said Tom.

"She just made it." She stared at him as if he'd said something rude.

"Okay then, thank you. But you keep watching the movie and I'll get it."

"I've seen it. It's boring."

She picked up her cane and went off into the kitchen. Tom waited a moment then followed. She shot him a glance when he came in and made more noise than she needed to with the cups. He walked over to the window.

"What does your mother do?"

"What?"

"Your mother. I wondered what line of work she was in."

"She edits a magazine." She handed him a cup of coffee. "Cream and sugar?"

"No thanks. Must be a pretty stressful kind of job."

Grace laughed. Tom was surprised by how bitter it sounded.

"Yeah. I guess you could say that."

There was an awkward silence. Grace turned away and was about to pour another cup but instead she stopped and looked at him. He could see the surface of the coffee in the glass pot trembling from the tension in her. It was plain to see she had something important to say.

"Just in case she hasn't told you, I don't want to know anything about this, okay?"

Tom nodded slowly and waited for her to go on. She'd good as spat the words at him and was a little thrown by the calm reaction. She abruptly poured the coffee but did it too fast so that she spilled some. She clunked the pot down on the table and picked up the cup, not looking at him as she went on.

"This whole thing was her idea. I think it's totally stupid. They should just get rid of him."

She stomped past him and out of the room. Tom watched her go, then he turned and looked out into the forlorn little backyard. A cat was eating something sinewy by an upturned garbage can.

He had come here to tell this girl's mother, for the last time, that the horse was beyond help. It was going to be tough after they had come all this way. He had thought a lot about it since Annie's visit to the ranch. To be precise, he'd thought a lot about Annie and the sadness in those eyes of hers. It had occurred to him that if he took the horse on, he might be doing it not to help the horse but to help her. He never did that. It was the wrong reason.

"I'm sorry. It was important."

He turned to see Annie coming in. She was wearing a big denim shirt and her hair was combed back, still wet from the shower. It made her look boyish.

"That's okay."

She went to get the coffee and topped up her cup. Then she came over to him and did the same to his without asking.

"You've been to see him?"

She put the coffeepot down but stayed standing in front of him. She smelled of soap or shampoo, something expensive anyway.

"Yes. I just came from there."

"And?"

Tom still didn't know how he was going to break it to her, even as he started to speak.

"Well, he's about as wretched as a horse can get."

He paused a moment and saw something flicker in her eyes. Then over her shoulder he saw Grace in the doorway, trying to look as if she didn't care and failing miserably. Meeting this girl just now had been like seeing the last picture of a triptych. The whole had become clear. All three—mother, daughter and horse—were inextricably connected in pain. If he could help the horse, even a little, maybe he could help them all? What could be wrong with that? And truly, how could he walk away from such suffering?

He heard himself say, "Maybe we could do something."

He saw the relief surge into Annie's face.

"Now hold on, ma'am, please. That was only a maybe. Before I could even think about it, I need to know something. It's a question for Grace here."

He saw the girl stiffen.

"You see, when I work with a horse, it's no good just me doing it. It doesn't work that way. The owner needs to be involved too. So, here's the deal. I'm not sure I can do anything with old Pilgrim, but if you'll help, I'm prepared to give it a go."

Grace gave that bitter little laugh again and looked away as if she couldn't believe he could make such a dumb suggestion. Annie looked at the floor.

"You have a problem with that Grace?" Tom said. She looked at him with what was no doubt meant as contempt but when she spoke, her voice quavered.

"Isn't it like, obvious?"

Tom considered this for a moment, then shook his head. "Nope. I don't think it is. Anyway, that's the deal. Thanks for the coffee." He put his cup down and walked toward the door. Annie looked at Grace who turned away into the living room. Then Annie came hurrying after him into the hall.

"What would she have to do?"

"Just be there, help out, be involved."

Something told him he shouldn't mention riding. He put his hat on and opened the front door. He could see the desperation in Annie's eyes.

"It's cold in here," he said. "You ought to get the heating checked out."

He was about to step out when Grace appeared in the living room doorway. She didn't look at him. She said something but it was so low he couldn't catch it.

"I'm sorry Grace?"

She shifted uncomfortably, her eyes flicking sideways.

"I said okay. I'll do it."

And she turned away and went back into the room.

Diane had cooked a turkey and was carving it as if it deserved it. One of the twins tried picking a piece and got his hand slapped. He was supposed to be ferrying the plates over from the sideboard to the table where everyone else was already seated.

"What about the yearlings?" she said. "I thought that was the whole idea of not doing clinics, so you could work with your own horses for a change."

"There'll be time for that," said Tom. He couldn't understand why Diane seemed so riled.

"Who does she think she is, coming out here like that? Just assuming she can force you into it. I think she's got one hell of a nerve. Get off!" She tried to slap the boy again but this time he got away with the meat. Diane raised the carving knife. "Next time you get this, okay? Frank, don't you think she's got a nerve?"

"Oh hell, I don't know. Seems to me it's up to Tom. Craig, will you pass the corn please?"

Diane made up the last plate for herself and came and sat down. They all went quiet for Frank to say grace.

"Anyway," Tom went on after it was said, "Joe here's going to be helping me with the yearlings. That right Joe?"

"Sure."

"Not while you're at school you're not," Diane said. Tom and Joe exchanged a look. No one spoke for a while, everyone just getting on with helping themselves to vegetables and cranberry sauce. Tom hoped Diane would let the matter drop, but she was like a dog with a bone.

"I guess they'll want feeding and all, out here all day long."

"I don't reckon they'll expect that," Tom said.

"What, they'll go forty miles into Choteau every time they want a cup of coffee?"

"Tea," Frank said. Diane shot him an unfriendly look.

"Huh?"

"Tea. She's English. They drink tea. Come on Diane, give the guy a break."

"Does the girl's leg look funny?" Scott said, through a mouthful of turkey.

"Funny!" Joe shook his head. "You are one weird kid."

"No I mean, is it like, made of wood or what?"

"Just eat your food Scott, okay?" Frank said.

They ate in silence for a while. Tom could see Diane's mood hanging above her like a cloud. She was a tall, powerful woman, whose face and spirit had been hardened by the place she lived in. Increasingly as she moved into her mid-forties, she had about her an air of lost opportunity. She'd grown up on a farm near Great Falls and it was Tom who'd first met her. They dated a few times, but he made it clear he wasn't ready to settle down and was anyway so seldom around, that it just petered out. So Diane married the younger brother instead. Tom was fond of her, though sometimes, especially since his mother moved to Great Falls, he found her a touch overprotective. He worried now and again that she gave him more attention than she did Frank. Not that Frank ever seemed to notice.

"When you figuring on branding?" he asked his brother.

"Weekend after next. If the weather picks up."

On a lot of ranches they left it until later, but Frank branded in April because the boys liked to help and the calves were still small enough for them to handle. They always made an event of it. Friends came over to help and Diane laid on a spread for everyone afterward. It was a tradition Tom's father had begun and one of many Frank kept going. Another was how they still used horses for much of the work other ranchers now used vehicles for. Rounding up cattle on motorcycles wasn't the same somehow.

Tom and Frank had always seen these things the same way. They never disagreed about the way the ranch was run, nor anything else for that matter. This was partly because Tom thought of the place as more Frank's than his. It was Frank who'd stayed here all these years while he traveled, doing his horse clinics. And Frank had always been the better businessman and knew more about cattle than he would ever know. The two of them were close and easy together and Frank was genuinely thrilled about Tom's plans to get more seriously into horse rearing because it meant he'd be around the place more. Though the cattle were mainly Frank's and the horses Tom's, they discussed things and helped each other out whenever they could. Last year, when Tom was off doing a chain of clinics, it was Frank who had supervised the building of an arena and exercise pool that Tom had designed for the horses.

Tom was aware suddenly that one of the twins had asked him a question.

"Sorry, what was that?"

"Is she famous?" It was Scott.

"Is who famous, for heavensakes?" Diane snapped.

"The woman from New York."

Diane didn't give Tom the chance to answer.

"Have you heard of her?" she asked the boy. He shook his head. "Well then, she isn't famous is she? Eat your food."

S I X T E E N

THE NORTHERN EDGE OF CHOTEAU WAS GUARDED BY a thirteen-and-a-half-foot-tall dinosaur. Pedants knew it to be an Albertasaurus but to everyone else it looked pretty much like a regular T. rex. It kept watch from the parking lot of the Old Trail Museum and you got to see it just after you passed the sign on Route 89 saying WELCOME TO CHOTEAU—NICE PEOPLE, GREAT COUNTRY. Conscious perhaps of the immediate damper this might put on such a welcome, the sculptor had shaped the creature's steak-knife teeth into a knowing grin. The effect was unsettling. You couldn't tell if it wanted to eat you or lick you to death.

Four times a day, for two weeks now, Annie had traversed this reptilian gaze as she drove to and from the Double Divide. They would go out at noon after Grace had done some schoolwork or spent a grueling morning at the physical therapist's. Annie would drop her off at the ranch, come back, hit the phones and the fax, then head out again at about six, as she was doing now, to collect her.

The trip took about forty minutes and she enjoyed it,

especially, since the weather had turned, the evening ride. For five days the skies had been clear and they were bigger and bluer than she'd ever known skies could be. After the afternoon frenzy of phone calls to New York, driving out into this landscape was like plunging into an immense, calming pool.

The trip was a long L shape and for the first twenty miles, north along 89, Annie's was often the only car. The plains stretched endlessly away to her right and as the sun arced low, toward the Rockies on her left, the winter-worn grass around her turned to pale gold.

She turned west onto the unmarked gravel road that went in a straight line for another fifteen miles to the ranch and the mountain wall beyond. The Lariat left a cloud of dust behind it that drifted slowly away in the breeze. Curlews strutted on the road in front then glided away at the last moment into the pasture. Annie lowered the visor against the sun's dazzle and felt something inside her quicken.

In the last few days she had started coming out to the ranch a little earlier so that she could watch Tom Booker at work. Not that the real work with Pilgrim had started yet. So far it had been mostly physical therapy, building up the horse's wasted shoulder and leg muscles in the swimming pool. Round and round he swam, with a look in his eyes as if he were being chased by crocodiles. He was staying out on the ranch now, in a stall right by the pool, and the only close contact Tom had so far had with him was getting him in and out of the water. Even so it was dangerous enough.

Yesterday Annie had stood beside Grace and watched him get Pilgrim from the pool. The horse hadn't wanted to come out, fearing a trap, so Tom had walked down the ramp till he was up to his waist. Pilgrim had thrashed around and soaked him and even reared up over him. But Tom was totally unfazed. It seemed miraculous to Annie how the man could stand so calmly close to death. How could one calculate such margins? Pilgrim too had seemed baffled by this lack of fear and soon staggered out and let himself be ushered to his stall.

Tom came back to Grace and Annie and stood dripping before them. He took off his hat and poured the water from its brim. Grace started to laugh and he gave her a wry look that made her laugh even more. Then he turned to Annie and shook his head.

"She's a heartless woman this daughter of yours," he said. "What she doesn't know is next time she's the one going in."

The sound of Grace's laughter had stayed in Annie's head ever since. On the way back to Choteau, Grace had told her what they had been doing with Pilgrim and the questions Tom had asked about him. She had told her about Bronty's foal, about Frank and Diane and the boys, how the twins were a pain but Joe was alright. It was the first time she'd talked freely and happily since they'd left New York and Annie had to try hard not to overreact and to just let it happen as though it were nothing special. It hadn't lasted. Driving past the dinosaur, Grace fell silent, as if it reminded her how nowadays she behaved toward her mother. But at least it was a start, thought Annie.

The Lariat's tires scrunched now on the gravel as she came around the ridge and curved down into the valley under the wooden Double D sign that marked the start of the ranch's driveway. Annie could see horses running in the big open arena by the stables and as she got nearer she could see Tom riding among them. In one hand he had a long stick with an orange flag on the end and he was waving it at them, making them run away from him. There were maybe a dozen colts in there and mostly they kept close to each other. There was one among them though who was always alone and now Annie could see it was Pilgrim.

Grace was leaning on the rail next to Joe and the twins, all of them watching. Annie parked and walked over to them, ruffling the heads of the dogs who no longer barked when she arrived. Joe smiled at her and was the only one who said hello.

"What's going on?" Annie asked.

"Oh, he's just driving them around some."

Annie leaned on the rail beside him and watched. The colts bolted and swerved from one end of the arena to the other, making long shadows on the sand and kicking up amber clouds of it that trapped the slanting sun. Tom moved Rimrock effortlessly after them, sometimes stepping sideways or backward to block them or open up a gap. Annie hadn't seen him ride before. The horse's white-socked feet made intricate steps without any visible guidance, steered, so it seemed to Annie, by Tom's thoughts alone. It was as if he and the horse were one. She couldn't take her eyes off him. As he came past, he tipped his hat and smiled.

"Annie."

It was the first time he hadn't called her ma'am or Mrs. Graves and to hear him, unprompted, speak her name pleased her, made her feel accepted. She watched him move off toward Pilgrim who had stopped like all the others at the far end of the arena. The horse stood separate and was the only one sweating. The scars on his face and chest stood out in the sunlight and he was tossing his head and snorting. He seemed as troubled by the other horses as he was by Tom.

"What we're doing here Annie, is trying to get him to learn how to be a horse again. All the others already know, see? That's how they are in the wild, herd animals. When they've got a problem, like they have now with me and this flag, they look to each other. But old Pilgrim here has plumb forgotten. I'm the rock and they're the hard place. He thinks he hasn't got a friend in the world. Turn 'em all loose in the mountains and these guys would be fine. Poor old Pilgrim though, he'd be bear bait. It's not that he doesn't want to make friends, he just doesn't know how."

He moved Rimrock in on them and lifted the flag sharply, making it crack in the air. The colts all broke away to the right and this time, instead of breaking left like before, Pilgrim went after them. As soon as he was clear of Tom though, he separated and again came to a halt on his own. Tom grinned.

"He'll get there."

The sun had long gone by the time they had Pilgrim back in his stall and it was getting cold. Diane called the boys in for their supper and Grace went in with them to pick up a coat she had left in the house. Tom and Annie walked slowly over to the Lariat. Annie felt suddenly very aware of their being alone together. For a while neither of them spoke. An owl flew low over their heads toward the creek and Annie watched it melt into the dark of the cottonwoods. She felt Tom's eyes on her and turned to look at him. He smiled calmly and quite without embarrassment and the look he gave her wasn't the look of a virtual stranger, but of someone who'd known her for a very long time. Annie managed to smile back and was relieved to see Grace coming toward them from the house.

"We're branding here tomorrow," Tom said. "If you two want to come and give a hand."

Annie laughed. "I think we'd just get in the way," she said.

He shrugged. "Maybe. But as long as you don't get in the way of the branding iron it doesn't matter too much. Even if you do, it's a nice-looking mark. Back in the city you might be proud of it."

Annie turned to Grace and could see she was keen but trying not to look it. She turned back to Tom.

"Okay, why not?" she said.

He told her they'd be starting around nine the next morning but they could show up whenever they liked. Then they said good-night. As she pulled away up the driveway, Annie looked in the rearview mirror. He was still standing there, watching them go.

SEVENTEEN

Tom rode up one side of the valley and Joe the other. The idea was to pick up stragglers but the cows needed little more inducement. They could see the old Chevy down in the meadow where it always parked at feeding time and they could hear Frank and the twins hollering and banging the bag of cow cake on its lowered rear end for them to come and get it. They streamed down from the hills, calling in reply while their calves scrambled after them, calling too, anxious not to be left behind.

Tom's father used to raise pure Herefords, but for some years now Frank had raised a Black Angus–Hereford cross. The Angus cows were good mothers and suited the climate better because their udders were black, not pink like the Herefords, so they didn't get burned by the sun bouncing off the snow. Tom watched for a while as they moved away from him down the hill, then he turned Rimrock to the left and dropped over into the shaded bed of the creek.

Steam rose off the water into the warming air and a dipper took off and flew straight upstream ahead of them fast and so low that its slate wings almost skimmed the surface. Down here the calling of the cattle was muted then lost in the soft splashing of the horse's feet as he moved up to the top of the meadow. Sometimes along here a calf would get tangled in the thick willow scrub. But today they found nothing and Tom eased Rimrock back onto the bank then loped him up into the sun at the top of the ridge and stopped.

He could see Joe on his brown and white paint pony way over on the other side of the valley. The boy waved and Tom waved back. Below, the cattle were funneling down to the Chevy, flooding around it so that it looked from here like a boat on a seething pool of black. The twins were tossing out a few pellets of cake to keep the cows interested while Frank clambered back into the driver's seat and started to pull slowly away back down the meadow. Lured by the cake, the cattle surged after it.

From this ridge you could see right down the valley to the ranch and the corrals to which the cattle were now being led. And as Tom looked, he saw what he realized he had been looking out for all morning. Annie's car was coming down the driveway, leaving a low, gray wake of dust. As it curved in front of the ranch house, the sun flashed on its windshield.

More than a mile separated him from the two figures that got out of the car. They were small and quite featureless. But Tom could picture Annie's face as if she were beside him. He saw her as she'd been last evening, as she watched the owl, before she sensed him watching her. She had looked so lost and beautiful that he'd wanted to take her in his arms. She's another man's wife, he'd told himself as the Lariat's tail-lights went off up the driveway. But it hadn't stopped him thinking about her. He nudged Rimrock forward and moved off down the hill to follow the cattle.

The air over the corral hung heavy with dust and the smell of scorched flesh. Separated from their mothers, who kept up a constant calling, the calves were moved through a series of connecting pens until they found themselves in a narrow chute from which there was no return. Emerging from here, one by one, they were clamped and lowered sideways onto a table where four pairs of hands went immediately to work. Before they knew it, they'd been given a shot, a yellow insect tag in one ear, a growth pellet in the other, then a burn on the butt with a branding iron. Then the table went vertical again, off came the clamp and suddenly they were free. They tottered off in a daze toward the call of their mothers at whose udders, at last, they found comfort.

All of this was witnessed, with a lazy, regal disinterest by their fathers, five enormous Hereford bulls, who lay chewing in an adjoining pen. It was witnessed by Annie with something approaching horror. She could see Grace felt the same. The calves squealed terribly and got what little revenge they could by spurting shit down their attackers' boots or kicking any careless shin they found. Some of the neighbors who had come to help had brought children along and those big or bold enough were trying their hand at roping and wrestling the smaller calves. Annie saw Grace watching them and thought what a terrible mistake it was to have come. There was such an extreme physicality about it all. It only seemed to make her own child's disability more blatant.

Tom must have read this on Annie's face because he came over and quickly found her a job. He put her to work in the feeder pen to the chute alongside a grinning

giant with reflector sunglasses and a T-shirt that said
CEREAL KILLER. He introduced himself as Hank and gave
Annie a handshake that made her knuckles crack. He
said he came from the next ranch down the valley.

"Our friendly neighborhood psycho," Tom said.

"It's okay, I already ate," Hank confided to Annie.

As she got to work, Annie saw Tom go over to Grace,
put his arm around her shoulders and lead her off,
though to where, Annie had no time to see because a
calf trod on her foot then kicked her hard on the knee.
She yelped and Hank laughed and showed her how to
shove them into the chute without getting too bruised
or shat upon. It was hard work and she had to concentrate and soon, what with Hank's jokes and the warm
spring sunshine, she started to feel better.

Later, when she had a moment to look, she saw Tom
had taken Grace right to the front line and had her
wielding the branding iron. To begin with she kept her
eyes closed. But soon he got her thinking so hard about
her technique that all squeamishness vanished.

"Don't press too hard," Annie heard him say. He
was standing behind Grace, with his hands resting
gently on her upper arms. "Just let it drop down
lightly." Flames flared up as the red-hot head of the
iron touched the calf's hide. "That's good, firm but
gentle. It hurts, but he'll get over it. Now let it roll a
little. Good. Now lift. Grace, that's a perfect brand.
Best Double D of the day."

Everyone cheered. The girl's face was flushed and her
eyes were shining. She laughed and made a little bow.
Tom saw Annie looking and grinned and pointed at her.

"Your turn next, Annie."

* * *

By late afternoon all but the smallest calves were branded and Frank announced it was time to eat. Everyone started heading for the ranch house, the younger children running on ahead, whooping. Annie looked around for Grace. No one had said anything about them being invited and Annie felt it was time to leave. She saw Grace up ahead, walking to the house with Joe, the two of them chatting easily about something. Annie called her name and she turned.

"We have to go now," Annie said.

"What? Why?"

"Yeah, why? You're not allowed to go." It was Tom. He'd come up alongside her. They were beside the bull pen. The two of them had hardly spoken all day. Annie shrugged.

"Well, you know. It's getting late."

"Yeah, I know. And you've got to get back and feed the fax machine and make all those calls and things, right?"

The sun was behind him and Annie put her head on one side and squinted at him, giving him a look. Men didn't normally tease her like this. She liked it.

"But you see, there's kind of a tradition here," he went on. "That whoever makes the best brand has to give a speech after dinner."

"What!" said Grace.

"That's right. Or drink ten jugs of beer. So, Grace, you better go on in and get yourself ready." Grace looked at Joe to make sure it was a joke. Tom nodded toward the house, deadpan. "Joe, you better show her the way." Joe led her off, doing his best not to grin.

"If you're sure we're invited," said Annie.

"You're invited."

"Thank you."

"You're welcome."

They smiled at each other and the silence between them was filled for a few moments by the lowing of cattle. Their calls were gentler now that the frenzy of the day had passed. It was Annie who first felt the need to speak. She looked at the bulls lazing in the last of the sunshine.

"Who'd be a cow when you could lie around like these guys all day?" she said.

Tom looked at them and nodded.

"Yep. They spend all summer making love and winter just lying around and eating." He paused, considering something as he watched them. "On the other hand, not too many of them get to do it. Get born as a bull and you've got a ninety-nine percent chance of getting castrated and served up as a hamburger. On balance, I reckon I'd choose being a cow."

They sat at a long table covered with a starched white cloth and laid with glazed hams, turkey, and steaming dishes of corn, beans, and sweet potato. The room it stood in was clearly the main living room but seemed to Annie more like a large hall that divided the two wings of the house. Its ceiling was high and its floor and walls were of dark, stained wood. There were paintings of Indians chasing buffalo and old sepia photographs of men with long moustaches and plainly dressed women with serious faces. On one side, an open staircase curved up to a wide, railed landing that overlooked the entire room.

Annie had felt embarrassed when they came in. She realized that while she had been out branding, most of the other women had been inside preparing the meal. But no one seemed to mind. Diane, who till today had never seemed overly friendly, made her feel welcome and even offered her a change of clothes. As all the men were equally dusty and muckstained, Annie thanked her and declined.

The children sat at one end of the table and the clamor they made was so loud that the adults at the other had to strain to hear themselves talk. Every so often Diane yelled at them to pipe down but it had little or no effect and soon, led by Frank and Hank who sat on either side of Annie, the uproar was general. Grace sat next to Joe. Annie could hear her telling him about New York and about a friend of hers who got mugged on the subway for his new Nike trainers. Joe listened with widening eyes.

Tom sat across from Annie, between his sister Rosie and their mother. They'd driven up from Great Falls this afternoon with Rosie's two daughters who were five and six years old. Ellen Booker was a gentle, fine-boned woman with perfectly white hair and eyes the same vivid blue as Tom's. She spoke little, just listened and smiled at what was going on around her. Annie noticed how Tom looked after her and talked quietly to her about the ranch and the horses. She could see from the way Ellen watched him that this was her favorite child.

"So Annie, you gonna do a big piece about us all in your magazine?" said Hank.

"That's right, Hank. You're the centerfold."

He gave a great bellow of laughter.

Frank said, "Hey Hank, you better get yourself some of that—what do they call it? Lipsuction."

"Liposuction, you fool," Diane said.

"I'll go for the lipsuction," Hank said. "Though I guess it depends who's doing the sucking."

Annie asked Frank about the ranch and he told her how they had moved here when he and Tom were boys.

He took her over to look at the photographs and told her who all the people were. There was something about this gallery of solemn faces that Annie found moving. It was as though their mere survival in this daunting land were in itself some mighty triumph. While Frank was telling her about his grandfather, Annie happened to glance back at the table and saw Tom look up and see her and smile.

When she and Frank went back and sat down, Joe was telling Grace about a hippie woman who lived farther up on the mountains. She'd bought some Pryor Mountain mustangs a few years back, he said, and just let them run wild. They'd bred and now there was quite a herd of them up there.

"She's got all these kids too and they run around with nothing on. Dad calls her Granola Gay. Came here from L.A."

"Californication!" Hank chanted. Everyone laughed.

"Hank, do you mind!" Diane said.

Later, over a dessert of pumpkin pie and homemade cherry ice cream, Frank said, "You know what, Tom? While you're working on that horse of theirs, Annie and Grace here ought to move into the creek house. Seems crazy them doing all that shuttling to and fro."

Annie just caught the sharp look Diane gave her husband. It was obviously something they hadn't discussed. Tom looked at Annie.

"Sure," he said. "It's a good idea."

"Oh, that's very nice of you, but really . . ."

"Hell, I know that old house you're staying in down there in Choteau," said Frank. "It's good as falling down around your ears."

"Frank, the creek house isn't exactly a palace, for heavensakes," said Diane. "Anyway, I'm sure Annie wants her privacy."

Before Annie could speak, Frank leaned forward and looked down the table. "Grace? What do you think?"

Grace looked at Annie, but her face gave her answer and it was all Frank needed.

"That's settled then."

Diane got up. "I'll make some coffee," she said.

EIGHTEEN

A QUARTER MOON THE COLOR OF DAPPLED BONE STILL stood in the dawning sky when Tom stepped out through the screen door and onto the porch. He stopped there, pulling on his gloves, feeling the cold air on his face. The world was white and brittle with frost and no breeze ruffled the clouds made by his breath. The dogs came rushing up to greet him, their bodies wagging with their tails and he touched their heads and with no more than a nod sent them racing off toward the corrals, nipping and jostling each other, their feet scuffing tracks in the magnesium grass. Tom turned up the collar of his green wool jacket and stepped down off the porch to follow them.

The yellow blinds on the upstairs windows of the creek house were closed. Annie and Grace were probably still asleep. He'd helped them move in the previous afternoon after he and Diane had cleaned the place up a little. Diane had barely said a word all morning but he could tell how she felt by the jutting of her jaw and the methodically violent way she wielded the vacuum cleaner and made up the beds. Annie was to sleep in the main front bedroom, overlooking the creek. It was where Diane and Frank had slept and, before them, he and Rachel. Grace was to have Joe's old bedroom at the back of the house.

"How long are they planning on staying?" Diane said as she finished making Annie's bed. Tom was by the door, checking that a radiator worked. He turned but she wasn't looking at him.

"I don't know. Guess it depends how things go with the horse."

Diane didn't say a thing, just shunted the bed back into position with her knees so that the headboard banged against the wall.

"If you have a problem with it, I'm sure—"

"Who said I had a problem? I don't have a problem." She stomped past him out onto the landing and scooped up a pile of towels she'd left there. "I just hope the woman knows how to cook, that's all." And she went off down the stairs.

Diane wasn't around later when Annie and Grace arrived. Tom helped them unload the Lariat and took their bags upstairs for them. He was relieved to see they'd brought two big boxes of groceries. The sun was streaming through the big front window in the living room and made the place seem light and airy. Annie said how pretty it was. She asked if it would be okay to move the long dining table over to the window so that she could use it as her desk and look out on the creek and the corrals while she worked. Tom took one end and she took the other and when they'd moved it he helped her bring in all her computers and fax machines and some other electronic gadgetry whose purpose he couldn't begin to guess.

It had struck him as odd that the first thing Annie should want to do in this new place, before unpacking, before even seeing where she was to sleep, was to set up somewhere to work. He could tell from the look on Grace's face as she watched that to her it wasn't odd at all. It had always been like this.

Last night before he turned in, he'd walked out, as he always did, to check on the horses and on the way back he'd looked up at the creek house and seen the lights on and wondered what they were doing, this woman and her child, and of what if anything they spoke. Seeing the house standing there against the clear night sky, he'd thought of Rachel and the pain those walls had encased so many years ago. Now pain was encased there again, pain of the highest order, finely wrought by mutual guilt and used by wounded souls to punish those they love the most.

Tom made his way past the corrals, the frosted grass scrunching under the soles of his boots. The branches of the cottonwoods along the creek were laced with silver and over their heads he could see the eastern sky starting to glow pink where soon the sun would show. The dogs were waiting for him outside the barn door, all eager. They knew he never let them go in with him but they always thought it worth a try. He shooed them away and went in to see to the horses.

An hour later, when the sun had melted black patches on the barn's frost-veneered roof, Tom led out one of the colts he'd started the previous week and swung himself up into the saddle. The horse, like all the others he'd raised, had a good soft feel and they rode an easy walk up the dirt road toward the meadows.

As they passed below the creek house, Tom saw the blinds of Annie's bedroom were now open. Farther on he found footprints in the frost beside the road and he followed them until they were lost among the willows where the road crossed the creek in a shallow ford.

There were rocks you could use as stepping-stones and he could see from the wet criss-cross marks on them that whoever it was had done just that.

The colt saw her before he did and, prompted by the pricking of its ears, Tom looked up and saw Annie running back down from the meadow. She was wearing a pale gray sweatshirt, black leggings and a pair of those hundred-dollar shoes they advertised on TV. She hadn't yet seen him and he brought the colt to a stop at the water's edge and watched her come nearer. Through the low rush of the water, he could just make out the sound of her breathing. She had her hair tied back and her face was pink from the cold air and the effort of her running. She was looking down, concentrating so hard on where she was putting her feet that if the colt hadn't softly snorted, she might have run right into them. But the sound made her look up and she stopped in her tracks, some ten yards away.

"Hi!"

Tom touched the brim of his hat.

"A jogger, huh?"

She made a mock haughty face. "I don't jog, Mr. Booker. I run."

"That's lucky, the grizzlies around here only go for the joggers."

Her eyes went wide. "Grizzly bears? Are you serious?"

"Well, you know, we keep 'em pretty well fed and all." He could see she was worried and grinned. "I'm kidding. Oh, they're around but they like to stay higher. You're safe enough." He thought about adding, except for the mountain lions, but if she'd heard about that woman in California she might not think it too funny.

She gave him a narrow-eyed look for teasing her, then grinned and came closer so that the sun fell full on her face and she had to shield her eyes with one hand to look up at him. Her breasts and shoulders rose and fell to the rhythm of her breathing and a slow steam curled off her and melted in the air.

"Did you sleep okay up there?" he said.

"I don't sleep okay anywhere."

"Is the heating okay? It's been a while since—"

"It's fine. Everything's fine. It's really very kind of you to let us stay out here."

"It's good to have the old place lived in."

"Well, anyway. Thank you."

For a moment, neither of them seemed to know what to say. Annie reached out to touch the horse, but did it a little too suddenly so that the animal tossed his head away and took a couple of steps back.

"I'm sorry," Annie said. Tom reached down and rubbed the colt's neck.

"Just hold your hand out. A little lower, there, so he can get the smell of you." The colt lowered his muzzle to Annie's hand and explored it with the tips of his whiskers, snuffling it now. Annie watched, a slow smile starting, and Tom noticed again how the corners of her mouth seemed to have some mysterious life of their own, qualifying each smile for its occasion.

"He's beautiful," she said.

"Yeah, he's doing pretty good. Do you ride?"

"Oh. A long time ago. When I was Grace's age."

Something in her face changed and at once he regretted asking the question. And he felt dumb because it was clear that in some way she blamed herself for what had happened to her daughter.

"I'd better get back, I'm getting cold." She moved off, giving the horse space as she passed, squinting up at Tom. "I thought it was supposed to be spring!"

"Oh well, you know what they say, if you don't like the weather in Montana, wait five minutes."

He turned in the saddle and watched her make her way back across the stepping-stones of the ford. She slipped and cursed to herself as one shoe went briefly under the icy water.

"Need a lift?"

"No, I'm fine."

"I'll come by around two o'clock and collect Grace," he called.

"Okay!"

She reached the far side of the creek and turned to give him a little wave. He touched his hat and watched her turn away again and break into a run, still not looking at what lay around her or ahead of her, but only where she placed her feet.

Pilgrim burst into the arena as though fired from a cannon. He ran straight to the far end and stopped there, sending up a splash of red sand. His tail was clenched and it twitched and his ears moved back and forward. His eyes were wild and fixed on the open gate through which he'd come and through which he knew the man would now follow him.

Tom was on foot and had in his hands an orange flagstick and a coiled rope. He came in and shut the gate and walked to the middle of the arena. The sky above him rushed with small white clouds so that the light shifted constantly from gloom to glare.

For almost a minute they stood there, quite still, the horse and the man, assessing each other. It was Pilgrim who moved first. He snorted and lowered his head and took some small steps back. Tom stayed like a statue, with the tip of his flag resting on the sand. Then at last he took a step toward Pilgrim and at the same time lifted the flag in his right hand and made it crack. Immediately the horse launched off to the left and ran.

Round and round the arena he went, kicking up the sand, snorting loudly and tossing his head. His cocked and tangled tail splayed out behind him, flicking and swishing in the wind. He ran with his rear skewed in and his head skewed out and every ounce of every muscle in his body was clenched and focused only on the man. Such was the angle of his head, he had to strain his left eye backward to see him. But it never strayed, held there by a line of fear so enthralling that, in his other eye, the world was but a circling blur of nothingness.

Soon his flanks began to shine with sweat and flecks of foam flew from the corners of his mouth. But still the man drove him ever on and every time he slowed, up the flag would go and crack, forcing him forward and forward again.

All this Grace watched from the bench Tom had set up for her outside the rails of the arena. It was the first time she'd seen him work like this on foot and there was an intensity about him today that she'd noticed right away when he came by in the Chevy on the stroke of two to drive her down to the barn. For today, they both knew, was when the real work with Pilgrim was to start.

The horse's leg muscles had grown strong again with all the swimming he'd been doing and the scars on his chest and face were looking better by the day. It was the scars inside his head that now needed seeing to. Tom had parked outside the barn and let Grace lead the way down the avenue of stalls to the big one at the end where Pilgrim now lived. There were bars on the top half of the door and they could see him watching them all the way. When they reached the door, he always backed away into the far corner, lowering his head and flattening his ears. But he no longer charged when they came in and lately Tom had let Grace take in his feed and water. His coat was matted and his mane and tail filthy and tangled and Grace longed to get a brush on him.

The far wall of the stall had a sliding door which opened onto a bare concrete lobby where there were doors both to the pool and the arena. Getting him to and from either one was a matter of opening the appropriate door and crowding him so that he bolted through. Today, as if sensing some new plot, he hadn't wanted to go and Tom had had to get in close and slap his hindquarters.

Now, as Pilgrim went by, for maybe the hundredth time, Grace saw him turn his head to look square at Tom, wondering why all of a sudden he was being allowed to slow without the flag being raised. Tom let him come right down to a walk and then stop. The horse stood there, looking about, blowing. Wondering what was going on. After a few moments Tom started to walk toward him. Pilgrim's ears went forward, then back, then forward again. His muscles quivered in wavelike spasms down his sides.

"You see that, Grace? See those muscles all knotted up there? You've got yourself one hell of a determined horse here. Gonna need a whole lot of cooking, old fella, ain't you?"

She knew what he meant. He'd told her the other day about an old man called Dorrance from Wallowa County, Oregon, the best horseman Tom had ever met, and how, when he was trying to get a horse to unwind, he'd poke his finger into its muscles and say he wanted to check if the potatoes were cooked yet. But Grace could see Pilgrim wasn't going to allow any such thing. He was moving his head to one side, assessing the man's approach with one fearful eye and when Tom was about five yards away, he broke away in the same direction as before. Only now Tom stepped in and blocked him with the flag. The horse braked hard in the sand and swerved to the right. He turned outward, away from Tom, and as his rear end swung past, Tom stepped smartly in and whacked it with the flag. Pilgrim lunged away forward. And now he was circling clockwise and the process began all over again.

"He wants to be alright," Tom said. "He just doesn't know what alright is."

And if he ever gets to be alright, Grace thought, what then? Tom had said nothing about where all this was leading. He was taking each day as it came, not forcing things, just letting Pilgrim take his time and make his choices. But what then? If Pilgrim got better, was it she who was expected to ride him?

Grace knew quite well that people rode with worse disabilities than hers. Some even started from scratch that way. She'd seen them at events and once she'd even taken part in a sponsored show-jump where all the money went to the local Riding for the Disabled group. She'd thought how brave these people were and felt sorry for them. Now she couldn't bear the idea that people might feel the same about her. She wouldn't give them the chance. She'd said she would never ride again and that was that.

Some two hours later, after Joe and the twins had come back from school, Tom opened the arena gate and let Pilgrim run back into his stall. Grace had already cleaned the place out and put new shavings down and Tom stood guard and watched her bring in the bucket of feed and hang up a fresh net of hay.

As he drove her back up the valley to the creek house, the sun was low and the rocks and limber pine on the slopes above them cast long shadows on the pale grass. They didn't speak and Grace wondered why silence with this man she'd known so short a time never seemed uncomfortable. She could tell that he now had something on his mind. He circled the Chevy to the back of the house and pulled up by the back porch. Then he cut the engine off, sat back and turned to look her right in the eye.

"Grace, I've got a problem."

He paused and she didn't know whether she was supposed to say something, but he went on.

"You see, when I'm working with a horse, I like to know the history. Now most times the horse can tell you pretty much the whole deal just by himself. In fact a sight better than his owner might tell it. But sometimes he can be so messed up in his head that you need more to go on. You need to know what went wrong. And often it's not the obvious thing but something that went wrong just before that, maybe even some little thing."

Grace didn't understand and he saw her frown.

"It's like if I was driving this old Chevy and I hit a tree and someone asks me what happened, well, I wouldn't say, 'Well, you know, I hit a tree.' I'd say maybe I'd had too many beers or there was oil on the road or maybe the sun was in my eyes or something. See what I mean?"

She nodded.

"Well, I don't know how you feel about talking about it and I can sure understand you might not want to. But if I'm going to figure out what's going on in Pilgrim's head, it'd help me a whole lot if I knew something about the accident and what exactly happened that day."

Grace heard herself take a breath. She looked away from him to the house and noticed you could see right through the kitchen to the living room. She could see the blue-gray glow of the computer screen and her mother sitting there, on the phone, framed in the fading light of the big front window.

She hadn't told anyone what she really remembered about that day. To the police, lawyers, doctors, even to her parents, she'd gone on pretending that much of what had happened was a blank. The problem was Judith. She still didn't know if she could handle talking about Judith. Or even about Gulliver. She looked back at Tom Booker and he smiled. In his eyes there was not a trace of pity and she knew in that instant that she was accepted, not judged. Perhaps it was because he only knew the person she now was, the disfigured, partial one, not the whole she once had been.

"I don't mean now," he said gently. "When you're ready. And only if you want to." Something beyond her caught his eye and she followed his glance and saw her mother coming out onto the porch. Grace turned back to him and nodded.

"I'll think about it," she said.

Robert propped his glasses up on the top of his forehead, leaned back in his chair and rubbed his eyes for a long time. He had his shirtsleeves rolled up and his tie lay crumpled among the layers of papers and law books that covered his desk. Along the corridor he could hear the cleaners moving systematically through the other offices, talking to each other now and then in Spanish. Everyone else had gone home four or five hours ago.

Bill Sachs, one of the younger partners, had tried to persuade him to come with him and his wife to see some new Gerard Depardieu movie everyone was talking about. Robert said thanks but he had too much work to get through and anyway he always found something faintly disturbing about Depardieu's nose.

"It looks, you know, kind of penile," he said.

Bill, who could have passed as a psychiatrist anyway, had peered at him over his hornrims and asked in a comic Freudian accent, why Robert should find such an association disturbing. Then he got Robert laughing about two women he'd heard talking the other day on the subway.

"One of them had been reading this book that tells you what your dreams mean and she was telling the other girl how it had said if you dreamed about snakes it meant you were really obsessed by penises and the other one said, phew, that was a relief 'cause all she ever dreamed about was penises."

Bill wasn't the only one who seemed to be making a special effort to cheer him up at the moment. Robert was touched but on the whole he wished they wouldn't. Being on your own for a few weeks didn't justify this level of sympathy and so he suspected his colleagues sensed in him some deeper loss. One had even offered to take over the Dunford Securities case. God, that was about the only thing that kept him going.

Every night for nearly three weeks now he'd been up till way past midnight working on it. The hard disk on his laptop was almost bursting with it. It was one of the most complicated cases he'd ever worked on, involving bonds worth billions of dollars being shuffled endlessly through a maze of companies across three continents. Today he'd had a two-hour conference call with lawyers and clients in Hong Kong, Geneva, London and

Sydney. The time differences were a nightmare. But curiously it kept him sane and, more important, too busy to dwell too much on how he missed Grace and Annie.

He opened his sore eyes and leaned across to press the redial button on one of his phones. Then he settled back, staring out of the window at the illuminated coronets on the spire of the Chrysler Building. The number Annie had given him, for this new place they'd moved into, was still busy.

He'd walked to the corner of Fifth and Fifty-ninth before he flagged a cab. The cold night air felt good and he'd toyed with the idea of walking all the way home across the park. He'd done it before at night though only once did he make the mistake of telling Annie. She'd yelled at him for a full ten minutes and told him he was insane going in there at night, did he want to get himself disemboweled? He wondered if he'd missed something in the newspapers about this particular hazard, but it didn't seem the right time to ask.

From the name posted on the dashboard of the cab, he could tell the driver was Senegalese. There were quite a few of them nowadays and Robert always enjoyed blowing their minds by casually addressing them in Wolof or Jola. This young man was so amazed he almost drove smack into a bus. They talked about Dakar and places they both knew and the driving got so bad that Robert began to think the park might have been a safer bet after all. When they pulled up outside the apartment building, Ramón came down and opened the cab door and the driver said how grateful he was for the tip and that he would pray that Allah bless Robert with many strong sons.

After Ramón had given him an apparently white-hot

piece of news about a star player just signed by the Mets, Robert took the elevator and let himself into the apartment. The place was dark and the clunk of the door as he shut it echoed through the lifeless labyrinth of rooms.

He walked through to the kitchen and found the supper Elsa had cooked for him and the usual note saying what it was and how long it needed in the microwave. He did what he always did and scooped it guiltily into the garbage. He'd left her notes thanking her but saying please not to bother cooking for him, he could get takeout or cook something himself. But there it still was every night, bless her.

The truth was, the aching emptiness of the apartment made him morose and he avoided being here as much as he could. He felt it most acutely at weekends. He'd tried going up to Chatham but the loneliness there had been even worse. It hadn't been helped by arriving to find that the thermostat on Grace's tropical fish tank had failed and all the fish had died of cold. The sight of their tiny, faded corpses floating in the tank had upset him profoundly. He hadn't told Grace, nor even Annie, but had pulled himself together, made careful notes and ordered identical impostors from the pet store.

Since Annie and Grace had left, talking to them on the phone had become the high point of Robert's day. And tonight, having tried for hours and failed to reach them, he felt a sharper need than ever for the sound of their voices.

He sealed the garbage bag so that Elsa wouldn't discover the shameful destiny of the supper she'd cooked. As he was dumping the bag outside the service door, he heard the phone and he ran back down the corridor as fast as he could. The answering machine had already clicked in by the time he got there and he had to speak loudly to compete with his own recorded voice.

"Hold on, I'm here." He found the off button. "Hi. I just got in."

"You're all out of breath. Where were you?"

"Oh, out partying. You know, doing the bars and clubs and things. God, it's tiring."

"Don't tell me."

"I wasn't going to. So how're things where the deer and the antelope play? I tried calling all day."

"I'm sorry. There's just the one line here and the office has been trying to bury me in fax paper."

She said Grace had tried calling him half an hour ago at the office, probably just after he'd left for home. She'd gone to bed now but sent him her love.

As Annie told him about her day, Robert walked through to the sitting room and, without turning the lights on, settled himself on the sofa by the window. Annie sounded weary and downcast and he tried, without much success, to cheer her up.

"And how's Gracie?"

There was a pause and he heard Annie sigh.

"Oh. I don't know." Her voice was low now, presumably so that Grace wouldn't hear. "I see how she is with Tom Booker and Joe, you know, the twelve-year-old? They get on really well. And with them, she seems fine. But when it's just the two of us, I don't know. It's gotten so bad she won't even look at me." She sighed again. "Anyway."

They were silent for a while and in the distance he heard a wail of sirens out in the street, on their way to another nameless tragedy.

"I miss you, Annie."

"I know," she said. "We miss you too."

NINETEEN

A NNIE DROPPED GRACE AT THE CLINIC A LITTLE BE-
fore nine and wove her way back to the gas station in
Choteau center. She filled up alongside a little man with
a face like leather and a hat brimmed wide enough to
shelter a horse. He was checking the oil of a Dodge
pickup which was hitched to a trailerload of cattle.
They were Black Angus like the herd at the Double
Divide and Annie had to fight the urge to confide some
knowing remark about them based on the little she'd
gleaned from Tom and Frank on branding day. She re-
hearsed it in her head. Good-lookin' cattle. No, you
wouldn't say cattle. Healthy-lookin' beasts? Fellas? She
gave up. In all truth she had no idea if they were good,
bad or flea-bitten, so she kept her mouth shut and just
gave the man a nod and a smile instead.

As she came out from paying, someone called her
name and she looked around and saw Diane getting out
of her Toyota at the other row of pumps. Annie waved
and walked over.

"So you do sometimes give yourself a break from

that telephone after all," Diane said. "We were beginning to wonder."

Annie smiled and told her she had to bring Grace into town three mornings a week for physical therapy. She was going back to the ranch now to do some work and would come back in at midday to pick her up.

"Heck, well I can do that for you," Diane said. "I've got a bunch of things to do in town. Is she up at the Bellview Medical Center?"

"Yes, but honestly, you don't want—"

"Don't be silly. It's crazy you driving all that way."

Annie demurred but Diane would have none of it, it was no problem she said, and in the end Annie gave way and thanked her. They chatted for a few more minutes about how things were going up at the creek house and whether Annie and Grace had everything they needed, then Diane said she'd better get going.

On her way back to the ranch Annie puzzled over the encounter. The substance of Diane's offer had been friendly enough, but the manner in which it had been made was something less. There had been just the faintest hint of accusation, almost as though she were saying that Annie was much too busy to bother herself with being a mother. Or maybe Annie was just being paranoid.

She traveled north and looked out over the plains to her right where the black shapes of the cattle stood out against the pale grass like the ghosts of buffalo from another age. Ahead on the blacktop, the sun was already making pools of mirage and she lowered the window and let the wind blow her hair back. It was the second week in May and at last it felt as if spring had really come and wasn't just kidding. When she swung left off 89, the Rocky Mountain Front loomed before her, topped with cloud that seemed squeezed from some galactic can of chantilly. All that was missing, she thought, was a cherry and one of those little paper umbrellas. Then she remembered all the faxes and phone messages that would be waiting for her when she got back to the ranch and realized a moment or two later that the thought had eased her foot on the gas pedal.

She'd already used up much of the month's leave she'd asked Crawford Gates to give her. She would have to ask him for more and she wasn't looking forward to it. For despite all his talk about how she should feel free to take off as much time as she needed, Annie was under no illusion. In the last few days there had been clear signs that Gates was getting restless. There had been a series of small interferences, not one of them on its own enough for her to make a real fuss about, but which, when viewed collectively, signaled danger.

He had criticized Lucy Friedman's lounge lizard piece which Annie considered quite brilliant; he'd queried the design team over two front covers—not in a heavy-handed way but enough to make an impression; and he'd sent Annie a long memo about how he thought their coverage of Wall Street was slipping behind the competition. That would have been okay, except that he'd copied it to four other directors before even speaking to her. But if the old bastard wanted a fight, so be it. She hadn't phoned him. Instead she wrote an immediate and robust reply, full of facts and figures, and copied it to the same people plus, for good measure, a couple of others she knew to be her allies. Touché. But God, it took such a lot of effort.

When she drove over the hill and down past the corrals, she saw Tom's yearlings running in the arena, but there was no sign of Tom and she felt disappointed, then amused that she should feel so. As she came around the back of the creek house she saw there was a phone company truck parked there and as she got out, a man in blue coveralls came out of the house onto the porch. He wished her good-day and said he'd fitted the new lines.

Inside, she found two new phones beside her computer. The answering machine showed four messages and there were three faxes, one of them from Lucy Friedman. As she began to read it, one of the new phones rang.

"Hi." It was a man's voice and for a moment she didn't recognize it. "Just wanted to see if it worked."

"Who is this?" Annie said.

"I'm sorry. It's Tom, Tom Booker. I just saw the phone guy leaving and I wanted to see if the new lines worked."

Annie laughed.

"I can hear they do, one of them anyway. I hope you don't mind him letting himself in."

"Of course not. Thank you. You really needn't have."

"It's no big deal. Grace said her dad sometimes had trouble getting through."

"Well, it's very kind of you."

There was a pause and then, just for something to say, Annie told him how she'd bumped into Diane in Choteau and how she'd kindly offered to bring Grace back.

"She could have taken her in too if we'd known."

Annie thanked him again for the phones and offered to pay for them but he brushed it aside and said he'd leave her to get on with using them and hung up. She started to read Lucy's fax again but for some reason found it hard to concentrate and went off to the kitchen to make some coffee.

Twenty minutes later she was back at her table and

had one of the new lines rigged up for the modem and the other exclusively for the fax. She was just about to call Lucy who was in a new fury about Gates, when she heard footsteps on the back porch and a light tapping on the screen door.

Through the haze of the screen she could see Tom Booker standing there and he started to smile as he caught sight of her. He stepped back when Annie opened the door and she saw he had with him two saddled horses, Rimrock and another of the colts. She folded her arms, leaned against the door frame and gave him a skeptical smile.

"The answer's no," she said.

"You don't yet know what the question is."

"I think I can guess."

"You can?"

"I think so."

"Well, I kind of reckoned seeing as you've just saved yourself forty minutes driving down to Choteau and then some forty more driving back and all, you might feel inclined to blow a little of it on taking some air."

"On horseback."

"Well. Yeah."

They looked at each other for a moment, just smiling. He was wearing a faded pink shirt and over his jeans those old patched leather chaps he always rode in. Maybe it was just the light, but his eyes seemed as clear and blue as the sky behind him.

"Truth is, you'd be doing me a favor. I got all these eager young colts to ride and poor old Rimrock here is feeling kind of left out. He'd be that grateful, he'd take real good care of you."

"Is this how I get to pay for the phones?"

"No ma'am, I'm afraid that's extra."

* * *

The physical therapist who looked after Grace was a tiny woman with a shock of streaked curls and gray eyes so large they made her seem permanently surprised. Terri Carlson was fifty-one and a Libra; both her parents were dead and she had three sons which her husband had given her in rapid succession some thirty years ago before running off with a Texan rodeo queen. He'd insisted the boys be called John, Paul and George and Terri thanked the Lord he'd gone before there was a fourth. All this Grace had found out on her very first visit here and on each subsequent visit Terri had taken up where she left off so that now, had Grace been asked, she could have filled several notebooks on the woman's life. Not that Grace minded in the least. She liked it. It meant she could simply lie on the workout bench, as she was doing now, and surrender herself entirely not just to the woman's hands but to her words as well.

Grace had protested when Annie told her she'd arranged for her to come here three mornings a week. She knew that after all these months it was more than she strictly needed. But the therapist in New York had told Annie that the harder you worked at it, the less likely it was you'd end up with a limp.

"Who cares if I have a limp?" Grace said.

"I do," Annie said, so that was it.

In fact, Grace enjoyed the sessions here more than in New York. First they did the workout. Terri had her doing everything. On top of all the exercises, she strapped Velcro weights on her stump, got her sweating on the arm bicycle, even had her disco dancing in front of the mirrors that lined the walls. That first day she'd seen Grace's expression when the tape came on.

"You don't like Tina Turner?"

Grace said Tina Turner was fine. Just kind of . . .

"Old? Get outa here! She's my age!"

Grace blushed and they laughed and from then on things were fine. Terri told her to bring in some of her own tapes and these had now become the source of much joking between them. Whenever Grace brought in a new one Terri would examine it, shake her head and sigh, "More gloom from the tomb."

After the workout, Grace would relax for a while and then get to work on her own in the pool. Then, for the last hour, it was back in front of the mirrors for some walk practice or "gait training" as Terri called it. Grace had never felt fitter in her whole life.

Today Terri had pressed the pause button on her life story and was telling her about an Indian boy she visited each week up on the Blackfeet Reservation. He was twenty years old and proud and beautiful, she said, like something out of a Charlie Russell picture. That was, until last summer when he'd gone swimming in a pool with some friends and dived headfirst into a concealed shelf of rock. It had clean snapped his neck and now he was paralyzed from there on down.

"First time I visited with him, boy was he angry," she said. She was working Grace's stump like a pump handle. "He told me he didn't want anything to do with me and if I didn't go then he'd go, he wasn't sticking around to be humiliated. He didn't actually say 'by a woman,' but that's what he meant. I thought, what does he mean 'go'? He wasn't going anywhere, all he could do was lie there. But you know what? He did go. I got to work on him and after a while I looked at his face and he was—gone."

She saw Grace didn't understand.

"His mind, his spirit, whatever you care to call it.

Just upped and gone. Like that. And he wasn't faking it, you could tell. He was away somewhere. And when I was through, he just kind of came back. Now he does it every time I visit him. Over you go now honey, let's do a few Jane Fondas."

Grace turned on her left side and started doing scissor lifts. "Does he say where he goes?" she asked. Terri laughed.

"You know, I asked him that and he said he wouldn't tell me 'cause I'd only come busybodying after him. That's what he calls me, Ol' Busybody. Makes out he doesn't like me, but I know he does. It's just his way of keeping his pride. I guess we all do that some way or other. That's good, honey. A little higher now? Good!"

Terri took her to the pool room and left her there. It was a peaceful place and today Grace had it to herself. The air was laced with the clean smell of chlorine. She changed into her swimsuit and settled herself to rest awhile in the small whirlpool. The sun was angling down from the skylight onto the surface of the swimming pool. Some bounced back to dance in shimmering reflection on the ceiling, while the rest slanted through to the bottom of the pool where it formed undulating patterns, like a colony of pale blue snakes that lived and died and were constantly reborn.

The swirling water felt good on her stump and she lay back and thought about the Indian boy. How good to be able to do that, to leave your body whenever you wanted and go off somewhere. It made her wonder about when she was in the coma. Perhaps that's what had happened then. But where had she gone and what had she seen? She couldn't remember a thing about it, not even a dream, only the coming out of it, swimming through the tunnel of glue toward her mother's voice.

She had always been able to remember her dreams. It

was easy, all you had to do was tell someone about them the moment you woke, even if it was only yourself. When she was younger, in the mornings, she used to climb into her parents' bed and snuggle under her father's arm and tell him. He'd ask her all sorts of detailed questions and sometimes she'd have to invent things to fill in the gaps. It was always only her father because by that hour Annie was already up and out running or in the shower yelling for Grace to get dressed and go do her piano practice. Robert used to tell her she should write all her dreams down because she'd have fun reading about them when she was grown up, but Grace could never be bothered.

She had expected to have terrible, bloody dreams about the accident. But she hadn't dreamed about it once. And the only one she'd had about Pilgrim was two nights ago. He was standing on the far side of a great brown river and it was odd because he was younger, little more than a foal, but it was definitely Pilgrim. She'd called him and he'd tested the water with his foot then walked right in and started to swim toward her. But he wasn't strong enough for the current and it started to sweep him away and she'd watched his head getting smaller and smaller and she felt so powerless and filled with anguish because all she could do was keep on calling his name. Then she was aware that someone was standing beside her and she turned and saw Tom Booker and he said she shouldn't worry, Pilgrim would be okay, because downstream the river wasn't so deep and he would be sure to find a place to cross.

Grace hadn't told Annie about Tom Booker asking if she'd talk about the accident. She feared Annie might make a fuss or resent it or try and make the decision for her. It was none of Annie's business. It was something private between her and Tom, about her and her horse and it was for her to decide. And she realized now that she had already decided. Although the prospect daunted her, she would talk to him. Maybe she would tell Annie later.

The door opened and Terri came back in and asked her how she was doing. She said Grace's mom had just called. Diane Booker would be there at midday to pick her up.

They rode up along the creek and crossed at the ford where they'd met the other morning. As they moved up into the lower meadow the cattle stepped lazily aside to let them pass. The cloud had broken away and scattered from the snow-covered tops of the mountains and the air smelled new, of roots uncoiling. There were pink crocus and shooting star already showing in the grass and a first hint of leaf hung like a green haze on the cottonwoods.

He let her go before him for a while and watched the breeze in her hair. She'd never ridden western before and said the saddle felt like a boat. Back at the house she'd got him to shorten Rimrock's stirrups so they were now more the length you'd ride a cutting horse or if you were roping, but she said she felt more in control that way. He could see she was a rider from the way she held herself and from the easy way her body moved with the rhythm of the horse.

When it was clear she had the feel of it, he eased alongside and they rode together, neither one of them speaking except when she asked him the name of some tree or plant or bird. She'd fix him with those green eyes of hers while he told her and then nod, all serious, storing the information away. They rode past stands of as-

pen which he told her they called quakin' asp on account of the way the wind fluttered in their leaves and
he showed her the black scars in their pale trunks where
in the winter foraging elk had stripped away the bark.

They rode up a long, sloping ridge, strewn with pine
and potentilla, and came to the rim of a high bluff from
where you could look down the twin valleys that gave
the ranch its name and there they stopped and sat the
horses awhile.

"That's quite a view," Annie said. He nodded.

"When my daddy moved us all out here, Frank and I
would come up here sometimes and have ourselves a
race back down to the corral for a dime or maybe a
quarter if we were feeling rich. He'd take one creek and
I'd take the other."

"Who won?"

"Well, he was younger and mostly he went so darn
fast he fell off and I'd have to hang around in the trees
down there and time it just right so we finished neck
and neck. It made him real happy to win, so most times
that's what happened."

She smiled at him.

"You ride pretty good," he said. She made a face.

"This horse of yours would make anyone look
good."

She reached down and rubbed Rimrock's neck and
for a moment the only sound was the soft frupping of
the horses' nostrils. She sat back up and looked down
the valley again. You could just see the tip of the creek
house above the trees.

"Who's R.B.?" she said.

He frowned. "R.B.?"

"On the well, by the house. There are some initials,
T.B.—which I guessed was you—and R.B."

He laughed. "Rachel. My wife."

"You're married?"

"My ex-wife. We got divorced. A long time ago."

"Do you have children?"

"Uh-huh, one. He's twenty years old. Lives with his mother and stepfather in New York City."

"What's his name?"

She sure asked a whole lot of questions. That was her job, he guessed, and he didn't mind at all. In fact he liked the way she was so direct, just looked you right in the eye and came out with it. He smiled.

"Hal."

"Hal Booker. That's nice."

"Well, he's a nice guy. You look kind of surprised."

Right away he felt bad for saying it for he could tell from the way she colored up that he'd embarrassed her.

"No, not at all. I just—"

"He was born right down there in the creek house."

"Is that where you lived?"

"Yup. Rachel didn't take to it out here. The winters can get kind of hard if you're not used to it."

A shadow passed over the heads of the horses and he looked up at the sky and so did she. It was a pair of golden eagles and he told her how you could know this from their size and the shape and color of their wings. And together, in silence, they watched them soar slowly up the valley until they were lost beneath the massive gray wall of mountain beyond.

"Been there yet?" Diane said, as the Albertasaurus watched them go by the museum on their way out of town. Grace said she hadn't. Diane drove brusquely, handling the car as though it needed to be taught a lesson.

"Joe loves it. The twins prefer Nintendo."

Grace laughed. She liked Diane. She was sort of spiky but she'd been nice to her right from the start. Well, they all had, but there was something special about the way Diane talked with her, something confiding, almost sisterly. It occurred to Grace that it might be to do with her having only had sons.

"They say dinosaurs used this whole area as a breeding ground," she went on. "And you know what Grace? They're still around. You just meet some of the men hereabouts."

They talked about school and Grace told her how, on the mornings she didn't have to come in to the clinic, Annie made her do schoolwork. Diane agreed that was tough.

"How does your dad feel about you both being out here?"

"He gets a little lonely."

"I bet he does."

"But he's got some big important case on at the moment so I maybe wouldn't see too much of him anyway."

"They're a real glitzy pair your mom and dad, huh? These big careers and all."

"Oh, Dad's not like that." It came right out and the silence that followed made it sound worse. Grace hadn't meant to imply any criticism of her mother but she knew from the way Diane looked at her that this was how it had sounded.

"Does she ever get to take a vacation?"

The tone was knowing, sympathetic and it made Grace feel like a traitor, that she'd handed Diane some kind of weapon and she wanted to say no, you've got it wrong, it's not like that at all. But instead she just shrugged and said, "Oh yes, sometimes."

Grace looked away and for some miles neither of

them spoke. There were some things other people could never understand, she thought. It always had to be one way or the other and it was more complicated than that. She was proud of her mother, for heavensakes. Although she'd never dream of letting her know, Annie was how she herself wanted to be when she grew up. Not exactly maybe, but it seemed natural and right that women should have such careers. She liked the way all her friends knew about her mother, how successful she was and everything. She wouldn't want it any other way and though she sometimes gave Annie a hard time for not being around as much as other people's moms, if she was honest, she never felt she was missing out. It was often just her and her dad, but that was okay. It was more than okay, sometimes she even preferred it that way. It was just that Annie was, well, so sure about everything. So extreme and purposeful. It made you want to fight her even when you agreed.

"Pretty, isn't it?" Diane said.

"Yes." Grace had been staring out at the plains but she hadn't taken anything in and, now that she did, pretty didn't seem the right word at all. It seemed a desolate kind of place.

"You wouldn't dream there's enough nuclear weapons buried out there to blow up the entire planet would you?"

Grace looked at her. "Really?"

"You betcha." She grinned. "Missile silos all over the place. We may not have too many people out here but bombs and beef, oh boy, we're second to none."

Annie had the phone tucked into her neck and was half listening to Don Farlow while she played around on the keyboard with a sentence she'd just typed. She was trying to write an editorial, the only writing she got to do nowadays. Today she was rubbishing a new street crime initiative just announced by the mayor of New York City but she was having trouble finding the old mix of wit and vitriol that used to characterize Annie Graves at her best.

Farlow was getting her up to speed on assorted things he and his legal hitmen had been working on, none of which interested Annie remotely. She gave up on the sentence and looked out of the window. The sun was getting low and down at the big arena she could see Tom leaning on the rail talking with Grace and Joe. She saw him throw his head back and laugh at something. Behind him the barn threw a long wedge of shadow on the red sand.

They'd been working all afternoon with Pilgrim, who now stood watching from the other end of the arena, the sweat shining on his back. Joe had only just got back from school and had as usual gone right out to join them. Every now and then, over the past few hours, Annie had looked down there at Tom and Grace and felt just an inkling of something that, if she didn't know herself better, she might have mistaken for jealousy.

Her thighs ached from the morning's ride. Muscles she hadn't used for thirty years were making their complaints known and Annie relished the pain like a keepsake. It was years since she'd felt the exhilaration that had been there this morning. It was like someone had let her out of a cage. Still excited, she'd told Grace all about it as soon as Diane dropped her home. The girl's face had fallen a little before clicking on the disinterest with which lately she greeted all her mother's news and Annie cursed herself for blurting it out. It had been insensitive, she thought; although later, on reflection, she wasn't quite sure why.

"And he said to call a halt," Farlow was saying.

"What? Sorry Don, could you say that again?"

"He said to drop the lawsuit."

"Who did?"

"Annie! Are you feeling okay?"

"I'm sorry Don, I'm just fiddling around with something here."

"Gates told me to drop the Fiske case. Remember? Fenimore Fiske? 'And who, pray, is Martin Scorsese?' "

It was one of Fiske's many immortal gaffes. He'd dug himself in even deeper some years later by calling *Taxi Driver* a squalid little film from a trifling talent.

"Thanks Don, I remember him well. Gates really said to drop it?"

"Yes. He said it was costing too much and it would do you and the magazine more harm than good."

"That son of a bitch! How dare he do that without talking to me. Jesus!"

"For Godsake don't tell him I told you."

"Jesus."

Annie swung around in her chair and her elbow knocked a cup of coffee off the desk.

"Shit!"

"You alright?"

"Yeah. Listen Don, I've got to think about this. I'll call you back, okay?"

"Okay."

She hung up and for a long moment stared down at the broken cup and the spreading stain of coffee.

"Shit."

And she went off to the kitchen to get a cloth.

TWENTY

"I THOUGHT IT WAS THE SNOWPLOW, YOU SEE. I HEARD it a long, long way off. We had all the time in the world. If we'd known what it was, we could have taken the horses right off the road, out into the field or somewhere. I should have said something about it to Judith but I just didn't think. Any case, when we were out with the horses, she was always the boss, you know? Like if there was a decision to be made, she'd be the one who got to make it. And it was like that with Gulliver and Pilgrim too. Gully was the boss, the sensible one."

She bit her lip and looked away to one side so that the light on the back of the barn caught the side of her face. It was getting dark and a cool breeze was coming in off the creek. The three of them had put Pilgrim away for the night and then Joe, with no more than a look from Tom, had made himself scarce, saying he had homework to do. Tom and Grace had strolled over to the back pen where he kept the yearlings. Once she'd caught the foot of her false leg in a rut and stumbled a little and Tom had nearly reached out to stop her from falling, but she'd righted herself and he was glad he hadn't. Now the two of them were leaning on the fence of the pen watching the horses.

She'd taken him step by snowy step through the morning of the accident. How they'd gone up through the woods and how funny Pilgrim had been, playing with the snow and how they'd lost the trail and had to make that steep descent beside the stream. She talked without looking at him, keeping her eyes on the horses, but he knew all she saw was what she'd seen that day, another horse and a friend both now dead. And Tom watched her talk and felt for her with the whole of his heart.

"Then we found the place we'd been looking for. It was like this steep bank leading up to the railroad bridge. We'd been up there before, so we knew where the path was. Anyway. Judith went first and you know, it was weird, it was like Gully knew something was wrong because he didn't want to go and Gully isn't like that."

She heard her own words and how she'd got the tense wrong and she looked at him briefly and he gave her a smile.

"So up he went and I asked her if it was okay and she said it was but to be careful, so I started up after her."

"Did you have to make Pilgrim go?"

"No, not at all. It wasn't like with Gully. He was happy to go."

She looked down and for a moment stayed silent. One of the yearlings nickered softly at the far end of the pen. Tom put a hand on her shoulder.

"You okay?"

She nodded. "Then Gully started to slip." She looked at him, earnest suddenly. "You know, they found out later that the ice was only on that one side of the path? If he'd been like, a few inches to the left, it wouldn't have happened. But he must have just put one foot on it and that was it."

She looked away again and he could tell from the way her shoulders moved that she was fighting to calm her breathing.

"So he started to slide. He was trying so hard, you could see, jabbing his feet to try and make them hold but the more he did it the worse it got, they just wouldn't hold. They were coming right at us and Judith yelled for us to get out of the way. She was like clinging on to Gully's neck and I tried to get Pilgrim to turn and I know I did it too hard, you know, really yanked on him? If only I'd kept my head and done it more gently, he'd have gone. But I guess I scared him even worse than he was already and he wouldn't . . . he just wouldn't move!"

She stopped for a moment and swallowed.

"Then they hit us. How I stayed on I don't know." She gave a little laugh. "Would've been a whole lot smarter not to. Unless I'd got hooked up like Judith. When she came off it was like, you know, somebody was waving a flag or something, like she was all flimsy and made of nothing. She kind of flipped as she fell, anyway her leg got caught in the stirrup and down we all went, together, sliding on down. It seemed like it took forever. And you know? The weirdest thing, as we went down I remember thinking, with all this blue sky above us and the sun shining and the snow on the trees and everything and I'm thinking, my, what a beautiful day it is." She turned to look at him. "Isn't that the weirdest thing you ever heard?"

Tom didn't think it was weird at all. There were such moments, he knew, when the world chose thus to reveal itself not, as it might seem, to mock our plight or our irrelevance but simply to affirm, for us and for all life, the very act of being. He smiled at her and nodded.

"I don't know if Judith saw it right away, the truck I mean. She must have hit her head really hard and Gully had totally freaked and was just, you know, thrashing her all over the place. But as soon as I saw it, coming through that place where the bridge used to be I thought, there's no way this guy's going to stop and I thought if I could just get hold of Gully I can get everybody out the way. I was so stupid. God I was stupid!"

She clamped her head in her hands, screwing her eyes shut, but only for a few moments. "What I should have done was got off. It would have been a lot easier to get hold of him. I mean, he was freaked alright, but he'd hurt his leg and he wasn't going anywhere in a hurry. I could have given Pilgrim a whack on the butt and sent him off and then led Gully off the road. But I didn't."

She sniffed, regathered herself.

"Pilgrim was incredible. I mean, he was pretty freaked too, but he got it back together right away. It was like he knew what I wanted. I mean, he could have stepped on Judith or anything, God, but he didn't. He knew. And if the guy hadn't blown his horn, we'd have done it, we were so close. My fingers were that far away, that far. . . ."

Grace looked at him and her face was all distorted with the pain of knowing what might have been and at last the tears came. Tom put his arms around her and held her and she placed the side of her face against his chest and sobbed.

"I saw her face looking up at me, down by Gully's feet, just before the horn sounded. She looked so little, so scared. I could have saved her. I could have saved us all."

He didn't speak, for he knew the futility of words to

change such things and that even the passing of years might leave her certainty undimmed. For a long time they stood that way, with the night folding around them and he cupped his hand on the back of her head and smelled the fresh young smell of her hair. And when her crying was done and he felt her body slacken, he asked her gently if she wanted to go on. She nodded and sniffed and took a breath.

"Once the horn sounded, that was it. And Pilgrim, he kind of turned to face the truck. It was crazy, but it was like he wasn't going to allow it. He wasn't going to let this great monster come and hurt us all, he was going to fight. Fight a forty-ton truck for heavensakes! Isn't that something? But he was going to, I could feel it. And when it was right in front of us he reared up at it. And I fell and hit my head. That's all I remember."

The rest Tom knew, at least in outline. Annie had given him Harry Logan's number and a couple of days ago he'd called and listened to the man's account of what happened next. Logan told him how it had ended for Judith and Gulliver and how Pilgrim had run off and how they'd found him down in the water with that great hole in his chest. Tom had asked him a lot of detailed questions, some of which he could tell Logan found baffling. But the man sounded bighearted and patiently catalogued the horse's injuries and what he'd done to treat them. He told Tom of how they'd taken Pilgrim to Cornell, whose fine reputation Tom knew of, and all they'd done for him there.

When Tom said, in all truth, that he'd never heard of a vet being able to save a horse so sorely injured, Logan laughed and said he dearly wished he hadn't. He said things had gone all wrong later at the Dyer place and the Lord only knew what those two boys had done to the poor creature. He said he even blamed himself for going along with some of it, like trapping the animal's head in the door to give him those shots.

Grace was getting cold. It was late and her mother would be wondering where she was. They walked slowly back to the barn and passed through its dark, echoing emptiness and out the other end to the car. The beam of the Chevy's headlights tilted and dipped as they bumped along the track toward the creek house. For a while the dogs ran ahead, throwing pointed shadows before them and when they turned their heads to look back at the car, their eyes flashed ghostly and green.

Grace asked him if what he now knew would help him make Pilgrim better and he said he'd have to do some thinking but that he hoped so. When they pulled up he was glad to see she no longer looked like she'd been crying and when she got out she smiled at him and he could tell she wanted to thank him but was too shy to say it. He looked beyond her to the house, hoping he might see Annie but there was no sign of her. He gave Grace a smile and touched his hat.

"I'll see you tomorrow."

"Okay," she said and swung the door shut.

By the time he got in, the others had already eaten. Frank was helping Joe with some math problem at the big table in the living room and telling the twins for the last time to turn down the sound on some comedy show they were watching or he'd come and switch it off. Without a word, Diane took the supper she'd saved him and put it in the microwave while Tom went through to the downstairs bathroom to clean up.

"Did she like her new phones then?" Through the

open door he could see her settling herself back at the kitchen table with her needlework.

"Yeah, she was real grateful."

He dried his hands and came back in. The microwave was pinging and he took his supper out and went to the table. It was chicken potpie, with green beans and a vast baked potato. Diane always thought it was his favorite meal and he never had the heart to disabuse her. He wasn't at all hungry but didn't want to upset her so he sat down and ate.

"What I can't work out is what she's going to do with the third one," Diane said, not looking up.

"How do you mean?"

"Well, she's only got two ears."

"Oh, she's got a fax machine and other things that use lines of their own and with people calling her all the time, that's what she needs. She offered to pay for the lines being put in."

"And you said no, I'll bet."

He didn't deny it and saw Diane smile to herself. He knew better than to argue when she was in this kind of mood. She'd made it plain from the start that she wasn't crazy about Annie being here and Tom thought it best just to let her have her say. He got on with his meal and for a while neither one of them spoke. Frank and Joe were arguing about whether some figure should be divided or multiplied.

"Frank says you took her out on Rimrock this morning," Diane said.

"That's right. First time since she was a kid. She rides good."

"That little girl. What a thing to happen."

"Yeah."

"She seems so lonely. Be better off in school, I reckon."

"Oh, I don't know. She's okay."

After he'd eaten and gone out to check the horses, he told Diane and Frank he had some reading to do and bade them and the boys good-night.

Tom's room took up the whole northwest corner of the house and from its side window you could look right up the valley. The room was large and seemed more so because there was so little in it. The bed was the one his parents had slept in, high and narrow with a scrolled maple headboard. There was a logcabin quilt on it that his grandmother had made. It had once been red and white but the red had faded a pale pink and in places the fabric had worn so thin that the lining showed through. There was a small pine table with one simple chair, a chest of drawers and an old hidecovered armchair that stood under a lamp by the black iron woodstove.

On the floor were some Mexican rugs Tom had picked up some years back in Santa Fe, but they were too small to make the place seem cozy and had more the opposite effect, stranded like lost islands on a dark-stained sea of floorboard. Set into the back wall were two doors, one to the closet where he kept his clothes and the other leading to a small bathroom. On the top of the chest of drawers stood a few modestly framed photographs of his family. There was one of Rachel holding Hal as a baby, its colors now grown saturate and dark. There was a more recent one of Hal beside it, his smile uncannily like Rachel's in the first. But for these and the books and back issues of horse magazines that lined the walls, a stranger might have wondered how a man could live so long yet own so little.

Tom sat at the table going through a stack of old *Quarter Horse Journals,* looking for a piece he remembered reading a couple of years back. It was by a Californian horse trainer he'd once met and was about a young mare who'd been in a bad wreck. They'd been shipping her over from Kentucky along with six other horses and somewhere in Arizona the guy towing the trailer had fallen asleep, driven off the road and the whole rig had flipped clean over. The trailer ended up lying on the side where the door was so the rescue folk had to get chainsaws and cut their way in. When they did they found the horses had been tied into their boxes and were hanging in the air by their necks from what was now the roof, all but the mare dead.

This trainer, Tom knew, had a pet theory that you could use a horse's natural response to pain to help it. It was complicated and Tom wasn't sure he fully grasped it. It seemed to be based on the notion that though a horse's first instinct was to flee, when it actually felt pain, it would turn and face it.

The man backed this up with stories of how horses in the wild would run from a pack of wolves but when they felt teeth touch their flanks they would "turn in" and confront the pain. He said it was like a baby teething; he doesn't avoid the pain, but bites on it. And he claimed this theory had helped him sort out the traumatized mare who'd survived the wreck.

Tom found the right issue and read the piece again, hoping it might shed some light on what to do with Pilgrim. It was kind of short on detail but it seemed all the guy had really done was take the mare back to basics as if he were starting her afresh, helping her find herself, making the right thing easy and wrong thing difficult. It was fine, but there was nothing new there for Tom. He was doing that already. As for the turning-in-to-pain thing, he still couldn't make a lot of sense of it. But what was he doing? Looking for a new trick? There were no tricks, he should know that by now. It was just you and the horse and understanding what was going on in both your heads. He pushed the magazine away, sat back and sighed.

Listening to Grace this evening and earlier to Logan, he'd searched every corner of what they said for something to latch on to, some key, some lever he could use. But there was none. And now at last he understood what he'd been seeing all this time in Pilgrim's eyes. It was a total breakdown. The animal's confidence, in himself and all around him, had been shattered. Those he had loved and trusted had betrayed him. Grace, Gulliver, everyone. They'd led him up that slope, pretended it was safe and then screamed at him and hurt him when it turned out not to be.

Maybe Pilgrim even blamed himself for what happened. For why should humans think they had a monopoly on guilt? So often Tom had seen horses protect their riders, children especially, from the dangers that inexperience led them into. Pilgrim had let Grace down. And when he'd tried to protect her from the truck, all he'd gotten in return was pain and punishment. Then all those strangers, who'd tricked him and caught him and hurt him and jabbed their needles in his neck and locked him up in the dark and the filth and the stench.

Later, as he lay sleepless with the light out and the house long fallen quiet, Tom felt something float heavily within him and settle on his heart. He now had the picture he'd wanted or as much of it as he was likely to get and it was a picture as dark and devoid of hope as he'd ever known.

There was no delusion, nothing foolish or fanciful about the way Pilgrim had assessed the horrors that had befallen him. It was simply logical and it was this that made helping him so hard. And Tom wanted so very much to help him. He wanted it for the horse itself and for the girl. But he knew too—and knew at the same time that it was wrong—that above all he wanted it for the woman he'd ridden with that morning and whose eyes and mouth he could see as clearly as if she were lying there beside him.

TWENTY-ONE

THE NIGHT MATTHEW GRAVES DIED, ANNIE AND HER brother were staying with friends in the Blue Mountains of Jamaica. It was the end of the Christmas holiday and her parents had gone back down to Kingston and left them up there for a few more days because they were having such fun. Annie and George, her brother, were sharing a double bed, tented by a vast mosquito net into which, in the middle of the night, their friends' mother came in her nightgown to wake them. She turned on the bedside light and sat on the end of the bed waiting for Annie and George to rub the sleep from their eyes. Dimly through the gauze of the mosquito net, Annie could see the woman's husband, hovering in his striped pajamas, his face in shadow.

Annie would always remember the strange smile on the woman's face. Later she understood it was a smile born of fear at what she had to say, but in that moment when sleep and consciousness elide, her expression seemed humorous, so when the woman said she had bad news and that their father was dead, Annie thought it was a joke. Not a very funny one, but still a joke.

Many years later, when Annie thought she should do something about her insomnia (an urge that came upon her every four or five years and led only to large amounts of money being paid to hear things she already knew), she had been to see a hypnotherapist. The woman's technique was "event oriented." This apparently meant that she liked her clients to come up with some incident that marked the onset of whatever particular mess they were in. She would then pop you into a trance, take you back and resolve it.

After the first hundred-dollar session the poor woman was clearly disappointed that Annie couldn't come up with an appropriate incident, so for a week Annie had racked her brain to find one. She'd talked it over with Robert and it was he who came up with it: Annie being woken at the age of ten to be told her father was dead.

The therapist nearly fell off her chair with excitement. Annie felt pretty pleased too, like one of those girls she'd always hated at school who sat in the front row with their hands in the air. Don't go to sleep because someone you love might die. It didn't come much neater. The fact that for the next twenty years Annie had slept each night like a log didn't seem to bother the woman.

She asked Annie what she felt about her father and then what she felt about her mother, and after Annie had told her, she asked how she felt about doing "a little separation exercise." Annie said that would be fine. The woman then tried to hypnotize her but was so excited she did it too fast and there wasn't a hope in hell it would work. Not to disappoint her, Annie did her best to fake a trance but had a lot of trouble keeping a straight face when the woman stood her parents on spinning silver discs and dispatched them one by one, waving serene farewells, into outer space.

But if her father's death, as Annie actually believed, had no connection with her inability to sleep, its effect on almost everything else in her life was immeasurable.

Within a month of the funeral, her mother had packed up the house in Kingston and disposed of things around which her children had felt their lives revolved. She sold the small boat in which their father had taught them to sail and had taken them to deserted islands to dive among the coral for lobsters and run naked on the palmed white sand. And their dog, a black Labrador cross called Bella, she gave to a neighbor they hardly knew. They saw the dog watching from the gate as the taxi took them to the airport.

They flew to England, a strange, wet, cold place where nobody smiled and their mother left them in Devon with her parents while she went up to London to sort out, she said, her husband's affairs. She lost no time in sorting one out for herself too, for within six months she was to marry again.

Annie's grandfather was a gentle, ineffectual soul who smoked a pipe, did crossword puzzles and whose main concern in life was avoiding the wrath or even mild displeasure of his wife. Annie's grandmother was a small, malicious woman with a tight white perm through which the pink of her scalp glowed like a warning. Her dislike of children was neither greater nor less than her dislike of almost everything else in life. But whereas most of these things were abstract or inanimate or simply unaware of her dislike, from these, her only grandchildren, she derived a much more gratifying return and set about making their stay, over the ensuing months, as miserable as possible.

She favored George, not because she disliked him less

but in order to divide them and thus make Annie, in whose eye she was quick to spot defiance, all the more unhappy. She told Annie her life in "The Colonies" had given her vulgar, slovenly ways which she set about curing by sending her to bed with no supper and smacking her legs, for the most trivial of crimes, with a long-handled wooden spoon. Their mother, who traveled down by train to see them each weekend, listened impartially to what her children told her. Inquests of stunning objectivity were held and Annie learned for the first time how facts could be so subtly rearranged to render different truths.

"The child has such a vivid imagination," her grandmother said.

Reduced to mute contempt and acts of petty vengeance, Annie stole cigarettes from the witch's purse and smoked them behind dripping rhododendrons, greenly contemplating how unwise it was to love, for those you loved would only die and leave you.

Her father had been a bounding, joyous man. The only one who ever thought she was of value. And since his death, her life had been a ceaseless quest to prove him right. Through school and through her student days and on through her career, she'd been driven by that single purpose: to show the bastards.

For a while, after having Grace, she'd thought the point proven. In that pinched pink face, hungering so blind and needy at her nipple, came calm, as if the journey were complete. It had been a time for definitions. Now, she told herself, now I can be what I am, not what I do. Then came the miscarriage. Then another and another and another, failure compounding failure and soon Annie was again that pale, angry girl behind the rhododendrons. She'd shown them before and she'd show them again.

But it wasn't like before. Since her early days at *Rolling Stone,* those parts of the news media that followed such matters had dubbed her "brilliant and fiery." Now, reincarnated as boss of her own magazine—the kind of job she'd vowed never to take—the first of these epithets stuck. But, as if in recognition of the colder fuel that drove her, "fiery" transmuted to "ruthless." In fact, Annie had surprised even herself with the casual brutality she'd brought to her latest post.

Last fall she'd met an old friend from England, a woman who'd been at the same boarding school and when Annie told her about all the bloodletting at the magazine she'd laughed and said did Annie remember playing Lady Macbeth in the school play? Annie did. In fact, though she didn't say this, she remembered being rather good.

"Remember how you stuck your arms in that bucket of fake blood for the 'Out, damned spot' speech? You were red right up to the elbows!"

"Yep. Sure was one hell of a spot."

Annie laughed along but went away and worried about the image for a whole afternoon, until she decided it wasn't even remotely relevant to her present situation because Lady Macbeth was doing it for her husband's career not her own and in any case was clearly out of her tree. The following day, perhaps to prove a point, she had fired Fenimore Fiske.

Now, from the fatuous vantage of her office in exile, Annie reflected on such deeds and on the losses within her that had prompted them. Some of these things she had glimpsed that night at Little Bighorn when she'd slumped by the stone etched with the names of dead men and wept. Here, in this place of sky, she now came to see them more clearly, as if their secrets were unfurling with the season itself. And with a bereaved stillness born of this knowledge, as May slipped by, she watched the separate world outside grow warm and green.

Only when she was with him did she feel part of it. Three times more he had come to her door with the horses and they had ridden out together to other places he wanted to show her.

It had become routine that on Wednesdays Diane collected Grace from the clinic and sometimes on other days she or Frank might take her there too if they had to go to town. These mornings, Annie would catch herself waiting for Tom's call to ask if she wanted to ride and when it came she would try not to sound too eager.

The last time, she'd been in the middle of a conference call and she'd looked down toward the corrals and seen him leading Rimrock and a colt, both saddled, from the barn and she'd quite lost the drift of the conversation. She was suddenly aware that everyone in New York had gone silent.

"Annie?" one of the senior editors said.

"Yeah, sorry," Annie said. "I'm getting all this static this end. I lost that last bit."

When Tom arrived, the conference was still going and she waved him in through the screen door. He took off his hat and came through and Annie mouthed to him that she was sorry and to help himself to coffee. He did and settled himself on the arm of the couch to wait.

There were a couple of recent issues of her magazine lying there and he'd picked one up and looked through it. He found her name at the top of the page where it listed everyone who worked there and he made an impressed face. Then she saw him grinning to himself over another style piece of Lucy Friedman's, called "The New Rednecks." They'd taken a couple of models to some godforsaken place in Arkansas and shot them draped over the real thing, unsmiling men with beer guts, tattoos and guns slung in their pickup windows. Annie wondered how the photographer, a brilliant, outrageous man who wore mascara and liked to show everyone his pierced nipples, had escaped with his life.

It was ten minutes before the conference call finished and Annie, aware of Tom listening, became more and more self-conscious. She realized she was talking in a more dignified way than normal to impress him and immediately felt foolish. Gathered around the speaker phone in her office in New York, Lucy and the others must have wondered what she was on. When it was over she hung up and turned to him.

"I'm sorry."

"It's okay, I liked hearing you work. And now I know what to wear next time I go down to Arkansas." He tossed the magazine onto the couch. "It's a lot of fun."

"It's a lot of pain. Mostly in the ass."

She was already in her riding clothes and they went right out to the horses. She said she'd try the stirrups a little longer and he came and showed her how to do it because the straps were different from those she was used to. She stepped in close to watch how he did it and for the first time she was aware of the smell of him, a warm clean smell of leather and some functional brand of soap. All the while, the tops of their arms touched lightly and neither of them moved away.

That morning they'd crossed over to the southern creek and made their way slowly up beside it to a place he said they might see beavers. But they saw none, only the two intricate new islands they'd built. They dismounted and sat on the gray bleached trunk of a fallen cottonwood while the horses drank their own reflections from the pool.

A fish or a frog broke the surface in front of the colt and he leapt back scared like some character in a cartoon. Rimrock gave him a weary look and went on drinking. Tom laughed. He got up and walked over and when he got there he put one hand on the colt's neck and another on his face. For a while he just stood there holding him. Annie couldn't hear if he spoke but she noticed that the horse seemed to be listening. And without any coaxing, he went back to the water and after a few wary sniffs, drank as if nothing had happened. Tom came back and saw her smile and shake her head.

"What's the matter?"

"How do you do that?"

"Do what?"

"Make him feel it was okay."

"Oh, he knew it was okay." She waited for him to go on. "He gets a little melodramatic sometimes."

"And how do you know that?"

He gave her the same amused look he'd given her that day when she'd asked him all those questions about his wife and son.

"You get to learn." He stopped and something in her face must have told him she felt rebuked because he smiled and went on.

"It's only the difference between looking and seeing. Look long enough and if you're doing it right you get to see. Same with your job. You know what makes a good piece for your magazine because you've spent time making it your business to know."

Annie laughed. "Yeah, like designer rednecks?"

"Yeah, that's right. I wouldn't guess in a million years that's what people want to read about."

"They don't."

"Sure they do. It's funny."

"It's dumb."

It came out harsh and with a finality that left a silence hanging between them. He was watching her and she softened and gave him a self-deprecating smile.

"It's dumb and patronizing and phony."

"There's some serious stuff there too."

"Oh, yeah. But who needs it?"

He shrugged. Annie looked over at the horses. They'd drunk their fill and were browsing the new grass at the water's edge.

"What you do is real," she said.

As they rode back, Annie told him about the books she'd found in the public library, about whisperers and witchcraft and so forth and he laughed and said sure, he'd read some of that stuff too and he'd sure wished a fair few times that he was a witch. He knew about Sullivan and J. S. Rarey.

"Some of those guys—not Rarey, he was a real horseman—but some of the others, they did things that looked like magic but were just downright cruel. You know, things like pouring lead shot in a horse's ear, so the sound of it would paralyze him with fear and people would say wow, look, he's tamed that crazy horse! What they didn't know was that he'd probably killed it too."

He said that many times a troubled horse would get worse before he got better and you had to let him do that, let him go beyond the brink, to hell and back even. And she didn't answer because she knew he wasn't just talking about Pilgrim but about something greater that involved them all.

She knew that Grace had talked to Tom about the accident, not from him but from overhearing Grace tell Robert on the phone a few days later. This had become one of Grace's favorite tricks, letting Annie learn things by proxy so she could gauge the precise extent of her exclusion. On the night in question, Annie had been taking a bath upstairs and lay there listening through the open door—as Grace knew she must be, for she made no attempt to lower her voice.

She hadn't gone into detail, simply told Robert she'd remembered more than she expected about what had happened and that she felt better for having talked about it. Later, Annie had waited to be told herself but knew it wasn't going to happen.

For a while she'd felt angry with Tom, as if somehow he'd invaded their lives. She'd been curt with him the next day.

"I hear Grace told you all about the accident?"

"Yes, she did," he said, almost matter-of-fact. And that was all. It was clear he saw it as something between him and Grace and when Annie got over her anger, she respected him for this and remembered that it wasn't he who'd invaded their lives but the other way around.

Tom rarely spoke to her about Grace and when he did it was about things that were safe and factual. But Annie knew he saw how it was between them, for who could not?

TWENTY-TWO

THE CALVES HUDDLED AT THE FAR END OF THE MUDDY corral, trying to hide behind each other and using their wet black noses to push each other forward. When one of them got shunted to the front you could see panic set in and when it got too much he'd break around to the back and the whole thing would start over again.

It was the Saturday morning before Memorial Day and the twins were showing Joe and Grace how good they'd gotten at roping. Scott, whose turn it was, had on a pair of brand-new chaps and a hat that was a size too big for him. He'd already knocked it off a couple of times swinging the loop. Each time Joe and Craig had whooped with laughter and Scott had got red and done his best to look as if he found it funny too. He'd been swinging the rope in the air so long that Grace was getting dizzy watching.

"Shall we come back next week?" Joe said.

"I'm picking, okay?"

"They're over there. Black, with four legs and a tail?"

"Okay, smartass."

"Well jeez, just throw the damn thing."

"Okay! Okay!"

Joe shook his head and gave Grace a grin. They were sitting side by side on the top rail and Grace still felt proud of herself for having climbed up there. She did it like it was nothing and though it hurt like hell where the bar now pressed into her stump she wasn't going to budge.

She had on a new pair of Wranglers she and Diane had spent a long time finding in Great Falls and she knew they looked good because she'd spent half an hour in front of the bathroom mirror this morning checking them out. Thanks to Terri, the muscles in her right butt filled them out well. It was funny, back in New York she wouldn't have been seen dead in anything other than Levi's, but out here everyone wore Wranglers. The guy in the store said it was because the seams on the inside leg were more comfy for riding.

"I'm better'n you are anyway," Scott said.

"You sure swing a bigger loop."

Joe jumped down into the corral and walked across the mud toward the calves.

"Joe! Get out the way will ya?"

"Don't pee your pants. I'm gonna make it easier for you, break 'em up some."

As he got nearer, the calves moved off till they were bunched in the corner. Their only escape now was to make a break and Grace could see the worry grow among them till it was set to erupt. Joe stopped. One more step and they'd go.

"Ready?" he called.

Scott bit on his bottom lip and swung the loop a little quicker so it made a whirring noise in the air. He nodded and Joe stepped forward. Right away the calves broke for the other corner. Scott gave a little unintended cry of effort as he threw it. The rope snaked through the air and landed with its loop clean over the head of the leading calf.

"Yeah!" he yelled and yanked it tight.

But the triumph lasted only a second, for as soon as the calf felt the loop tighten he was away and Scott went with him. He left his hat hanging in the air and slapped headfirst onto the mud like a diver in a swimming race.

"Let go! Let it go!" Joe kept hollering, but maybe Scott didn't hear or maybe his pride didn't let him because he hung on to the rope as if his hands were glued to it and off he went. What the calf lacked in size he made up for in spirit and he jumped and bucked and kicked like a steer in a rodeo show, sledging the boy behind him through the mud.

Grace put her hands to her face in alarm and nearly toppled back off the rail. But once they could see Scott was only hanging in there because he wanted to, Joe and Craig started to whoop and laugh. And still he didn't let go. The calf took him from one end of the corral to the other and back again while the other calves stood bemused.

The noise brought Diane running from the house but Tom and Frank, from the barn, beat her to it. They got to the rail beside Grace just as Scott let go.

He lay quite still, face down in the mud and everyone went quiet. Oh no, Grace thought, oh no. At the same moment Diane arrived and gave a frightened cry.

One hand slowly lifted itself from the mud, in a kind of comical salute. Then, theatrically, the boy lifted himself up and turned to face them, standing before them in the middle of the corral to let them have their laugh. And so they did. And when Grace saw Scott's teeth show white in an otherwise perfect coat of brown, she joined in. And together they laughed loud and long and

Grace felt part of them and that life perhaps might yet be good.

A half-hour later everyone had dispersed. Diane had taken Scott back into the house to clean up and Frank, who wanted Tom's opinion on a calf he was worried about, had driven him and Craig up to the meadow. Annie had gone down to Great Falls to buy food for what she insisted on calling, to Grace's embarrassment, "the dinner party" to which she'd invited the Booker family that evening. So now it was just the two of them, Grace and Joe, and it was Joe who suggested they go down to see Pilgrim.

Pilgrim now had a corral to himself next to the colts Tom was starting and whose interest, over the double fence, he returned with a mix of suspicion and disdain. He saw Grace and Joe from a long way off and started snorting and nickering and trotting up and down the neurotic, muddy track he'd churned along the far side of the corral.

The rutted grass made walking a little tricky but Grace concentrated on swinging her leg through and although she knew Joe walked more slowly than he normally would, it didn't worry her. She felt as easy with him as she did with Tom. They reached the gate to Pilgrim's corral and leaned there to watch him.

"He was such a beautiful horse," she said.

"He still is."

Grace nodded. She told him about that day, almost a year ago, when they went down to Kentucky. And while she spoke, across the corral, Pilgrim seemed to be acting out some perverse parody of the events she described. He paced the rail in a mocking strut with his tail held high, but it was matted and twitched and was angled, Grace knew, by fear not pride.

Joe listened and she saw in his eyes the same contained calm that was in Tom's. It was startling sometimes how like his uncle he was, both in looks and manner. That easy smile and the way he took off his hat and pushed back his hair. Now and again Grace had caught herself wishing he was just a year or two older—not that he'd be interested in her, of course. Not in that way, not now, what with her leg. Anyway, it was fine as it was, just being friends.

She had learned a lot from watching Joe handle the younger horses, especially Bronty's foal. He never forced himself on them but instead let them come and offer themselves and then he would accept them with an ease that Grace could see made them feel both welcome and secure. He'd play with them, but if they ever got unsure he'd back off and leave them be.

"Tom says you gotta give them direction," he'd told her one day when they were with the foal. "But push too hard and they get real squirmy. You gotta let them kind of fill in. Tom says it's all about self-preservation."

Pilgrim had stopped and stood watching them from as far away as he could get.

"So, you gonna ride him?" Joe said. Grace turned to him and frowned.

"What?"

"When Tom's got him straightened out."

She gave a laugh that sounded hollow even to her.

"Oh, I'm not going to ride again."

Joe shrugged and nodded. There was a thump of hooves from the neighboring corral and they both turned to watch the colts playing some equine version of tag. Joe bent and plucked a stem of grass and stood sucking it awhile.

"Pity," he said.

"What?"

"Well, couple of weeks' time, Dad'll be driving the cattle up there to the summer pastures and we all go along. It's kinda fun, real pretty up there, you know?"

They went over to the colts and gave them some feed nuts Joe had in his pocket. As they walked back to the barn, Joe sucked his grass stem and Grace wondered why she went on pretending she didn't want to ride. Somehow she'd got herself trapped. And she felt, as with most things, that it probably had something to do with her mother.

Annie had surprised her by supporting the decision, so much so that Grace was suspicious. It was, of course, the stiff-upper-lip English way that when you fell off you climbed right back on so you didn't lose your nerve. And though what had happened was clearly more than a tumble, Grace had come to suspect Annie was playing some devious double-bluff, agreeing with Grace's decision only in order to prompt the opposite. The only thing that made her doubt this was Annie herself, after all these years, starting to ride again. Grace privately envied these morning rides with Tom Booker. But what was weird was that Annie must know it was almost guaranteed to put Grace off riding again herself.

Where though, Grace now wondered, did all this second-guessing get her? What was the point in denying her mother some maybe imaginary triumph, when it meant denying herself something she was now almost sure she wanted?

She knew she'd never ride Pilgrim again. Even if he got better, there would never be that trust between them again and he'd be sure to sense some lurking fear within her. But she could try riding some lesser horse maybe. If only she could do it without it all being a big deal, so that if she failed or looked stupid or something, it wouldn't matter.

They got to the barn and Joe opened the door and led the way in. All the horses were turned out now that the weather was warmer and Grace didn't know why he was bringing her in here. The click of her cane on the concrete floor echoed loudly. Joe took a left turn into the tack room and Grace stopped in the doorway, wondering what he was doing.

The room smelled of its new pine paneling and dressed leather. She watched him walk over to the rows of saddles that stood on their rests on the wall. When he spoke, it was over his shoulder, with the grass stem still in his teeth and his voice matter-of-fact, as if he were offering her a choice of sodas from the icebox.

"My horse or Rimrock?"

Annie regretted the invitation almost as soon as she'd issued it. The kitchen in the creek house wasn't exactly built for high cuisine, not that her cuisine was all that high anyway. Partly because she believed it more creative but mainly because she was too impatient, she cooked by instinct rather than recipe. And, apart from three or four stock dishes she could cook with her eyes shut, it was fifty-fifty whether something turned out brilliant or botched. This evening, she already felt, the odds were tilting more toward the latter.

She'd opted, safely she thought, for pasta. A dish they'd done to death last year. It was chic but easy. The kids would like it and there was even a chance Diane might be impressed. She'd also noticed Tom avoided eating too much meat and, more than she cared to admit to herself, she wanted to please him. There were no fancy ingredients. All she needed was penne regata, mozzarella and some fresh basil and sun-dried tomatoes, all of which she thought she'd be able to pick up in Choteau.

The guy in the store had looked at her as if she'd spoken in Urdu. She'd had to drive on down to the big supermarket in Great Falls and still couldn't find all she needed. It was hopeless. She'd had to rethink it on the spot and trudged the aisles, getting more and more annoyed, telling herself she'd be damned if she'd give in and serve them steak. Pasta she'd decided and pasta it would be. She ended up getting dried spaghetti, bottled bolognese sauce and a few trusty ingredients to spice it up so she could pretend it was her own. She checked out with two bottles of good Italian red and just sufficient pride intact.

By the time she'd got back to the Double Divide she felt better. She wanted to do this for them, it was the least she could do. The Bookers had all been so kind, even if Diane's kindness always seemed to have an edge to it. Whenever Annie had brought up the question of payment, for the rent and for the work he was doing with Pilgrim, Tom had brushed it aside. They'd settle up later, he said. She'd got the same response from Frank and Diane. So the dinner party tonight was Annie's interim way of thanking them.

She put the food away and carried the stack of newspapers and magazines she'd bought in Great Falls over to the table under which there was already a small mountain of them. She'd already checked her machines for messages. There had been only one, on E-mail, from Robert.

He'd been hoping to fly out and spend the holiday weekend with them but at the last minute was summoned to a meeting on Monday in London. From there he had to go on to Geneva. He'd phoned last night and spent half an hour apologizing to Grace, promising he'd come out soon. The E-mail note was just a jokey one he'd sent as he was about to leave for JFK, written in some cryptic language he and Grace called cyberspeak which Annie only half understood. At the bottom he'd drawn a computer-generated picture of a horse with a big smile on its face. Annie printed it out without reading it.

When Robert had told her last night that he wouldn't be coming, her first reaction had been relief. Then it had worried her that she should feel this and ever since she'd busily avoided analyzing further.

She sat down and wondered idly where Grace was. There had been nobody about down at the ranch when she drove back in from Great Falls. She guessed they were all indoors or around by the back corrals. She'd go and look when she'd caught up with the weeklies, the Saturday ritual she persisted with here, though it seemed to require a lot more effort. She opened *Time* magazine and bit into an apple.

It took Grace about ten minutes to make her way down below the corrals and through the grove of cottonwoods to the place Joe had told her about. She hadn't been down here before but when she came through the trees she understood why he'd chosen it.

Below her, at the foot of a curving bank, lay a perfect ellipse of meadow, moated beyond by an elbow of the creek. It was a natural arena, secluded from all but trees and sky. The grass stood deep, a lush blue-green, and wildflowers grew among it of a kind Grace had never seen.

She waited and listened for him. There was barely a

breeze to worry the leaves of the cottonwoods that tow-
ered behind her and all she could hear was the hum of
insects and the beating of her heart. No one was to
know. That was the deal. They'd heard Annie's car and
watched her go by through a crack in the barn door.
Scott would be out again soon, so in case they were
seen, Joe had told her to go on ahead. He'd saddle the
horse, check the coast was clear and follow.

Joe said he knew Tom wouldn't mind if she rode
Rimrock, but Grace wasn't happy about it so they settled on Gonzo, Joe's little paint. Like every other horse
she'd met here, he was sweet and calm and Grace had
already made friends with him. He was also a better
size for her. She heard a branch snap and the soft blow
of the horse and she turned and saw them coming
through the trees.

"Anybody see you?" she said.

"Nope."

He rode by her and steered Gonzo gently down the
bank to the meadow. Grace followed but the slope was
difficult and a yard or so from the bottom she caught
her leg and fell. She finished in a tangle that looked
worse than it was. Joe got down and came to her.

"You okay?"

"Shit!"

He helped her up. "Are you hurt?"

"No. I'm okay. Shit, shit, shit!"

He let her curse and without a word dusted down her
back for her. She saw there was a muddy mark all
down one side of her new jeans.

"Your leg okay?"

"Yes. I'm sorry. It just makes me so angry sometimes."

He nodded and for a moment or two said nothing,
letting her sort herself out.

"Still want to try?"

"Yes."

Joe led Gonzo and the three of them walked out into the meadow. Butterflies lifted before them, making way in the shin-high grass which smelled warm and sweet with the sun and the crushing of their boots. The creek here ran shallow over gravel and as they came nearer, Grace could hear the water. A heron lifted up and banked lazily away, adjusting his legs as he went.

They reached a low stump of cottonwood, gnarled and overgrown, and Joe stopped beside it and coaxed Gonzo around so that it formed a platform for Grace to mount.

"That any good?" he said.

"Uh-huh. If I can get up there."

He stood at the horse's shoulder, holding him steady with one hand and Grace with the other. Gonzo shifted and Joe gave him a stroke on the neck and told him it was okay. Grace put a hand on Joe's shoulder and hoisted herself with her good leg up onto the tree stump.

"Okay?"

"Yes. I think so."

"Are the stirrups too short?"

"No, they're fine."

Her left hand was still on his shoulder. She wondered whether he could feel in it the banging of her blood.

"Okay. Keep hold of me and, when you're ready, put your right hand on the horn of the saddle."

Grace took a deep breath and did as he said. Gonzo moved his head a little but his feet stayed rooted. When he was sure she was steady, Joe took his hand off her, reached down, and took hold of the stirrup.

This was going to be the difficult part. To put her left foot in the stirrup, all her weight would have to be on her prosthetic. She thought she might slip but she could feel Joe brace himself and take a lot of the weight and in no time she had her foot safely in the stirrup as if they'd done it many times before. All that happened was that Gonzo shifted a little again but Joe whoaed him, calm but firmer this time, so that he steadied on the instant.

All she had to do now was swing her prosthetic leg over, but it felt so strange having no feeling there and she suddenly remembered that the last time she'd done this was on the morning of the accident.

"Okay?" Joe said.

"Yes."

"Go on then."

She braced her left leg, letting the stirrup take her weight, then tried to lift her right leg over the horse's rear.

"I can't get it high enough."

"Here, lean on me some more. Lean out, so you get more of an angle."

She did and, summoning all her strength as if her life depended on it, she lifted the leg and swung. And as she did so, she pivoted and hauled herself up with the saddle horn and she felt Joe hoist her too and she swung the leg high and sideways and over it went.

She settled herself into the saddle and was surprised it didn't feel more alien. Joe saw her looking for the other stirrup and so he went quickly around and helped her into it. She could feel the inside thigh of her stump on the saddle and though tender, it was impossible to know precisely where feeling ended and nothingness began.

Joe stepped aside with his eyes fixed on her in case something happened, but she was too much in her own head to notice this. She gathered the reins and nudged Gonzo forward. He moved out without question and she walked him in a long curve along the rim of the creek and didn't look back. She could give more pressure with the leg than she'd imagined possible, though without calf muscles she had to generate it with her stump and measure its effect by the horse's response. He moved as if he knew all this and by the time they'd reached the end of the meadow and turned, without a foot misplaced, the two of them were one.

Grace lifted her eyes for the first time and saw Joe standing there among the flowers waiting for her. She rode an easy S shape back to him and stopped and he grinned up at her with the sun in his eyes and the meadow spreading away behind him and Grace suddenly wanted to cry. But she bit hard on the inside of her lip and grinned back down at him instead.

"Easy as pie," he said.

Grace nodded and as soon as she could trust her voice said yeah, it was easy as pie.

TWENTY-THREE

THE CREEK HOUSE KITCHEN WAS A SPARTAN AFFAIR, LIT by cold fluorescent strips whose casing had become coffins for an assortment of insects. When Frank and Diane had moved to the ranch house, they'd taken all the best equipment with them. The pots and pans were all from broken families and the dishwasher needed a thump in the right place to click through its cycle. The only thing Annie hadn't quite yet mastered was the oven which seemed to have a mind of its own. The door seal was rotten and the heat dial loose so that cooking required a blend of guesswork, vigilance and luck.

Baking the French-style apple tart she was serving for dessert however, hadn't been half the task of working out how they all might get to eat it. Too late Annie had discovered there weren't enough plates, cutlery or even enough chairs. And, embarrassed—because it somehow seemed to defeat the whole object—she'd had to call Diane and drive down and borrow some. Then she'd realized that the only table big enough to use was the one she was using for her desk, so she'd had to clear it and now all her machinery was stacked on the floor with her papers and magazines.

The evening had started in panic. Annie was used to entertaining people who thought the later you arrived the cooler you were, so it hadn't occurred to her that they'd arrive on the dot. But at seven, when she hadn't even changed, there they were, all but Tom, walking up the hill. She yelled to Grace, flew upstairs and threw on a dress she now had no time to press. By the time she heard their voices down by the porch, she'd done her eyes and lips, brushed her hair, given herself a blast of perfume and was downstairs to greet them.

Seeing them all standing there, Annie thought what a stupid idea this was, entertaining these people in their own house. Everyone seemed to feel awkward. Frank said Tom had been delayed by some problem with one of the yearlings but he was in the shower when they left and wouldn't be long. She asked them what they wanted to drink and remembered as she did so that she'd forgotten to get any beer.

"I'll have a beer," Frank said.

It got better though. She opened a bottle of wine while Grace took Joe and the twins off and sat them on the floor in front of Annie's computer where soon she had them surfing spellbound on the Internet. Annie, Frank and Diane carried chairs out onto the porch and sat talking in a fading glow of evening light. They laughed over Scott's adventure with the calf, assuming Grace had told her all about it. Annie pretended she had. Then Frank told a long story about a disastrous high school rodeo where he'd humiliated himself in front of a girl he was trying to impress.

Annie listened with feigned attention, all the while waiting for the moment she would see Tom come around the end of the house. And when he did, his smile and the way he took off his hat and said he was sorry for being late were just as she'd imagined.

She led him into the house, apologizing before he even asked for one that there wasn't any beer. Tom said wine would be fine and he stood and watched her pour it. She handed him the glass and looked him full in the eyes for the first time and whatever she'd been going to say flew right out of her head. There was a beat of embarrassed silence before he came to the rescue.

"Something smells good."

"Nothing spectacular I'm afraid. Is your horse alright?"

"Oh yeah. Her temperature's running a little high but she'll be okay. Have you had a good day?"

Before she could answer, Craig ran in calling Tom's name and telling him he had to come and see something they had on the computer.

"Hey, I'm having a talk here with Grace's mom."

Annie laughed and told them to go ahead, Grace's mom needed to see to the food anyway. Diane came in to help and the two of them chatted about the children while they got things ready. And every so often Annie would glance through into the living room and see Tom in his pale blue shirt, hunkered down among the kids, all of them vying for his attention.

The spaghetti was a hit. Diane even asked for the sauce recipe and Annie would have owned up if Grace hadn't beaten her to it and told them all it was out of a bottle. Annie had set the table in the middle of the living room and lit it with candles she'd bought in Great Falls. Grace had said this was overdoing it but Annie had persisted and now was glad she had because their light gave the room a warm glow and cast flickering shadows on the walls.

And she thought how good it was to hear the silence

of this house filled with talk and laughter. The kids sat at one end and the four adults the other, she and Frank facing Tom and Diane. A stranger, it occurred to Annie, would have assumed them couples.

Grace was telling everyone about the things you could access on the Internet, like The Visible Man, a murderer in Texas who had been executed and donated his body to science.

"They froze him and sliced him up into two thousand little pieces and photographed each one of them," she said.

"That's gross," Scott said.

"Do we want to hear about this while we're eating?" Annie said. She'd meant it only lightly but Grace decided to take it as a rebuke. She gave Annie a withering look.

"It's the National Library of Medicine, Mom. It's education for Godsake, not some stupid beat-'em-up game."

"Slice 'em up, more like," Craig said.

"Go on Grace," Diane said. "It's fascinating."

"Well that's it really," Grace said. She spoke without enthusiasm now, signaling to everyone that her mother had, as usual, deflated not just her but the topic too of both interest and fun. "They just put him back together again and you can call it up on the screen and dissect him, like in three-D, you know."

"You can do all that right here on that little screen?" Frank said.

"Yes."

The word was so flat and final that only silence could follow it. It lasted but a moment, though it seemed to Annie an eternity, and Tom must have seen the desperation in her eyes, because he gave Frank a sardonic nod and said, "Well, there you go little brother, your chance for immortality."

"Lord have mercy," Diane said. "Frank Booker's body on view to the nation."

"Oh, and what's wrong with my body may I ask?"

"Where d'you want us to start?" Joe said. Everyone laughed.

"Hell," said Tom. "With two thousand pieces, you could put them back in a different way and get a prettier result."

The mood began to flow again and once she was sure of it Annie gave Tom a look of relief and thanks, which he acknowledged with just the smallest softening of his eyes. It struck her as uncanny that this man who'd never fully known a child of his own should so understand each wounding nuance that passed between her and Grace.

The apple tart wasn't so great. Annie had forgotten the cinnamon and she could tell as soon as she cut the first slice that it could have done with another fifteen minutes. But no one seemed to mind and the kids all had ice cream instead anyway and were soon off to the computer again while the adults sat and had coffee at the table.

Frank was complaining about the conservationists, the *greenos* as he called them, and how they didn't understand the first damn thing about ranching. He addressed himself to Annie because the others had clearly heard it a hundred times. These maniacs were letting wolves go, shipping the damn things in from Canada so they could come and help the grizzlies eat the cattle. A couple of weeks back, he said, a rancher down near Augusta had two heifers taken.

"And all these *greenos* flew up from Missoula with their choppers and consciences and all and said, sorry old buddy, we'll airlift him out for ya, but don't you go trapping or shooting him or we'll nail your hide in court. Damn thing's probably lazing by the pool now at some five-star hotel, you and me footing the bill."

Tom was grinning at Annie and Frank saw and pointed a finger at him.

"This guy's one of 'em, Annie, I tell ya. Ranching in his blood and he's green as a seasick frog on a pool table. You wait till Mr. Wolf takes one of his foals, oh boy. It'll be the three big S's."

Tom laughed and saw Annie's frown.

"Shoot, shovel and shut the hell up," he confided. "The caring rancher's response to nature."

Annie laughed and was suddenly aware of Diane's eyes on her. And when Annie looked at her, Diane smiled in a way that only emphasized that she hadn't been smiling before.

"What do you think, Annie?" she asked.

"Oh, I don't have to live with it."

"But you must have an opinion."

"Not really."

"Oh surely. You must cover this kind of thing all the time in your magazine."

Annie was surprised to be so pursued. She shrugged.

"I suppose I think every creature has a right to live."

"What, even plague rats and malarial mosquitoes?"

Diane was still smiling and the tone was light but there was something beneath it that made Annie cautious.

"You're right," she said after a moment. "I guess it depends who they bite."

Frank gave a roar of laughter and Annie allowed herself a glance at Tom. He was smiling at her. So too, in a less fathomable way, was Diane who seemed at last prepared to let the subject drop. Whether that was so remained a mystery because suddenly there was a yell and Scott was behind her grabbing her shoulder, his cheeks hot with outrage.

"Joe won't let me use the computer!"

"It's not your turn," Joe called from where the others were all still huddled around the screen.

"It is too!"

"It's not your turn Scott!"

Diane called Joe over and tried to mediate. But the yelling got worse and soon Frank was involved too and the fight shifted from the particular to the general.

"You never let me have a turn!" Scott said. He was near tears.

"Don't be such a baby," Joe said.

"Boys, boys." Frank had his hands on their shoulders.

"You think you're so great—"

"Oh shut up."

"—giving Grace riding lessons and all."

Everyone went quiet except for some cartoon bird squawking on oblivious on the computer screen. Annie looked at Grace who immediately looked away. No one seemed to know what to say. Scott was a little daunted by the effect his revelation had produced.

"I saw you!" His voice was more taunting but less certain. "Her on Gonzo, down by the creek!"

"You little shit!" Joe said it through his teeth and at the same time made a lunge. Everyone erupted. Scott was knocked back against the table and coffee cups and glasses went flying. The two boys fell in a tangle to the floor, with Frank and Diane above them yelling and trying to lever them apart. Craig came running, feeling he should somehow be involved here too but Tom put out a hand and took gentle hold of him. Annie and Grace could only stand and watch.

The next moment Frank was marching the boys out of the house, Scott wailing, Craig crying in sympathy and Joe in a silent fury which spoke louder than both. Tom went with them as far as the kitchen door.

"Annie I'm so sorry," Diane said.

They were standing by the wreckage of the table like dazed hurricane survivors. Grace stood pale and alone across the room. As Annie looked at her, something that was neither fear nor pain, but a hybrid of both, seemed to cross the girl's face. Tom saw it too when he came back from the kitchen and he went over to her and put a hand on her shoulder.

"You okay?"

She nodded without looking at him.

"I'm going upstairs."

She picked up her cane and made her way with awkward haste across the room.

"Grace . . ." Annie said gently.

"No Mom!"

She went out and the three of them stood and listened to the sound of her uneven footsteps on the stairs. Annie saw the embarrassment on Diane's face. On Tom's there was a compassion that, if she'd let it, would have made her weep. She inhaled and tried to smile.

"Did you know about this?" she said. "Did everyone know except me?"

Tom shook his head. "I don't think any of us knew."

"Maybe she wanted it to be a surprise," Diane said. Annie laughed.

"Yeah, well."

She wanted them only to go, but Diane insisted on staying to clear the place up and so they stacked the dishwasher and cleared the broken glass from the table. Then Diane rolled up her sleeves and got going on the pots and pans. She clearly thought it best to be chirpy and chattered on at the sink about the barn dance Hank had invited them all to on Monday.

Tom said barely a word. He helped Annie haul the table back to the window and waited while she switched off the computer. Then, working side by side, they started to load all her work things back onto the table.

What prompted her, Annie didn't know, but suddenly she asked how Pilgrim was. He didn't answer right away, just went on sorting some cables, not looking at her, while he considered. His tone, when at last he spoke, was almost matter-of-fact.

"Oh, I reckon he'll make it."

"You do?"

"Uh-huh."

"Are you sure?"

"No. But you see Annie, where there's pain, there's still feeling and where there's feeling, there's hope."

He fixed the last cable.

"There you go." He turned to face her and they looked each other in the eye.

"Thanks," Annie said quietly.

"Ma'am, it's my pleasure. Don't let her turn you away."

When they came back to the kitchen, Diane had finished and all except the things she'd lent was put away in places she knew better than Annie. And when Diane had brushed aside Annie's thanks and apologized again for the boys, she and Tom said their good-nights and went.

Annie stood under the porch light and watched them walk away. And as their figures were swallowed by the darkness, she wanted to call after him to stay and hold her and keep her from the cold that fell again upon the house.

* * *

Tom said good-night to Diane outside the barn and went on in to check the sick filly. Walking down from the creek house, Diane had gone on about how dumb Joe was to take the girl riding like that without telling a soul. Tom said he didn't think it was dumb at all, he could understand why Grace might want to keep such a thing secret. Joe was being a friend to her, that was all. Diane said it was none of the boy's business and frankly she'd be glad when Annie packed up and took the poor girl back home to New York.

The filly hadn't gotten any worse, though she was still breathing a little fast. Her temperature was down to a hundred and two. Tom rubbed her neck and talked to her gently while with his other hand he felt her pulse behind the elbow. He counted the beats for twenty seconds, then multiplied by three. It was forty-two beats per minute, still above normal. She was clearly running some kind of fever and maybe he'd have to get the vet up to see her in the morning if there was no change.

The lights of Annie's bedroom were on when he came out and they were still on when he finished reading and switched off his own bedroom light. It was a habit now, this last look up at the creek house where the illuminated yellow blinds of Annie's window stood out against the night. Sometimes he'd see her shadow pass across them as she went about her unknown bedtime rituals and once he'd seen her pause there, framed by the glow, undressing and he'd felt like a snooper and turned away.

Now though, the blinds were open and he knew it meant something had happened or was happening even as he looked. But he knew it was something only they could resolve and, though it was foolish, he told himself that maybe the blinds were open not to let darkness in but to let it out.

Never, since he first laid eyes on Rachel so many years ago, had he met a woman he wanted more.

Tonight was the first time he'd seen her in a dress. It was a simple cotton print, black dotted with tiny pink flowers, and there were pearl buttons all down the front. It reached well below her knees and it had little cap sleeves that showed the tops of her arms.

When he arrived and she'd told him to come into the kitchen to get a drink, he couldn't take his eyes off her. He'd followed her inside and breathed deep the waft of her perfume and while she poured the wine he'd watched her and noticed how she kept her tongue between her teeth to concentrate. He noticed too a glimpse of satin strap at her shoulder which he'd tried all evening not to look at and failed. And she'd handed him the glass and smiled at him, creasing the corners of that mouth in a way he wished was only for him.

Over supper he'd almost got to believe it was, because the smiles she gave Frank and Diane and the kids were nothing like it. And maybe he'd imagined it, but when she talked, no matter how generally, it always seemed somehow directed at him. He'd never seen her with her eyes made up before and he watched how they shone green and trapped the candle flame when she laughed.

When everything had exploded and Grace stormed out, it was only Diane being there that had stopped him from taking Annie in his arms and letting her cry as he could see she wanted to. He didn't fool himself that the urge was merely to console her. It was to hold her and know closely the feel and the shape and the smell of her.

But nor did Tom think this made it shameful, though

he knew others might. This woman's pain and her child and the pain of that child were all part of her too, were they not? And what man was God enough to judge the fine divisions of feeling appropriate to each or all or any of these?

All things were one, and like a rider in harmony, the best a man could do was recognize the feel and go with it and be as true to it as his soul let him.

She switched all the downstairs lights off and as she went up the stairs, she saw Grace's door was closed and beneath it that her room was dark. Annie went to her own room and switched on the light. She paused in the doorway, knowing that crossing the threshold somehow had significance. How could she let this pass? Allow another layer to settle unquestioned with the night between them, as if there were some inexorable geology at work? It didn't have to be so.

Grace's door creaked when Annie opened it, pivoting light into the room from the landing. She thought she saw the bedclothes shift but couldn't be sure, for the bed was beyond the angle of light and Annie's eyes took time to adjust.

"Grace?"

Grace was facing the wall and there was a studied stillness to the shape of her shoulders beneath the sheet.

"Grace?"

"What." She didn't move.

"Can we talk?"

"I want to go to sleep."

"So do I, but I think it would be good if we talked."

"What about?"

Annie walked over to the bed and sat down. The prosthetic leg was propped against the wall by the bedside table. Grace sighed and turned over on her back, staring at the ceiling. Annie took a deep breath. Get it right, she kept telling herself. Don't sound hurt, go easy, be nice.

"So you're riding again."

"I tried."

"How was it?"

Grace shrugged. "Okay." She was still looking at the ceiling, trying to look bored.

"That's terrific."

"Is it?"

"Well isn't it?"

"I don't know, you tell me."

Annie fought the beating of her heart and told herself, keep calm, keep going, just take it. But instead she heard herself say, "Couldn't you have told me?"

Grace looked at her and the hate and hurt in her eyes almost took Annie's breath away.

"Why should I tell you?"

"Grace—"

"No why? Huh? Because you care? Or just because you have to know everything and control everything and not let anybody do anything unless you say so! Is that it?"

"Oh Grace." Annie suddenly felt she needed light and she reached across to turn on the lamp on the bedside table but Grace lashed out.

"Don't! I don't want it on!"

The blow hit Annie's hand and sent the lamp crashing to the floor. The ceramic base broke into three clean pieces.

"You pretend you care but all you really care about is you and what people think of you. And your job and your big-shot friends."

She propped herself up on her elbows as if to bolster

a rage already made worse by the tears distorting her face.

"Anyway, you said you didn't want me to ride again so why the hell should I tell you? Why should I tell you anything! I hate you!"

Annie tried to take hold of her but Grace pushed her away.

"Get out! Just leave me alone! Get out!"

Annie stood up and felt herself sway so that for a moment she thought she might fall. Almost blindly, she made her way across the pool of light that she knew would take her to the door. She had no clear idea of what she would do when she got there. She merely knew that she was obeying some final separating command. As she reached the door she heard Grace say something and she turned and looked back toward the bed. She could see Grace was facing the wall again and that her shoulders were shaking.

"What?" Annie said.

She waited and whether it was her own grief or Grace's that shrouded the words a second time she didn't know, but there was something about the way they were spoken that made her go back. She walked to the bed and stood close enough to touch but didn't, for fear her hand might be struck away.

"Grace? I didn't hear what you said."

"I said . . . I've started."

It came amid sobs and for a moment Annie didn't understand.

"You've started?"

"My period."

"What, tonight?"

Grace nodded.

"I felt it happen downstairs and when I came up

there was blood in my panties. I washed them in the bathroom but it wouldn't come out."

"Oh Gracie."

Annie reached down and put a hand on Grace's shoulder and Grace turned. There was no anger in her face now, only pain and sorrow and Annie sat on the bed and took her daughter in her arms. Grace clung to her and Annie felt the child's sobs convulse them as if they were but one body.

"Who's going to want me?"

"What, honey?"

"Whoever's going to want me? Nobody will."

"Oh Gracie, that's not true. . . ."

"Why should they?"

"Because you're you. You're incredible. You're beautiful and you're strong. And you're the bravest person I ever met in my whole life."

They held each other and wept. And when they could speak again, Grace told her she hadn't meant the terrible things she'd said and Annie said she knew, but there was truth there too, and how as a mother, she had got so many, many things wrong. They sat with their heads on each other's shoulder and let flow from their hearts words they'd barely dared utter to themselves.

"All those years you and Dad were trying for another baby? Every night I used to pray this time let it be okay. And it wasn't for your sake or because I wanted a brother or a sister or anything like that. But just so I wouldn't have to go on being so . . . oh I don't know."

"Tell me."

"So special. Because I was the only one, I felt you both expected me to be so good at everything, so perfect and I wasn't, I was just me. And now I've gone and spoiled it all anyway."

Annie held her more tightly and stroked her hair and told her this wasn't so. And she thought, but didn't say, what a perilous commodity love was and that the proper calibration of its giving and taking was too precise by far for mere humans.

How long they sat there Annie couldn't tell. But it was long after their crying had ceased and the wetness of their tears had grown cold on her dress. Grace fell asleep in her arms and didn't wake even when Annie laid her down then laid herself beside her.

She listened to her daughter's breathing, even and trusting, and for a while watched the breeze stirring the pale drapes at the window. Then Annie slept too, a deep and dreamless sleep, while outside the earth rolled vast and silent under the sky.

TWENTY-FOUR

ROBERT LOOKED OUT THROUGH THE RAIN-STREAKED window of the black cab at the woman on the billboard who'd been waving the same wave at him for the last ten minutes. It was one of those electronically animated jobs, where the arm actually moved. She was wearing Ray-Bans and a bright pink bathing suit and in her other hand had what was probably meant to be a piña colada. She was doing her best to persuade Robert and several hundred other traffic-snarled, rain-soaked travelers that they'd be better off buying an air ticket to Florida.

It was debatable. And a harder sell than it seemed, Robert knew, because the English newspapers had been going to town on stories about British tourists in Florida being mugged, raped and shot. As the cab crawled forward, Robert could see some wag had scrawled by the woman's feet *Don't forget your Uzi.*

He realized too late that he should have taken the Underground. Every time he'd been to London in the last ten years they'd been digging up some new section of the road out to the airport and he was pretty sure they didn't just save it up for when he came. The flight to Geneva was due to leave in thirty-five minutes and at this rate he'd miss it by about two years. The cabdriver had already informed him, with something suspiciously approaching relish, that out at the airport there was a "right peasouper."

There was. And he didn't miss his flight; it was canceled. He sat in the business-class lounge and for a couple of hours enjoyed the camaraderie of a growing band of harassed executives, each pursuing his or her own self-important path to a coronary. He tried calling Annie but got the answering machine and he wondered where they were. He'd forgotten to ask their plans for this first Memorial Day in years they hadn't spent together.

He left a message and sang a few bars of the "Halls of Montezuma" for Grace, something he did over breakfast on this day as a cue for groans and missiles. Then he took a final look at the notes of today's meeting (which had gone well) and the paperwork for tomorrow's (which might also if he ever got there) and then he put it all away and went for another walk around the departure area.

As he was looking idly and for no good reason at a rack of cashmere golf sweaters that he wouldn't have wished upon his worst enemy, someone said hello and he looked up and saw a man who came as close to that category as anyone he knew.

Freddie Kane was something medium-to-small in publishing, one of those people you never questioned too closely about the exact nature of their business, for fear of embarrassing not them but yourself. He compensated for whatever deficiencies might lie in that murky area by making it clear that he had a personal fortune and furthermore knew every piece of gossip there was to know about anyone who was anyone in New York. By forgetting Robert's name on each of the four or five occasions they'd been introduced, Freddie had made it equally clear that he didn't count Annie Graves's husband among this number. Annie, on the other hand, he very much did.

"Hi! I thought it was you! How're you doing!"

He thumped one hand on Robert's shoulder and used the other to pump his hand in a way that somehow managed to be simultaneously both violent and flaccid. Robert smiled and noted that the man had on a pair of those glasses movie stars were all now wearing in the hope that it made them look more intellectual. He'd clearly forgotten Robert's name again.

They chatted for a while over the golf sweaters, swapping information on destinations, estimated arrivals and the properties of fog. Robert was oblique and guarded about why he was in Europe, not because it was secret but because he could see how frustrated it made Freddie. And so it was perhaps revenge for this that motivated the man's closing remarks.

"I hear Annie's got herself a Gates problem," he said.

"I'm sorry?"

Freddie put a hand to his mouth and made a face like a guilty schoolboy.

"Oops. Maybe we're not supposed to know."

"I'm sorry Freddie, you're way ahead of me."

"Oh, it's just a little bird told me Crawford Gates is out headhunting again. Probably not a word of truth in it."

"How do you mean, headhunting?"

"Oh, you know how it's always been at that place, musical chairs and shoot the pianist. I just heard he was giving Annie a hard time, that's all."

"Well, it's the first I've—"

"Just gossip. Shouldn't have mentioned it."

He gave a satisfied grin and, having fulfilled what may indeed have been the sole purpose of the encounter, said he'd better get back to the airline desk to do some more complaining.

Back in the business lounge Robert helped himself to another beer and flipped through a copy of *The Economist*, mulling over what Freddie had said. Although he'd played ingenuous, he'd known right away what the man was getting at. It was the second time in a week that he'd heard it.

The previous Tuesday he'd been at a reception given by one of his firm's big clients. It was the kind of do he normally made excuses to avoid but which, with Annie and Grace away, he'd actually found himself looking forward to. It was held in several sumptuous acres of office near Rockefeller Center with mountains of caviar high enough to ski on.

Whatever the latest collective noun for a gathering of lawyers was (they came up with a new and more disparaging one each week), there was certainly one of them here. There were many faces from other law firms that Robert recognized and he guessed the hosts' motive for inviting them all was to keep his own firm on their toes. Among the other lawyers was Don Farlow. They'd only met once before but Robert liked him and knew Annie did too and that she rated him highly.

Farlow greeted him warmly and Robert was pleased to find as they chatted that they shared not just an appetite bordering on greed for caviar, but a wholesomely cynical attitude about those who'd provided it. They staked a claim beside the nursery slopes and Farlow listened sympathetically while Robert told him how the litigation over Grace's accident was progressing—or rather not progressing, for it was getting so complicated it seemed destined to drag on for years. Then the talk moved on. Farlow asked after Annie and how things were going out west.

"Annie's sensational," said Farlow. "The very best. The crazy thing is, that asshole Gates knows that."

Robert asked him what he meant and Farlow looked surprised and then embarrassed. He quickly changed the subject and the only other thing he said, as he went, was that Robert should tell Annie to come back soon. Robert had gone straight home and called Annie. She'd made light of it.

"That place is Paranoia Palace," she said. Oh sure, Gates had been giving her a hard time, but no more than usual. "The old bastard knows he needs me more than I need him."

Robert had let it drop, even though he felt that her bravado seemed intended more to convince herself than him. Now if Freddie Kane knew about it, it was a safe bet that most of New York knew too or soon would. And though this wasn't Robert's world, he'd seen enough of it to know which was more important: what was said or what was true.

TWENTY-FIVE

HANK AND DARLENE NORMALLY HELD THEIR BARN dance on the Fourth of July. But this year Hank was scheduled to have his varicose veins fixed at the end of June and didn't fancy hobbling around so they'd hauled it back a month or so to Memorial Day.

There was risk involved. A few years back, two feet of snow had fallen this very weekend. And some Hank had invited felt a day set aside to honor those who'd died for their country wasn't a suitable day for a celebration at all. Hank said shit, come to that, celebrating independence was pretty dumb too when you'd been married as long as him and Darlene, and anyway, all those he knew who'd gone to Vietnam liked a damn good party, so what the hell?

Just to show him, it rained.

Rivers of it slid off billowing tarpaulins to hiss among the burgers, ribs and steaks on the barbecue and a fuse box exploded with a flash and snuffed all the colored lights strung around the yard. No one seemed to mind too much. They all just packed into the barn. Someone gave Hank a T-shirt which he immediately put on; it had I TOLD YOU printed on the front in big black letters.

Tom was late arriving because the vet couldn't get out to the Double Divide till after six. He'd given the little filly another shot and thought that would do it. They were still busy with her when the others left for the party. Through the open doors of the barn he'd seen all the kids piling into the Lariat with Annie and Grace. Annie had waved to him and asked if he was coming. He told her he'd be along later. He was pleased to see she was wearing the dress she'd worn two nights before.

Neither she nor Grace had spoken a word about what had happened that night. On Sunday he'd risen before dawn and dressed in the dark and seen Annie's blinds still open and the lights still on. He'd wanted to go on up and see if everything was okay but thought he'd leave it awhile in case it seemed nosy. When he'd finished seeing to the horses and came in for breakfast, Diane said Annie had just called to ask if it would be alright if she and Grace came with them to church.

"Probably just wants to write it up in her magazine," Diane said. Tom told her he thought that was unfair and that she should give Annie a break. Diane hadn't spoken to him for the rest of the day.

They'd all driven to church in two cars and it was clear at once, to Tom at least, that something had changed between Annie and Grace. There was a still-ness there. He noticed how when Annie spoke Grace now looked her in the eyes and how, after they'd parked the cars, the two of them linked arms and walked together all the way to the church.

There wasn't room for them all in one row, so Annie and Grace had sat a row in front where a shaft of sun angled down from a window, trapping slow convec-

tions of dust. Tom could see the other churchfolk looking at the newcomers, the women as much as the men.
And he found his own eyes kept returning to the nape
of Annie's neck when she stood to sing or tilted her
head in prayer.

Back at the Double Divide later, Grace had ridden
Gonzo again, only this time in the big arena with everyone watching. She walked him awhile then, when Tom
told her to, took him up to a trot. She was a little tight
at the start, but once she relaxed and found the feel,
Tom could see how sweetly she rode. He told her a
couple of things about the way she was using her leg
and when it all clicked, he said to go ahead and move
on up to a lope.

"A lope!"

"Why not?"

So she did and it was fine and as she opened her hips
and moved with the motion he saw the grin break out
on her face.

"Shouldn't she be wearing a hat?" Annie had asked
him quietly. She meant one of those safety helmets people wore in England and back east and he'd said well
no, not unless she was planning on falling off. He knew
he should have taken it more seriously, but Annie
seemed to trust him and left it at that.

Grace slowed in perfect balance and brought Gonzo
to an easy stop before them and everyone clapped and
cheered. The little horse looked like he'd won the Kentucky Derby. And Grace's smile was wide and clear as a
morning sky.

After the vet had left, Tom showered, put on a clean
shirt and set off through the rain for Hank's place. It
was coming down so thick, the old Chevy's wipers all
but gave in and Tom had to peer with his nose to the
glass to negotiate a way through the flooded craters of

the old gravel road. There were so many cars when he got there that he had to park right out on the driveway and if he hadn't worn his slicker he'd have been soaked by the time he got to the barn.

As soon as he walked in, Hank saw him and came over with a beer. Tom laughed at the T-shirt and even as he took off his slicker, realized he was already scanning the faces for Annie. The barn was large but still too small for all the folk packed into it. There was country music playing, almost drowned by the sound of talk and laughter. People were still eating. Every now and then the wind would drive a cloud of smoke from the barbecue in through the open doors. Mostly people ate standing up because the tables hauled in from outside were still wet.

While he chatted with Hank and a couple of other guys, Tom let his eyes travel the room. One of the empty stalls on the far side had been turned into a bar and he could see Frank helping out behind it. Some of the older kids, including Grace and Joe, were gathered around the sound system, going through the box of tapes and groaning at the embarrassing prospect of their parents trying to dance to the Eagles and Fleetwood Mac. Nearby Diane was telling the twins for the last time to quit throwing food or she'd take them right home. There were many faces Tom knew and many who greeted him. But there was only one he was looking for and at last he saw her.

She stood in the far corner with an empty glass in her hand, talking with Smoky who'd come up from New Mexico where he'd been working since Tom's last clinic. It was Smoky who seemed to be doing most of the talking. Every so often Annie glanced around the room and Tom wondered if she was looking for anyone in particular and if so, whether it might be him. Then he told himself not to be such a damn fool and went and got himself some food.

Smoky knew who Annie was as soon as they were introduced. "You're the one done call him when we were doing the Marin County clinic!" he said. Annie smiled.

"That's right."

"Hell, I remember him calling me when he came back from New York saying there was no way he was going to work with that horse. Now here y'all are."

"He changed his mind."

"Ma'am, he sure must of. Ain't never seen Tom do something he didn't want."

Annie asked him questions about his work with Tom and what went on at the clinics and it was clear from the way he spoke that Smoky worshiped the ground Tom walked. He said there were quite a few people now doing clinics and things but not one of them was in the same league, or even close. He told her about things he'd seen Tom do, horses he'd helped that most folk would have taken out and shot.

"When he lays his hands on them you can see all the trouble just kind of fall out of them."

Annie said he hadn't done this yet with Pilgrim and Smoky said that must be because the horse wasn't yet ready.

"It sounds like magic," she said.

"No ma'am. It's more than magic. Magic's just tricks."

Whatever it was, Annie had felt it. She'd felt it when she watched Tom work, when she rode with him. In truth, she felt it almost every moment she was with him. It was this that she had contemplated yesterday morning when she woke with Grace still sleeping beside her and saw the dawn spilling in through the faded drapes that now hung unmoving. For a long time she'd lain quite still, cradled in the calm of her daughter's breathing. Once, from a distant dream, Grace murmured something that Annie labored in vain to decipher.

It was then she'd noticed, among the pile of books and magazines beside the bed, the copy of *Pilgrim's Progress* Liz Hammond's cousins had given her. She hadn't opened it nor had she any idea that Grace had brought it in here. Annie slipped quietly from the bed and took it to the chair by the window where there was just enough light to read.

She remembered listening wide-eyed to the story as a child, captivated on a simple literal level by the story of little Christian's heroic journey to the Celestial City. Reading it now, the allegory seemed obvious and clumsy. But there was a passage near the end that made her pause.

> *Now I saw in my dream that by this time the pilgrims were got over the Enchanted Ground and entering into the country of Beulah, whose air was very sweet and pleasant; the way lying directly through it, they solaced themselves there for a season. Yea, here they heard continually the singing of birds and saw every day the flowers appear in the earth and heard the voice of the turtle in the land. In this country the sun shineth night and day; wherefore this was beyond the Valley of the Shadow of Death and also out of the reach of Giant Despair; neither could they from this place so much as see Doubting Castle. Here they were within sight of the City they were going to, also here met some of the inhabitants thereof. For in*

this land the Shining Ones commonly walked, because it was upon the borders of Heaven.

Annie read the passage three times and read no farther. It was this that had led her to call Diane to ask if she and Grace could come to church. However, the urge—so wildly out of character that it made even Annie laugh—had little, if anything, to do with religion. It had to do with Tom Booker.

Annie knew that somehow he had set the scene for what had happened. He had unlocked a door through which she and Grace had found each other. "Don't let her turn you away," he'd told her. And she hadn't. Now she simply wanted to give thanks, but in a ritualized way that wouldn't embarrass anyone. Grace had teased her when she told her, asking how many centuries it was since she'd last seen the inside of a church. But she said it with affection and was plainly happy to come along.

Annie's head refocused on the party. Smoky didn't seem to have noticed her drifting. He was in the middle of some long, involved story about the man who owned the ranch he was working at down in New Mexico. While Annie listened she went back to doing what she'd spent most of the evening doing, looking out for Tom. Maybe he wasn't coming after all.

Hank and the other men cleared the tables out into the rain again and the dancing began. The music was louder now and still country so that, led by the most streetwise among them, the kids could keep up their groaning, no doubt secretly relieved at not having to dance themselves. Laughing at your parents was a whole lot more fun than having them laugh at you. One or two of the older girls had broken ranks and were dancing and the sight suddenly had Annie worried. Stupidly, until now, it hadn't occurred to her that seeing others dance might upset Grace. She made an excuse to Smoky and went to find her.

Grace was sitting by the stalls with Joe. They saw Annie coming and Grace whispered something to him that made him grin. It was gone from his face by the time Annie got there. He stood up to greet her.

"Ma'am, would you like to dance?"

Grace burst out laughing and Annie gave her a suspicious glance.

"This is entirely unprompted of course," she said.

"Of course ma'am."

"And not, by any remote chance, a dare?"

"Mom! That's so rude!" Grace said. "What a terrible thing to suggest!" Joe kept a perfect straight face.

"No ma'am. Absolutely not."

Annie looked again at Grace who now read her mind.

"Mom, if you think I'm going to dance with him to this music, forget it."

"Then thank you Joe. I'd be delighted."

So they danced. And Joe danced well and even though the other kids hooted, he didn't turn a hair. It was while they were dancing that she saw Tom. He was watching her from the bar and waved and the sight of him gave her such a teenage thrill that at once she felt embarrassed because maybe it showed.

When the music stopped Joe gave a courteous bow and escorted her back to Grace who hadn't stopped laughing. Annie felt a touch on her shoulder and turned. It was Hank. He wanted the next dance and wouldn't take no for an answer. By the time they'd finished he had Annie laughing so much her sides ached. But there was no respite. Frank was next, then Smoky.

As she danced, she looked over and saw Grace and Joe were now doing a jokey kind of dance with the twins and some other kids, jokey enough anyway to allow Grace and Joe the illusion that they weren't really dancing with each other.

She watched Tom dance with Darlene, then Diane, then more closely with some pretty, younger woman Annie didn't know and didn't much want to know. Perhaps it was some girlfriend she hadn't heard about. And every time the music stopped, Annie looked for him and wondered why he didn't come and ask her to dance.

He saw her making her way across to the bar after she'd danced with Smoky and as soon as he could do so politely he thanked his partner and followed. It was the third time he'd tried to reach her but someone always got there first.

He weaved his way behind her through the hot crowd and saw her wipe the sweat from her brow with both hands, back through her hair, just as she'd done when he met her out running. There was a dark patch on her back where the fabric of her dress had grown wet and clung to her skin. As he got near he could smell her perfume mixed with another more subtle and potent that was all her own.

Frank was back serving behind the bar and he saw Annie and asked her over other people's heads what she wanted. She asked him for a glass of water. Frank said sorry there wasn't any, only Dr Peppers. He handed her one and she thanked him and turned and Tom was standing right there in front of her.

"Hi!" she said.

"Hi. So Annie Graves likes to dance."

"As a matter of fact I can't stand it. It's just that here no one gives you the choice."

He laughed and decided therefore that he wouldn't ask her, though he'd looked forward to it all evening. Someone pushed between them, cutting them off from each other for a moment. The music had started up again so they had to shout to make each other hear.

"You obviously do," she said.

"What?"

"Like to dance. I saw you."

"I guess. But I saw you too and I reckon you like it more than you say."

"Oh, you know, sometimes. When I'm in the mood."

"You want some water?"

"I would die for water."

Tom called to Frank for a clean glass and handed back the Dr Peppers. Then he put a hand lightly on Annie's back to steer her through the crowd and felt the warmth of her body through the damp dress.

"Come on."

He found a path for them among all the people and all she could think of was the feel of his hand on her back, just below her shoulder blades and the clasp of her bra.

As they skirted the dance floor, she chided herself for telling him she didn't like to dance, for otherwise he'd surely have asked and there was nothing she wanted more.

The great barn doors stood open and the disco lights lit the rain outside like a bead curtain of ever-changing color. There was no longer any wind but the rain fell so hard it made a breeze of its own and others had gathered in the doorway for the cool Annie now felt on her face.

They stopped and stood together on the brink of shelter and peered out through the rain whose roar made distant the music behind them. No longer was there reason for his hand to be on her back and though she hoped he wouldn't, he took it away. Across the yard she could just make out the lights of the house like a lost ship where she assumed they were headed for her drink of water.

"We'll get drenched," she said. "I'm not that desperate."

"I thought you said you'd die for water?"

"Yes, but not in it. Though they say drowning's the best way to go. I always thought, how on earth do they know that?"

He laughed. "You sure do a lot of thinking don't you?"

"Yep, always fizzing away up there. Can't stop it."

"Kind of gets in the way sometimes, don't it?"

"Yep."

"Like now." He saw she didn't understand. He pointed toward the house. "Here we are, looking out through the rain and you're thinking, too bad, no water."

Annie gave him a wry look and took the glass from his hand. "Kind of a forest-and-trees situation, you mean."

He shrugged and smiled and she reached out into the night with the glass. The pricking of the rain on her bare arm was startling, almost painful. The roar of its falling excluded all but the two of them. And while the glass filled they held each other's eyes in a communion of which humor was only the surface. It took less time than it seemed or than either seemed to want.

Annie offered it first to him, but he just shook his head and kept watching her. She watched him back over the rim of the glass as she drank. And the water tasted cool and pure and so purely of nothing that it made her want to cry.

TWENTY-SIX

GRACE COULD TELL SOMETHING WAS GOING ON AS SOON as she climbed into the Chevy beside him. The smile gave it away, like a kid who'd hidden the candy jar. She swung the door shut and Tom pulled away from the back of the creek house and headed down toward the corrals. She'd only just got back from her morning session with Terri in Choteau and was still eating a sandwich.

"What is it?" she said.

"What's what?"

She narrowed her eyes at him but he was all innocence.

"Well, for a start, you're early."

"I am?" He shook his wristwatch. "Darn thing."

She saw it was a lost cause and sat back to finish her sandwich. Tom gave her that funny smile again and kept driving.

The second clue was the rope he picked up from the barn before they went down to Pilgrim's corral. It was much shorter than the one he used as a lasso and of a narrower gauge, plied in an intricate crisscross of purple and green.

"What's that?"

"It's a rope. Pretty, isn't it?"

"I meant, what is it for?"

"Well, Grace, there's no end of things a hand could do with a rope like this."

"Like swing from trees, tie yourself up . . ."

"Yep, that kind of thing."

When they got to the corral Grace leaned on the rail where she usually did and Tom went in with the rope. Away in the far corner, as usual too, Pilgrim started snorting and trotting to and fro as if marking out some futile last resort. His tail, ears and the muscles on his sides seemed wired to a convulsive current. He watched Tom every step of the way.

But Tom didn't look at him. As he walked, he was doing something with the rope, though what, because his back was to her, Grace couldn't tell. Whatever it was, he went on with it after he stopped in the center of the corral and still he didn't look up.

Grace could see Pilgrim was as intrigued as she was. He'd stopped his pacing and now stood watching. And though every so often he tossed his head and pawed the ground, his ears reached out at Tom as if pulled by elastic. Grace moved slowly along the rails to get a better angle on what Tom was doing. She didn't have to go far because Tom turned toward her so that his shoulder masked what he was doing from Pilgrim. But all Grace could see was that he seemed to be tying the rope into a series of knots. Briefly, he looked up and smiled at her from under the brim of his hat.

"Kinda curious, ain't he?"

Grace looked at Pilgrim. He was more than curious. And now that he couldn't see what Tom was doing, he did what Grace had done and took a few small steps to get a better look. Tom heard him and at the same time moved a couple of steps farther away, turning too, so that now he had his back to the horse. Pilgrim stood awhile and looked off to one side, taking stock. Then he looked at Tom again and took a few more tentative steps toward him. And Tom heard him again and moved off so the space between them stayed almost but not quite the same.

Grace could see he'd finished tying the knots, but he went on pulling them and working at them and suddenly she saw what it was he'd made. It was a simple halter. She couldn't believe it.

"Are you going to try and get that on him?"

Tom gave her a grin and said in a stage whisper, "Only if he begs me."

Grace was too involved to know how long it took. Ten, maybe fifteen minutes, but not a lot more. Every time Pilgrim came nearer, Tom would move off, denying him the secret and fueling his desire to know it. And then Tom would stop and with every stop reduce by a fraction the gap between them. By the time they'd twice circled the corral and Tom had worked his way back to the center, they were only some dozen paces apart.

Now Tom turned so that he stood at right angles, still calmly working away at the rope and though once he looked up at Grace and smiled, never did he look at the horse. Thus ignored, Pilgrim blew and looked to one side then the other. Then he took two or three more steps toward Tom. Grace could see he expected the man to move off again but this time he didn't. The change surprised him and he stopped and looked around again to see if anything else in the world, including Grace, could help him make sense of this. Finding no answer, he stepped closer. Then closer still, blowing and craning his nose to get a whiff of whatever danger this man might have up his sleeve and balancing the risk against a now overwhelming need to know what he had in his hands.

At last he was so close that his whiskers almost brushed the brim of Tom's hat and Tom must have felt the snuffling breath on the back of his neck.

Now Tom moved away a couple of steps and though the movement wasn't sudden, Pilgrim jumped like a startled cat and nickered. But he didn't go away. And when he saw Tom was now facing him, he calmed. Now he could see the rope. Tom was holding it in both hands for him to have a good look. But looking wasn't enough, as Grace knew. He'd have to get a smell of it too.

For the first time, Tom was now looking at him and he was saying something too, though what, Grace was too far off to hear. She bit her lip as she watched, willing the horse forward. Go on, he won't hurt you, go on. But he needed no urging other than his own curiosity. Hesitantly, but with a confidence that grew with every step, Pilgrim walked to Tom and put his nose to the rope. And once he'd sniffed the rope, he started sniffing Tom's hands and Tom just stood there and let him.

In that moment, in that quivering touch between horse and man, Grace felt many things connect. She couldn't have explained it, even to herself. She simply knew that some seal had been set on all that had happened in the days just passed. Finding her mother again, riding, the confidence she'd felt at the party, all this Grace hadn't quite dared trust, as though at any second someone might snatch it all away. There was such hope however, such a promise of light in this tentative act of trust by Pilgrim that she felt something shift and open within her and knew that it was permanent.

With what was plainly consent, Tom now slowly moved one hand to the horse's neck. There was a quiver and for a moment Pilgrim seemed to freeze. But it was only caution and when he felt the hand upon him and realized it brought no pain, he eased and let Tom rub him.

It went on a long time. Slowly Tom worked his way up until he'd covered the whole of his neck and Pilgrim let him. And then he let him do the same on the other side and even feel his mane. It was so matted it stood like spikes between Tom's fingers. Then, gently and still without hurry, Tom slipped the halter on. And Pilgrim did not balk nor even for a moment demur.

The only thing that bothered him about showing this to Grace was that she might make too much of it. It was always fragile when a horse took this step and with this horse it was more than fragile. Not the eggshell but the membrane within it. He could read in Pilgrim's eyes and in the quiver of his flanks how close he was to rejecting it. And if he rejected it, the next time—if there was one—would be worse.

For many days Tom had worked for this, in the mornings, without Grace knowing. He did different things when she was watching in the afternoons, mainly flagging and driving and getting the horse used to the feel of a thrown rope. But working toward the halter was something he wanted to do alone. And until this very morning he hadn't known whether it would ever happen, whether the spark of hope he'd told Annie about was truly there. Then he'd seen it and stopped, because he wanted Grace to be there when he blew on it and made it glow.

He didn't have to look at her to know how much it

moved her. What she didn't know, and maybe he should have told her before instead of being such a smartass, was that it wasn't all now going to be sweetness and light. There was work to come that might make Pilgrim seem cloaked yet again in madness. But that could wait. Tom wasn't going to start now. This moment belonged to Grace and he didn't want to spoil it.

So he told her to come in, as he knew she must long to. He watched her prop her cane against the gatepost and come carefully with only the slightest sign of a limp across the corral. When she was nearly up to them, Tom told her to stop. It was better to let the horse come to her than her to him and with barely a nudge on the halter rope he did so.

He could see Grace biting her lip, trying not to tremble as she held her hands out below the horse's nose. There was fear on both sides and it was surely a greeting of a lesser kind than Grace must remember. But in the sniffing of her hands, then later of her face and hair, Tom thought he saw at least a glimpse of what they once had been together and yet might be again.

"Annie this is Lucy. Are you there?"

Annie let the question hang for a while. She was composing an important memo to all her key people on how they should handle interference from Crawford Gates. The basic message was tell him to go fuck himself. She'd switched the answering machine on to give herself peace so that she could find an only slightly more veiled way of saying it.

"Shit. You're probably out chopping off cow's balls or whatever the hell it is they do out there. Listen, I . . . Oh, just call me will you?"

There was a troubled note in her voice that made Annie pick up.

"Cows don't have balls."

"Speak for yourself kiddo. So we were lurking there, were we?"

"Screening, Luce, it's called screening. What's up?"

"He fired me."

"What?"

"The son of a bitch fired me."

Annie had seen it coming for weeks. Lucy was the first person she'd hired, her closest ally. By firing her, Gates was sending the clearest possible signal. Annie listened with a dull sinking in her chest while Lucy told her how it happened.

The pretext had been a piece on women truck drivers. Annie had seen the copy and though predictably preoccupied with sex, it was a lot of fun. The pictures were terrific too. Lucy had wanted a big headline that said simply MOTHERTRUCKERS. Gates had vetoed it, saying Lucy was "obsessed with sleaze." They'd had a stand-up fight in front of the whole office during the course of which Lucy had told Gates bluntly to do what Annie was trying to find a euphemism for in her memo.

"I'm not going to let him do this," Annie said.

"Kiddo, it's done. I'm gone."

"No you're not. He can't do it."

"He can Annie. You know he can and, shit, I'd had enough anyway. It's no fun anymore."

There were a few seconds of silence while they both thought about that. Annie sighed.

"Annie?"

"What?"

"You better get back here, you know? And quick."

*　*　*

Grace came home late, bubbling with all that had happened with Pilgrim. She helped Annie serve supper and told her while they ate how it had felt to touch him again, how he'd trembled. He hadn't let her stroke him as he'd let Tom and she'd felt a little upset at how briefly he tolerated her near him. But Tom said it would come, you just had to take it a step at a time.

"Pilgrim wouldn't look at me. It was weird. Like he was ashamed or something."

"Of what happened?"

"No. I don't know. Maybe just of the way he is."

She told Annie how, later, Tom had led him up to the barn and they'd washed him down. He'd allowed Tom to pick up his feet and clean some of the compacted filth out of them and though he wouldn't let his mane or tail be cleaned, they'd at least managed to get a brush to most of his coat. Grace suddenly stopped and gave Annie a look of concern.

"You okay?"

"I'm fine. Why?"

"I dunno. You looked sort of worried or something."

"Just tired I guess, that's all."

When they were almost through eating, Robert called and Grace went and sat at Annie's desk and told the same story all over again while Annie cleared the dishes.

She stood at the sink washing pans and listening to the frenzied clatter of a bug trapped among corpses he maybe recognized in one of the fluorescent lights. Lucy's call had cast a reflective shadow that even Grace's news had failed fully to dispel.

Her spirits had lifted briefly when she heard the scrunch of the Chevy's wheels outside bringing Grace back from the corrals. She and Tom hadn't spoken since the barn dance though he'd scarcely been out of her thoughts and she'd quickly checked her reflection in the glass door of the oven, thinking, hoping, that he'd come in. But he'd just waved and driven off.

Lucy's call had hauled her back—as in a different way Robert's did now—into what she knew with dulling acknowledgment to be her real life. Though what she meant by "real," Annie no longer knew. Nothing, in a sense, could be more real than the life they'd found here. So what was the difference between these two lives?

One, it seemed to Annie, was comprised of obligations and the other of possibilities. Hence, perhaps, the notion of reality. For obligations were palpable, soundly rooted in reciprocal deeds; possibilities on the other hand were chimeras, flimsy and worthless, dangerous even. And as you grew older and wiser, you realized this and closed them off. It was better that way. Of course it was.

The bug in the light was trying a new tactic, taking long rests then hurling himself at the plastic casing with doubled effort. Grace was telling Robert how, the day after tomorrow, she was going to help drive the cattle up to the summer pastures and how they'd all be sleeping rough. Yes, she said, of course she'd be riding, how else was she supposed to go?

"Dad, you don't have to worry okay? Gonzo's fine."

Annie finished in the kitchen and switched off the lights to give the bug a break. She walked slowly into the living room and stopped to stand behind Grace's chair, idly arranging the girl's hair on the back of her shoulders.

"She's not coming," Grace said. "She says she's got too much work to do. She's right here, do you want to talk to her? Okay. I love you too, Daddy."

She vacated the chair for Annie and went off upstairs

to run a bath. Robert was still in Geneva. He said he would probably be flying back to New York the following Monday. He'd told Annie two nights ago what Freddie Kane had said and now, wearily, she told him about Gates firing Lucy. Robert listened in silence and then asked her what she was going to do about it. Annie sighed.

"I don't know. What do you think I should do?"

There was a pause and Annie sensed he was thinking carefully about what he was about to say.

"Well, from out there, I don't think there's a whole lot you can do."

"You're saying we should come back?"

"No, I'm not saying that."

"With everything going so well with Grace and Pilgrim?"

"No, Annie. I didn't say that."

"That's what it sounded like."

She could hear him inhale deeply and suddenly she felt guilty about twisting his words when she wasn't being honest about her own motives for staying. His voice, when he resumed, was measured.

"I'm sorry if that's how it sounded. It's wonderful about Grace and Pilgrim. It's important you all stay out there as long as you need to."

"More important than my job you mean?"

"Christ, Annie!"

"I'm sorry."

They talked about other, less contentious things and by the time they said good-bye they were friends again, though he didn't tell her he loved her. Annie hung up and sat there. She hadn't meant to attack him like that. It was more that she was punishing herself for her own inability—or reluctance—to sort out the tangle of half-realized desires and denials that churned within her.

Grace had the radio on in the bathroom. An oldies station was doing what they kept calling a Major Monkees Retrospective. They'd just played "Daydream Believer" and now it was "Last Train to Clarksville." Grace must have fallen asleep or have her ears underwater.

Suddenly, and with suicidal clarity, Annie knew what she was going to do. She would tell Gates that if he didn't reinstate Lucy Friedman she would resign. She would fax him the ultimatum tomorrow. If it was still okay with the Bookers, she would, after all, go on the damned cattle drive. And when she came back, she would either have a job or she wouldn't.

TWENTY-SEVEN

THE HERD CURLED UP TOWARD HIM AROUND THE SHOULder of the ridge like a spilling black river in reverse. Here the contours of the land gave all the marshaling required, forcing the cattle upward on a curving trail which, though neither fenced nor marked, was yet their only option. Tom always liked to ride ahead here and stop high on the slope to watch them come.

The other riders were coming now, set strategically above and about the edge of the herd, Joe and Grace to the right, Frank and the twins on the left and appearing now at the rear, Diane and Annie. Beyond them, the plateau they had just crossed was a sea of wildflowers through which their passage had churned a wake of green and at whose distant shore they'd rested under a noon sun and watched the cattle drink.

From where Tom now stood his horse, you could see but the faintest shimmer of the pool and nothing at all of the valley beyond where the land fell away to the meadows and cottonwood creeks of the Double Divide. It was as if the plateau shelved seamless and straight to the vast plains and the eastern rim of the sky.

The calves looked dapper and strong, with a fine luster to their coats. Tom smiled to himself when he thought of the sorry beasts they'd driven that spring some thirty years ago when his father first brought them to live out here. Some had been so scrawny you could almost hear the rattle of their ribs.

Daniel Booker had ranched some serious winters back at Clark's Fork but nothing as harsh as he found on the Front. In that first winter he lost near as many calves as he saved and the cold and the worry etched marks yet deeper in a face already changed forever by the forced sale of his home. But on the ridge where Tom was now, his father had smiled at what he saw about him and known for the first time that his family could survive in this place and even might prosper.

Tom had told Annie about this while they rode across the plateau. During the morning and even when they stopped to eat, there'd been too much going on for them to speak. But now both cattle and riders had the hang of things and there was time. He'd ridden up alongside her and she'd asked him the names of the flowers. He'd shown her blue flax and cinquefoil and balsamroot and the ones they called rooster heads and Annie had listened in that serious way of hers, storing it all away as if one day she might be tested.

It had been one of the warmest springs Tom could remember. The grass was lush and made a wet slicking sound against the legs of their horses. Tom had pointed out the ridge ahead and told her how he'd ridden with his father to its crest that long ago day to see if they were on the right line for the high pastures.

Today Tom was riding one of his young mares, a pretty strawberry roan. Annie rode Rimrock. All day he'd thought how good she looked on him. She and Grace were wearing the hats and boots he'd helped them buy yesterday after Annie said she was coming. At the store they'd laughed side by side at the sight of themselves in the glass. Annie had asked did they get to wear guns too and he said that depended on who she was going to shoot. She said the only candidate was her boss back in New York so maybe a Tomahawk missile might be better.

Their crossing of the plateau was leisurely. But as the cattle reached the foot of the ridge they seemed to sense that from here on it was one long climb and they quickened the pace and called to each other as if to summon some collective effort. Tom had asked Annie to ride ahead with him but she'd smiled and said she'd better drop back to see if Diane needed help. So he'd come up here alone.

Now the herd was almost up to him. He turned his horse and rode over the crest of the ridge. A small crowd of mule deer vaulted away in front of him. At a safe distance they stopped to look back. The does were heavy-bellied with their fawns and assessed him with their great tilted ears before the buck moved them off again. Beyond their bobbing heads, Tom could see the first of the narrow pine-fringed passes that led to the high pastures and, leaning massively above them, the snowpatched peaks of the divide.

He'd wanted to be beside Annie and see her face when this view was revealed to her and he'd felt a loss when she declined and went back to Diane. Maybe she sensed in his offer an intimacy he hadn't meant, or rather one he yearned for but hadn't meant to convey.

By the time they reached it, the pass was already in the shadow of the mountains. And as they moved slowly up between the darkening banks of trees, they looked back and saw the shadow spread east like a stain behind them until only the distant plains retained the sun. Above the trees on either side, sheer gray walls of rock encompassed them, making echoes of the children's calls and the murmur of the cattle.

Frank threw another bough on the fire and its impact sent a volcano of sparks into the night sky. The wood was from a fallen tree they'd found and so dry it seemed to thirst for the flames that beset it, tonguing high into the windless air.

Through the dodging of the flames, Annie watched the glow on the children's faces and noticed how their eyes and teeth flashed when they laughed. They were telling riddles and Grace had them all guessing feverishly at one of Robert's favorites. Grace had her new hat tipped rakishly forward and her hair, cascading from it to her shoulders, trapped the firelight in a spectrum of reds and ambers and golds. Never, Annie thought, had her daughter looked more lovely.

They'd finished eating, a simple meal cooked on the fire, of beans, chops and salty bacon with jacket potatoes baked in the embers. It had tasted wonderful. Now, while Frank saw to the fire, Tom went to get water from the stream across the meadow so they could make coffee. Diane was joining in the riddle game now. Everyone assumed Annie knew the answer and though she'd forgotten it, she was happy to keep quiet, lean back against her saddle and observe.

They'd reached this place just before nine when the last of the sun was fading from the far-off plains. The final pass had been steep, with the mountains tilting over their heads like cathedral walls. At last they'd followed the cattle through an ancient gateway of rock and seen the pasture open up before them.

The grass was thick and dark in the evening light and

because spring, Annie supposed, came later here, there were fewer flowers yet among it. Above, only the highest peak remained and its angle had rolled to give a glimpse of a western slope where a sliver of snow glowed golden pink in the long-gone sun.

The pasture was encircled by forest and on one side, where the ground was slightly raised, stood a small log cabin with a simple pen for the horses. The stream looped in and out of the trees along the other side and it was here first that they'd all gone to let the horses drink beside the jostling cattle. Tom had warned them that it could freeze up here at night and that they should bring warm clothes. But the air had stayed balmy.

"Howya doing there, Annie?" Frank had stacked the fire and was settling himself beside her. She could see Tom materializing from the darkness beyond where now and then the invisible cattle called.

"Frank, apart from my aching butt, I'm doing just great."

He laughed. It wasn't just her butt. Her calves ached too and the insides of her thighs were so sore she winced every time she moved. Grace had lately ridden less even than she had, but when Annie had asked her earlier if she was sore too, she said she was fine and, no, the leg didn't hurt at all. Annie didn't believe a word of it but left it at that.

"Remember those Swiss folk last year Tom?"

Tom was pouring water into the coffeepot. He laughed and said yeah, he did, then set the pot on the fire and sat back beside Diane to listen.

Frank said he and Tom had been driving through the Pryor Mountains and found their road blocked by a herd of cattle. Behind them came these cowboys, all dressed to the nines in fancy new gear.

"One of them had on a pair of hand-tooled chaps

must have set him back a thousand bucks. Funny thing was, they weren't riding, they were all walking, leading their horses behind them and they looked real miserable. Anyway, me and Tom wind down the window and ask is everything okay and they don't understand a word we're saying."

Annie watched Tom across the corner of the fire. He was watching his brother and smiling his easy smile. He seemed to sense her gaze, for his eyes moved from Frank to her and in them there was no surprise, only a calm so knowing it faltered her heart. She held his look for as long as she dared, then smiled and turned again to Frank.

"We don't understand a word they're saying neither, so we just wave and let them go by. Then up the road we find this old guy dozing behind the wheel of a brand-new Winnebago, top of the range. And he lifts his hat and I know the guy. It's Lonnie Harper, has a big spread over that way but never could run it to save his life. Anyway, we say howdy and ask is that his herd back there and he says, yeah, it sure is and the cowboys are from Switzerland, all over here on vacation.

"Said he'd set himself up as a dude ranch and these folks were paying him thousands of bucks to come and do what he used to have to pay hands to do. We said why're they walking? And he laughed and said that was the best part, 'cause after one day they all got too saddle-sore to ride, so there wasn't even no wear on the horses."

"Way to go," Diane said.

"Yep. These poor Swiss fellas get to sleep on the ground and cook their own beans on the fire while he sleeps in the Winnie, watches TV and eats like a king."

When the water boiled, Tom made coffee. The twins

were through with riddles and Craig asked Frank to show Grace his match trick.

"Oh no," Diane groaned. "Here we go."

Frank took two matches from the box he kept in his vest pocket and placed one on the upturned palm of his right hand. Then, with a serious face, he leaned over and rubbed the head of the other match in Grace's hair. She laughed, a little uncertainly.

"You do physics and all that stuff at school Grace, I guess."

"Uh-huh."

"Well then, you'll know about static electricity and all. That's all this really is. I'm just kinda charging up here."

"Oh yeah," Scott said sarcastically. Joe promptly shushed him. Holding the charged match between finger and thumb with his left hand, Frank now drew it slowly up the palm of his right hand so that its head approached the head of the first match. As soon as they touched there was a loud snap and the first match jumped clean off his hand. Grace shrieked in surprise and everyone laughed.

She made him do it again and again and then had a go herself and, of course, it didn't work. Frank shook his head theatrically, as if baffled why it didn't. The kids were loving it. Diane, who must have seen it a hundred times, gave Annie a tired, indulgent smile.

The two women were getting on well, better than ever, Annie believed, though only yesterday she'd been aware of a coolness no doubt caused by Annie changing her mind at the last minute about coming on the cattle drive. Riding together today, they'd talked easily about all sorts of things. But still, somewhere beneath Diane's friendliness, Annie sensed a wariness that was less than dislike yet more than mistrust. More than anything, she noticed the way Diane watched her when she was around Tom. It was this that had led Annie, against all desire, to decline Tom's invitation this afternoon to ride with him to the top of the ridge.

"What d'you reckon Tom?" Frank said. "Try some water?"

"Reckon so, brother." A dutiful conspirator, he passed Frank the can he'd filled from the stream and Frank told Grace to roll up her sleeves and immerse both arms up to the elbows. Grace was giggling so much she poured half of it down her shirt.

"Kind of gets the charge going, you know?"

Ten minutes later, none the wiser and much the wetter, Grace gave up. During that time both Tom and Joe successfully made the match jump and Annie had a go but couldn't make it move. The twins couldn't do it either. Diane confided to Annie that the first time Frank tried it on her, he'd got her sitting fully clothed in a cattle trough.

Then Scott asked Tom to do his rope trick.

"It ain't a trick," Joe said.

"Is too."

"It ain't, is it Tom?"

Tom smiled. "Well, it kind of depends what you mean by trick." He pulled something from the pocket of his jeans. It was a simple piece of gray cord about two feet long. He tied the ends together to make a loop. "Okay," he said. "This one's for Annie." He got up and came toward her.

"Not if it involves pain or death," Annie said.

"Ma'am, you won't feel a thing."

He knelt down beside her and asked her to hold up the first finger of her right hand. She did and he put the loop over it then told her to watch carefully. Holding the other end of the loop taut with his left hand, he drew one side of the cord over the other with the middle finger of his right hand. Then he rolled the hand over so it was under the loop, then back over it again and put the same finger tip to tip with Annie's.

It seemed now that the loop circled their touching fingertips and that it could only be removed if the touch were broken. Tom paused and she looked up at him. He smiled and the nearness of his clear blue eyes almost overwhelmed her. "Look," he said softly. And she looked down again at their touching fingers and gently he pulled the cord and it slipped away and was free, still knotted and without ever breaking their touch.

He showed her a few more times and then Annie tried and Grace tried and the twins tried and none of them could do it. Joe was the only one who could, though Annie could see from his grin that Frank also knew how. Whether Diane knew too it was hard to tell, for all she did was sip her coffee and watch with a sort of half-amused detachment.

When everyone was through trying, Tom stood up and wound the loop around his fingers to make a neat coil of it. He handed it to Annie.

"Is this a gift?" she said as she took it.

"Nope," he said. "Just till you get the hang of it."

She woke and for a moment had no idea what she was looking at. Then she remembered where she was and realized she was staring at the moon. It seemed close enough for her to reach out and place her fingers in its craters. She turned her head and saw Grace's sleeping face beside her. Frank had offered them the cabin, which normally they only used if it was raining. Annie was tempted but Grace had insisted they sleep outside with the others. Annie could see them lying in their sleeping bags beside the dimming glow of the fire.

She felt thirsty and so alert it was hopeless to try again for sleep. She sat up and looked around. She couldn't see the water can and would be sure to wake the others in the search. Across the meadow the black shapes of the cattle cast shadows yet blacker on the pale moonlit grass. She slipped her legs quietly from the sleeping bag and felt again the havoc done to her muscles by the riding. They'd slept in their clothes, only taking off their boots and socks. Annie was wearing jeans and a white T-shirt. She stood up and set off barefoot toward the stream.

The dew-drenched grass felt cool and thrilling on her feet, though she took care where she placed them for fear of stepping in something less romantic. Somewhere high among the trees an owl was calling and she wondered if it was this or the moon or plain habit that had woken her. The cattle lifted their heads to look as she passed among them and she whispered a greeting, then felt foolish for doing so.

The grass on the near bank of the stream was churned by the cattle's hooves. The water moved slow and silent, its glass surface reflecting only the black of the forest beyond. Annie walked upstream and found a place where the flow divided smoothly around an island tree. With two long steps she reached the far side and walked downstream again to a tapered overhang of bank where she could kneel to drink.

Viewed from here, the water now reflected only sky. And so perfect was the moon that Annie hesitated to disturb it. The shock of the water, when at last she did, made her gasp. It was colder than ice, as if it flowed from the ancient glacial heart of the mountain. Annie cupped it in ghost-pale hands and bathed her face. Then she cupped some more and drank.

She saw him first in the water when he loomed across the reflected moon that had so transfixed her gaze she'd lost all sense of time. It didn't startle her. Even before she looked up she knew it was him.

"Are you okay?" he said.

The other bank where he stood was higher and she had to squint up at him against the moon. She could read the concern on his face. She smiled.

"I'm fine."

"I woke up and saw you weren't there."

"I was just thirsty."

"The bacon."

"I suppose."

"Does the water taste as good as that glass of rain the other night?"

"Almost. Try it."

He looked down at the water and saw it would be easier to reach from where she was.

"Mind if I come over? I'm disturbing you."

Annie almost laughed. "Oh no you're not. Be my guest."

He walked to the island tree and crossed and Annie watched and knew that more was being crossed than water. He smiled as he came close and when he reached her he knelt beside her and without a word cupped his hand to the water and drank. Some slipped between his fingers, quickening the moonlight in silver trickles.

It seemed to Annie, and would always seem, that in what followed there was no element of choice. Some things simply were and could not be rendered otherwise. She trembled now at its doing and would tremble later at the thought of it, though never once with regret.

He finished drinking and turned to her and as he was

about to brush the water from his face, she reached out and did it for him. She felt the cold of the water on the back of her fingers and might have taken it as rejection and removed her hand had she not then felt through it the confirming warmth of his flesh. And with this touch, the world went still.

His eyes had only the unifying pale of the moon. Clarified of color, they seemed to have some limitless depth into which she now traveled with wonder but quite without misgiving. He gently raised his hand to the hand she yet held to his cheek. And he took it and turned it and pressed her palm to his lips, as if sealing some long-awaited welcome.

Annie watched him and took a long quiver of breath. Then she reached out with her other hand and ran it across the side of his face, from his harsh unshaven cheek to the softness of his hair. She felt his hand brush the underside of her arm and stroke her face as she had stroked his. At his touch she closed her eyes and blindly let his fingers trace a delicate path from her temples to the corners of her mouth. When his fingers reached her lips she parted them and let him tenderly explore their rim.

She dared not open her eyes for fear she might see in his some reticence or doubt or even pity. But when she looked, she found only calm and certainty and a need as legible as her own. He put his hands to her elbows and smoothed them up inside the sleeves of her T-shirt to hold her upper arms. Annie felt her skin contract. She had both her hands in his hair now and she gently drew his head toward her and felt an equal pressure on her arms.

In the instant before their mouths touched, Annie had a sudden urge to say she was sorry, that he should please forgive her, this wasn't what she'd meant to do.

He must have seen the thought take shape in her eyes, for before she could utter it he shushed her softly with but the smallest moving of his lips.

When they kissed, it seemed to Annie she was coming home. That somehow she had always known the taste and the feel of him. And though she almost quaked at the touch of his body against her, she could not tell at what precise point her own skin ended and his began.

How long they kissed, Tom could only guess from his own changed shadow on her face when they stopped and moved apart a little to look at each other. She gave him a sad smile then looked up at the moon in its new place and trapped pieces of it in her eyes. He could still taste the sweet wetness of her glistening mouth and feel the warmth of her breath on his face. He ran his hands down her bare arms and felt her shiver.

"Are you cold?"

"No."

"I've never known a June night so warm up here."

She looked down then took one of his hands in both of hers and cradled it palm upward in her lap, tracing the calluses with her fingers.

"Your skin's so hard."

"Uh-huh. It's a sorry hand for sure."

"No it's not. Can you feel me touching it?"

"Oh yes."

She didn't look up. Through the dark arch made by her falling hair he saw a tear run on her cheek.

"Annie?"

She shook her head and still didn't look at him. He took hold of her hands.

"Annie, it's okay. Really, it's okay."

"I know it is. It's just that, it's so okay I don't know how to handle it."

"We're just two people, that's all."

She nodded. "Who met too late."

She looked at him at last and smiled and wiped her eyes. Tom smiled back but didn't answer. If what she said was true he didn't want to endorse it. Instead, he told her what his brother had said on a night much the same yet under a thinner moon so many years ago. How Frank had wished that now could last forever and how their father had said forever was but a trail of nows and the best a man could do was live each one fully in its turn.

Her eyes never left him while he spoke and when he'd finished she stayed silent so that suddenly he worried she might have taken his words amiss and seen in them some self-serving incitement. Behind them in the pines, the owl began to call again and was answered now, far across the meadow, by another.

Annie leaned forward and found his mouth again and he felt in her an urgency that wasn't there before. He tasted the salt of her tears in the corner of her lips, that place he'd yearned so long to touch and never dreamed he'd kiss. And as he held her and moved his hands on her and felt the press of her breasts against him, he thought not that this was wrong but only concern that she might come to feel it so. But if this were wrong, then what in the whole of life was right?

At last she broke away and leaned back from him, breathing hard, as if daunted by her own hunger and where it would surely lead.

"I'd better go back," she said.

"You'd better."

She kissed him gently once more, then laid her head on his shoulder so that he couldn't see her face. He brushed his lips on her neck and breathed the warm smell of her as if to store it, perhaps forever.

"Thank you," she whispered.

"What for?"

"For what you've done for all of us."

"I've done nothing."

"Oh Tom, you know what you've done."

She disengaged herself and stood in front of him with her hands resting lightly on his shoulders. She smiled down at him and stroked his hair and he took her hand and kissed it. Then she left him and walked to the island tree and crossed the stream.

Once only did she turn to look at him, though with the moon behind her, what look it was he could but guess. He watched her white shirt go back across the meadow, its shadow trailing footprints in the gray of the dew, while the cattle glided about her, black and silent as ships.

The last glow had gone from the fire by the time she got back. Diane stirred but only in sleep, Annie thought. She quietly slipped her wet feet back into her sleeping bag. The owls soon ceased their calling and the only sound was Frank's soft snoring. Later, when the moon had gone, she heard Tom come back and didn't dare look. She lay for a long time looking at the reasserted stars, thinking of him and what he must be thinking of her. It was that hour when routine doubt would settle heavily upon her and Annie waited to feel shame at what she'd just done. But it never came.

In the morning, when at last she found the courage to look at him, she saw no betraying trace of what had passed between them. No secret glance, and, when he spoke, no layer laced beneath his words for her alone to understand. In fact his manner, like everyone else's, was so seamlessly and happily the same as before that Annie felt almost disappointed, so utter was the change she felt in herself.

As they ate breakfast, she looked across the meadow for the place where they had knelt, but daylight seemed to have altered its geography and she couldn't find it. Even the footprints they'd made had been scuffed by the cattle and soon were lost forever under the morning sun.

After they'd eaten, Tom and Frank went to check the adjoining pastures while the children played over by the stream and Annie and Diane washed up and packed. Diane told her about the surprise she and Frank had lined up for the kids. Next week they were all flying down to L.A.

"You know, Disneyland, Universal Studios, the works."

"That's great. They don't have any idea?"

"Nope. Frank was trying to get Tom to come too, but he's promised to go down to Sheridan to sort some old guy's horse out."

She said it was about the only time of year they could get away. Smoky was going to keep an eye on things for them. Otherwise the place would be empty.

The news came as a shock to Annie and not just because Tom had failed to mention it. Maybe he expected to have finished with Pilgrim by then. More shocking was the message implicit in what Diane had said. In kinder words, she was clearly telling Annie that it was time to take Grace and Pilgrim home. Annie realized how, for so long now, she had deliberately avoided confronting the issue, letting each day pass untallied in the hope that time might return the favor and ignore her too.

By midmorning they were already down below the lowest pass. The sky had clouded over. Without the cattle, their progress was quicker, though in the steeper parts descent was harder than the climb and crueler by far to Annie's battered muscles. There was none of the exhilaration of the day before and in their concentration even the twins grew quiet. As she rode, Annie reflected long on what Diane had told her and longer still on what Tom had said last night. That they were just two people and that now was now and only now.

When they broke the skyline of the ridge up which Tom had wanted her to ride with him, Joe called and pointed and they all stopped to look. Far away to the south, across the plateau, there were horses. Tom told her they were the mustangs set free by the hippie woman, the one Frank called Granola Gay. It was almost the only thing he said to her all day.

It was evening and starting to rain when they reached the Double Divide. They were all too tired to talk as they unsaddled the horses.

Annie and Grace said their good-nights to the Bookers outside the barn and got into the Lariat. Tom said he'd go and check that Pilgrim was okay. His goodnight to Annie seemed no more special than the one he gave to Grace.

On the way up to the creek house, Grace said the sleeve of her prosthetic leg felt tight on her stump and they agreed to have Terri Carlson take a look tomorrow. While Grace went up for the first bath, Annie checked her messages.

The answering machine was full, the fax machine had spewed a whole new roll of paper over the floor and her E-mail was humming. Mostly the messages expressed varying degrees of shock, outrage and commiseration. There were two others and these were the only ones

Annie bothered to read in full, one with relief and the other with a mix of emotion she had yet to name.

The first, from Crawford Gates, said that with the greatest possible regret he must accept her resignation. The second was from Robert. He was flying out to Montana to spend the coming weekend with them. He said he loved them both very much.

FOUR

TOM BOOKER WATCHED THE LARIAT DISAPPEAR OVER THE ridge and wondered, as he had so many times before, about the man Annie and Grace were going to collect. What he knew of him he knew mainly from Grace. As if by some unspoken consent, Annie had talked of her husband only rarely and even then impersonally, more of his job than of his character.

Despite the many good things Grace had told him (or perhaps because of them) and despite his own best efforts to the contrary, Tom could not fully dislodge a predisposed dislike that was not, he knew, in his nature. He'd tried to rationalize it, in the hope of finding some more acceptable reason. The guy, after all, was a lawyer. How many of them had he ever met and liked? But of course, it wasn't that. There was sufficient cause in the simple fact that this particular lawyer was Annie Graves's husband. And in a few short hours he would be here, openly possessing her again. Tom turned and went into the barn.

Pilgrim's bridle hung on the same peg in the tack room where he'd put it the day Annie first brought the horse out here. He took it down and looped it over his shoulder. The English saddle too was on the same rest. There was a thin layer of hay dust on it which Tom wiped away with his hand. He lifted the saddle off with its rug and carried them out and down the avenue of empty stalls to the back door.

Outside the morning was hot and still. Some of the yearlings in the far paddock were already seeking the shade of the cottonwoods. As Tom made his way down toward Pilgrim's corral, he looked at the mountains and knew from their clarity and a first wafting of cloud that later there would be thunder and rain.

All week he had avoided her, shunning the very moments he had always sought, when he might be alone with her. He had learned from Grace that Robert was coming. But even before then, even as they rode down from the mountains, he'd decided this was what he must do. Not an hour had gone by that he hadn't remembered the feel and smell of her, the touch of her skin on his, the way their mouths had melded. The memory was too intense, too physical, for him to have dreamed it, but he would treat it as if he had, for what else could he do? Her husband was coming and soon, in a matter of days now, she would be gone. For both of their sakes, for all of their sakes, it was best that until then he keep his distance and see her only when Grace was there too. Only thus might his resolve endure.

It had been sorely tested the very first evening. When he dropped Grace back at the house, Annie was waiting out on the porch. He waved and would have pulled away but she came toward the car to speak to him while Grace went off inside.

"Diane tells me they're all going to L.A. next week."

"Yes. It's all a big secret."

"And you're off to Wyoming."

"That's right. I promised a while back I'd go visit down there. Friend of mine's got a couple of colts he wants starting."

She nodded and for a moment the only sound was the impatient rumble of the Chevy's engine. They smiled at each other and he felt she was equally unsure of the territory they had stepped into. Tom tried hard to let nothing show in his eyes that might make things difficult for her. In all likelihood she regretted what had happened between them. Maybe one day he would too. The screen door banged and Annie turned.

"Mom? Okay if I call Dad?"

"Sure."

Grace went in again. When Annie turned back to him, he saw in her eyes that there was something she wanted to say. If it was regret, he didn't want to hear it so he spoke to stem it.

"I hear he's coming out this weekend?"

"Yes."

"Grace is like a cat with ten tails, been going on about it all afternoon."

Annie nodded. "She misses him."

"I'll bet. We'll have to see if we can lick old Pilgrim into shape by then. Get Grace up there riding him."

"Are you serious?"

"Don't see why not. We've got some hard work this week but if things work out, I'll give it a go and if he's okay with me, Grace can do it for her daddy."

"Then we can take him home."

"Uh-huh."

"Tom—"

"Of course, you're welcome to stay as long as you like. Just because we're all away, doesn't mean you have to leave."

She smiled bravely. "Thank you."

"I mean, packing up all your computer and fax and all's going to take a week or two." She laughed and he had to look away from her for fear of betraying the ache in his chest at the thought of her leaving. He shoved the car into gear and smiled and bade her good-night.

Since then Tom had done better in avoiding being alone with her. He'd thrown himself into the work with Pilgrim with an energy he hadn't been able to summon since his earliest clinics.

In the mornings he worked him on Rimrock, moving him around and around the corral until he could go from a walk to a lope and back again as smoothly as Tom was sure he once had and until his hind feet fit faultlessly the prints of his fore. In the afternoons Tom went on foot and worked him on a halter. He worked him in circles, stepping in close and turning him, making him roll his hindquarters across.

Sometimes Pilgrim would try and fight it and back away, and when he did this Tom would run with him, keeping in the same position until the horse knew there was no point running because the man would always be there and that maybe after all it was okay to do what was being asked of him. His feet would come still and the two of them would stand there awhile, drenched in their own and each other's sweat and leaning on each other and panting, like a pair of punched-out boxers waiting for the bell.

At first Pilgrim had found his new urgency puzzling, for even Tom had no way of telling him there was a deadline now. Not that Tom could have explained why he should be so determined to make the horse right when in so doing he would deprive himself forever of what he most wanted. But whatever he made of it, Pilgrim seemed to draw on this strange and relentless new vigor and soon he was as much a party to the endeavor as Tom.

And today, at last, Tom would ride him.

Pilgrim watched him shut the gate and walk to the middle of the corral carrying the saddle with the bridle looped over his shoulder.

"That's right old pal, that's what it is. But don't you take my word for it."

Tom laid the saddle down on the grass and stepped away from it. Pilgrim looked off to one side for a moment, pretending it was no big deal and he wasn't interested. But he couldn't stop his eyes from coming back to the saddle and after a while he stepped forward and walked toward it.

Tom watched him come and never moved. The horse stopped about a yard away from where the saddle lay and reached out almost comically with his nose to sniff the air above it.

"What d'you reckon? Gonna bite ya?"

Pilgrim gave him a baleful look then looked back at the saddle. He was still wearing the rope halter Tom had made for him. He pawed the ground a couple of times then stepped in closer and nudged the saddle with his nose. With an easy movement, Tom took the bridle off his shoulder and held it in both hands, sorting it. Pilgrim heard it clink and looked up.

"Don't you go looking all surprised. You saw this coming a hundred miles away."

Tom waited. It was hard to imagine this was the same animal he'd seen in that hellish stall in upstate New York, severed from the world and all that he was. His coat gleamed, his eyes were clear and the way his nose had healed gave him a look that was almost noble, like some battle-scarred Roman. Never, Tom thought, had a horse been so transformed. Nor so many lives around one.

Now Pilgrim came to him, as Tom knew he would, and gave the bridle the same ritual sniffing he'd given the saddle. And when Tom undid the halter and put the bridle on him, not once did he flinch. There was still some tightness and the faintest quivering in his muscles, but he let Tom rub his neck and then move his hand along and rub the place where the saddle would go and neither did he step away nor even toss his head at the feel of the bit in his mouth. However fragile, the confidence and trust Tom had been working for were set.

Tom led him around with the bridle as they'd done so often with the halter, circling the saddle and stopping eventually right by it. Easily, and making sure Pilgrim could see his every move, he lifted it and placed it on the horse's back, soothing him all the while with either hand or word or both. Lightly he fastened the cinch, then walked him to let him know how it felt when he moved.

Pilgrim's ears were working all the time but his eyes showed no white and every now and then he made that soft blowing sound that Joe called "letting the butterflies out." Tom leaned down and tightened the cinch, then laid himself across the saddle and let the horse walk some more to know his weight, all the time soothing him. And when, at last, the horse was ready, he eased his leg over and sat in the saddle.

Pilgrim walked and he walked straight. And though his muscles still trembled to some deep untouchable vestige of fear that perhaps would always be there, he walked bravely and Tom knew that if the horse sensed no mirrored trace of it in Grace, then she might ride him too.

And when she had, there would be no need for her or her mother to stay.

Robert had bought a travel guide to Montana at his favorite bookstore on Broadway and by the time the FASTEN SEAT BELTS sign pinged on and they started their descent into Butte, he probably knew more about the city than most of the thirty-three thousand, three hundred and thirty-six people who lived there.

A few more minutes and there it was below him, "the richest hill on earth," elevation five thousand, seven hundred and fifty-five feet, the nation's largest single source of silver in the 1880s and of copper for another thirty years. The city today, Robert now knew, was a mere skeleton of what it then was, but "had lost nothing of its charm," none of which, however, was immediately apparent from the vantage of Robert's window seat. It looked like someone had stacked luggage on a hillside and forgotten to collect it.

He'd wanted to fly to Great Falls or Helena, but at the last minute something had cropped up at work and he'd had to change his plans. Butte had been the best he could do. But even though it looked on the map a huge distance for Annie to drive, she'd still insisted on coming to meet him.

Robert had no clear picture of how the loss of her job had affected her. The New York papers had slavered over the story all week. GATES GARROTES GRAVES, one of them blazed, while others gave new spin to the old gag, the best of which was GRAVES DIGS ONE FOR HERSELF. It was odd to see Annie cast as victim or martyr, as the more sympathetic pieces had it. It was even odder how nonchalant she had been about it on the phone when she got back from playing cowboy.

"I don't give a damn," she'd said.

"Really?"

"Really. I'm glad to be shut of it. I'll do something new."

Robert wondered for a moment if he'd called the wrong number. Perhaps she was just putting on a brave face. She said she was tired of all the power games and the politics, she wanted to get back to writing, to what she was good at. Grace, she said, thought it was terrific news, the best thing that could have happened. Robert had then asked about the cattle drive and Annie said, simply, that it had been beautiful. Then she'd handed him over to Grace, fresh from her bath, to tell him all about it. They would both be there to meet him at the airport.

There was a small crowd of people waving as he walked across the asphalt, but he couldn't see Annie or Grace among them. Then he looked more closely at the two women in blue jeans and cowboy hats who he'd noticed laughing at him, rather rudely he thought, and saw it was them.

"My God," he said as he came up to them. "It's Pat Garrett and Billy the Kid!"

"Howdy stranger," Grace drawled. "What brings you into town?" She took off her hat and threw her arms around his neck.

"My baby, how are you? How ARE you?"

"I'm good." She clung so tight Robert choked up with emotion.

"You are. I can see. Let me look at you."

He held her away from him and had a sudden memory of that limp, lusterless body he'd sat watching in the hospital. It was hardly credible. Her eyes brimmed with life and the sun had brought out all the freckles on her face. She seemed almost to glow. Annie looked on and smiled, clearly reading his thoughts.

"Notice anything?" Grace said.

"You mean apart from everything?"

She did a little twirl for him and he suddenly got it.

"No cane!"

"No cane."

"You little star."

He gave her a kiss and at the same time reached out for Annie. She too had taken off her hat now. Her tan made her eyes seem clear and so very green. She, too, seemed transformed. More beautiful than he could ever recall. She stepped in close and put her arms around him and kissed him. Robert hugged her till he felt he had control of himself and wouldn't embarrass them all.

"God, it seems a long time," he said at last.

Annie nodded. "I know."

The journey back to the ranch took about three hours. But though she was impatient to show her father around and let him see Pilgrim and introduce him to the Bookers, Grace enjoyed every mile of it. She sat in the back of the Lariat and put her hat on Robert's head. It was too small for him and looked funny, but he left it perched there and soon had them laughing with an account of his connecting flight to Salt Lake City.

Virtually every other seat had been taken by a touring tabernacle choir who had sung the entire way. Robert had sat squeezed between two voluminous women altos with his nose buried in his Montana guidebook while everyone around him boomed "Nearer My God to Thee." Which, at thirty thousand feet of course, they were.

He got Grace to rummage in his bag for the presents he'd bought for them both in Geneva. For her, he'd got a massive box of chocolates and a miniature cuckoo clock with the strangest-looking cuckoo she'd ever laid eyes on. Its call, Robert conceded, was more like a parrot with piles. But it was absolutely authentic, he swore; he knew for a fact Taiwanese cuckoos, especially hemorrhoidal ones, looked and sounded precisely like that. Annie's presents, which Grace also unwrapped, were the usual bottle of her favorite perfume and a silk scarf all three of them knew she'd never wear. Annie said it was lovely and leaned across and kissed him on the cheek.

Looking at her parents, united side by side before her, Grace felt true contentment. It was as though the final pieces of her fractured jigsaw life were falling back in place. The only space that remained was riding Pilgrim. And that, if all had gone well today at the ranch, would soon be filled too. Until they knew for sure, neither she nor Annie was going to mention it to Robert.

It was a prospect that both thrilled and troubled Grace. It wasn't so much that she wanted to ride him again but that she knew she must. Since she'd been riding Gonzo, no one seemed to doubt that she would do so—provided, that is, Tom thought it safe. Only she, secretly, had doubts.

They were not to do with fear, at least not in its simple sense. She worried that when the moment came she might feel fear but was fairly sure that if she did, she would at least be able to control it. She worried more however that she might let Pilgrim down. That she wouldn't be good enough.

Her prosthetic leg was now so tight it gave her constant pain. On the last few miles of the cattle drive it had been almost unbearable. She hadn't told a soul. When Annie noticed how often now she left the leg off when they were alone, Grace had made light of it. It had been harder to pretend to Terri Carlson. Terri could see how inflamed the stump was and told her she urgently needed a new fitting. The trouble was, nobody out west did this type of prosthetic. The only place it could be done was New York.

Grace was determined to hold out. It would only be a week or two at most. She would just have to hope that the pain wouldn't distract her too much and make her less good when the moment came.

It was the cusp of evening when they left Route 15 and headed west. Before them the Rocky Front was stacked high with thunderheads which seemed to reach out over the gathering sky toward them.

They drove through Choteau so that Grace could show Robert the dump they'd first lived in and the dinosaur outside the museum. Somehow he'd come to seem neither as big nor as mean as he had when they arrived. Nowadays Grace almost expected him to wink.

By the time they reached the turn off 89, the sky was vaulted with blackening cloud like a ruined church, through which the sun found fitful access. Cruising out along the straight gravel road to the Double Divide, they all fell silent and Grace began to feel nervous. She wanted so much for her father to be impressed by the place. Perhaps Annie felt the same way, because when they came over the ridge and saw the Double Divide open up before them, she stopped the car to let Robert take in the view.

The dust-cloud they had stirred from the road overtook them and drifted slowly ahead, dispersing gold on a stark burst of sun. Some horses grazing down by the cottonwoods that fringed the nearest bend of the creek raised their heads to watch.

"Wow," Robert said. "Now I know why you guys don't want to come home."

TWENTY-NINE

ANNIE HAD BOUGHT THE FOOD FOR THE WEEKEND ON the way to the airport and should, of course, have done it on the way back. Five hours in a hot car had done the salmon no good at all. The supermarket in Butte was the best she'd found since coming to Montana. They even had sun-dried tomatoes and small pots of rooted basil which had wilted badly on the journey home. Annie had watered them and stood them on the windowsill. They might just survive. Which was more than could be said for the salmon. She took it to the sink and ran it under cold water in the hope of washing away the ammonia smell.

The rush of water drowned the constant low rumble of thunder outside. Annie doused the fish's sides and watched its loosened scales shiver and twirl and disappear with the water. Then she opened its gutted belly and sluiced the blood from its clotted membranous flesh till it glistened a lurid pink. The smell became less pungent, but the feel of the fish's flaccid body in her hands brought such a wave of nausea that she had to leave the fish on the draining board and go quickly through the screen door out onto the porch.

The air was hot and heavy and brought no relief. It was almost dark, though long before it should be. The clouds were a bilious black veined with yellow and so low they seemed to compress the very earth.

Robert and Grace had been gone almost an hour. Annie had wanted to leave it until morning but Grace had insisted. She wanted to introduce Robert to the Bookers and let him see Pilgrim right away. She hardly gave him time to look inside the house before getting him to drive her down to the ranch. She'd wanted Annie to come along too, but Annie said no, she'd get supper and have it ready for when they got back. Tom meeting Robert was something she'd rather not see. She wouldn't know where to look. Even the thought of it now made her nausea worse.

She'd bathed and changed into a dress but already felt sticky again. She stepped out onto the porch and filled her lungs with the useless air. Then she walked slowly around to the front of the house where she could look out for them.

She'd seen Tom and Robert and all the kids piling into the Chevy and watched the car go by below her on its way up to the meadows. The angle was such that she could only see Tom in the driver's seat as they passed. He didn't look up. He was turned talking to Robert who sat beside him. Annie wondered what he made of him. It was as though she herself were being judged by proxy.

All week Tom had avoided her and although she thought she knew why, she felt his distance like a widening space within her. While Grace was in Choteau seeing Terri Carlson, Annie had waited for him to call as he always did to ask her to go riding, knowing in her heart that he wouldn't. When she went with Grace to watch him working with Pilgrim, he was so involved he barely seemed to notice her. Afterward, their conversation had been trivial, polite almost.

She wanted to talk to him, to say she was sorry for what had happened, though she wasn't. At night, alone in her bed, she'd thought of that tender mutual exploring, taking it further in fantasy until her body ached for him. She wanted to say she was sorry simply in case he thought badly of her. But the only chance she'd had was that first evening when he had brought Grace home. And when she'd started to speak he'd cut her off, as if he knew what she was going to say. The look in his eyes as he drove away had almost made her run calling after him.

Annie stood with her arms folded, watching the lightning flicker somewhere above the shrouded mass of the mountains. She could see the headlights of the Chevy now among the trees up by the ford and as they leveled and headed down the track she felt a heavy drop of rain on her shoulder. She looked up and another smacked the center of her forehead and trickled down her face. The air was suddenly cooler and filled with the fresh smell of wet on dust. Annie could see the rain coming down the valley toward her like a wall. She turned and hurried back inside to grill the salmon.

He was a nice guy. What else did Tom expect? He was lively and funny and interesting and, more important, he was interested. Robert leaned forward to squint through the futile arc made by the wipers. They had to shout to make themselves heard through the drumming of the rain on the car's roof.

"If you don't like the weather in Montana, wait five minutes," Robert said. Tom laughed.

"Did Grace tell you that?"

"I read it in my guidebook."

"Dad's the ultimate guidebook nerd," Grace yelled from the back.

"Well thanks sweetie, I love you too."

Tom smiled. "Yep, well. Sure looks like rain."

He'd taken them up pretty well as far as you could comfortably go in a car. They'd seen some deer, a hawk or two and then, high on the far side of the valley, a herd of elk. The calves, some no more than a week old, sheltered beside their mothers from the thunder. Robert had brought along some binoculars and they watched for ten minutes or more, the kids all clamoring for their turn. There was a big bull with a wide six-point sweep of antlers and Tom tried bugling to it but got no reply.

"How much would a bull like that weigh?" Robert asked.

"Oh, seven hundred pounds, maybe a little more. Come August his antlers alone could weigh fifty."

"Ever shoot them?"

"My brother Frank hunts now and then. Me, I'd sooner see their heads moving about up here than hung on some wall."

He asked a whole lot more questions on the way home, Grace teasing him all the while. Tom thought of Annie and all her questions when he'd brought her up here those first few times and he wondered if Robert had gotten the habit from her or she from him or whether they were both like that by nature and just suited each other. That must be it, Tom decided. They just suited each other. He tried to think of something else.

Water was torrenting down the track up to the creek

house. Around the back, the rain was gushing in spouts from every corner of the roof. Tom said he and Joe would bring the Lariat up from the ranch later on. He pulled up as close as he could to the porch so Robert and Grace wouldn't get drenched when they got out. Robert got out first. He shut the door and from the backseat Grace asked Tom in a quick whisper how it had gone with Pilgrim. Though they'd been to see the horse earlier, they'd had no time alone to speak.

"It went good. You'll be okay."

She beamed from ear to ear and Joe gave her a little gleeful punch on the arm. She had no time to ask more because Robert opened the rear door for her to get out.

It should have occurred to Tom that the rain on the dust at the edge of the porch would have made it slippery. But it didn't, until Grace stepped out of the car and her feet went from under her. She gave a little cry as she fell. Tom leapt out and ran around the front of the car.

Robert was bent anxiously over her.

"God, Gracie, are you okay?"

"I'm fine." She was already trying to get up and seemed more embarrassed than hurt. "Dad, really, I'm fine."

Annie came running out and nearly fell herself.

"What happened?"

"It's okay," Robert said. "She just slipped."

Joe was out of the car now too, all concerned. They helped Grace to her feet. She winced as she took her own weight. Robert kept his arm around her shoulders.

"Are you sure you're okay baby?"

"Dad please, don't make a fuss. I'm fine."

She limped but tried to hide it as they took her into the house. Fearing they were missing out on the drama, the twins were about to come inside too. Tom stopped them and with a gentle word sent them back to the car. He could see from Grace's mortified face that it was time to leave.

"See you all in the morning then."

"Okay," Robert said. "Thanks for the tour."

"You're welcome."

He winked at Grace and told her to get a good night's sleep and she smiled bravely and said she would. He steered Joe out through the screen door then turned to say good-night and his eyes met Annie's. The look between them lasted less than a moment but in it was contained all their hearts would utter.

Tom tipped his hat to them and said good-night.

She knew something had broken as soon as she hit the deck of the porch and in a moment of horror thought it was her own thighbone. Only when she stood up was she certain it wasn't. She was shaken and, God, so embarrassed but she wasn't hurt.

It was worse. The sleeve of the prosthetic was cracked from top to bottom.

Grace was sitting on the rim of the bathtub with her blue jeans dropped crumpled around her left ankle and the prosthetic in her hands. The inside of the cracked sleeve was warm and damp and smelled of sweat. Maybe they could glue it or tape it or something. But then she'd have to tell them about it and if it didn't work there was no way they'd let her ride Pilgrim tomorrow.

After the Bookers left, she'd had to put on a major act to make light of the fall. She'd had to smile and joke and tell her mom and dad at least a dozen more times that she was okay. At last they seemed to believe her. When she thought it safe, she'd claimed the first bath and escaped up here to examine the damage behind closed doors. She could feel the damn thing move on her stump as she walked across the living room and getting up the stairs was really tricky. If she couldn't even do that with it, how on earth could she ride Pilgrim? Shit! Falling like that was so dumb. She'd gone and spoiled everything.

She sat and thought for a long time. She could hear Robert downstairs talking excitedly about the elk. He was trying to imitate the call Tom had made. It didn't sound anything like it. She could hear Annie laughing. It was so great to have him here at last. If Grace told them now what had happened it would wreck the whole evening.

She decided what to do. She stood up, maneuvered herself over to the basin and got a box of Band-Aids out of the medicine cabinet. She'd make as good a repair with them as she could and in the morning try riding Gonzo. If it felt okay, she wouldn't tell anyone until she'd ridden Pilgrim.

Annie switched off the bathroom light and walked quietly across the landing to Grace's room. The door was ajar and creaked softly as she opened it wider. The bedside lamp was still on, the one they'd bought together in Great Falls to replace the broken one. The night it broke now seemed to Annie to belong to a different life.

"Gracie?"

There was no answer. Annie went over to the bed and switched off the light. She noted casually that Grace's leg wasn't propped in its usual place against the wall, but lay instead on the floor, tucked in the shadow between bed and table. Grace was asleep, her breathing so soft that Annie had to strain to hear it. Her hair lay swirled like the mouth of a dark river across the pillow. Annie stood for a while, watching her.

She'd been so brave about the fall. Annie knew it must have hurt. Then at supper and all evening she'd been so funny and bright and cheerful. She was an incredible kid. Before dinner, in the kitchen, while Robert was upstairs taking a bath, she'd told Annie what Tom had said about riding Pilgrim. She was buzzing with excitement, had it all worked out how she was going to surprise her dad. Joe was going to take him off to see Bronty's foal and then bring him back at just the right moment to find her on Pilgrim. Annie was not without qualms about it and nor, she guessed, would Robert be. But if Tom thought it safe, it would be.

"He seems like a real nice fellow," Robert had said, helping himself to another piece of salmon, which surprisingly tasted alright.

"He's been very kind to us," Annie said, as blandly as she could. There was a short silence and her words seemed to hang there as if for inspection. Mercifully, Grace started to talk about some of the things she'd seen Tom do this week with Pilgrim.

Annie leaned over now and kissed her daughter softly on the cheek. From some far-off place, Grace murmured a response.

Robert was already in bed. He was naked. As she came in and started to undress, he put down his book and watched her, waiting for her. It was a signal he'd used for years and in the past she'd often enjoyed undressing before him, even been aroused by it. Now though, she found his silent gaze unsettling, almost unbearable. She'd known, of course, he would expect to make love tonight, after so long apart. All evening she had dreaded it.

She took off her dress and laid it on the chair and felt suddenly so acutely aware of his eyes on her and the intensity of the silence that she stepped over to the window and parted the blind to look out.

"The rain's stopped."

"It stopped about half an hour ago."

"Oh."

She looked down toward the ranch house. Though she'd never been in Tom's room, she knew the window and could see the light was on. Oh God, she thought, why can't it be you? Why can't it be us? The thought filled her with a kind of yearning surge so near to desperation that she quickly had to shut the blind and turn away. She hurriedly took off her bra and panties and reached for the big T-shirt she normally wore to sleep in.

"Don't put it on," Robert said softly. She turned to look at him and he smiled. "Come here."

He held out his arms to her and she swallowed and did her best to smile back, praying he couldn't read what she feared was in her eyes. She put the T-shirt down and walked to the bed, feeling shockingly exposed in her nakedness. She sat on the bed beside him and couldn't help the shiver of her skin as he slipped one hand around the back of her neck and the other to her left breast.

"Are you cold?"

"Only a little."

He gently pulled her head down to him and kissed her, in the way he always kissed her. And she tried, with every atom she could muster, to blank her mind of all comparison and lose herself in the familiar contours of his mouth and its familiar taste and smell and the familiar cradling of his hand on her breast.

She closed her eyes but could not subdue the welling

sense of betrayal. She had betrayed this good and loving man not so much by what she'd done with Tom but by what she longed to do. More powerfully however, and even though she told herself how foolish it was, she felt she was betraying Tom by what she was doing now.

Robert opened the sheets and shifted to let her in beside him. She saw the familiar pattern of russet hair on his stomach and the engorged pink sway of his erection. It slid hard against her thigh as she lay herself down beside him and found his mouth again.

"Oh God, Annie, I've missed you."

"I've missed you too."

"Have you?"

"Shh. Of course I have."

She felt the flat of his hand travel down her side and over her hip to her belly and knew he would stroke between her legs and would find how unaroused she was. Just as his fingers reached the rim of her hair, she slipped away a little down the bed.

"Let me do this first," she said. And she eased herself over between his legs and took him in her mouth. It was a long time, years even, since she'd done it and the thrill of it made him take a sudden shuddering breath.

"Oh, Annie. I don't know if I can take this."

"It doesn't matter. I want to."

What wanton liars love makes of us, she thought. What dark and tangled paths it has us tread. And as he came, she knew with a flooding sad certainty that whatever happened they would never be the same again and that this guilty act was secretly her parting gift.

Later, when the light was off, he came inside her. So dark was the night, they could not see each other's eyes. And thus protected, Annie at last was stirred. She turned herself loose to the liquid rhythm of their coupling and found beyond its sorrow some brief oblivion.

THIRTY

Robert drove Grace down to the barn after breakfast. The rain had cleared and cooled the air and the sky was a faultless wide curve of blue. He'd already noticed Grace was quieter this morning, more serious, and he asked her on the way down if she was okay.

"Dad, you've got to stop asking me that. I'm fine. Please."

"I'm sorry."

She smiled and patted his arm and he left it at that. She'd called Joe before they left and by the time they got there he'd already fetched Gonzo from the paddock. He gave them a big grin as they got out of the Lariat.

"Good morning, young man," Robert said.

"Morning Mr. Maclean."

"It's Robert, please."

"Okay sir."

They led Gonzo into the barn. Robert saw that Grace seemed to be walking with more of a limp than yesterday. Once she even seemed to lose her balance and had to reach for the gate of a stall to steady herself. He stood to watch them saddle Gonzo, asking Joe all about him, how old the pony was, how many hands, whether paints had a special kind of temperament. Joe gave full and courteous answers. Grace didn't say a word. Robert could see in the gathering of her brow that something was troubling her. He guessed from Joe's glances at her that he saw it too, though both knew better than to ask.

They led Gonzo out the back of the barn and into the arena. Grace prepared to mount.

"No hat?" Robert asked.

"You mean no hard hat?"

"Well, yes."

"No, Dad. No hat."

Robert shrugged and smiled. "You know best."

Grace narrowed her eyes at him. Joe looked from one of them to the other and grinned. Then Grace gathered the reins and, with Joe's shoulder for support, put her left foot in the stirrup. As she took the weight on her prosthetic leg, something seemed to give and Robert saw her wince.

"Shit," she said.

"What is it?"

"Nothing. It's okay."

With a grunt of effort she swung the leg over the cantle and sat in the saddle. Even before she'd settled he could see something was wrong and then he saw her face screw up and realized she was crying.

"Gracie, what is it?"

She shook her head. He thought at first she was in pain, but when at last she spoke it was clear they were tears of anger.

"It's no damn good." The words were almost spat. "It's not going to work."

*   *   *

It took Robert the rest of the day to get hold of Wendy Auerbach. The clinic had an answering machine with an emergency number which, curiously, seemed permanently busy. Maybe every other prosthetic in New York had cracked in sympathy or through some lurking defect whose time had suddenly come. When at last he got through, a weekend duty nurse said she was sorry but it wasn't clinic policy to give out home numbers. If however it really was as urgent as Robert said, which by her tone she seemed to doubt, she would try to contact Dr. Auerbach on his behalf. An hour later the nurse called back. Dr. Auerbach was out and wouldn't be home till late afternoon.

While they waited, Annie called Terri Carlson, whose number—unlike Wendy Auerbach's—was listed in the phone book. Terri said she knew someone over in Great Falls who might be able to rig up another kind of prosthetic at short notice but she advised against it. Once you'd gotten used to a particular type of leg, she said, changing to another was tricky and could take time.

Although Grace's tears had upset him and he felt for her in her frustration, Robert felt also a secret relief that he was to be spared what, it now emerged, was to have been a surprise staged specially for him. The sight of Grace climbing up on Gonzo had been nerve-racking enough. The thought of her on Pilgrim, whose calmer demeanor he didn't quite trust, was downright scary.

He didn't query it however. The failing, he knew, was his. The only horses he'd ever felt at ease with were those little ones in shopping malls that you slotted coins in to make them rock. Once it was apparent the idea had the backing not just of Annie but more crucially of Tom Booker too, Robert had set about salvaging it as though it had his full support.

By six o'clock they had a plan.

Wendy Auerbach at last called and got Grace to describe precisely where the crack was. She then told Robert that if Grace could get back to New York and come in for a new molding late on Monday, they could do a fitting on Wednesday and have the new prosthetic ready by the weekend.

"Alrighty?"

"Alrighty," Robert said and thanked her.

In family conference in the creek house living room, the three of them decided what they'd do. Annie and Grace would fly back with him to New York and the following weekend they'd fly out here again for Grace to ride Pilgrim. Robert couldn't return with them because he had to go again to Geneva. He tried to look convincingly sad that he'd be missing all the fun.

Annie called the Bookers and got Diane, who'd earlier been so sweet and concerned when she heard what had happened. Of course it would be okay to leave Pilgrim here, she said. Smoky could keep an eye on him. She and Frank were getting back from L.A. on Saturday, though when Tom would be back from Wyoming she wasn't sure. She invited them to join them all that evening for a barbecue. Annie said they'd love to.

Then Robert called the airline. They had a problem. There was only one other seat on the return flight he'd booked himself on from Salt Lake City to New York. He asked them to hold it.

"I'll get a later flight," Annie said.

"Why?" Robert said. "You may as well stay here."

"She can't fly back here on her own."

Grace said, "Why not? Come on Mom, I flew to England on my own when I was ten!"

"No. It's a connection. I'm not having you wandering around an airport on your own."

"Annie," Robert said. "It's Salt Lake City. There are more Christians per square yard than in the Vatican."

"Mom, I'm not a kid."

"You are a kid."

"The airline'll take care of her," Robert said. "Look, if it comes to it, Elsa can fly out with her."

There was a silence, he and Grace both watching Annie, waiting on her decision. There was something new, some indefinable change in her that he'd noticed first on the way back from Butte the previous day. At the airport he'd put it down simply to the way she looked, this new healthy radiance she had. On the journey she'd listened to the banter between him and Grace with a kind of amused serenity. But later, beneath it, he'd thought he glimpsed something more wistful. In bed, what she'd done for him was blissful, yet also somehow shocking. It had seemed to have its source not in desire but in some deeper, more sorrowful intent.

Robert told himself that whatever change there was doubtless stemmed from the trauma and release of losing her job. But now, while he watched her making up her mind, he acknowledged to himself that he found his wife unfathomable.

Annie was looking out of the window at the perfect late spring afternoon. She turned back to them and pulled a comic sad face.

"I'll be here all on my own."

They laughed. Grace put an arm around her.

"Oh poor little Mommy."

Robert smiled at her. "Hey. Give yourself a break. Enjoy it. After a year of Crawford Gates, if anyone deserves some time it's you."

He called the airline to confirm Grace's reservation.

* * *

They built the fire for the barbecue in a sheltered bend of the creek below the ford, where two rough-hewn wooden tables with fixed benches stood the year round, their tops warped and runneled and bleached the palest gray by the elements. Annie had come across them on her morning run from whose tyrannical routine she seemed, with no apparent ill effect, to have all but escaped. Since the cattle drive, she had only run once and even then was shocked to hear herself tell Grace she'd been out jogging. If she was now a jogger, she might as well quit.

The men had gone up earlier to get the fire going. It was too far for Grace to walk with her taped-up leg and resurrected cane, so she went with Joe in the Chevy, ferrying the food and drink. Annie and Diane trailed after on foot with the twins. They walked at a leisurely pace, enjoying the evening sun. The trip to L.A. had just ceased to be a secret and the boys babbled with excitement.

Diane was friendlier than ever. She seemed genuinely pleased that they'd sorted Grace's problem out and wasn't at all spiky, as Annie had feared, about her staying on.

"Tell you the truth, Annie, I'm glad you're going to be around. That young Smoky's okay, but he's only a kid and I'm not too sure how much goes on in that head of his."

They walked on while the twins ran ahead. Only once did their conversation pause, when a pair of swans flew over their heads. They watched the sun on their earnest white necks craning up the valley and listened to the moan of their wings fading on the still of the evening.

As they drew nearer, Annie heard the crackle of firewood and saw a curl of white smoke above the cottonwoods.

The men had built the fire on a close-cropped spit of grass that jutted into the creek. To one side of it, Frank was showing off to the children how he could skim stones and earning only derision. Robert, beer in hand, had been put in charge of the steaks. He was taking the job as seriously as Annie would have predicted, chatting to Tom with one side of his brain while the other monitored the meat. He nagged away at it constantly, readjusting it piece by piece with a long-handled fork. In his plaid shirt and loafers, standing alongside Tom, Annie thought with affection how out of place he looked.

Tom saw the women first. He waved and came over to get them a drink from the cooler. Diane had a beer and Annie a glass of the white wine she'd supplied. She found it hard to look Tom in the eyes as he handed it to her. Their fingers touched briefly on the glass and the sensation made her heart skip.

"Thanks," she said.

"So, you're running the ranch for us next week."

"Oh, absolutely."

"At least there'll be someone here smart enough to use a telephone if something comes up," Diane said.

Tom smiled and looked confidingly at Annie. He wasn't wearing a hat and he pushed back a fall of blond hair from his brow as he spoke.

"Diane reckons poor old Smoke can't count to ten."

Annie smiled. "It's very kind of you. We've way outstayed our welcome."

He didn't answer, just smiled again and this time Annie managed to hold his gaze. She felt that if she let herself, she could dive into the blue of his eyes. At that moment, Craig came running up to say Joe had pushed him into the creek. His pants were soaked up to the knees. Diane yelled for Joe and went off to investigate. Left alone with Tom, Annie felt panic rise within her. There was so much she wanted to say but not a word of it trivial enough for the occasion. She couldn't tell if he shared or even sensed her awkwardness.

"I'm real sorry about Grace," he said.

"Yes, well. We sorted it out. I mean, if it's okay with you, she can ride Pilgrim when you get back from Wyoming."

"Sure."

"Thank you. Robert won't get to see it but, you know, to have got this far and then not—"

"No problem." He paused. "Grace told me about you quitting your job."

"That's one way of putting it."

"She said you weren't too cut up about it."

"No. I feel good about it."

"That's good."

Annie smiled and swallowed some more wine, hoping to diffuse the silence that now fell between them. She glanced toward the fire and Tom followed her look. Left to himself, Robert was giving the meat his undivided attention. It would be done, Annie knew, to perfection.

"He's a top hand with a steak, that husband of yours."

"Oh yes. Yes. He enjoys it."

"He's a great guy."

"Yes. He is."

"I was trying to work out who was the luckier." Annie looked at him. He was still looking at Robert. The sun was full on Tom's face. He looked at her and smiled. "You for having him, or him for having you."

They sat and ate, the children at one table and the adults at the other. The sound of their laughter filled the space among the cottonwoods. The sun went down and between the silhouetted trees Annie watched the molten surface of the creek take on the pinks and reds and golds of the dimming sky. When it was dark enough, they lit candles in tall glass sleeves to shield them from a breeze that never came and watched the perilous fluttering of moths above them.

Grace seemed happy again, now that her hopes of riding Pilgrim were restored. After everyone had finished eating, she told Joe to show Robert the match trick and the children gathered around the adults' table to watch.

When the match jumped the first time, everyone roared. Robert was intrigued. He got Joe to do it again, and then again more slowly. He was sitting across the table from Annie, between Diane and Tom. She watched the candlelight dance on his face while he concentrated, scrutinizing every move of Joe's fingers, searching as he always did for the rational solution. Annie found herself hoping, almost praying, that he wouldn't find it or that if he did, he wouldn't let on.

He had a couple of attempts himself and failed. Joe was giving him the whole spiel about static electricity and was doing it well. He was about to get him to put his hand in water to "boost the charge" when Annie saw Robert smile and knew he had it. Don't spoil it, she said to herself. Please don't spoil it.

"I get it," he said. "You flick it with your nail. Is that right? Here, let me have another go."

He rubbed the match in his hair and drew it slowly up his palm toward the second one. When they touched, the second one jumped away with a crack. The children cheered. Robert grinned, like a boy who'd caught the biggest fish. Joe was trying not to look disappointed.

"Too darn smart these lawyers," Frank said.

"What about Tom's trick!" Grace called. "Mom? Have you still got that piece of string?"

"Of course," Annie said. She'd kept it in her pocket ever since Tom gave it to her. She treasured it. It was the only piece of him she had. Without thinking, she took it out and handed it to Grace. Immediately, she regretted it. She had a sudden, fearful premonition, so strong she almost cried out. She knew that if she let him, Robert would demystify this too. And if he did, something precious beyond all reason would be lost.

Grace handed the cord to Joe who told Robert to hold his finger up. Everyone was watching. Except for Tom. He was sitting back a little, watching Annie over the candle. She knew he could read what she was thinking. Joe now had the cord looped over Robert's finger.

"Don't," Annie said suddenly.

Everyone looked at her, startled to silence by the anxious note in her voice. She felt the heat rising to her cheeks. She smiled desperately, seeking help among the faces in her embarrassment. But the floor was still hers.

"I—I just wanted to figure it out myself first."

Joe hesitated a moment to see if she was serious. Then he lifted the loop from Robert's finger and handed it back to her. Annie thought she saw in the boy's eyes that he, like Tom, understood. It was Frank who came to the rescue.

"Good for you Annie," he said. "Don't you go showing no lawyers till you've got yourself a contract."

Everyone laughed, even Robert. Though when their

eyes met she could see he was puzzled and perhaps even hurt. Later, when the talk had moved safely on, it was only Tom who saw her quietly coil the cord and slip it back into her pocket.

THIRTY-ONE

LATE SUNDAY NIGHT, TOM DID A FINAL CHECK ON THE horses then came inside to pack. Scott was in his pajamas on the landing getting a final warning from Diane who wasn't buying his story that he couldn't sleep. Their flight was at seven in the morning and the boys had been put to bed hours ago.

"If you don't cut it out, you don't come, okay?"

"You'd leave me here on my own?"

"You betcha."

"You wouldn't do that."

"Try me."

Tom came up the stairs and saw the jumble of clothes and half-filled suitcases. He winked at Diane and steered Scott off to the twins' room without a word. Craig was already asleep and Tom sat on Scott's bed and they whispered about Disneyland and which order they'd do the rides until the boy's eyelids grew heavy and he slept.

On his way to his own room, Tom walked past Frank and Diane's and she saw him and thanked him and said good-night. Tom packed all he needed for the week, which wasn't much, then tried to read for a while. But he couldn't concentrate.

While he was out with the horses, he'd seen Annie arrive back in the Lariat from taking her husband and Grace to the airport. He walked to the window now and looked up toward the creek house. The yellow blinds of her bedroom were lit and he waited a few moments, hoping he'd see her shadow cross, but it didn't.

He washed, undressed and got into bed and tried reading again with no greater success. He turned off the light and lay on his back with his hands tucked behind his head, picturing her up there in the house all alone, as she would be all week.

He'd have to leave for Sheridan around nine and would go up and say good-bye before he left. He sighed and turned over and forced himself at last into a sleep that brought no peace.

Annie woke around five and lay for a while watching the luminescent yellow of the blinds. The house contained a silence so delicate she felt it might shatter with but the slightest shift of her body. She must then have dozed off, for she woke again at the distant sound of a car and knew it must be the Bookers leaving for their flight. She wondered if he'd got up with them to see them off. He must have. She got out of bed and opened the blinds. But the car had gone and there was no one outside the ranch house.

She went downstairs in her T-shirt and made herself a coffee. She stood cradling the cup in her hands by the living room window. There was mist along the creek and in the hollows of the valley's far slope beyond. Maybe he was already out with the horses, checking them one more time before he went. She could go for a run and just happen to find him. But then what if he came here to say good-bye, as he'd said he would, when she was out?

She went upstairs and ran herself a bath. Without Grace, the house seemed so empty and its silence oppressive. She found some bearable music on Grace's little radio and lay in the hot water without much hope that it might calm her.

An hour later she was dressed. She'd taken much of that time deciding what to wear, trying one thing then another and in the end getting so cross with herself for being such an idiot that she punished herself by pulling on the same old jeans and T-shirt. What the hell did it matter, for Christsakes? He was only coming to say good-bye.

At last, at the twentieth time of looking, she saw him come out of the house and throw his bag into the back of the Chevy. When he stopped at the fork, she thought for an anguished moment that he was going to turn the other way and head off up the drive. But he nosed the car toward the creek house instead. Annie went into the kitchen. He should find her busy, getting on with her life, as if his going was really no big deal. She looked around in alarm. There was nothing to do. She'd done it all already, emptied the dishwasher, cleared the garbage, even (heaven help her) put sparkle on the sink, all to pass the time till he came. She decided to make some more coffee. She heard the scrunch of the Chevy's tires outside and looked up to see him swing the car in a circle so it was pointing ready to leave. He saw her and waved.

He took his hat off and gave a little knock on the frame of the screen door as he came in.

"Hi."

"Hi."

He stood there turning the brim of his hat in his hands.

"Grace and Robert get their flight okay?"

"Oh yes. Thanks. I heard Frank and Diane go."

"Did you?"

"Yes."

For a long moment the only sound was the drip of the coffee coming through. They could neither talk nor even look each other in the eye. Annie stood leaning against the sink trying to look relaxed as she dug her fingernails into her palms.

"Would you like a coffee?"

"Oh. Thanks, but I better be going."

"Okay."

"Well." He pulled a small piece of paper out of his shirt pocket and stepped closer to hand it to her. "It's the number I'll be at down in Sheridan. Just in case there's a problem or something, you know."

She took it. "Okay, thanks. When will you be back?"

"Oh, sometime Saturday I guess. Smoky'll be by tomorrow, see to the horses and all. I told him you'd be feeding the dogs. Feel free to ride Rimrock anytime."

"Thanks. I might." They looked at each other and she gave him a little smile and he nodded.

"Okay," he said. He turned and opened the screen door and she followed him out onto the porch. She felt as if there were hands on her heart, slowly twisting the life from it. He put his hat on.

"Well, bye Annie."

"Bye."

She stood on the porch and watched him get back in the car. He started the engine, tipped his hat to her and pulled away down the track.

* * *

He drove for four and a half hours but he measured it not by time but only by how each mile seemed to make the ache deepen in his chest. Just west of Billings, lost in thoughts of her, he almost drove into the back of a cattle truck. He decided to take the next exit and go the slower route to the south, through Lovell.

It took him near Clark's Fork, through land he'd known as a boy, though there was little now to know it by. Every trace of the old ranch was gone. The oil company had long taken what it wanted and pulled out, selling off the land in plots too small for a man to make a living. He drove past the remote little cemetery where his grandparents and great-grandparents were buried. On another day he would have bought flowers and stopped, but not today. Only the mountains seemed to offer some slim hope of comfort and south of Bridger he turned left toward them and headed up on roads of red dirt into the Pryor.

The ache in his chest only got worse. He lowered the window and felt the blast of the hot sage-scented air on his face. He cussed himself for a lovelorn schoolboy. He would find somewhere to stop and get himself back together.

They'd built a fancy new viewing place above the Bighorn Canyon since he was last there, with a big parking lot and maps and signs that told you about the geology and all. He supposed it was a good thing. Two carloads of Japanese tourists were having their pictures taken and a young couple asked him to take one for them so they could both be in it. He did and they smiled and thanked him four times and then everyone piled back into their cars and left him alone with the canyon. He leaned on the metal rail and looked down a thousand feet of yellow and pink striated limestone to the snaking, garish green water below.

Why hadn't he just taken her in his arms? He could tell she wanted him to, so why hadn't he? Since when had he been so goddamn proper about these things? He'd conducted this area of his life till now with the simple notion that if a man and a woman felt the same way about each other they should act on it. Okay, so she was married. But that hadn't always stopped him in the past, unless the husband was either a friend or potentially homicidal. So what was it? He searched for an answer and found none, except that there was no precedent to judge it by.

Below him, maybe five hundred feet below, he saw the spanned black backs of birds he couldn't name, soaring against the green of the river. And, quite suddenly, he identified what it was he felt. It was need. The need that Rachel, so many years ago, had felt for him and that he'd found himself unable to return, nor felt for any being or thing before or since. Here at last he knew. He had been whole and now he was not. It was as if the touch of Annie's lips that night had stolen away some vital part of him that only now he saw was missing.

It was for the best, Annie thought. She was grateful— or at least believed she would be—that he had been stronger than she was.

After Tom left, she had been firm with herself, setting herself all sorts of resolutions for the day and the days to come. She would make good use of them. She would call friends to whose faxed condolences she hadn't yet responded; she would call her lawyer about the tedious details of her severance and she would tidy all the other loose ends she'd left hanging last week. Then she would enjoy her isolation; she would walk, she would ride, she would read; she might even write something, though what she had no idea. And by the time Grace came back, her head, and possibly her heart, would be level.

It wasn't quite that easy. After the early high cloud had burned away, the day was another perfect one, clear and warm. But though she tried to be part of it, performing every task she set herself, she could not shift the listless hollow inside her.

At around seven, she poured herself a glass of wine and stood it on the side of the tub while she bathed and washed her hair. She'd found some Mozart on Grace's radio and though it crackled, it helped to banish a little of the loneliness that had crept upon her. To cheer herself further, she put on her favorite dress, the black one with the little pink flowers.

As the sun went behind the mountains she got into the Lariat and drove down to feed the dogs. They came bounding from nowhere to meet her and escorted her like a best friend into the barn where their food was kept.

Just as she finished filling their bowls, she heard a car and thought it odd that the dogs paid it no attention. She put the bowls down before them and went to the door.

She saw him but a moment before he saw her.

He was standing in front of the Chevy. Its door hung open and its headlights behind him shone lambent in the dusk. As she stopped in the doorway of the barn, he turned and saw her. He took off his hat, though he didn't twist it nervously in his hands as he had this morning. His face was grave. They stood quite still, perhaps five yards apart, and for a long moment neither of them spoke.

"I thought . . ." He swallowed. "I just thought I'd come back."

Annie nodded. "Yes." Her voice was fainter than air.

She wanted to go to him but found she couldn't move and he knew it and put his hat on the hood of the car and came toward her. Watching him draw near, she feared that all that was welling within her would engulf and sweep her quite away before he got to her. Lest it did, she reached out like a drowning soul to grasp him and he stepped into the circle of her arms and circled her in his and held her and she was saved.

The wave broke over her, convulsing her with sobs that shook her very bones as she clung to him. He felt her quake and held her more tightly to him, burrowing his face to find hers, feeling the tears that streamed on her cheek and smoothing, soothing them with his lips. And when she felt the quaking subside, she slid her face through the pressing wetness and found his mouth.

He kissed her as he'd kissed her on the mountain, but with an urgency from which neither of them now would turn back. He held her face in his hands that he might kiss her more deeply and she moved her hands down his back and took hold of him below his arms and felt how hard his body was and so lean that she could lay her fingers in the grooved caging of his ribs. Then he held her in the same way and she trembled at the touch.

They leaned apart to catch their breath and look at one another.

"I can't believe you're here," she said.

"I can't believe I ever went."

He took her by the hand and led her past the Chevy, with its door still open and its lights now finding purchase in the fading light. The sky above them domed a deepening orange till it met the black of the mountains in a roar of carmine and vermilion cloud. Annie waited on the porch while he unlocked the door.

He didn't turn on any lights but led her through the shadows of the living room where their footsteps creaked and echoed on the wooden floor and penumbral sepia faces watched their passage from the pictures on the walls.

She had a longing for him so powerful that as they climbed the wide staircase it felt almost like sickness. They reached the landing and walked hand in hand past the open doors of rooms strewn like an abandoned ship with discarded clothes and toys. The door of his room was also open and he stood aside for her to go in then followed her and closed the door.

She saw how wide and bare the room was, not how she'd imagined it those many nights she'd seen the light at his window. Through that same window now, she could see the creek house, shaped black against the sky. The room was filled with a waning glow that turned all it touched to coral and gray.

He reached out and drew her to him to kiss her again. Then, without a word, he started to undo the long line of buttons at the front of her dress. She watched him do it, watched his fingers and then his face, the little concentrating frown. He looked up and saw her watching but didn't smile, just held her look as he undid the last button. The dress fell open and when he slid his hands inside it and touched her skin, she gasped and shivered. He held her by her sides as before and bent his head and gently kissed the tops of her breasts above her bra.

And Annie leaned back her head and closed her eyes and thought, there is nothing but this. No other time, nor place nor being than now and here and him and us. And no earthly point in calculating consequence or permanence or right or wrong, for all, all else, was as nothing to the act. It had to be and would be and was.

Tom led her to the bed and they stood beside it while she stepped from her shoes and started to unbutton his shirt. Now it was his turn to watch and he did so as if from some reaching crest of wonder.

Never before had he made love in this room. Nor never, since Rachel, in a place that he could call his home. He had gone to women's beds but never let them come to his. He had casualized sex, kept it distant that he might keep himself free and protect himself from the kind of need he'd seen in Rachel and which now he felt for Annie. Her presence, in the sanctum of this room, thus took on a significance that was both daunting and wondrous.

The light from the window set aglow her glimpsing skin where her dress fell open. She undid his belt and the top of his jeans and pulled his shirt clear so she could roll it off his shoulders.

In the momentary blindness as he pulled off his T-shirt, he felt her hands on his chest. He lowered his head and kissed again between her breasts and breathed the smell of her deep into his lungs as if he would drown in it. He eased the dress gently from her shoulders.

"Oh Annie."

She parted her lips but said nothing, just held his gaze and reached behind her back and unhooked her bra. It was plain and white and edged above with simple lace. She lifted the straps from her shoulders and let it fall away. Her body was beautiful. Her skin pale, except at the neck and arms where the sun had turned it a freckled gold. Her breasts were fuller than he'd thought they'd be, though still firm, her nipples large and set high. He put his hands to them and then his face and felt the nipples gather and stiffen at the brush of his lips. Her hands were at the zipper of his jeans.

"Please," she breathed.

He pulled the faded quilt from the bed and opened the sheets and she laid herself down and watched him take off his boots and socks and then his jeans and shorts. And he felt no shame nor saw any in her, for why should they feel shame at what was not of their making but of some deeper force that stirred not just their bodies but their souls and knew naught of shame nor of any such construct?

He knelt on the bed beside her and she reached out and took his erection in her hands. She bent her head and brushed her lips around the rim of it so exquisitely that he shuddered and had to close his eyes to find some lower, more tolerable key.

Her eyes, when he ventured to look at her again, were dark and glazed with the same desire he knew glazed his own. She let go of him and lay back and lifted her hips for him to take off her panties. They were of a pale, functional gray cotton. He ran his hand over the soft bulge within them then pulled them gently down.

The triangle of revealed hair was deep and thick and of the darkest amber. Its curling tips trapped the last glimmer of the light. Just above it ran the paled scar of a caesarean. The sight of it moved him, though he knew not why, and he lowered his head and traced its length with his lips. The brush of her hair on his face and the warm, sweet smell he found there moved him more powerfully and he lifted his head and leaned back on his heels that he might catch his breath and see her more fully.

They surveyed each other now in their nakedness, letting their eyes roam and feed with an incredulous, suspended, mutual hunger. The air was filled with the urgent synchrony of their breathing and the room seemed to swell and fold to its rhythm like an enclosing lung.

"I want you inside me," she whispered.

"I don't have anything to—"

"It doesn't matter. It's safe. Just come inside me."

With a little frown of need, she reached for the tilt of him again and as she closed her fingers on it, he felt she had possession of the very root of his being. He came forward again on his knees, letting her steer him in toward her.

As he saw Annie open herself before him and felt the soft collision of their flesh, Tom saw suddenly again in his mind those birds, wide-winged and black and nameless, soaring below him against the green of the river. He felt he was returning from some distant land of exile and that here, and only here, he could be whole again.

It seemed to Annie, when he entered her, that he dislodged in her loins some hot and vivid surge that swept slowly the entire length of her body to lap and furrow around her brain. She felt the swell of him within her, felt the gliding fusion of their two halves. She felt the caress of his hard hands on her breasts and opened her eyes to see him bend his head to kiss them. She felt the travel of his tongue, felt him take her nipple in his teeth.

His skin was pale, though not as pale as hers, and on his rib-furrowed chest the cruciform of hair was darker than the sunbleach of his head. There was a kind of supple angularity to him, born of his work, which somehow she had expected. He moved on her with that same centered confidence she'd seen in him all along; only now, focused exclusively on her, in this new domain, it was both more overt and intense. She wondered how this body that she'd never seen, this flesh, these parts of him she'd never touched, could yet feel so known and fit her so well.

His mouth delved the open hollow of her arm. She felt his tongue slick the hair that since coming here she'd let grow long and soft again. She turned her head and saw the framed photographs on top of the chest of drawers. And for a fleeting moment, the sight of them threatened to connect her to another world, a place which she was in the act of altering and which she knew she would find sullied with guilt if she were to let herself but look. Not now, not yet, she told herself and she lifted his head between her hands and quested blindly for the oblivion of his mouth.

When their mouths parted, he leaned back and looked down at her and for the first time smiled, moving on her to the slow rasp of their coupled selves.

"You remember that first day we rode?" she said.

"Every moment."

"That pair of golden eagles? Do you remember?"

"Yes."

"That's what we are. Now. That's what we are."

He nodded. Their eyes locked into each other, unsmiling now, in a growing preoccupied urgency, until at last she saw the flicker in his face and felt him quiver and then the spurt and flood of him within her. And she arched herself into him and at the same time felt in her loins a shocking, protracted imploding of flesh that rushed to her core then jolted and spread in waves to the furthest corners of her being, bearing him there with it, until he filled every place within her and they were one and indistinguishable.

THIRTY-TWO

HE WOKE WITH THE DAWN AND FELT AT ONCE THE SLEEP-
ing warmth of her beside him. She lay along his body,
nestled in the shelter of his arm. He could feel her
breath on his skin and the soft rise and fall of her
breasts against him. Her right leg was tucked over his.
He could feel the gentle prickle of her belly on his thigh.
The palm of her right hand lay on his chest above his
heart.

It was that clarifying hour when normally men left
and women wanted them to stay. He'd known it many
times himself, the urge to slip away like a thief with the
dawn. It seemed prompted not so much by guilt as by
fear, fear that the comfort or companionship that
women seemed often to want, after a night spent more
carnally, was somehow too committing. Maybe there
was some primordial force at work. You sowed your
seed and got the hell out.

If so, this morning, Tom felt not a trace of it.

He lay quite still so as not to wake her. And it occurred to him that maybe he was afraid to. Never in the
night, not once in the long hours of their tireless hun-

ger, had she shown any sign of regret. But he knew that with the dawn would come, if not regret, some colder new perspective. And so he lay in the unfolding light and treasured the slack and guiltless warmth of her beneath his arm.

He slept again and woke the second time to the sound of a car. Annie had turned over and he lay now with his front molded to the contours of her back, his face tucked into the scented nape of her neck. As he eased himself away from her, she murmured though didn't wake and he slipped from the bed and silently gathered his clothes.

It was Smoky. He'd pulled up beside their two cars and was inspecting Tom's hat, which had stood all night on the hood of the Chevy. The worry on his face changed to a grin of relief when he heard the clack of the screen door and saw Tom heading out toward him.

"Hiya, Smoke."

"Thought you was upped and gone down to Sheridan."

"Yeah. There was a change of plan. Sorry, I meant to call you." He'd called the man with the colts from a gas station in Lovell to say sorry he couldn't make it, but had clean forgotten about Smoky.

Smoky handed him his hat. It was damp from the dew.

"Thought for a minute there you'd been kidnapped by aliens or somethin'." He looked at Annie's car. Tom could see he was trying to figure things out.

"Annie and Grace didn't go back east then?"

"Well, Grace did, but her mother couldn't get a flight. She's staying over till the weekend when Grace gets back."

"Right." Smoky nodded slowly but Tom could see he wasn't altogether sure what was going on. Tom glanced at the Chevy's open door and remembered the lights must have been on all night too.

"Had some trouble last night with the battery here," he said. "Maybe you could help me give it a jump?"

It didn't explain a whole lot but it did the trick, for the prospect of a task seemed to drive all lingering doubt from Smoky's face.

"Sure," he said. "I got some leads in the truck."

Annie opened her eyes and took only a moment to remember where she was. She turned over, expecting to see him and felt a small leap of panic on finding herself alone. Then she heard voices and the slam of a car door outside and felt a larger leap. She sat up and swung her legs out from the tangle of sheets. She stood and walked to the window and, as she did so, had to stem the moist run of him between her legs. She felt a bruised aching there that was also somehow delicious.

Through a narrow gap in the drapes she saw Smoky's truck pulling away from the barn and Tom waving after him. Then he turned and headed back to the house. She knew he wouldn't see her if he looked up and, watching him, she wondered how the night might have changed them both. What now might he think of her, having seen her so wanton and shameless? What now did she think of him?

He squinted up at the sky where already the clouds were burning off. The dogs came bounding around his legs and he ruffled their heads and spoke to them as he walked and Annie knew that, for her at least, nothing had changed.

She showered in his little bathroom, waiting to be seized by guilt or remorse, but neither came, only trepidation at what he might be feeling. She found the sight of his few simple toilet things beside the basin oddly touching. She used his toothbrush. There was a big blue toweling bathrobe slung by the door and she put it on, wrapping herself in the smell of him, and went back into his room.

He'd opened the drapes and was looking out of the window when she came in. He heard her and turned and she recalled him doing the same that day in Choteau when he'd come to the house to give her his verdict on Pilgrim. There were two cups steaming on the table beside him. She could see the apprehension in his smile.

"I made some coffee."

"Thanks."

She went over and took the cup, casing it in her hands. Alone together in the big empty room, they seemed suddenly formal, like strangers arrived too early at a party. He nodded at the robe.

"It suits you." She smiled and sipped the coffee. It was black and strong and very hot. "There's a better bathroom along the way there if you—"

"Yours is just fine."

"That was Smoky dropped by. I forgot to call him."

There was silence. Somewhere down by the creek a horse whinnied. He looked so worried, she was suddenly afraid he was going to say sorry, it was all a mistake and could they just forget it ever happened.

"Annie?"

"What?"

He swallowed. "I just wanted to say, that whatever you feel, whatever you think or want to do, it's okay."

"And what do you feel?"

He said simply, "That I love you." Then he smiled and gave a little shrug that almost broke her heart. "That's all."

She put her cup down on the table and went to him and they clung to each other as if the world were already bent on their division. She covered his lowered face with kisses.

They had four days before Grace and the Bookers returned, four days and four nights. One protracted moment along the trail of nows. And that was all she would live and breathe and think of, Annie resolved, nothing beyond nor nothing past. And whatever came to pass, whatever brutal reckonings were forced upon them, this moment would be there, indelibly written in their heads and hearts forever.

They made love again while the sun eased over the corner of the house and angled knowingly in upon them. And afterward, cradled in his arms, she told him what she wanted. That the two of them should ride again to the high pastures where first they had kissed and where now they might be alone together, with nothing but the mountains and the sky to judge them.

They forded the creek a little before noon.

While Tom had saddled the horses and loaded a packhorse with all they might need, Annie had driven back up to the creek house to change and get her things. They would both bring food. Though she didn't say and he didn't ask, he knew she would also have called her husband in New York to lay some pretext for her coming absence. He'd done the same with Smoky, who was getting a little dazed with all these changes of plan.

"Going up to check on the cattle, huh?"

"Yes."

"On your own or . . . ?"

"No, Annie's coming too."

"Oh. Right." There was a pause and Tom could hear two and two coalescing in Smoky's mind.

"I'd appreciate it, Smoke, if you kept it to yourself."

"Oh sure, Tom. You bet."

He said he'd drop by as previously planned to see to the horses. Tom knew he could be trusted on both issues.

Before leaving, Tom went down to the corrals and put Pilgrim into the field with some of the younger horses he'd started to get along with. Normally Pilgrim would go running off with them right away, but today he stood by the gate and watched Tom walk back to where he'd left the saddled horses.

Tom was going to ride the same mare he'd taken on the cattle drive, the strawberry roan. As he rode up toward the creek house, leading Rimrock and the little paint packhorse behind him, he looked back and noticed Pilgrim was still standing alone by the gate, watching him go. It was almost as if the horse knew something in their lives had changed.

Tom waited with the horses on the track below the creek house and watched Annie come in long strides down the slope toward him.

The grass in the meadow beyond the ford had grown lush and long. Soon the contractors would be here for haymaking. It slushed against the legs of the horses as Tom and Annie rode through it side by side, with no other sound but the rhythmic creak of their saddles.

For a long time neither of them seemed to feel the need to talk. She asked no questions now about the land through which they passed. And it seemed to Tom that this was not because at last she knew the names of things, but rather that their names no longer mattered. It only mattered that they were.

They stopped in the heat of the midafternoon and

watered the horses at the same pool as before. They ate a simple meal she had brought, of crusted bread and cheese and oranges. She peeled hers deftly in one unbroken curl and laughed when he tried to do the same and failed.

They crossed the plateau where the flowers had begun to fade and this time rode together to the crest of the ridge beyond. They startled no deer but saw instead, maybe a half-mile on toward the mountains, a small band of mustangs. Tom signed to Annie to stop. They were downwind and the mustangs hadn't yet sensed them. It was a family band of seven mares, five of them with foals. There were also a couple of colts, too young yet to have been driven away. The band stallion Tom had never seen before.

"What a beautiful animal," Annie said.

"Yeah."

He was magnificent. Deep-chested and strong in the quarters, he weighed maybe more than a thousand pounds. His coat was a perfect white. The reason he hadn't yet seen Tom and Annie was that he was too busy seeing off a more pressing intruder. A young stallion, a bay, was making a bid for the mares.

"Things get kind of heated this time of year," Tom said quietly. "It's the mating season and this young fella thinks it's time he had a go. He'll have been trailing this band for days, probably with a few other young studs." Tom craned in the saddle to peer around. "Yep, there they are." He pointed them out to Annie. There were nine or ten of them another half-mile or so to the south.

"That's what they call a bachelor band. They spend their time hanging out, you know, getting drunk, bragging to each other, carving their names on trees, till they're big enough to go steal some other guy's mares."

"Oh. I see." Her tone made him realize what he'd

said. She was giving him a look but he didn't return it. He knew exactly what the corners of her mouth would be doing and the knowing of it pleased him.

"That's right." He kept his eyes firmly on the mustangs.

The two stallions were standing nose to nose, while the mares and foals and the challenger's distant friends looked on. Then suddenly both stallions exploded, tossing their heads and squealing. This was when the weaker one would normally concede. But the bay didn't. He reared up and screamed and the white stallion reared too, but higher, and thrashed at him with his hooves. Even from here you could see the white of their bared teeth and hear the thwack as their kicks struck home. Then, within moments, it was over and the bay scuttled off defeated. The white stallion watched him go. Then, with a glance at Tom and Annie, he ushered his family away.

Tom felt her eyes on him again. He shrugged and gave her a grin.

"You win some, you lose some."

"Will the other one be back?"

"Oh yes. He's gonna have to spend some more time at the gym, but he'll be back."

They built a fire by the stream, just next to the place where they had kissed. They buried potatoes as before in its embers and while these cooked, they made a bed, laying their bedrolls side by side with the saddles for a headboard then zipping their two single sleeping bags together. An inquisitive huddle of heifers stood with lowered heads on the other bank to watch.

When the potatoes were done, they ate them with sausage fried in an old iron pan and some eggs Annie thought would never survive the journey. They mopped the dark yolks from their plates with the rest of the bread. The sky had clouded over. They washed their plates in the moonless stream and laid them on the grass to dry. Then they took off their clothes and, with the flicker of the fire on their skin, made love.

There was a gravity to their union which seemed to Annie somehow to befit the place. It was as though they'd come to dignify the promise here witnessed.

Later, Tom sat propped against his saddle and she lay folded in his arms with her back and head against his chest. The air had grown much colder. Somewhere high on the mountain above them there was the yip and wail of what he told her were coyotes. He draped a blanket over his shoulders and drew it around them, cocooning her against the night and all encroachment. Nothing, Annie thought, nothing in that other world can touch us here.

For many hours, staring into the fire, they talked about their lives. She told him about her father and all the exotic places where they'd lived before he died. She told him about meeting Robert and how he'd seemed so clever and dependable, so grown up and yet so sensitive. And he was still all of those things, a fine, fine man. Their marriage had been good, still was, in many ways. But looking back now, she realized that what she'd wanted from him was actually what she'd lost in her father: stability, security and unquestioning love. These Robert had given her spontaneously and without condition. What she had given him in return was loyalty.

"I don't mean by that I don't love him," she said. "I do. I really do. It's just that it's a love that feels more like, I don't know. Like gratitude or something."

"For his loving you."

"Yes. And Grace. It sounds awful doesn't it?"

"No."

She asked him if it was like that with Rachel and he said no, it was different. And Annie listened in silence while he told her the story. She conjured life in her mind from the photograph she'd seen in Tom's room, the beautiful face with its dark eyes and glossy tumble of hair. The smile was hard to reconcile with the sorrow Tom now spoke of.

It was not the woman but the child in her arms that had moved Annie most. It gave her a pang of what, at the time, she refused to acknowledge as jealousy. It was the same feeling she'd had when she saw Tom's and Rachel's initials in the concrete of the well. Oddly, the other photograph, of the grown Hal, gave full mitigation. Though he was dark like his mother, his eyes were Tom's. Even frozen in time, they disarmed all animosity.

"Do you ever see her?" Annie asked when he'd finished.

"Not for some years. We talk on the phone now and then, about Hal mostly."

"I saw the picture in your room. He's beautiful."

She could hear Tom smile behind her head. "Yeah, he is." There was a silence. A branch, white-crusted with ash, collapsed in the fire, hoisting a flurry of orange sparks into the night.

He asked, "Did you want more children?"

"Oh yes. We tried. But I could never hold on to them. In the end we just, gave up. More than anything, I wanted it for Grace. A brother or a sister for Grace."

They fell silent again and Annie knew, or thought she knew, what he was thinking. But it was a thought too sorrowful, even on this outside rim of world, for either one of them to utter.

The coyotes kept up their chorus all night. They mated for life, he told her, and were so devoted that if ever one were caught in a trap, the other would bring it food.

For two days they rode the bluffs and gullies of the high front. Sometimes they would leave the horses and go on foot. They saw elk and bear and once Tom thought he saw, watching from a high crag, a wolf. It turned and went before he could be sure and he didn't mention it to Annie in case it worried her.

They came across hidden valleys filled with beargrass and glacier lily and waded up to their knees through meadows turned to lakes of brilliant blue with lupine.

The first night it rained and he pitched the little tent he'd brought in a flat green field, strewn all about with the bleached poles of fallen aspen. They got soaked to the skin and sat huddled together, shivering and laughing in the mouth of the tent with blankets over their shoulders. They sipped scalding coffee from blackened tin mugs while outside the horses grazed unbothered, the rain sleeking off their backs. Annie watched them, her wet face and neck lit from below by the oil lamp and he thought he'd never seen, nor ever would he see, any living creature so beautiful.

That night, while she slept in his arms, he lay listening to the drumming of the rain on the tent roof and tried to do what she'd told him they must, not to think beyond the moment, just to live it. But he couldn't.

The following day was clear and hot. They found a pool, fed by a narrow twist of waterfall. Annie said she wanted to swim and he laughed and said he was too old and the water way too cold. But she wouldn't take no for an answer, so under the dubious gaze of the horses, they stripped and leapt in. The water was so icy it made them shriek and they had to scramble right out and stood hugging each other, bare-assed and blue, jabbering like a couple of loopy kids.

That night the sky shimmered green and blue and red with aurora borealis. Annie had never seen it before and he had never seen it so clear and so bright. It rippled and spread in a vast luminous arch, trailing folded striations of color in its wake. He saw its crenelate reflection in her eyes as they made love.

It was the last night of their blinkered idyll, though neither gave it name, other than by the plangent joining of their bodies. By tacit compact forged only of their flesh, they took no rest. There was to be no squandering in sleep. They fed upon each other like creatures foretold of some dreadful, limitless winter. And they only ceased when the bruising of their bones and the raw traction of their coupled skin made them cry out in pain. The sound floated through the luminous stillness of the night, through shadowed pine and on and up until it reached the listening peaks beyond.

Some time after that while Annie slept, he heard, like some distant echo, a high primeval call which made every creature of the night fall silent. And Tom knew he'd been right and that it was a wolf he'd seen.

THIRTY-THREE

SHE PEELED THE ONIONS THEN CUT THEM IN HALF AND finely sliced them, breathing through her mouth so the fumes wouldn't make her cry. She could feel his eyes upon her every move and she found it curiously empowering, as if his watching somehow invested her with skills she'd never thought to possess. She'd felt it too when they made love. Maybe (she smiled at the thought), maybe that was how horses felt in his presence.

He was leaning back against the divider on the far side of the room. He hadn't touched the glass of wine she'd poured him. In the living room, the music she'd found on Grace's radio had given way to a learned discussion about some composer she'd never heard of. All these people on public radio seemed to have the same cream-calm voices.

"What are you looking at?" she said gently.

He shrugged. "You. Does it bother you?"

"I like it. It makes me feel I know what I'm doing."

"You cook fine."

"I can't cook to save my life."

"That's okay, you can cook to save mine."

She had been worried when they got back to the ranch this afternoon that reality would come crashing in around their ears. But, strangely, it hadn't. She felt clothed in a kind of inviolable calm. While he'd seen to the horses, she'd checked her messages and found none among them to disturb her. The most important was from Robert, giving Grace's flight numbers and arrival time in Great Falls tomorrow. It had all gone alrighty, he said, with Wendy Auerbach—in fact Grace was so alrighty about her new leg, she was thinking of putting in for the marathon.

Annie's calm had even survived when she called and spoke to them both. The message she'd left on Tuesday, that she was going to spend a couple of days up at the Bookers' mountain cabin, seemed to have stirred not the smallest ripple. Throughout their marriage she had often taken time on her own somewhere and Robert presumably now saw this as part of the process of getting her head back together after losing her job. He simply asked how it had been and, simply, she replied that it had been lovely. Except by omission, she didn't even have to lie.

"It worries me, all this back-to-nature, big-outdoors stuff you're getting into," he joked.

"Why's that?"

"Well, soon you'll be wanting to move out there and I'll have to switch to livestock litigation or something."

When they hung up Annie wondered why the sound of his voice or of Grace's hadn't plunged her into the sea of guilt she surely knew awaited her. It just hadn't. It was as though that susceptible part of her nature were in suspense, with its eye on the clock and mindful that she had owing yet some few, fleeting hours with Tom.

She was cooking him the pasta dish she'd wanted to make that evening they'd all come for supper. The little pots of basil she'd bought in Butte were flourishing. As she chopped the leaves, he came up behind her and rested his hands lightly on her hips and kissed the side of her neck. The touch of his lips made her catch her breath.

"It smells good," he said.

"What, me or the basil?"

"Both."

"You know, in ancient times they used basil to embalm the dead."

"Mummies you mean?"

"Daddies too. It prevents mortification of the flesh."

"I thought that was about banishing lust."

"It does that too, so don't eat too much."

She tipped it into the pan where the onions and tomatoes were already cooking, then swiveled slowly in his hands to face him. Her forehead was against his lips and he kissed her there gently. She looked down and slotted her thumbs into the front pockets of his jeans. And in the sharing quiet of that moment, Annie knew she could not leave this man.

"Oh Tom. I love you so much."

"I love you too."

They lit the candles she'd bought for the supper party and turned off the fluorescents so they could eat at the little table in the kitchen. The pasta was perfect. When they were through eating, he asked her if she'd figured out the string trick. She said according to Joe it wasn't a trick but in any case, no, she hadn't.

"Do you still have it?"

"What do you think?"

She pulled it from her pocket and gave it to him and he told her to hold up her finger and watch closely because he was only going to show her once. She did and followed every intricate maneuver of his hand until the loop circled and seemed trapped by their touching fingers. Then, as he slowly pulled the loop, the moment before it came free, she suddenly saw how it was done.

"Let me try," she said. She found she could picture exactly the movements his hands had made and translate them in mirror image to her own. And sure enough, when she pulled, the cord came free.

He sat back in his chair and gave her a smile that was both loving and sad.

"There you are," he said. "Now you know."

"Do I get to keep the cord?"

"You don't need it anymore." And he took it and put it in his pocket.

Everyone was there and Grace wished they weren't. Such though had been the buildup to this moment, that a full turnout was only to be expected. She looked at the waiting faces along the rail of the big arena: her mom, Frank and Diane, Joe, the twins in their matching Universal Studios caps, even Smoky had come by. And what if it all went wrong? It wouldn't, she told herself firmly. She wasn't going to let it.

Pilgrim stood saddled in the middle of the arena while Tom adjusted the stirrups. The horse looked beautiful, though Grace still couldn't get used to the sight of him in a western saddle. Since riding Gonzo she'd come to prefer it to her old English one. It made her feel more secure, so that's what they were going to use today.

Earlier, she and Tom had managed to weed out the last tangles from his mane and tail and they'd brushed him till he shone. Scars aside, she thought, he looked

like a show horse. He'd always had a sense of occasion.
It was almost a year to the day, she recalled, that she'd
seen the first photograph of him, the one they'd sent up
from Kentucky.

They had all just watched Tom ride him gently
around the arena a few times. Grace had stood beside
her mother and tried with deep breathing to subdue her
fluttering stomach.

"What if it's only Tom he'll let ride him?" she hissed.

Annie gave her a hug. "Honey, Tom wouldn't let you
if it wasn't safe, you know that."

It was true. But it didn't make her any less nervous.

Tom had left Pilgrim alone and was now heading
over to them. She stepped forward. The new leg felt
good.

"All set?" he said. She swallowed and nodded. She
wasn't sure she could trust her voice. He saw the worry
in her face and when he got to her he said, so no one
else could hear, "You know, Grace, we don't have to do
this now. Tell you the truth, I didn't know there was
going to be this kind of circus."

"It's okay. I don't mind."

"Sure?"

"Sure."

He put his arm around her shoulders and they
walked out to where Pilgrim stood waiting. She saw
him prick up his ears as they came.

Annie's heart was thumping so loud she thought Diane, next to her, must be able to hear. It was hard to
know how many of its beats were for Grace and how
many for herself. For what was going on across the
strip of red sand was too momentous. It was both a
beginning and an end, though of what and for whom,

Annie had no clear perception. It was as though everything were swirling in some vast, climactic centrifuge of
emotion and only when it stopped would she see what
it had done to them all and what was then to become of
them.

"She's one brave kid, that daughter of yours," Diane
said.

"I know."

Tom had Grace stop a short distance from where Pilgrim was standing, so as not to crowd him. He went the
final few paces alone, stopped beside him then reached
gently to take hold of him. He held him by the bridle
and put his head beside Pilgrim's while he soothed the
horse's neck with the flat of his other hand. Pilgrim
never took his eyes off Grace.

Even from a distance, Annie could tell something was
wrong.

When Tom tried to ease him forward, he resisted,
lifting his head and looking down at Grace so that you
could see white at the top of his eye. Tom turned him
away and walked him in circles, as she'd seen him do
on a halter, bending him, making him yield to pressure
and roll his hindquarters across. This seemed to calm
him. But as soon as Tom led him back toward Grace, he
became edgy again.

Grace was facing the other way, so Annie couldn't
see her face. But she didn't need to. She could feel from
here the worry and hurt that had surely taken hold of
the girl.

"I don't know if this is a good idea," Diane said.

"He'll be alright." Annie said it too quickly. It
sounded harsh.

"I reckon," said Smoky. But even he didn't seem too
sure.

Tom took Pilgrim away and did some more circles

and when that didn't work either, he climbed up on him and took him a few times around the arena at a lope. Grace turned slowly, following them with her eyes. She looked briefly at Annie and they swapped a smile neither could make convincing.

Tom didn't speak or concern himself with anyone but Pilgrim. He was frowning and Annie couldn't tell if it was only in concentration or if there was worry there too, though he never showed worry, she knew, when he was with horses.

He dismounted and led Pilgrim again toward Grace. And again the horse balked. This time Grace turned on her heel and almost fell. As she walked back across the sand, her mouth quivered and Annie could see she was fighting tears.

"Smoke?" Tom called. Smoky climbed over the rail and went to him.

Frank said, "He'll be okay, Grace. Just you hang on there a minute or two. Tom'll get him okay, you'll see."

Grace nodded and tried to smile but couldn't look at him or anyone else, least of all Annie. Annie wanted to hug her but held off. She knew Grace wouldn't be able to take it and the tears would come and then she'd be embarrassed and angry at both of them. Instead, when the girl came near enough, Annie said quietly, "Frank's right. It'll be okay."

"He saw I was scared," Grace said under her breath.

Out in the arena, Tom and Smoky were huddled, having some urgent, hushed discussion none but Pilgrim could hear. After a while, Smoky turned and jogged over to the gate at the end of the arena. He climbed over it and disappeared into the barn. Tom left Pilgrim where he was and came over to where everyone was waiting.

"Okay Gracie," he said. "We're going to do something now that I'd kind of hoped we wouldn't have to. But there's still something going on inside him that I can't reach in any other way. So me and Smoke here, we're going to try laying him down. Okay?"

Grace nodded. Annie could see the girl had no clearer idea of what this meant than she had herself.

"What does it involve?" Annie asked. He looked at her and she had a sudden vivid image of their joined bodies.

"Well, it's more or less how it sounds. Only I have to tell you that it's not always pretty to watch. Sometimes a horse'll fight it real hard. That's why I don't like doing it unless I have to. This fella's already shown us he likes a good fight. So if you'd sooner not watch, I suggest you go inside and we'll call you when we're done."

Grace shook her head. "No. I want to watch."

Smoky came back into the ring with the things Tom had sent him to get. They'd had to do this a few months back at a clinic down in New Mexico, so Smoky pretty much knew the score. Quietly though, away from all those watching, Tom took him through the process again so there wouldn't be any mistakes and nobody would get hurt.

Smoky listened gravely, nodding now and again. When Tom saw he had it straight in his head, the two of them went over toward Pilgrim. He'd moved away to the far side of the arena and you could tell by the way he worked his ears that he sensed something was about to happen and that it might not be fun. He let Tom come to him and rub his neck but didn't take his eyes off Smoky who stood a few yards off with all those ropes and things in his hand.

Tom unhitched the bridle and in its place slipped on

the rope halter Smoky handed him. Then, one at a time, Smoky passed him the ends of two long ropes that were coiled over his arm. Tom fastened one under the halter and the other to the horn of the saddle.

He worked calmly, giving Pilgrim no cause for fear. The subterfuge made him feel bad, knowing what was to come and how the trust he'd built with the horse would now have to be broken before it could be restored. Maybe he'd got it wrong just now, he thought. Maybe what had happened between him and Annie had affected him in some way that Pilgrim sensed. Most likely all the horse had sensed was Grace's fear. But you could never be quite sure, even he, what else was going on in their minds. Maybe from somewhere deep inside him, Tom was telling the horse he didn't want it to work, for when it worked that was the end and Annie would be gone.

He asked Smoky for the hobble. It was made out of an old strip of sacking and rope. Smoothing his hand down Pilgrim's left foreleg, he lifted the hoof. The horse only shifted slightly. Tom soothed him all the time with his hand and his voice. Then, when the horse was still, he slipped the sling of sacking over the hoof and made sure it was snug. The other end was rope and with it he hoisted the weight of the raised hoof and made it fast to the horn of the saddle. Pilgrim was now a three-legged animal. An explosion waiting to happen.

It happened, as he knew it would, as soon as Tom moved away and took one of the lines, the halter one, from Smoky. Pilgrim tried to move and found himself crippled. He lurched and hopped on his right foreleg and the feeling scared him so badly that he jolted and hopped again and scared himself even worse.

If he couldn't walk, then maybe he could run, so now he tried and his eyes filled with panic at the feel of it.

Tom and Smoky braced themselves and leaned back on their lines, forcing him around them in a circle maybe fifteen feet in radius. And around and around he went, like a crazed rocking horse with a broken leg.

Tom glanced at the faces that watched from the rail. He could see Grace had grown pale and that Annie was now holding her, and he cussed himself for giving them the choice and not insisting they go inside and save themselves the pain of this sorry sight.

Annie had her hands on Grace's shoulders and the knuckles had gone white. Every muscle in their two bodies was clenched and jerked at each agonized hop that Pilgrim made.

"Why's he doing this!" Grace cried.

"I don't know."

"It'll be okay Grace," Frank said. "I saw him do this one time before." Annie looked at him and tried to smile. His face belied the comfort of his words. Joe and the twins looked almost as worried as Grace.

Diane said quietly, "Maybe you'd better take her inside."

"No," Grace said. "I want to watch."

By now Pilgrim was covered in sweat. But still he kept going. As he ran, his hobbled foot jabbed the air like a wild, deformed flipper. His jolting gait sent up a burst of red sand at every step and it hung over the three of them like a fine red mist.

It seemed to Annie so wrong, so out of character, for Tom to be doing this. She had seen him be firm with horses before but never causing pain or suffering. Everything he'd done with Pilgrim had been designed to build up trust and confidence. And now he was hurting him. She just couldn't understand.

At last the horse stopped. And as soon as he did Tom nodded to Smoky and they let the two lines go slack. Then off he went again and they tightened the lines and kept the pressure on until he stopped. They gave him slack again. The horse stood there, his wet sides heaving. He was panting like some desperate asthmatic smoker and the sound was so rasping and terrible that Annie wanted to block her ears.

Now Tom was saying something to Smoky. Smoky nodded and handed him his line then went to get the coiled lasso he'd left lying on the sand. He swung a wide loop in the air and at the second attempt got it to fall over the horn of Pilgrim's saddle. He pulled it tight then took the other end to the far side of the arena and tied it in a quick-release to the bottom rail. He came back and took the other two lines from Tom.

Now Tom went to the rail and started putting pressure on the lasso line. Pilgrim felt it and braced himself. The pressure was downward and the horn of the saddle tilted.

"What's he doing?" Grace's voice was small and fearful.

Frank said, "He's trying to get him to go down on his knees."

Pilgrim fought long and hard and when at last he did kneel, it was only for a moment. He then seemed to summon some last surge of effort and stood again. Three times more he went down and got up again, like some reluctant convert. But the pressure Tom was putting on the saddle was too strong and relentless and finally the horse crashed down on his knees and stayed down.

Annie could feel the relief in Grace's shoulders. But it wasn't over. Tom kept the pressure on. He yelled to

Smoky now to drop the other lines and come and help him. And together they hauled on the lasso line.

"Why don't they let him be!" Grace said. "Haven't they hurt him enough?"

"He's got to lie down," Frank said.

Pilgrim snorted like a wounded bull. There was foam spewing at his mouth. His flanks were filthy where the sand had stuck to his sweat. Again he fought for a long time. But again it was too much. And at last, slowly, he keeled over on his side and lay his head on the sand and was still.

It seemed to Annie a total, humiliating surrender.

She could feel Grace's body start to shake with sobs. She felt tears well in her own eyes and was powerless to stop them. Grace turned and buried her face in Annie's chest.

"Grace!" It was Tom.

Annie looked up and saw he was standing with Smoky by Pilgrim's prone body. They looked like two hunters at the carcass of a kill.

"Grace?" he called again. "Will you come here please?"

"No! I won't!"

He left Smoky and headed toward them. His face was grim, almost unrecognizable, as though he were possessed by some dark or vengeful force. She kept her arms around Grace to shelter her. Tom stopped in front of them.

"Grace? I'd like you to come with me."

"No, I don't want to."

"You've got to."

"No, you'll only hurt him some more."

"He's not hurt. He's okay."

"Oh sure!"

Annie wanted to intervene, to protect her. But so

daunting was Tom's intensity that instead she let him take her daughter from her hands. He gripped the child by her shoulders and made her look at him.

"You've got to do this Grace. Trust me."

"Do what?"

"Come with me and I'll show you."

Reluctantly, she let him lead her across the arena. Driven by the same protective urge, Annie climbed unbidden over the rail and followed. She stopped a few yards short, but near enough in case she was needed. Smoky tried a smile but saw right away it was inappropriate. Tom looked at her.

"It'll be okay Annie." She barely nodded.

"Okay Grace," Tom said. "I want you to stroke him. I want you to start with his hindquarters and rub him and move his legs and feel him all over."

"What's the point? He's good as dead."

"Just do as I say."

Grace walked hesitantly to the horse's rear. Pilgrim didn't lift his head from the sand but Annie could see his one eye try to follow her.

"Okay. Now stroke him. Go on. Start with his leg there. Go on. Waggle it around. That's it."

Grace cried out, "His body feels all dead and limp! What have you done to him?"

Annie had a sudden vision of Grace in her coma in the hospital.

"He'll be okay. Now put your hand on his hip and rub him. Do it Grace. Good."

Pilgrim didn't move. Gradually Grace worked her way along him, smearing the dust on his heaving, sweaty sides, working his limbs to Tom's instruction. At last she rubbed his neck and the wet, silky side of his head.

"Okay. Now I want you to stand on him."

"What!" Grace looked at him as if he were mad.

"I want you to stand on him."

"No way."

"Grace . . ."

Annie took a step forward. "Tom . . ."

"Be quiet Annie." He didn't even look at her. And now he almost shouted, "Do as I say Grace. Stand on him. Now!"

It was impossible to disobey. Grace started to cry. He took her hand and led her into the curve of Pilgrim's belly.

"Now step up. Go on, step up on him."

And she did. And with the tears streaming on her face, she stood frail, like a maimed soul, on the beaten flank of the creature she loved most in all the world and sobbed at her own brutality.

Tom turned and saw Annie was crying too but he paid no attention and turned back to Grace and told her she could now get down.

"Why are you doing this?" Annie begged. "It's so cruel and humiliating."

"No, you're wrong." He was helping Grace to get down and didn't look at Annie.

"What?" Annie said scornfully.

"You're wrong. It's not cruel. He had the choice."

"What are you talking about?"

He turned and looked at her at last. Grace was still crying beside him, but he paid her no heed. Even in her tears, the poor girl seemed as unable as Annie to believe Tom could be like this, so hard and pitiless.

"He had the choice to go on fighting life or to accept it."

"He had no choice."

"He did. It was hard as hell, but he could have gone on. Gone on making himself more and more unhappy.

But what he chose to do instead was to go to the brink and look beyond. And he saw what was there and he chose to accept it."

He turned to Grace and put his hands on her shoulders. "What just happened to him, laying down like that, was the worst thing he could imagine. And you know what? He found out it was okay. Even you standing on him was okay. He saw you meant him no harm. The darkest hour comes before the dawn. That was Pilgrim's darkest hour and he survived it. Do you understand?"

Grace was wiping her tears and trying to make sense of it. "I don't know," she said. "I think so."

Tom turned and looked at Annie and she saw something soft and imploring in his eyes now, something at last that she knew and could latch on to.

"Annie? Do you understand? It's real, real important you understand this. Sometimes what seems like surrender isn't surrender at all. It's about what's going on in our hearts. About seeing clearly the way life is and accepting it and being true to it, whatever the pain, because the pain of not being true to it is far, far greater. Annie, I know you understand this."

She nodded and wiped her eyes and tried to smile. She knew there was some other message here, one that was only for her. It was not about Pilgrim but about them and what was happening between them. But although she pretended to, she didn't understand it and could only hope that the time would come when she might.

Grace watched them undo Pilgrim's hobble and the ropes tied to his halter and saddle. He lay there a moment, looking up at them with one eye, not moving his head. Then, a little uncertainly, he staggered to his feet. He shrugged and whinnied and blew and then took a few steps to see he was all in one piece.

Tom told Grace to lead him to the tank at the side of the arena and she stood beside him while he took a good long drink. When he'd finished he lifted his head and yawned and everyone laughed.

"There go the butterflies!" Joe called.

Then Tom put the bridle back on and told Grace to put her foot in the stirrup. Pilgrim stood still as a house. Tom took her weight on his shoulder and she swung her leg and sat in the saddle.

She felt no fear. She walked him first one way around the arena then the other. Then she took him up to a lope and it was fine and collected and smooth as silk.

It was a while before she realized everyone was cheering, just like they had the day she rode Gonzo.

But this was Pilgrim. Her Pilgrim. He'd come through. And she could feel him beneath her, like he always used to be, giving and trusting and true.

THIRTY-FOUR

THE PARTY WAS FRANK'S IDEA. HE SAID HE HAD IT from the horse's mouth: Pilgrim had told him he wanted a party so a party there would be. He phoned Hank and Hank said he was up for it. What's more, he said, he had a houseful of bored cousins up from Helena and they were up for it too. By the time they'd called everyone they could think of, it had gone from being a small party to a midsize party to a big one and Diane was having fifty fits wondering how she was going to feed them all.

"Hell, Diane," Frank said. "We can't let Annie and Grace drive two thousand miles home with that old horse of theirs without giving them a good send-off."

Diane shrugged and Tom could see her thinking why the hell not?

"And dancing," Frank said. "We gotta have dancing."

"Dancing? Oh come on!"

Frank asked Tom what he thought and Tom said he thought dancing would be fine. So Frank called Hank again and Hank said he'd bring his sound system over and they could have the colored lights too if they wanted. He was there within the hour and the men and the kids rigged it all up outside the barn while Diane, shamed at last to better humor, drove Annie down to Great Falls to get the food.

By seven, everything was ready and they all went off to clean up and change.

As he came out of the shower, Tom caught sight of the blue robe by the door and felt a dull lurching inside him. He thought the robe might still smell of her but when he pressed it to his face it smelled of nothing.

He hadn't had a chance to be alone with Annie since Grace came back and he felt their separation like some cruel physical excision. The sight of her tears for Pilgrim had made him want to run to her and hold her. Not being able to touch her was almost more than he could bear.

He dressed slowly and lingered in his room, listening to the cars arriving and the laughter and the music starting up. When he looked out he saw there was already a crowd. It was a fine clear evening. The lights were finding a glow in the fading light. Clouds of smoke drifted slowly from the barbecue where he should be helping Frank. He searched the faces and found her. She was talking with Hank. She was wearing a dress he hadn't seen before, dark blue and sleeveless. As he watched, she threw her head back and laughed at something Hank said. Tom thought how beautiful she was. He'd never felt less like laughing in his life.

She saw him as soon as he stepped out onto the porch. Hank's wife was going in with a tray of glasses and he held the screen door for her and laughed at something she said as she passed. Then he looked out and found her eyes at once and smiled. She realized that Hank had just asked her a question.

"Sorry Hank, what was that?"

"I said, I hear you're headin' home?"

"Yes, afraid so. Packing up tomorrow."

"Can't tempt you city gals to stay, huh?"

Annie laughed, a little too loudly, as she'd been doing all evening. She told herself again to calm down. Across the crowd, she saw Tom had been hijacked by Smoky who wanted to introduce him to some friends.

"Jeez, that food smells good," Hank said. "How 'bout it, Annie, shall we get us some? You jus' come along with me."

She let herself be led, as if she had no will of her own. Hank got her a plate and piled it high with chunks of blackened meat, then flooded it with a dollop of chili beans. Annie felt sick but kept on smiling. She'd already decided what to do.

She would get Tom on his own—ask him to dance if that's what it took—and tell him she was going to leave Robert. She would go back to New York next week and break the news. First to Robert and then to Grace.

Oh God, Tom thought, it's going to be like last time. The dancing had been going on for over half an hour and every time he tried to get near her either she got waylaid or he did. Just when he thought he was clear, he felt a tap on his shoulder. It was Diane.

"Don't sister-in-laws get to dance?"

"Diane, I thought you'd never ask."

"I knew you never would."

He took hold of her and his heart sank a little when the new number turned out to be a slow one. She had on the new red dress she'd bought in L.A. and had tried painting her lips to match but it didn't quite work. She smelled pungently of perfume with an undertow of booze that he could detect too in her eyes.

"You look terrific," he said.

"Thank you, kind sir."

It had been a long time since he'd seen Diane drunk. He didn't know why, but it made him sad. She was pressing her hips into him and arching her back so much that if he were to let go of her she'd topple over. She was giving him a kind of knowing, teasing look he neither understood nor much liked.

"Smoky tells me you didn't go to Wyoming after all."

"He did?"

"Uh-huh."

"Well, that's right, I didn't. One of the guys down there got sick, so I'm going next week instead."

"Uh-huh."

" 'Uh-huh.' Diane, what is this?"

He knew, of course. And he chided himself for now giving her the chance to say it. He should have just closed the conversation.

"I just hope you were a good boy, that's all."

"Diane, come on. You've had too much to drink."

It was a mistake. Her eyes flashed.

"Have I? Don't think we haven't all noticed."

"Noticed what?" Another mistake.

"You know what I'm talking about. You can good as smell the steam rising off the pair of you."

He just shook his head and looked away as if she was crazy, but she saw it hit home because she grinned in victory and wagged a finger at him.

"Good job she's going home, brother-in-law."

They didn't exchange another word for the rest of the number. And when it was over she gave him that knowing look again and went off, swinging her hips like a hooker. He was still recovering when Annie came up behind him at the bar.

"Pity it's not raining," she whispered.

"Come and dance with me," he said. And he took hold of her before anyone else could and steered her off.

The music was quick and they danced apart, only uncoupling their eyes when the intensity threatened to overwhelm or betray them. To have her so close and yet so inaccessible was like some exquisite form of torture. After the second number, Frank tried to take her away but Tom made a joke of being the older brother and wouldn't yield.

The next number was a slow ballad in which a woman sang about her lover on death row. At last they could get their hands on each other. The touch of her skin and the light press of her body through their clothes almost made him reel and he had for a moment to close his eyes. Somewhere, he knew, Diane would be watching but he didn't care.

The dusty dance-floor was crammed. Annie looked about her at the faces and said quietly, "I need to talk to you. How can we get to talk?"

He felt like saying what is there to talk about? You're going. That's all there is to say. Instead he said, "The exercise pool. In twenty minutes. I'll meet you."

She only had time to nod, because the next moment Frank came up again and took her away from him.

Grace's head was spinning and it wasn't just from the two glasses of punch she'd had. She had danced with almost everyone—Tom, Frank, Hank, Smoky, even dear sweet Joe—and the image she'd had of herself was thrilling. She could whirl, she could shimmy, she could even jive. She didn't once lose her balance. She could do anything. She wished Terri Carlson was here to see it. For the first time in her new life, perhaps even her whole life, she felt beautiful.

She needed to pee. There was a toilet at the side of the barn but when she got there she found a line of people waiting to use it. She decided no one would mind if she used one of the bathrooms indoors—she was family enough and after all it was her party, kind of—so she headed for the porch.

She came through the screen door, instinctively keeping her hand on it so it didn't slam. As she walked through the narrow L-shaped boot-room that led to the kitchen, she heard voices. Frank and Diane were having a row.

"You've just had too much to drink," he said.

"Fuck you."

"It's none of our business, Diane."

"She's had her sights on him ever since she got here. Just take a look out there, she's like a bitch in heat."

"That's ridiculous."

"God, you men are so dumb."

There was an angry clatter of dishes. Grace had stopped in her tracks. Just as she decided she'd better go back to the barn and wait in line, she heard Frank's footsteps heading for the open door to the boot-room. She knew she wouldn't have time to leave before he saw her. And if he caught her sneaking out he'd know for sure she'd been eavesdropping. All she could do was head on in and bump into him as if she'd just come in.

As Frank appeared in front of her in the doorway, he stopped and turned back to Diane.

"Anyone'd think you were jealous or something."

"Oh give me a break!"

"Well, you give him a break. He's a grown man for Christsakes."

"And she's a married woman with a kid, for Christsakes!"

Frank turned and came into the boot-room, shaking his head. Grace stepped toward him.

"Hi," she said brightly. He seemed a lot more than just startled but he recovered instantly and beamed.

"Hey, it's the belle of the ball! Howya doing sweetheart?" He put his hands on her shoulders.

"Oh I'm having a great time. Thanks, for doing it and everything."

"Grace it's a real pleasure, believe me." He gave her a little kiss on the forehead.

"Is it okay if I use the bathroom in here? Just that there's a whole line of—"

"Course you can! You go right on in."

When she went through into the kitchen there was no one there. She heard footsteps going upstairs. Sitting on the toilet, she wondered who it was they'd been arguing about and got a first uneasy inkling that perhaps she knew.

Annie got there before him and walked slowly around to the far side of the pool. The air smelled of chlorine. The strike of her shoes on the concrete floor echoed in the caverning darkness. She leaned against the whitewashed block wall and felt its soothing cool on her back. A sliver of light was spilling in from the barn and she watched its reflection on the dead calm water of the pool. In the other world outside, one country song ended and another, barely distinguishable, began.

It seemed impossible that it was only last night that

they'd stood there in the creek house kitchen with no one to trouble them or keep them apart. She wished that she'd said then what she was going to tell him now. She hadn't trusted herself to find the right words. This morning when she'd woken in his arms, she had been no less sure, even in that same bed which only a week ago she'd shared with her husband. Her only shame was that she felt none. Still however, something had restrained her from telling him; and now she wondered if it was the fear of how he would react.

It wasn't that she doubted for one moment his love. How could she? There was just something about him, some sad foreshadowing that was almost fatalistic. She had seen it today, in his desperate intent that she should understand what he had done to Pilgrim.

There was a brief flooding of light now at the end of the passageway to the barn. He stopped and scanned for her in the darkness. She stepped toward him and at the sound he saw her and came to meet her. Annie ran the last few separating steps as if suddenly he might be snatched away. She felt in his embrace the same shuddering release of what all evening she had tried herself to contain. Their breathing was as one, their mouths, their blood as if pulsed through interlacing veins by the same heart.

When at last she could speak, she stood in the safety of his arms and told him that she was going to leave Robert. She spoke with such calm as she could muster, her cheek pressed to his chest, fearful perhaps of what she might see in his eyes were she to look. She said she knew how terrible the pain would be for all of them. Unlike the pain of losing Tom however, it was a pain she could at least imagine.

He listened in silence, holding her to him and stroking her face and hair. But when she had finished, still he didn't speak and Annie felt the first cold finger of dread steal upon her. She lifted her head, daring at last to look at him, and saw he was too filled with emotion yet to speak. He looked away across the pool. Outside the music thumped on. He looked back at her and gave a small shake of his head.

"Oh Annie."

"What? Tell me."

"You can't do that."

"I can. I'll go back and tell him."

"And Grace? You think you can tell Grace?"

She peered at him, searching his eyes. Why was he doing this? She'd hoped for validation and he'd proffered only doubt, thrusting at her immediately the one issue she'd dared not confront. And now Annie realized that in her deliberation she'd resorted to that old self-shielding habit of hers and rationalized it: of course children were upset by these things, she'd told herself, it was inevitable; but if it was done in a civilized, sensitive way there need be no lasting trauma; neither parent was lost, only some obsolete geography. In theory Annie knew this to be so; more than that, the divorces of several friends had proven it possible. Applied here and now, to them and Grace, it was of course nonsense.

He said, "After what she's suffered—"

"You think I don't know!"

"Of course you do. What I was going to say is that because of that, because you know, you'll never let yourself do this, even if now you think you can."

She felt tears coming and knew she couldn't stop them.

"I have no choice." It was uttered in a small cry that echoed around the bare walls like a lament.

He said, "That's what you said about Pilgrim, but you were wrong."

"The only other choice is losing you!" He nodded. "That's not a choice, can't you see? Could you choose to lose me?"

"No," he said simply. "But I don't have to."

"Remember what you said about Pilgrim? You said he went to the brink and saw what was beyond and then chose to accept it."

"But if what you see there is pain and suffering, then only a fool would choose to accept it."

"But for us it wouldn't be pain and suffering."

He shook his head. Annie felt a rush of anger now. At him for uttering what she knew in her heart to be right and at herself for the sobs now racking her body.

"You don't want me," she said and hated herself at once for her maudlin self-pity, then even more for the triumph she felt as his eyes welled with tears.

"Oh Annie. You'll never know how much I want you."

She cried in his arms and lost all sense of time and place. She told him she couldn't live without him and saw no portent when he told her this was true for him but not for her. He said that in time she would assess these days not with regret but as some gift of nature that had left all their lives the better.

When she could cry no more, she washed her face in the cool water of the pool and he found a towel and helped her mop the mascara that had swum from her eyes. They waited, saying little more, while the blotching faded from her cheeks. Then separately, when all seemed safe, they left.

THIRTY-FIVE

ANNIE FELT LIKE SOME MUDBOUND CREATURE VIEWING the world from the bottom of a pond. It was the first time she had taken a sleeping pill in months. They were the ones airline pilots were rumored to use, which was supposed to make you confident about the pills, not doubtful of the pilots. It was true that in the past, when she'd taken them regularly, the after-effects seemed minimal. This morning they lay draped over her brain like a thick, dulling blanket she was powerless to shrug, though sufficiently translucent for her to remember why she'd taken the pill and be grateful that she had.

Grace had come up to her soon after she and Tom came out of the barn and said bluntly that she wanted to go. She looked pale and troubled, but when Annie asked what was wrong she said nothing was, she was just tired. She didn't seem to want to look her in the eyes. On the way back up to the creek house, after they'd said their good-nights, Annie tried to chat about the party but barely got a sentence in reply. She asked her again if she was alright and Grace said she felt tired and a little sick.

"From the punch?"

"I don't know."

"How many glasses did you have?"

"I don't know! It's no big deal, don't go on about it."

She went straight up to bed and when Annie went in to kiss her good-night she just muttered and stayed facing the wall. Just as she used to when they first got here. Annie had gone straight to her sleeping pills.

She reached for her watch now and had to force her muffled brain to focus on it. It was coming up to eight o'clock. She remembered Frank, as they left last night, asking if they'd be coming to church this morning and because it seemed appropriate, somehow punishingly final, she'd said yes. She hauled her reluctant body out of bed and along to the bathroom. Grace's door was slightly ajar. Annie decided to have a bath, then take in a glass of juice and wake her.

She lay in the steaming water and tried to hold on to the last lacing of the sleeping pill. Through it she could feel already a cold geometry of pain configuring within her. These are the shapes which now inhabit you, she told herself, and to whose points and lines and angles you must become accustomed.

She dressed and went to the kitchen to get Grace's juice. It was eight-thirty. Since her drowsiness had gone she'd sought distraction in compiling mental lists of what needed to be done on this last day at the Double Divide. They had to pack; clean the house up; get the oil and tires checked; get some food and drink for the journey; settle up with the Bookers . . .

As she came to the top of the stairs, she saw Grace's door hadn't moved. She tapped on it as she went in. The drapes were still closed and she went across and drew them a little apart. It was a beautiful morning. Then she turned to the bed and saw it was empty.

It was Joe who first discovered Pilgrim was missing too. By then they'd searched every cobwebbed corner of every outbuilding on the ranch and found no trace of her. They split up and combed both sides of the creek, the twins hollering her name over and over and getting no reply but birdsong. Then Joe came yelling from down by the corrals, saying the horse was gone and they all ran to the barn and found the saddle and bridle were gone too.

"She'll be okay," Diane said. "She's just taken him for a ride somewhere." Tom saw the fear in Annie's eyes. They both already knew it was something more.

"She done anything like this before?" he said.

"Never."

"How was she when she went to bed?"

"Quiet. She said she felt a little sick. Something seemed to have upset her."

Annie looked so scared and frail, Tom wanted to hold her and comfort her, which would have looked only natural, but under Diane's gaze he didn't dare and it was Frank who did it instead.

"Diane's right," Frank said. "She'll be okay."

Annie was still looking at Tom. "Is Pilgrim safe enough for her to take out? She's only ridden him the once."

"He'll be alright," Tom said. It wasn't quite a lie; the real issue was whether Grace would be. And that depended on the state she was in. "I'll go with Frank and we'll see if we can find her."

Joe said he wanted to come too but Tom told him no and sent him off with the twins to get Rimrock and their dad's horse ready while he and Frank went to change out of their church clothes.

Tom was first out. Annie left Diane in the kitchen and followed him out over the porch to walk beside him to the barn. They only had the time it took to get there for the two of them to talk.

"I think Grace knows." She spoke low, looking straight ahead. She was trying hard to keep control. Tom nodded gravely.

"I reckon so."

"I'm sorry."

"Don't ever be sorry Annie. Ever."

That was all they said, because Frank came running up alongside and the three of them walked in silence to the rail by the barn where Joe had the horses waiting.

"There's his tracks," Joe called. He pointed at their clear outline in the dust. Pilgrim's shoes were different from those of every other shod horse on the ranch. There was no doubt the prints were his.

Tom looked back just the once as he and Frank loped up the track toward the ford, but Annie was no longer there. Diane must have taken her inside. Only the kids still stood there watching. He gave them a wave.

It wasn't till she found the matches in her pocket that Grace had the idea. She'd put them there after practicing the trick with her father at the airport while they waited for her flight to be called.

She didn't know how long they'd ridden. The sun was high so it must be some hours. She rode like a madwoman, consciously so, wholeheartedly, embracing madness and urging its return in Pilgrim. He'd sensed it and ran and ran all morning, mouth afoam, like a witch's nag. She felt that if she asked he would even fly.

At first she'd had no plan, only a blind, destructive rage whose purpose and direction were not yet set and might be turned as easily on others as herself. Saddling him and shushing him in the gathering light of the corral, all she knew was that somehow she would punish them. She would make them sorry for what they'd done. Only when she reached the meadows and galloped and felt the cold air in her eyes did she start to cry. Then the tears took over and streamed and she leaned forward over Pilgrim's ears and sobbed out loud.

Now, as he stood drinking at the plateau pool, she felt her fury not lessen but distill. She slicked his sweating neck with her hand and saw again in her head those two guilty figures slinking one by one from the dark of the barn, like dogs from a butcher's yard, thinking themselves unseen and unsuspected. And then her mother, with her makeup smeared by lust and still flushed from it, sitting there calmly at the wheel of the car and asking, as if butter wouldn't melt in her mouth, why she felt sick.

And how could Tom do this? Her Tom. After all that caring and kindness, this was what he was really like. It had all been an act, a clever excuse for the two of them to hide behind. It was only a week, a week for Godsake, since he'd stood chatting and laughing with her dad. It was sick. Adults were sick. And everyone knew about it, everyone. Diane had said so. Like a bitch in heat, she said. It was sick, it was all so sick.

Grace looked over the plateau and beyond the ridge to where the first pass curved up like a scar into the mountains. Up there, in the cabin where they'd all had such fun together on the cattle drive, up there, that's where they'd done it. Soiling, spoiling the place. And then her mother lying like that. Making out she was going there all alone to "get her head together." Jesus.

Well, she'd show them. She had the matches and she'd show them. It would go up like paper. And they would find her charred black bones in the ashes and then they'd feel sorry. Oh yes, then they'd feel sorry.

It was hard to know how much of a start she had on them. Tom knew a young guy on the reservation who could look at a track and tell you how old it was, near as damn it, to the minute. Frank knew more than most about such things because of his hunting, a lot more than Tom, but still not enough to know how far ahead she was. What they could tell however, was that she was riding the horse as hard as hell and that if she kept it up he'd soon be on his knees.

It seemed pretty clear she was heading for the summer pastures, even before they found his hoofmarks in the caked mud at the lip of the pool. From riding out with Joe, she knew the lower parts of the ranch pretty well, but the only time she'd been up here was on the cattle drive. If she wanted a bolt hole, the only place she'd know to head for was the cabin. That is, if she could remember the way when she got up into the passes. After two more weeks of summer, the place would look different. Even without the whirlwind that —judging by her progress—was going on in her head, she could easily get lost.

Frank got down from his horse to take a closer look at the prints at the water's edge. He took off his hat and wiped the sweat from his face with his sleeve. Tom got down too and held the horses so they wouldn't spoil what evidence there was in the mud.

"What do you reckon?"

"I don't know. It's kind of crusted already but with a sun this hot that don't say too much. A half-hour, maybe more."

They let the horses drink and stood mopping their brows and looking out across the plateau.

Frank said, "Thought we might get a sight of her from here."

"Me too."

Neither spoke for a while, just listened to the lap of the horses drinking.

"Tom?" Tom turned to look at him and saw his brother shift and smile uneasily. "This is none of my business, but last night, Diane . . . well, you know she'd had a drink or two and, anyway, we was in the kitchen and she was going on about how you and Annie were, well . . . Like I say, it's none of our business."

"It's okay, go on."

"Well. She said one or two things, and anyway, Grace came in, and I'm not sure, but I think maybe she heard."

Tom nodded. Frank asked him if that's what was going on here and Tom told him he reckoned so. They looked at each other and some refraction of the pain in Tom's heart must have shown in his eyes.

Frank said, "In pretty deep, huh?"

"About as deep as it gets."

They said no more, merely turned the horses from the water and set off across the plateau.

So Grace knew, though how she knew he didn't care. It was as he'd feared, even before Annie had voiced the fear this morning. When they were leaving the party last night he'd asked Grace if she'd had a good time and she'd barely looked at him, just nodded and forced a token smile. What pain she must be in to have gone off like this, Tom thought. Pain of his making. And he took it inside him and embraced it in his own.

At the crest of the ridge they expected again to see

her but didn't. Her tracks, where they could see them,
showed only a slight slackening of pace. Only once had
she stopped, some fifty yards from the mouth of the
pass. It looked as if she'd pulled Pilgrim up short then
walked him in a small circle, as if she was deciding or
looking at something. Then she'd gone on again at a
lope.

Frank reined to a halt just where the land began to
tilt sharply upward between the pines. He pointed at
the ground for Tom to look.

"What do you make of that?"

There were not one set of hoofmarks now but many,
though you could read Pilgrim's clearly among them
because of his shoes. It was impossible to tell whose
were the fresher.

"Must be some of old Granola's mustangs," Frank
said.

"I guess so."

"Ain't never seen 'em this far up before. You?"

"Nope."

They heard it as soon as they reached the bend about
halfway up the pass and they stopped to listen. There
was a deep rumble which at first Tom took to be a slide
of rocks somewhere up in the trees. Then they heard a
high-pitched clamor of screams and knew it was horses.

They rode, fast but cautious, to the top of the pass,
expecting any moment to come face to face with a
stampede of mustangs. But aside from their upward
tracks, there was no sign of them. It was hard to tell
how many there were. Maybe a dozen, Tom thought.

At its highest point, the pass forked like a pair of
tight pants into two diverging trails. To get to the high
pastures you had to go right. They stopped again and
studied the ground. It was so churned with hooves in all

directions, you could neither pick Pilgrim's among them nor know which way he or any other horse had gone.

The brothers split up, Tom taking the right and Frank the lower one left. About twenty yards up, Tom found Pilgrim's prints. But they were heading down, not up. A little farther up was another great churning of earth and he was about to inspect it when he heard Frank call out.

When he reined up next to him Frank told him to listen. For a few moments there was nothing. Then Tom heard it too, another frenzied call of horses.

"Where does this trail go?"

"I don't know. Ain't never been down here."

Tom put his heels into Rimrock and launched him into a gallop.

The trail went up then down then up again. It was winding and narrow and the trees crowded so close on either side that they seemed to be whipping back the other way with a motion all their own. Here and there one had fallen across the trail. Some they could duck and others jump. Rimrock never faltered but measured his stride and cleared them all without brushing a branch.

After maybe half a mile the ground fell away again then opened up under a steep, rock-strewn slope into which the trail had etched itself in a long upward crescent. Below it, the ground fell sheer, many hundreds of feet, to a dark netherworld of pine and rock.

The trail led to what appeared to be some vast and ancient quarry, carved into the limestone like a giant's cauldron that had cracked and spilled its contents down the mountain. From this place now, above the hammering of Rimrock's hooves, Tom heard again the scream of horses. Then he heard another and knew, with a sudden sickening, that it was Grace. It wasn't until he pulled Rimrock up in the cauldron's gaping mouth that he could see into it.

She was cowering at the back wall, trapped by a turmoil of shrieking mares. There were seven or eight of them and some colts and foals too, all running in circles and scaring each other more at every turn. Their clamor echoed back at them from the walls, only to redouble their fear. And the more they ran, the more dust they churned and the blindness only made them panic more. At the center, rearing and screaming and striking at each other with their hooves, were Pilgrim and the white stallion Tom had seen that day with Annie.

"Jesus Christ." Frank had arrived alongside. His horse balked at the sight and he had to rein him hard and circle back beside Tom. Rimrock was troubled but stood his ground. Grace hadn't seen them. Tom got down and handed Rimrock's reins to Frank.

"Stay here in case I need you, but you're gonna have to make way pretty quick when they come," he said. Frank nodded.

Tom walked to his left with his back to the wall, never taking his eyes off the horses. They swirled in front of him like a crazed carousel. He could feel the bite of the dust in his throat. It was clouding so thick that beyond the mares Pilgrim was only a dark blur against the rearing white shape of the stallion.

Grace was now no more than twenty yards away. At last she saw him. Her face was very pale.

"You hurt?" he yelled.

Grace shook her head and tried to call back to him that she was okay. But her voice was too frail to carry through the din and the dust. She'd bruised her shoulder and twisted her ankle when she fell, but that was all. All that paralyzed her was fear—and fear more for Pilgrim than herself. She could see the bared pink of the stallion's gums above his teeth as he hacked away at Pilgrim's neck, where already there was the black glint of blood. Worst of all was the sound of their screams, a sound she'd heard only once before, on a snowy, sunlit morning in another place.

She saw Tom now take off his hat and step out among the circling mares, waving it high in front of them. They skidded and shied away from him, colliding with those behind them. Now they'd all turned and he moved in quickly behind them, driving them before him, away from Pilgrim and the stallion. One tried to break away to the right but Tom dodged and headed it off. Through the dust cloud Grace could see another man, Frank maybe, moving two horses clear of the gap. The mares, with the colts and foals at their tails, bolted past and made good their escape.

Now Tom turned and worked his way around the wall again, giving space to the fighting horses, Grace supposed, so as not to drive them nearer to her. He stopped more or less where he'd been before and again called out.

"Stay right there Grace. You'll be okay."

Then, without any sign of fear, he walked toward the fight. Grace could see his lips moving but couldn't hear what he said over the horses' screams. Perhaps he was speaking to himself or maybe not at all.

He didn't stop until he was right up to them and only then did they seem to register his presence. She saw him reach for Pilgrim's reins and take hold of them. Firmly, but without any violent jerking of his hand, he drew the horse down off his hind legs and turned him from the stallion. Then he slapped him hard on his rump and sent him away.

Thus thwarted, the stallion turned his wrath on Tom.

The picture of what followed would stay with Grace till the day she died. And never would she know for sure what happened. The horse wheeled in a tight circle, tossing his head and kicking up a spray of dust and rock shards with his hooves. With the other horses gone, his snorting fury had dominion of the air and seemed to grow with each resounding echo from the walls. For a moment he appeared not to know what to make of the man who stood undaunted before him.

What was certain was that Tom could have walked away. Two or three paces would have taken him out of the stallion's reach and clear of all danger. The horse, so Grace believed, would simply have let him be and gone where the others had led. Instead, Tom stepped toward him.

The moment he moved, as he must have foreseen, the stallion reared up before him and screamed. And even now, Tom could have stepped aside. She had seen Pilgrim rear before him once and noted how deftly Tom could move to save himself. He knew where a horse's feet would fall, which muscle it would move and why, before it even knew itself. Yet on this day, he neither dodged nor ducked nor even flinched and, once more, stepped in closer.

The settling dust was still too thick for Grace to be sure, but she thought she now saw Tom open his arms a little and, in a gesture so minimal that she may have imagined it, show the horse the palms of his hands. It was as though he were offering something and perhaps it was only what he'd always offered, the gift of kinship and peace. But although she would never from this day forth utter the thought to anyone, Grace had a sudden, vivid impression that it was otherwise and that Tom, quite without fear or despair, was somehow this time offering himself.

Then, with a terrible sound, sufficient alone to ratify the passing of his life, the hooves came down upon his head and struck him like a crumbled icon to the ground.

The stallion reared again but not so high and only now to find some safer surface for his feet than the man's body. He seemed for a moment fazed by such prompt capitulation and pawed the dust uncertainly around Tom's head. Then, tossing his mane, he cried out one last time, then swerved toward the gap and was gone.

FIVE

THIRTY-SIX

SPRING CAME LATE TO CHATHAM THE FOLLOWING YEAR.
One night, in the closing days of April, there fell a full
foot of snow. It was of that heavy, languid kind and
gone within the day, but Annie feared it might have
withered the buds already forming on Robert's six
small cherry trees. When however in May the world at
last warmed, they seemed to reassert themselves and the
blossom when it came was full and unblemished.

Now the show was past its best, the pink of the petals
faded and delicately edged in brown. With each stir of
the breeze another flurry would dislodge, littering the
grass in wide circumference. Those that fell unbidden
were mostly lost among the longer grass that grew
around the roots. Some few however found a final brief
reprieve on the white gauze netting of a cradle which,
since the weather had grown mild, stood daily in the
dappled shade.

The cradle was old and made of woven wicker. It had
been handed down by an aunt of Robert's when Grace
was born and prior to her had sheltered the cranial
formation of several more or less distinguished lawyers.

The netting, across which Annie's shadow now loomed, was new. She had noticed how the child liked to watch the petals settle on it and she left those already there untouched. She looked in and saw he was sleeping.

It was too early to tell whose looks he had. His skin was fair and his hair a light brown, though in the sun it seemed to have a reddish tinge that was surely Annie's. From the day of his birth, now almost three months past, his eyes were never anything but blue.

Annie's doctor had told her she should sue. The coil had only been in four years, a year less than its recommended life. When he examined it, the copper was worn right through. The manufacturers would be sure to settle, he said, for fear of bad publicity. Annie had simply laughed and the sensation was so alien it had shocked her. No, she said, she didn't want to sue and neither, despite poor precedent and all his eloquent listing of the risks, did she want a termination.

Were it not for the steady configuration in her womb Annie doubted whether any of them, she or Robert or Grace, would have survived. It could, or should perhaps, have made things worse, become a bitter focus for their several sorrows. Instead, after the shock of its discovery, her pregnancy had, by slow degree, brought healing and a kind of clarifying calm.

Annie now felt a welling pressure in her breasts and for a moment thought of waking him to feed. He was so very different from Grace. She had rapidly grown restless at the breast as if it couldn't meet her needs and by this age she was already on bottles. This one just latched on and drank as if he'd done it all before. When he'd had his fill, he simply fell asleep.

She looked at her watch. It was nearly four. In an hour Robert and Grace would be setting off from the city. Annie briefly considered going back inside to do a little more work but decided against it. She'd had a good day and the piece she was working on, though in style and content quite unlike anything she'd ever written, was going well. She decided instead to walk up past the pond to the field and have a look at the horses. When she got back, the baby would most likely be awake.

They'd buried Tom Booker beside his father. Annie knew this from Frank. He'd written her a letter. It was sent to Chatham and arrived on a Wednesday morning in late July when she was alone and had just found out she was pregnant.

The intention, Frank said, had been to keep the funeral small, pretty much only for family. But on the day about three hundred people turned up, some from as far afield as Charleston and Santa Fe. There was room for only a few in the church, so they'd opened wide the doors and windows and everyone else stood outside in the sunshine.

Frank said he thought Annie would like to know this.

The main purpose of his writing, he went on to say, was that on the day before he died, Tom had apparently told Joe that he wanted to give Grace a present. The two of them had come up with the idea that she should have Bronty's foal. Frank wanted to know how Annie felt about it. If she thought it was a good idea, they'd ship him over in Annie's trailer along with Pilgrim.

It was Robert's idea to build the stable. Annie could see it now as she walked up toward the field, framed at the end of the long avenue of hazel that curved up from the pond. The building stood stark and new against a steep bank of fresh-leafed poplar and birch. It still surprised Annie every time she saw it. Its wood had barely weathered, nor that of the new gate and fence abutting. The different greens of the trees and of the grass in the field were so vivid and new and intense they seemed almost to hum.

Both horses lifted their heads at her approach then went calmly back to their grazing. Bronty's "foal" was now a boisterous yearling who in public was treated by Pilgrim with a kind of lofty disdain. It was mostly an act. Many times now, Annie had caught them playing. She folded her arms on the bar of the gate and leaned her chin to watch.

Grace worked with the colt every weekend. Watching her, it was so clear to Annie how much the girl had learned from Tom. You could see it in her movements, even in the way she talked to the horse. She never pushed too hard, just helped him find himself. He was coming on well. Already you could see in him that same soft feel that all the horses had at the Double Divide. Grace had named him Gully but had first asked Annie if she thought Judith's mom and dad would mind. Annie said she was sure they wouldn't.

She found it hard to think of Grace nowadays without a feeling of reverence and wonder. The girl, now nearly fifteen, was a constantly revealing miracle.

The week that followed Tom's death was still a blur and it was probably best for both of them that it remained so. They'd left as soon as Grace was fit to travel and flown back to New York. For days the girl was almost catatonic.

It was the sight of the horses that August morning which seemed to bring about the change. It unlocked a sluice gate in her and for two weeks she wept and poured forth her agony. It might have swept them all away. But in the flooded calm of its aftermath, Grace seemed to take stock and decide, like Pilgrim, to survive.

In that moment Grace became an adult. But sometimes now, when she didn't know she was being watched, you could catch a glimpse in her eyes of something that was more than merely adult. Twice gone to hell and twice returned. She had seen what she had seen and from it gleaned some sad and stilling wisdom that was as old as time itself.

In the fall Grace went back to school and the welcome she got there from her friends was worth a thousand sessions with her new therapist, whom nonetheless, even now, she still visited every week. When at last, with great trepidation, Annie had told her about the baby, Grace was overjoyed. She had never once, to this day, asked who the father was.

Neither had Robert. No test had established the fact, nor had he sought one. It seemed to Annie that he preferred the possibility of the child being his to the certainty that it wasn't.

Annie had told him everything. And just as guilts of variant cause and intricacy were etched forever in her own and Grace's hearts, so too was the hurt she had wrought in his.

For Grace's sake, they had adjourned all decision on what future, if any, their marriage might have. Annie stayed in Chatham, Robert in New York. Grace commuted between them, like some healing shuttle, restoring strand by strand the torn fabric of their lives. Once school had started, she came up to Chatham every weekend, usually by train. Sometimes however, Robert would drive her.

At first he would drop her off, kiss her good-bye and after a few formal words with Annie, drive all the way back to the city. One rain-soaked Friday night in late October, Grace prevailed on him to stay over. The three of them ate supper together. With Grace, he was as funny and loving as ever. With Annie he was reserved, never less and never more than courteous. He slept in the guest room and left early the following morning.

This was to become their unacknowledged Friday routine. And though on principle he had never yet stayed more than the one night, his departure the next day had gradually got later.

On the Saturday before Thanksgiving, the three of them had gone for breakfast at the Bakery. It was the first time they had been there as a family since the accident. Outside they bumped into Harry Logan. He made a big fuss of Grace and made her blush by telling her how grown up and gorgeous she looked. It was true. He asked if he could stop by and say hi to Pilgrim sometime and they said sure he could.

As far as Annie knew, no one in Chatham had any idea what had happened in Montana other than that their horse had gotten better. Harry looked at Annie's protruding belly and shook his head and smiled.

"You guys," he said. "Just the sight of you—all four of you—makes me feel so good. I'm really, really happy for you."

There was much marveling at how, after so many miscarriages, Annie had managed this time to go full term without trouble. The obstetrician said strange things often happened with elderly pregnancies. Annie said thanks very much.

The baby was born in early March by planned caesarean. They asked her if she wanted to have an epidural and watch and she said absolutely not, she wanted every kind of dope they had. She woke, as once she had before, to find the baby on the pillow beside her. Robert and Grace were there too and the three of them all wept and laughed together.

They named him Matthew, after Annie's father.

On the breeze now, Annie could hear the baby crying. When she turned away from the gate and started to walk back down toward the cherry trees, the horses didn't lift their heads.

She would feed him then take him inside and change him. Then she'd sit him in the corner of the kitchen so he could watch her with those clear blue eyes while she got the supper ready. Maybe she could persuade Robert to stay the whole weekend this time. As she came past the pond, some wild ducks took off, their wings clattering the water.

There was only one other thing Frank mentioned in the letter he had sent her last summer. Sorting out Tom's room, he said, he'd come across an envelope on the table. It had Annie's name on it and so he now enclosed it.

Annie looked at it a long time before she opened it. She thought how strange it was that never till now had she seen Tom's handwriting. Inside, folded in a sheet of plain white paper, was the loop of cord he'd taken back from her on that last night they spent together in the creek house. On the paper, all he'd written was, *In case you forget.*

Watch for
the new novel
by

NICHOLAS
EVANS

THE
LOOP

On sale everywhere
September 1998
from
Delacorte Press